THE OLD
MAN

THE OLD MAN

Thomas Perry

Grove Press UK

First published in the United States of America in 2017 by The Mysterious Press,
an imprint of Grove Atlantic
This paperback edition published in Great Britain in 2022 by Grove Press UK,
an imprint of Grove Atlantic

1 3 5 7 9 8 6 4 2

A CIP record for this book is available from the British Library.

Paperback ISBN 978 1 80471 020 3
E-book ISBN 978 1 80471 021 0

Printed and bound in Great Britain by Clays Ltd, Elcograf S.p.A.

Grove Press UK
Ormond House
26–27 Boswell Street
London
WC1N 3JZ

www.groveatlantic.com

To Jo, with love

1

"An old man should have a dog." Dan Chase's daughter had told him that ten years ago, after his wife died. The part that surprised him was the term "old man." He had just turned fifty then. But he supposed she was only giving him advance notice, time to get used to the idea and find a suitable dog. After a man's wife died, he had to do something not to die too.

After decades taking responsibility for a wife, then a daughter, then her husband and sons too, he woke up one morning and realized that the conditions he had been accustomed to seeing as permanent had changed. He was no longer at the center of things. After his wife died the house had gone silent. It wasn't the hearth where the clan gathered for warmth and sustenance anymore. It was just a solitary man's place.

The dogs were looking at him expectantly right now. He opened the door and the two big mutts, Dave and Carol, slipped out ahead of him into the yard, already galloping, a pair of black streaks. They always charged across the five hundred feet of yard to the back fence, their bodies elongated as they bounded along. When they reached the fence they stopped and trotted around the perimeter, patrolling. When they'd made one circuit and found nothing to pursue, they made one more circuit sniffing the ground before they returned to Dan Chase, hoping for an assignment.

After he had taken his daughter's advice he found there was much he remembered about dogs from when he was a boy. All dogs wanted to be good dogs, no matter how unpromising they seemed. You just had to help them find a way. And they were sunshine creatures. When their master opened his eyes in the morning it was their signal that the day had begun, and a day was to be greeted with joy and intense interest. They were a good example for an old man.

Chase started to walk and the two big dogs fell in beside him to skirt the side of the house to get to the gate. The two dogs were on his right at the moment, but they constantly changed positions, maintaining an orbit around him as he went. He opened the gate and, as always, they squeezed their sleek, muscular bodies through the opening ahead of him.

Dan Chase wore a pair of short leashes hanging from his neck, so if he saw a stranger walking toward him he could snap the leashes on Dave and Carol's collars. Even a person who loved dogs didn't necessarily want to meet two hairy, black eighty-pound beasts running free before he'd been introduced to them. Dave and Carol didn't mind. The big thing was to be out and going somewhere with Dan Chase.

Every day the three walked four or five miles, and did their errands on the way. About once a week Chase would take the car out, just to be sure the battery was charged and the oil got on the parts, but the rest of the time they walked. The walk was usually silent, except when they ran into somebody that Chase wanted to talk to, and there were some occasions when he spoke to the dogs. He had never believed in telling them what to do unless he had to, so the dogs generally got along by doing what Chase did. But when he did speak to them they stopped, their ears perked up, their heads turned, and their sharp, intent eyes focused on him.

Dave and Carol had been from the same litter, acquired together by animal control. The volunteer told him their mother had been a cross between a black Labrador and a standard poodle, but the father was something unknown. Nobody knew what he was except that he must have been bigger and hairier. Chase couldn't bear to split them up, so he didn't. When his daughter came to visit after he'd brought them home from the pound, she said, "Oh, Jesus. That's not the kind of dog I meant. Look at their feet. They're going to grow up big."

"I like big dogs," he said. "They're calmer and quieter. It's scared dogs that bite."

"I don't know," she said. "You really want to have two animals that could kill you? You're—"

"An old man. A stiff breeze could kill me."

"You know what I mean."

"I do," he said. "It's just another reason to make sure they never want to."

His relationship with Dave and Carol had worked that way, over time. This morning the three made their way along Norwich's Main Street past a succession of white clapboard houses and a couple of restaurants and hotels to the bridge over the Connecticut River that led to Hanover, New Hampshire. They were having a gentle early spring this year, after a winter that had hit early and held on, and kept most inhabitants of northern New England defending small areas of warmth for days at a time and going out only because there was somebody paying them to do it.

As Chase and his dogs stepped onto the bridge, Chase looked out over the river. Today the dark water was higher than yesterday, swelled by the early spring melt. The sun had been shining fairly steadily for a few days, and he judged that the big pockets of snow in the high places had begun to yield.

The first sign that something was wrong came just beyond the end of the bridge on the New Hampshire side. Chase's ears were attuned to the sounds of his world, and one of the sounds was the movement of cars. He had gotten used to the steady passage of cars across the long, narrow concrete bridge, about one every five seconds, going between twenty-five and thirty-five miles an hour, the sound approaching first from over his left shoulder, and then turning to a *whish* as it came abreast of him, and then fading far ahead. This vehicle came off the bridge just after he did and was moving much more slowly than cars usually did. Chase looked up the slight incline in the road ahead of him to detect a reason for a car to slow. The road ahead was clear, but the car drifted along on his left side, hanging behind him as he walked.

Chase pivoted to the right and walked up between the riverbank and the first house. The two dogs seemed to hesitate behind him, but he said quietly, "Come on." So they did. He didn't look back, but took out his cell phone and touched the camera symbol, held up the phone as though to take a shot of the river, but aimed it over his shoulder toward the car. He took a shot, and then hit the video symbol and kept the phone in his hand with his arm down at his side, pointing the lens behind him as he went.

Dave and Carol were happy enough to resume their walk, and in a moment the rhythm of car sounds was restored, with cars going up the incline toward Wheelock Street at the usual rate.

He looked at the picture he had taken. The shot was badly framed and at an angle, but the car was clear. It was a silver compact car, something like a Subaru Impreza. For the past few years those things had become as common as pigeons all over New England because they were cheap and had good traction on snow and ice.

His view of the driver's face was blocked by the car's roof. The one thing Chase could see from his high angle was the passenger seat, which had a lone object lying on it. Was that what it looked like? He squinted and stared, but he could think of nothing else it could be. It had to be a toy, a replica, or the real thing.

A part of his mind that he had kept dormant for a long time awakened. He changed his plan. The best time to walk back across the bridge was now, while the driver was still headed in the other direction and would have to turn around on a side street to follow. When that happened Chase wanted to be on the right side of the car where the driver couldn't shoot him easily. He muttered, "Come." Then he swung both arms to signal the dogs, trotted quickly across road, and headed back across the bridge.

When they returned to the Vermont side of the river, he moved off Main Street. If this person knew Chase was in Norwich, he or she would certainly know where he lived. He would be much safer if he got there first. He picked up his pace and cut across a couple of unfenced backyards and down an alley that led to the gravel parking lot behind the Norwich Inn.

Chase had not been ready. He had stayed here in this peaceful corner of the country for too long. When he came to the area he had bought guns and ammunition and hidden them in his house, his car, and his garage. But he hadn't carried one in ten years. There had been no sign of danger, and he had been out of sight for so long by then. He admitted to himself that what had ended the habit had been Anna's death. She had always been the one to remind him to stick a pistol into his coat before he went out. After she died he had not been very interested in protecting what was left of his life.

Chase's eyes and ears were now alert and sensitive, evaluating every sight and sound, trying to pick up anything that didn't belong, anything that had changed. He reminded himself that he couldn't be sure that there was anything to detect. A car had followed him across a bridge, its driver apparently slowing to look at him or the dogs. This might be nothing.

As Chase and the dogs moved along the paths and shortcuts toward his house, he checked the streets for the silver car. He was careful to check the parking lot in front of Dan and Whit's Country

Store. The Congregational Church's lot was visible across the green, and it was empty.

He reached the final block before his house and headed along the fence to the side opening near the back door. The dogs surged ahead of him and sniffed the ground, zigzagging as they did when following an invisible trail. Chase left them at it and stepped into his garage. He had placed a .45 Colt Commander under the seat of the car the day he bought it, and a second one in the spare tire bay under the floor of the trunk. The gun weighed thirty-six ounces and held only seven rounds, but there had been times when he'd bet his life that it would fire them all smoothly and accurately, and he was still aboveground. He took the pistol from under the seat and hid it beneath his coat.

When he emerged from the garage he saw that Dave and Carol were agitated, rushing to the distant fence and running back across the yard to the steps. Maybe someone had been here in their absence, and they resented the incursion. He stood with his back to the clapboards of the house and the gun in his belt under his jacket, waiting to see. After a short time, the dogs settled down. Whoever they had sensed must be gone. He put his hand on the gun and walked to the front steps. He looked in the window, and then opened the back door without stepping into the opening. There was no sound of feet sidestepping for a better angle. No shot. "Okay," he said, and the dogs leapt up on the porch and moved inside.

When Dave and Carol trotted across the floor, stopped on opposite sides of their big water bowl, and began to lap up the water, he let go of the gun. If anybody had been in the house, the dogs would have sniffed the air and gone to hunt for him.

Chase walked through the house, verifying that nothing had been changed or touched. He was almost certain this was unnecessary, but he had gotten lazy and irresponsible lately, so he made the extra effort. When he first moved to town he had taken lots of precautions, but over the years he had not bothered to stay ready.

Apparently today had been a false alarm, possibly even his sub-conscious producing a chimera to startle him into doing what he should. But he knew the real thing would seem just about as subtle and innocuous. Someone he didn't know would show an interest in him. But once the attack started, it would be loud and fast. Maybe today had been a blessing, a harmless event reminding him to make some corrections.

He patted the two dogs, gave them each a biscuit, and went to check on his preparations. He walked to the closet in one of the spare bedrooms where he kept his escape kit, opened the backpack, and looked inside. The money was there—ten thousand in US hundreds, another five thousand in Canadian hundreds, and ten thousand euros. The two guns were Beretta Nanos, and each was accompanied by four spare magazines full of 9mm rounds.

The three wallets contained the necessary credit cards and licenses for three different identities—Henry Dixon of Los Angeles, Peter Caldwell of Chicago, and Alan Spencer of Toronto. He had American passports for Dixon and Caldwell, and a Canadian passport for Spencer. The expiration dates on the cards were well spread out, and he checked and verified that he had not been inattentive enough to let any of the credit cards expire. He had known he could count on the companies to keep sending new cards. The companies paid themselves from bank accounts he'd held in those names for twenty-five years or more.

He went to the next hiding place in the small attic at the peak of the house, opened a box of Christmas ornaments, and pulled out the second kit, which included more money and female identities with the same surnames as the men. The photographs on the cards were of Anna. He took this second kit down to the spare bedroom with him.

He had three prepaid burner cell phones in his kit with the batteries removed. He plugged one of them into the surge suppressor under the bed to recharge the battery and stowed the others. He started to take the kit he'd made for Anna out of the room to throw it away, but then changed his mind. He took the contents of Anna's pack and added it to his pack. If he ever needed a kit at all it would be dangerous to leave anything here that revealed his next surnames. He and Anna used to call the packs bugout kits, because they were only to be used if they ever had to bug out—abandon their home and escape. The kit contained everything either of them would need to start over again somewhere else.

He let Dave and Carol out into the backyard again. Usually around this time they liked to have him throw a ball so they could race after it, but today none of them felt like playing. Instead, the dogs followed him as he walked around the yard looking for footprints, signs that the fence had been scuffed when someone had climbed it, or other indications that anyone had been there. The dogs could still be funny and puppyish when they felt like it, but today they were serious, even solemn. They stayed close, staring up at him now and then with their big, liquid eyes, as though to read his thoughts.

Chase spent the rest of the day watching for signs that never came, and making up for his neglected preparations. He checked and engaged all the locks on doors and windows and tested the alarm system. He spent a few minutes in the garage tying a piece of monofilament fishing line to a pair of tin cans from his recycling bin, and then tying another piece to the necks of two bottles.

They all had dinner at the usual time, and then the dogs went out while Chase did the dishes and cleaned up. After they came in he engaged the alarm and watched television for a while, keeping the volume very low so he or the dogs would hear any unusual sounds. At 11:30 p.m. after the weather report he took the dogs to bed. As usual, Dave and Carol jumped up and lay on the left side of the bed, nearest to the door.

When they were settled, Chase went to the end of the hallway that led from the kitchen and set up the two cans connected by the transparent fishing line. Then he did the same with the bottles at the beginning of the bedroom hallway. He was fairly sure the electronic alarm system would function well enough, but he knew making his own would help him sleep better.

It was nearly 3:00 a.m. when the clatter of tin cans broke the silence. He opened his eyes, and the dogs both lifted their heads from the bedcovers. Chase could see in silhouette that their heads were both turned toward the doorway, and their ears were pointed forward.

Dave launched himself off the bed. There was a heavy thud as his forepaws hit the hardwood, and then rapid scratching sounds as he accelerated down the hallway. Carol leapt after him, adding to the *scrit-scrit* of toenails down the hall.

Dan Chase was on his feet in a second, stepping into his pants. He picked up the Colt Commander and the flashlight from his nightstand and followed. He paused at the end of the hallway, leaned forward to let one eye show at the corner, but saw only dark shapes in motion. He turned on his flashlight in time to see Dave barrel into a man at the far end of the room and begin to growl.

The man went down, but he punched and kicked at Dave, trying to get the dog's jaw to open and release his arm.

"Lie still!" Chase shouted, and switched on the overhead lights. "Don't fight them."

Then the man had a gun in his hand, and Chase could see it had a long silencer attached to the barrel. The silencer was the man's enemy, because the extra eight inches made it too long for him to turn it around to fire into the dog. He managed to get it close, but the twisted arm gave Carol her opening. She ducked in beside Dave and bit.

This time the man was in trouble. Soon Carol was tearing at his shoulder, working her way up toward his throat. He knew it, and he struggled harder, using the unwieldy pistol to hammer at the dogs.

"*Lasst ihn los,*" said Chase. He aimed his gun at the man's torso.

The dogs released their jaws. The man hesitated.

"One chance," Chase called. "How are you going to use it?"

The man rolled to his side and got off a shot that went past Chase's ear. Within a half second Chase's shot pounded into the man's chest and he dropped the gun and lay still.

Chase had to do many things in a short time, so his movements were fast and efficient. He kicked the man's pistol a few feet away in case the man was alive. He patted each of the dogs while he ran his hand over them to see if they were hurt, and he spoke to them softly. "Dave, Carol. You're very, very good dogs. Thank you, my friends." They would probably be bruised, but there was no blood, and neither of them flinched at his touch. They licked his face as he knelt to check on the man.

The man on the floor had dark hair and olive skin. He was about thirty years old, with a widow's peak that showed he would have been bald in a few years if he had not come here tonight. Chase had never seen him before, unless he was the one in the silver Subaru.

There was no pulse at the man's carotid artery. The bullet hole in the chest was in the right position to go through the heart. The blood was draining under him from the exit wound, not being pumped out. Chase felt for a wallet, but found nothing in the man's pockets except a spare magazine for the pistol and a knife with a four-inch blade—not even a set of car keys. The lack of identification wasn't entirely a surprise. A man they'd send after Dan Chase would be one who could only succeed or die, because if he were caught he'd be more dangerous than Chase. Of course he had no phone, but Chase wasted a few seconds searching again for one.

Chase went to the upstairs closet for his escape kit, added the phones, took the pack outside, and hung it on a nail in the shed so it would be hard to distinguish from his fishing gear and the oars and motor for the aluminum boat turned over in the yard. On the way back he searched for the silver Subaru, but he didn't see it.

He went inside through the kitchen door, took the cans and bottles outside, disconnected the fishing line, and threw them in the recycling bin, picked up the phone, and dialed 9-1-1.

"Nine one one. What's your emergency?"

"This is Dan Chase at Ninety-two Neville Street in Norwich. A man just broke into my house with a gun, and woke up my dogs. He fired at me, so I shot him. He hasn't got a pulse."

"Please stay on the line, Mr. Chase. Help will be there in a few minutes."

"All right. Tell them there's no need for sirens. No use waking everybody in town." He stood in the kitchen with the phone to his ear for a moment until the dogs came in and sat on their haunches staring at him.

He cradled the phone on his shoulder while he opened the cookie jar and took out two dog treats and let their big jaws take them. He pulled out two more and bestowed those too, so the dogs would know that he appreciated them. All dogs wanted to do a good job.

Through the window he saw the flash of red and blue lights on the trees beside the house. Chase prepared himself for the next part. There would be a lot of talk. Then he and his dogs would go.

2

The police were about the way he'd expected them to be in this situation. A man who had owned a home in town for nineteen years, paid taxes, and lived without afflicting his neighbors was awakened by his dogs when an armed man broke into his house tonight. The armed man fired a round at the home owner, who shot him through the heart. The cops took the victim's statement, dusted the house for fingerprints, took photographs, and bagged the obvious stuff—both weapons, the ejected brass casings, and the bullet the attacker fired into the woodwork. Before the body was removed, they expressed the opinion that what had happened was unfortunate, but not very far out of the ordinary as home robberies went.

The only part that Chase regretted a little was not removing the silencer from the shooter's pistol. Having a silencer seemed unburglar-like to him, and sure as hell would make some cop scratch his head. The saving fact was that although silencers were illegal in Vermont, the house was half a mile from New Hampshire, where anybody who wanted a silencer could pay two hundred bucks for the federal transfer tax and have one.

The police had been sympathetic, and they hadn't even told him not to leave town. They would probably think of that in a day or two, but they wouldn't call him before midday tomorrow because he was a local man who'd had a shock and lost half a night's sleep. They would not be too far wrong, but right now the crime victim was driving at seventy-five miles an hour southbound down Interstate 89.

He took out the first of the prepaid cell phones and dialed his daughter Emily's number.

"Hello?" Her voice was raspy. She must be in bed stretching to reach the phone.

"Hi, kid. It's me. I'm really sorry to call at this hour. But it's finally happened. One of them found me at the house, so I'm on the road."

"Are you bringing the dogs to me?"

"Maybe eventually. Right now, no. Dave and Carol have been through a lot tonight. I think they need time with me before I do anything like that. Come to think of it, so do I."

"Jesus, Dad."

"I know, honey. I only called so you wouldn't think they got me or something. I can't help what's already happened. You'll be all right. There's nothing in the house that links me to you. No papers, no pictures, and to the extent I can accomplish it no prints of yours or DNA. I always clean the place after you leave. I'm going to be able to hold on to this phone a few more days, but no more than a week. If you need me, call it. Here's the number."

"I can see it on my screen."

"Oh, yeah."

"I hate this," she said. "I hate it, and it never had to happen."

"We're not sure yet if anything did happen."

"You just said it happened. I assume there's a dead man in your house?"

"They moved him pretty quickly. This happened in Vermont, honey. It was a slow night."

"Right. But it happened," she said.

"I'm sorry. But you're out of this mess and free from it. I'm glad."

"What bullshit. Nobody who loves anybody is ever free from anything."

"I meant you to be."

"I know you did. So now I have more money than a princess, only I'm still afraid to spend it, and my father is on a cell phone on a highway bullshitting me because he thinks he might not get to talk to me again."

"It probably won't be that bad."

"I hope not. But don't take any chances. If you have to, you can rent a motel room and leave the dogs in it, and I'll be there to pick them up as soon as a human being can take a plane there. If you're with them, I'll take all three of you."

"I've never doubted it," he said. He drove in silence for a few seconds.

"You're awfully quiet," she said.

"I'm really sorry."

"I get that," she said. "I've always gotten that."

"It doesn't hurt to repeat it."

"Yes it does. It all hurts."

"I guess you've got to get ready for work, don't you?"

"Yes."

"I love you."

"Obviously. And I love you. Call when you can."

He slipped the phone into his pocket and kept driving. As he drove, he listened to the deep, nasal snores of Dave and Carol, who were asleep together on the backseat.

3

Once a man has stolen something he is a thief. If what he stole is big enough, then always and forever, no matter what else he's done, he will always be a thief.

Again, for the ten thousandth time, he remembered standing in the North African sun, on the powdery dust of the road that ran along the desert's edge. He had just seen the car go by on its way from the office in the city to the place he had designated as the spot for the meeting he had demanded. At that moment, he could still have walked away. But if he kept going toward the meeting, he would die. He knew it would be a quiet death, not disturbing things on the surface. It would be so quiet it would seem civilized.

As Chase looked back on the day now, he could see it in its sun-bleached clarity. His first sin came right then. It was anger. He had risked his life bringing the shipment of money to Libya from the bank in Luxembourg. In order to preserve deniability he had been discharged from the army months earlier and moved into a civilian special ops status that left no records, and he carried a false passport. The military intelligence officers had ordered him to do everything the way a criminal would do it.

He had taken the freighter from Rotterdam to the Port of Algiers, watching his cargo container for the weeklong trip. On the last night out, he had caught a member of the crew sawing off the lock of the container, and had to choke him out and lock him, unconscious, in a storage bay, bound and gagged. For the rest of the trip he had needed to remain awake, crouching near the cargo container, clutching his gun and waiting for the others to find their shipmate and rush him.

When they were in sight of land he changed his plan. He opened the container and loaded the cartons of money into a lifeboat, then lowered the boat and drove it to shore alone. As soon as he hit the beach he hired the driver of a fish factory truck to carry him south, deep into the desert. After that he had begun the long trek east.

He had transported the money across two borders to smuggle it to the prearranged destination. He had paid for rides under canvas tarps in the backs of trucks, and twice stolen cars. In the middle of one night a pair of Algerian soldiers he had hired to drive him came to cut his throat, and he shot them both and drove on without them. When he had arrived at his destination, he set up the first meeting with the middleman, Faris Hamzah, and delivered the money. Then he had waited for the money to do its work. And he waited.

And then, that morning over two months later, when he had seen Faris Hamzah in the backseat of his new car, he had known. The money had not gone to the insurgents waiting in the Nafusa Mountains. The middleman in the city had absorbed it. The United States government had entrusted him with money to be delivered to the rebel army in the field. The fighters were short on food, on weapons and ammunition, and on parts and fuel for the cheap, tough little Japanese pickup trucks they drove through the remote areas where their strongholds were. Faris Hamzah had agreed to deliver it to them, but he had kept the money.

Hamzah's car was brand-new. It was a white Rolls-Royce Phantom. He didn't know what they cost, exactly, but he knew it was north of four hundred thousand in Los Angeles or New York. This one had made a much more complicated journey, probably by container ship to Dubai or Riyadh, where there were more people who could afford one, and then somehow transshipped across borders undercover. Ahead of it were two new Range Rovers, and a third came behind. Each of the Range Rovers had five men inside. The men he could see were wearing mismatched pieces of military battle dress. They were all on their way to his secret face-to-face meeting with Faris Hamzah in the empty land outside Hamzah's home village southeast of Benghazi.

He returned to the rented room where he had hidden his satellite phone. He climbed up on the roof of the building where he could see the streets nearby, and there would be no unseen listeners, and then he called the number that military intelligence had given him. When the voice came on and answered with the proper numeric ID, he said, "Faris Hamzah isn't passing the money to its intended end user. Right now he's sitting in the back of a Rolls-Royce and has three Range Rovers full of men who seem to be bodyguards."

The number on the other end said, "He was chosen very carefully."

"He's a thief."

The number sighed. "Everything we do in these situations is a gamble."

"I'm supposed to meet with him alone in about two hours," he said. "What do you want me to do?"

"You can meet with him if you want," said the number.

"I mean, should I try to get back what's left of the money?"

"If the first thing he bought was three Range Rovers full of armed men, you wouldn't have much luck. Is there any chance the fifteen men are insurgents?"

"He drove through town with them in brand-new cars."

"All right. You only gave him twenty million," the number said.

"We're letting him keep it?"

"He'll probably get his name moved to the shit list. This call is timed out. Call in again when you're out of the country." The line went dead.

He stood there staring at the phone for a few seconds. Then he realized not that he had already made his decision, but that there was no deciding to do. Then he was in motion.

Over the next few minutes he gathered the few belongings he had acquired, removed the phone's battery, and put it in his backpack with the rest. As he walked, he searched for a vehicle. He looked for one of the small Japanese pickup trucks like the ones the rebels in the desert used. When he found the right one, he paid the owner in cash, drove it to the police station, and parked it beside the lot where the policemen parked theirs. Then he walked on.

He never wavered, never lost sight of his destination. He thought through the details as he walked through the city. It was hot—terribly hot. But he bought bottled soft drinks from vendors as he went. The bottled water was too easy to refill with polluted tap water. Pepsi-Cola and Dr Pepper were much more expensive, but they were too difficult to counterfeit. He wore a baseball cap to keep himself from being sun blinded, and thought about how odd it was that people in these dreadful remote places all over the world sported caps that said Minnesota Twins and shirts labeled Seattle Mariners under a sun hot enough to suck the moisture from a person's eyeballs.

When he arrived at Faris Hamzah's house he had not thought about what would happen next, or who might get hurt. He had not even gotten around to thinking about how he would get out of the country. He had been trained with the expectation that he would do these things himself, making decisions as he came to them. He had gotten in, and so he would get out.

He could see beyond the stuccoed block wall that remodeling had begun at Faris Hamzah's house. He climbed the wall and dropped to the ground. There were colorful ceramic tiles in stacks waiting to be laid around a new fountain being built between the two scraggly olive trees he had noticed on his first visit. There was a high pile of pale newly milled lumber near the back of the house, probably for the framing of an addition. This was going to be a busy place, but it seemed to be empty of workmen at the moment. He climbed out of the compound.

He didn't return to the hotel where he had been staying. For the first twenty-four hours he watched Faris Hamzah's compound. There were still no workmen on the project, but there were armed watchmen around the compound at night. He observed them, and it seemed their job was to guard the growing cache of building materials. Part of the night they sat on the lumber and talked, but nobody walked the perimeter.

The second day he slept in the shade under a disabled truck propped up on blocks outside the bay of a mechanic's garage. There were about twenty other vehicles of various sorts in some state of disassembly or disrepair around the building. Any passing pedestrians who noticed him apparently assumed he was working on the truck or had taken a break in the shade. In those days he was good at sleeping until a particular sound reached his ears. He didn't hear it, so he slept about eight hours.

At dusk he crawled out and studied the compound from a distance. This time there were two guards at the gate in the wall, but no guards inside the compound that he could see. He knew Faris Hamzah must have come home. He came closer and saw the three Range Rovers parked outside the wall, and that confirmed it. He went to a smoke shop two blocks away and bought a pack of Gauloises cigarettes and matches.

He had noted many things during the sleepless part of his day. One was that the gas tank of the truck under which he had been sleeping was not empty. The truck had a bent axle and must have been towed to the mechanic's shop, but that had not emptied the tank. He went to the back of the compound and stole a dozen ten-penny nails, a hammer, and a bucket. He went back to the mechanic's shop, crawled under the truck, punched a hole in the gas tank, and drained it of a bucket of gasoline, then used the nail as a plug to stop the gas leaking out.

When the night was late and the moon was low, he climbed the back wall of Faris Hamzah's compound and walked up to the house. He poured gasoline along two sides of the house and had started along the third when he ran out of gasoline. He was careful to keep the entrance and the front door clear, so any people inside could get out.

He left the bucket, but kept the hammer and nails. When he judged the time was right he crouched to move forward and dragged himself under the first Range Rover. He reached up from below, disconnected the battery, and then cut one of the cables. Then he removed the pair of metal jerry cans for extra gasoline mounted on the rear door of each Rover, went under the vehicle, punched a hole in the gas tank, and filled the cans. He repeated the process with the other two Range Rovers. He hid the six twenty-liter cans at the back of Hamzah's compound.

He retreated, and began to walk through the darkened city. When he reached the police station he got into his white pickup truck, drove it to Hamzah's neighborhood, and parked it at the rear of his compound with the motor running. He loaded the six gasoline cans from the Range Rovers into the back of his truck.

He walked around the perimeter. When he reached the spot where the Range Rovers were parked he could see that the draining of their tanks was complete. They were sitting in a narrow lake of gasoline that reflected the light of the stars. He climbed the wall and locked the gate from the inside.

He stepped close to the rear of the house, lit a match, and started the first fire, then ran up the woodpile to vault over the wall to his truck. Within seconds the flames were licking up the sides of the house, and then billowing above it, throwing light throughout the compound. Soon he knew the guards had noticed the fire, because they began rattling the gate, then pounding on it, then throwing themselves against it. Finally they began to fire their guns at the lock. That seemed to work, because the shooting stopped and the two men ran inside to wake Faris Hamzah. Chase stood by the wall and waited.

The two guards had awakened the household with their gunfire. There was already a woman in the house screaming and shouting, and in a moment she emerged with two children and an elderly woman. They ran out under the sun roof that provided shade for the doorway during the day, and then out the gate.

Faris Hamzah came out a minute later carrying a sealed cardboard carton. His two guards came out after him, each carrying two more cartons, which they started to carry toward the gate, but Faris Hamzah yelled something in Arabic, and they put them near the woodpile instead. That way they wouldn't be tempting to neighbors who were attracted by the commotion and the fire. Faris Hamzah ran back inside to get more, and the two guards followed.

Chase recognized those five boxes, because he had packed them in Luxembourg. He took two of them and tossed them over the wall, and then the other three. He emptied the boxes into his truck's bed, closed them, brought them back into the compound, and placed them where Hamzah's guards had left them.

This time when Hamzah and his guards returned with five more cartons, they looked relieved and their confidence seemed to have returned. In the darkness, the fire, and the moving shadows, they could see the growing row of cardboard cartons and seemed to think that they had saved all the money. They ran back into the house, whether to save other valuables or to get water to fight the fire, it didn't matter. For the moment they were gone.

Chase hoisted himself back over the wall, threw the five full boxes over the wall into his truck and climbed after them, then covered the bed with its canvas tarp. He got into the driver's seat, lit a cigarette, and drove. He swerved close to the three Range Rovers. He stopped, tossed his burning cigarette into the pool of gasoline under the vehicles, and accelerated. In the rearview mirror he could see the fire flare into life, then streak along the row of cars, engulfing them in undulating light and flames twenty-five feet high.

Sometimes when he remembered the night, he imagined that he had seen Hamzah and his guards come out of the house to find that five boxes were empty and five gone, start shouting in amazement and anger, and then run to the gate to see the three vehicles aflame. He actually never saw that happen, because he was too far away by that time, and had already turned the corner at the first street. But his imagination had supplied the details, so they had become part of the story he had told only twice—once to Anna and once to Emily.

Now, as he stared ahead into the darkness of Interstate 89 beyond the range of his headlights, he thought about the time after the escape. He knew his enemies had assumed that when he reached the main highway he would head north for the port. Instead he turned south toward the desert. For the first few hours he was still checking his rearview mirrors every few seconds, pushing the gas pedal for every bit of extra speed. When he was far enough away he stopped on the desert road to secure the loose money under the tarp in the back of the truck by stuffing some into one box that was half-full, and the excess into his backpack and under the seats in the cab. Then he covered the bed again and drove on, going as far as he could while the night lasted.

He stopped again in a lonely spot at midday to fill the pickup's gas tank with two of the twenty-liter gas cans from the Range Rovers. Then he stopped at a garbage dump at the edge of an oil field and picked up some plastic bags of garbage to cover the cardboard boxes, so he would appear to be on his way to dump the trash.

He drove the next six hundred miles with the garbage in back, left the highway, and crossed into Algeria without seeing a checkpoint, and then made his way to the next paved road by bumping across deserted, rocky country until he felt the smooth pavement. Two days later he traded the truck to a fisherman on a beach in Morocco in exchange for a night trip along the coast to Rabat.

In a week he made the acquaintance of a man who imported hashish to Europe inside the bodies of fish. After another week he and his own boatload of fish made it into Gibraltar with plastic bags of money hidden in the bottoms of the fish crates.

The last call he made to his contact number for the intelligence service was brief. This time it was a female voice that said, "This number has been changed or disconnected. Please check your directory and dial again."

Tonight, so many years later, his taking back the money seemed like a story someone else had told him. He still saw snatches—the way Faris Hamzah's house looked in the firelight, the way the headlights of his little pickup truck bounced wildly into the air when he hit a bump, so they were just two beams aimed a little distance into the immensity of the sky, and the world below them was black. But the feelings seemed to belong to someone else, a misguided young man from long ago, his anger and self-righteousness preventing him from seeing clearly. Even the anger, the rage, had become abstract and bloodless. The emotion was simply a fact he acknowledged, a part of the record.

The rest of the record was no better. The Libyan government he had been sent to help topple had lasted another thirty years. Other men who had not yet been born on that night had overthrown it, and then the country had degenerated into anarchy, chaos, and civil war. The humanitarian purpose his mission had been intended to serve was relevant only to a particular, vanished set of circumstances, so irrelevant to the present that it was difficult for even Chase to reconstruct from memory.

He kept on Interstate 89 until he was past Manchester, New Hampshire, then merged onto 93, continued into Massachusetts, and then switched to 95. If he stuck with it, 95 could take him all the way to Florida. But he knew that was a route that carried every sort of traffic, including gunrunners and drug dealers bringing money south and merchandise north. Cops of many agencies were waiting along the way to spot a suspicious vehicle or a wanted license plate. He knew the best thing to do was move onto smaller, slower roads and stay on them as long as he could before he had to sleep.

He coasted off the interstate at a rest stop so he could use the men's room and let the dogs relieve themselves on the grassy margin off the parking area. He gave them food and water, and when they were ready to climb into the car again, he got back on the road. During their brief stop no other cars parked anywhere near them or even drove past them in the lot. He accelerated to the first exit and took it, so he would be on less-traveled roads as he headed south and west. He made his way to Route 20, which ran east and west across Massachusetts and New York State, and began the long drive through small towns and old rural districts, where there were no manned tollbooths or automatic cameras to take his picture.

In a few days his picture might be on television. He couldn't afford to be noticed now. Having some dutiful citizen out there who remembered seeing him in a particular location along the way could get him killed later. People had no idea what could happen to a man who had stolen millions of dollars that belonged to the intelligence services of the United States government.

4

He loved the dogs, but he had never allowed their veterinarian to insert ID chips under their skin. He had known that a chip could give a future pursuer one more way to find him. He had been working on ways to improve his odds for a long time. He regretted only that he had not been as rigorous about it for a few years as he had been at first.

When he got into the car around 4:00 a.m. he'd known that his name could no longer be Dan Chase. He decided to become Peter Caldwell, one of the identities he'd planted in his twenties, soon after he returned from North Africa. He had used the name at intervals to keep it current. Buying things and going to hotels and restaurants were what kept credit histories vigorous. From the beginning he had used many ways of planting his aliases in data banks.

He had used information from a death notice in an old newspaper to apply for a replacement birth certificate from the county clerk's office in the Texas town where one of the real Peter Caldwells was born. He'd used the birth certificate to apply for a driver's license in Illinois. Then he had opened a bank account, bought magazine subscriptions, joined clubs that mailed him a book a month, ordered mail-order goods by catalog and phone, and paid his bills by check. When he was offered a credit card, he took it and used it. Everything he had done as Daniel Chase, Peter Caldwell, Alan Spencer, or Henry Dixon had been calculated to increase their credit ratings and their limits and make them less vulnerable to challenge.

He had made a few preparations for the moment when his car had only one ride left in it. He had kept caffeine pills under the seat, along with tins of nuts and bottles of water and a contraption that would allow him to urinate into a bottle without stopping the car if he wanted to. None of these preparations was recent, and right now they simply irritated him. He could have done better than this.

By noon the second day he had already changed the license plates on his car. The major police forces all had automatic license plate readers, so he put on the Illinois license plates he had kept in the trunk in case the police were searching for him. On a trip to Illinois he had bought a wrecked car like his at an auction. He had kept the plates and donated the car to a charity. He had known they wouldn't try to fix the vehicle. The car was too badly damaged to be used for anything but parts.

For years he had maintained identities for his wife, Anna, and his daughter, Emily, as the wife and daughter of each of the three manufactured men. But when Anna died, he kept her identities. He'd told himself it was in case Emily needed to start over sometime, but the truth was that he simply couldn't bear to destroy them.

For Emily's protection he had invented separate identities for her when she was still a child. She had gotten married under the false name of Emily Harrison Murray. He had been at her wedding in Hawaii as a guest, and been introduced as Lou Barlow, a cousin of her late mother, Mrs. Murray. Her trust fund had been placed in her own hands when she turned eighteen, and then transferred to her new name, Emily Coleman, after the marriage. She had been walked down the aisle by a favorite professor from college, who had always believed the story that she had been orphaned in a car accident. She was living on the proceeds of a trust fund, wasn't she?

From the time she left home for college until yesterday he had bought six new burner cell phones once a month, and mailed her three. In the memory of each was another's number. The day after her boyfriend, Paul, proposed marriage, she told him her father existed. She also told Paul he was still welcome to withdraw his proposal, but whether he married her or not he had to keep her secret.

A bit after dark the night of the wedding he had met Paul. While the reception was going on inside the mansion they had rented for the wedding, Emily had conducted her new husband into the back garden. He and Paul had taken measure of each other that night. He had reassured himself that Emily had chosen a man who would die rather than betray her secrets. And Paul had seen that his father-in-law was the sort of man who was capable of holding him to it. He had been glad for Emily that Paul was intelligent and good-looking. He had been a swimmer in college, tall and lean, with an intense set of eyes. He had been a good husband to Emily so far.

Dave and Carol began to stir in the backseat again. He looked in the rearview mirror for a long time before he was sure nobody was following closely enough to be a problem, and then turned off onto a rural road and let the dogs out to explore a field for good spots to relieve themselves. Then he fed them again. When they were finished eating and drinking, he and the dogs got back in and moved ahead. He had driven the full stretch of daylight, and now it was dark again. The night felt friendly, but he knew he was only feeling the afterglow of having won the first fight. When this night was used up, most of the benefit of that victory would be too, so he kept pushing himself, putting more distance between him and Norwich, Vermont. He fought the increasing weight of his fatigue, keeping himself awake by will alone.

It was already late when he noticed the pair of headlights that wouldn't go away. He had not seen a persistent follower during the day, or these headlights earlier in the night, and now he was at least four hundred miles from Norwich, Vermont. To Peter Caldwell that meant that the follower must have tracked him using a global positioning system, and then slowly narrowed the distance between them. And the only reason he could think of for a chaser to follow so closely was to get eyes on him before making another attempt to kill him.

Caldwell glanced in the mirror at Dave and Carol. They were sleeping peacefully on the backseat, their barrel chests rising and falling in long, slow breaths. He was going to have to do something, and he knew it would be better for them if he did it while the world was still dark, and their black fur might give them a better chance to survive.

He reached under the seat and retrieved his pistol, ejected the magazine to be sure it was full, pushed it back in, and stuck the weapon in his belt, and then he felt for the spare magazine. The weight told him it was full. He kept going at the same speed for a few more minutes, until he saw a group of rectangular buildings ahead. As he drew closer he could read the green letters at the top of the nearest one, which said HOTEL. He supposed he must be approaching Buffalo, or at least its airport. When he reached the driveway leading to the building he swung abruptly into it and saw DAYS HOTEL flash above him as he went past the sign.

Dave and Carol slid a little and then sat up, always interested in any change. He said quietly, "Hello, my friends. Everything is going to be all right." He knew that they would determine the opposite from the tone of his voice or the smell of his sweat now that his heartbeat and respiration had accelerated.

He watched the headlights a quarter mile behind dip slightly as the follower applied his brakes, and noted that the driver was one of those who didn't coast much, but instead always had his foot on the gas or the brake trying to exert control. The man probably oversteered too. Caldwell wasn't sure if the information would be useful or not. In the long run those habits burned a lot of gas. But if the driver was following him by GPS that didn't matter, because he could always stop at a gas station and catch up with Caldwell later.

Caldwell took the next turn into the semicircular drive toward the hotel entrance, but then kept driving past it to move around to the back of the building. He turned off his headlights as soon as he was around the first corner and drove up the outer row of cars parked in the lot. He turned into the first empty space and stopped, so his brake lights didn't show for more than a second, and turned off the engine. He turned off the car's dome lights, pulled out the pistol, and ducked down.

The pursuing car came off the highway and disappeared toward the front of the building. Caldwell could see it was a black sedan, probably a Town Car. When it was no longer visible, he opened his door and the back door to let the dogs out. The dogs ran across the lane to the bushes. He lay down beside his car and used his cell phone's screen as a flashlight to look at the undercarriage.

He saw the transponder, a small black box stuck to the underside of the battery mount with a pair of wires taped to the leads of his battery. He reached up and tore it out, and then stayed low to move away from his car. The first vehicle he saw was the hotel's shuttle bus. He crawled under it and attached the transponder to the battery of the bus the same way it had been attached to his car.

He stood and moved between the rows of parked vehicles toward his car. But as he did, a man emerged from the rear entrance of the hotel. Caldwell ducked down beside the nearest car. His pursuers' car must have stopped at the front entrance to let this man go into the hotel to search for Caldwell inside. He had come through the lobby to the back of the hotel.

The man began to run. As he ran he took a pistol out of his coat. In the dim light, Caldwell saw the thin red line of a laser bobbing along the pavement as the man ran directly toward Caldwell's car. He had recognized it.

Caldwell stayed down behind the car where he had hidden and waited until the man had gone past him, and then moved after him. He took out his pistol, hoping there would be something different he could do, but not knowing what it would be. He was fairly sure that the one who had stayed in the Town Car would be on his way around the building to the lot right now.

Moving the transponder had been a waste of time. The man ran unerringly to Caldwell's car. Caldwell saw the red dot sweep up from the ground to the car's windshield, and then to the side, into the backseat.

Caldwell used the time to get behind the man. He was still about twenty feet away when he said, "Drop the gun."

The man's body gave a startle reflex, as though he'd received an electric shock. He became still, the pistol with its laser sight still in his hand, its red dot on the side window of Caldwell's car, with the beam passing through to the backseat.

Caldwell said, "Drop it. You won't have time to do anything else."

Caldwell felt despair. The man wasn't reacting correctly. Maybe he didn't even speak English. Caldwell went to one knee and used the left mirror of the car beside him to steady his aim on the man's torso. The red dot moved.

Just as Caldwell had expected, the man tried to spin around to fire at the spot where Caldwell's voice had come from, and as Caldwell had predicted, the laser sight went too high. The man saw his mistake and tried to lower his aim, but Caldwell's shot found his chest.

Caldwell ran to the place where the man lay, but the two dogs reached him first. They sniffed the burned propellant in the air, the man's body, the blood, the death, and began to whine. "Come on," he said. "Let's go." He turned to let the two dogs into his car, but as he shut the back door, he heard the sound of another car approaching. As he ducked down he noticed the dead man's gun lying beside the body, the laser sight still emitting the beam of red light. He snatched up the pistol and pocketed it, then slithered under his car and lay on his belly.

The car's engine was too loud, the driver's impatience with the laws of physics bringing him around the building too fast. Caldwell kept track of the turn by listening to the squeal of the tires. The man drove directly to Caldwell's car, stopped his Town Car in front of it to block it, and then slid out the passenger side of his car and crouched behind it for protection as he drew a pistol and aimed it over the hood.

Caldwell used the only opportunity he could see. He remained on his belly and aimed the pistol with the laser sight under the man's car. When the red dot settled on the man's ankle, he fired.

The man went down, and Caldwell could see that the man's leg and the right side of his torso were now on the pavement as he clutched at his wounded ankle. Caldwell fired beneath the car again, then twice more. Caldwell saw the man's body jump twice, and then lie still.

Caldwell got into the Town Car and swung it into a parking space, and then ran to look into the backseat of his own car to be sure the dogs were still where they should be. He got in and started the engine. In a moment the car was back on the road. "I'm sorry about that, my friends," he said. "You're safe now." He hoped they would take it as a kind thing to say, and not just a lie.

5

The difficulty at the hotel had cost him time. He couldn't proceed in a straight line on the same highway and hope nobody would be waiting for him somewhere ahead. He took the first southbound highway. He used the night as well as he could, driving as fast as possible and never slowing unless he needed to.

When he reached the place for sleep it was beginning to turn light again. He was on a flat road through farm country, and he had not seen another car for an hour. There was a barn made of boards that had been rough cut many years ago and erected on a foundation of mortared fieldstones. At some point the barn had been painted on one end with a broadside advertisement that might have been for tobacco, but the paint had worn to illegibility. The wood on the barn had turned gray, and right now it was almost uniform. There must have been a farmhouse and outbuildings once, but there was no vestige of them now.

The headlights swept across the fields as he turned off the highway onto what had once been the barnyard, and he could see that nothing had been planted here for a very long time. There were mature trees in places where rows of corn or wheat had once been.

Caldwell drove the car inside the barn and parked. He took out the bowls, gave Carol and Dave a big bowl of bottled water, and another bowl with dry kibble.

When they had gobbled up their breakfast, he talked to them for a while. He used the word "good" many times, and petted and stroked them, and when they wanted him to, he rubbed their bellies.

As they ventured out of the barn and trotted around the area sniffing the air and zigzagging across the untilled weedy fields, Peter went into the backseat of the car, opened both doors, and lay down to sleep.

He slept deeply in the shade of the ghostly gray-board barn. He dreamed a selection of his usual nightmares, in which he got into predicaments that made him fear a deception of his was about to be uncovered. This time, as often happened, he was with his daughter, Emily, who in his dream was still a toddler and prone to tripping or falling into holes or not quite making it through doorways in time to save herself. The worst part was when Anna made an appearance.

She was twenty-four years old when they met, and she had lived only until she was forty-five, so he always remembered her as a young woman, her face almost unlined and her eyes still sharp and bright and blue, her hair the color of dark chocolate. She came into his vision, not through a doorway, just there. She smiled at him and put her hands on his shoulders almost the way she would sometimes, and he tried to place his hands on her waist, but then she was gone.

Waking stung, like learning the terrible news all over again. No, this wasn't a repeal of her death, just his daily return to the world where she was dead. He sat up in the backseat of the car.

He turned his head and saw Carol and Dave trotting around in the field beyond the barn. He acknowledged that he had been aware of them out there for a long time, maybe all the time he'd been sleeping. They weren't impatient, just watching over him and patrolling while he slept.

Caldwell got out of the car and went to the trunk. He took out a bottle of water and some canned dog food and refilled their bowls. He used the rest of the water to brush his teeth, then wash his face and underarms. The dogs had never seen him do such things in this primitive way, and they were frankly curious. When he was ready to go, they were already sitting nearby watching him. He said okay and the dogs jumped up on the backseat and settled there again.

Now as he drove, he realized that he wasn't afraid. When Anna had been alive and Emily was a child he had always dreaded the possibility that one or another of the people who wanted him dead would find him. Now he seemed to have outgrown the dread.

The three men who had finally come for him were young. Some of them had certainly not been born when he committed his theft, and probably none of them knew much about what he'd done. His was a name on a list, or maybe even the whole list. At one time he would have said it was a shame for a shooter to die for something that had so little to do with him. Now he knew that the reason didn't matter very much. Everybody died for nothing.

The predicament he had created for himself when he was young had made him aware that life was precious. Not everyone understood living. What many people seemed not to remember was that a human being who got up under his own power on even one morning and saw the sun and had food to eat was a very lucky animal. Knowing that each day was a life in itself had led him to make a thousand good decisions. Marrying Anna had been the most important. The decision had seemed insane to both of them at the start. They expected it to end early and badly. And maybe his life had been sweeter because he had known that it could all be taken away at any second. Each gift might be the last gift.

As Caldwell drove west in the early evening, with the sun down ahead of him, he felt much improved. He'd had more than eight continuous hours of sleep, something he almost never got anymore.

There were problems Caldwell had to solve tonight. First, he needed to get rid of this car. People in Norwich knew it. The car was registered in the name Daniel Chase. The fact that it now had Illinois plates had probably helped him get as far as he had. But the idea that the new plates would be sufficient for much longer was a fantasy. The men who attacked him had probably reported the Illinois plate numbers to their comrades. He couldn't simply remove the plates and abandon the car. The vehicle identification number was a matter of record, and any division of motor vehicles would type it into a computer and see that the car was wanted by the police. He could sell the car to the sort of person who would not be in a hurry to register it, and that would give Caldwell some time, but only a few days. If the police could catch him they would catch anybody else who drove it. What he really needed to do was make the car disappear.

As Caldwell drove, he thought of various ways of making the car invisible. If he tried to burn it, the VIN would still be visible on the dash, the front of the engine block, and the driver's side doorjamb. He was not far from Lake Erie now. If he dumped the car into the lake, it would have to be somewhere out in deep water or it would be visible from shore, and be found quickly. There was no easy way to accomplish that.

He supposed that he was going to have to find a way to bury it. Burying a car like his Camry would require a hole at least six feet deep, seven feet wide, and sixteen feet long. It would be like digging five or six graves in one night, and then filling them in. He started to think about the various sorts of machines he could get that would make the work easier. The best would be a bulldozer, but how could he get one without drawing attention to himself? He had to think smaller. Maybe he could rent a rototiller to break up the ground, or maybe some sort of motorized posthole digger that worked like a big Archimedes' screw to bring the dirt up to the surface.

He was still thinking about the problem when he drove into the outskirts of Erie, Pennsylvania. As he studied the area, he passed by a possible solution. A large junkyard stretched for about two hundred yards from the fence to the back wall. He could clearly see the driveway running up to the gate, but he was fairly sure that was not going to be his best way in. He pulled over a few hundred yards past the driveway, got out of the car, and trotted to the fence.

Caldwell walked along the perimeter of the yard, looking for security cameras, breaks in the barbed wire, and the general organization of the place. There was a big, low building near the entrance, and he assumed that was the office and a workshop and warehouse for salvaged parts. The owners would certainly have whatever security there was up there to prevent theft. What he needed to find was a place in another part of the facility that wasn't so well protected. It took him fifteen minutes of walking and looking before he found something that he believed would do. He trotted back to the place where he had parked, got in, and drove into Erie.

He rented a room in a one-story motel off Route 6 that had no hallways, just a long row of identical doors under a roof facing the highway. He parked in front of the one he'd rented and brought the dogs into the room with him. He turned on the television set and watched the local news with some trepidation. He still wasn't able to tell whether the three men who had come after him were agents of the US government, freelance operatives hired by Faris Hamzah or his heirs, or representatives of some other force that had developed an interest in him. He dreaded the possibility that the news anchor would announce that three FBI agents had died in the line of duty, or that he would see his own face on the screen identified as a thief and a murderer. But there was nothing.

The next day he began looking through newspaper ads, visiting Laundromats and coffee shops to look at bulletin boards and pick up the latest issues of shoppers' guides. In the afternoon he found an older Toyota Corolla in the parking lot of a grocery store with a sign on one of the side windows that said $1,500. RUNS GOOD. He found that the car was as advertised, and the young woman who owned it was reassured by the fact that he could pay in cash.

Late that night he left the dogs in the motel with some food and water, and they lay sprawled on the bed with the television going. He drove to the junkyard outside town. When he got there, he pulled onto the gravel driveway, and then turned to drive along the tall chain link fence until he came to the place he had seen the night before.

The coils of barbed wire at the top of the fence were uniform, but here the fence was made of wooden boards. He backed his car up to the fence until its bumper was against the boards. He stepped on the trunk and looked inside the yard. This was a forlorn area where most of the cars were in fairly bad shape. Some had front ends that looked as though a giant hand had swept across the metal and smeared it to the side. Others were not misshapen by accidents, but were old and out of style.

He looked carefully at the inner side of the wooden section of the fence and realized how his purpose could be accomplished. The wooden section consisted of a frame with a row of boards nailed vertically to it. He eased the car into the wooden fence, listened to the creaking sounds as nails were wrenched from two-by-fours, and kept adding power until one ten-foot segment toppled inward to the ground. The coiled barbed wire hung across the opening.

He got out of his car, dragged the section of boards aside, and drove his car under the barbed wire and inside the junkyard. He drove slowly and carefully through this area of the yard until he found a spot that looked right. There was a row of pretty good cars, all of them up on blocks and ready to be stripped for parts. He pulled up beside the last one, found a set of blocks, and went to work. He went to the trunk, took out the jack and the tire iron, jacked up the car, put the first block in place, removed the wheel, and lowered the car onto the block. He kept at it until all four wheels had been removed and the car was up on blocks like the others. He popped off the hubcaps and put them in the backseat, then rolled the wheels a distance away where there were some tires, and left them.

It took him a few minutes to restore the wooden fence and restring the looped barbed wire along the top. Then he began to walk. It took him about an hour to walk to the space in the parking lot of the grocery store where his replacement Toyota was waiting, and another half hour in the grocery store to fill the car with supplies for himself and the dogs. When he got back to his motel room he moved the other items he had left into the trunk of the replacement car. He took the dogs out for a few minutes so they could relieve themselves, and then the three climbed back onto the king bed and slept.

6

Early in the morning Caldwell went to the office to check out of the motel. The night's work of scrapping his car without anyone's knowledge had left him worn, but he had to begin the next phase.

He had known from the beginning that the only way to survive would be to drop out of sight completely for a while. He took out his disposable cell phone and texted Emily. "Can you talk now?"

The answer came back about a minute later. "With a patient. I'll call."

He opened the door of the new car and let the dogs examine it. They were a bit hesitant at first, because it wasn't the car they considered theirs. Its smells were not their smells. But because he was holding the door for them they jumped up onto the seat, sniffed a little, flopped down, adjusted their positions, and then lay still.

He got in and drove out the far end of the parking lot so the motel owners wouldn't see he had a different car. Then he headed west through Erie and turned south onto Route 6 toward Cleveland and Sandusky. After a few minutes the phone rang.

"Hi," he said.

"Are you still all right?" Emily said.

"So far. You?"

"No changes yet."

"I wanted you to know that it's time to get rid of the phones we've been using. You can reach me on the second one from now on, if you need to."

"Okay," she said. "What prompted this?"

"I'm going to have to sink beneath the surface now. It will be months before I try to call again, so don't worry about the long silence. Don't ever go near the house. There's nothing left there that you want."

"I know," she said. "You're the only relic I have left."

"If you get the feeling that somebody's watching you, or anything like that, call. Otherwise, just wait. Don't look as though you're being watchful, but be watchful."

"I know all this. I've known it since I was ten. I'm going to be thinking about you every day if this takes thirty years. We all will be. You have a family that loves you. Now go get lost. With your heart and lungs, you could live to be a hundred and six. Do it."

"I'll try. Bye, kid."

"Bye, Dad."

He could almost see her standing up from the big leather chair in her office in her white coat and striding along with that straight posture and determined walk, ready to see her next patient. She looked a bit like her mother did at thirty, only taller and straighter.

He was going to settle somewhere. Traveling gave too many people a chance to notice him. And since the last time he had needed to disappear, a hundred new layers of danger had been added. The last time, right after he had returned from North Africa, technology had been more primitive.

When he got home from Libya he wrote a letter to his section of military intelligence. He told them he had made it home with the money he had recovered from Faris Hamzah. He included a few facts that an outsider could not have known, to prove he wasn't a fake. He asked them to reactivate the phone contact number so he could make arrangements to deliver the money to his section.

He had felt wary and very angry. He had not liked the way his contact people had treated him near the end of his mission. They had abandoned a comrade behind enemy lines. But he had also ignored his orders, so he was prepared for some kind of unpleasant reaction. He rented a small retail space in a Virginia shopping center and placed the money there before he mailed his letter to Fort Meade. He suspected that the minute he had given them a location they would put it under surveillance, so he didn't mention one.

On the day he had set for the delivery, he made a call to the contact number from a pay phone a hundred miles away. He never heard the ring, just heard the faint hiss of an open line and a male voice that said, "Hello."

He said, "Hello. Thank you for activating the number. I'm calling to turn the money from my mission over to army intelligence. I just need—"

"I advise you to be quiet and listen carefully. You are wanted for a number of serious offenses, and the United States government doesn't bargain with fugitives. There will be a team of federal officers for you to surrender yourself to at the rendezvous point. You will be taken into custody and transported to a secure facility where you can be interviewed regarding events that occurred during the past five months. You will be given ample opportunity to explain anything you like. Is this all clear?"

"I haven't done anything wrong. I just want to finish my mission and—"

"Quiet."

"Get the money back where it belongs."

"Here are your instructions. Proceed to Walter Reed National Military Medical Center at 8901 Rockville Pike in Bethesda. Park your vehicle, and walk to the front entrance. Step inside, and they'll be waiting for you. Do you understand?"

He hung up the phone. Two weeks later he parked behind the retail space he had rented, picked up the boxes of money, and drove away. He used some of the cash to live for the next few months while he worked on the first fake identities he built. It was easy for him to earn a license to work as a truck driver under the name Daniel Chase, because he had learned to drive a semi in the army, while he was training in false identities. The work kept him moving, mostly at night, and gave him plenty of time to think.

Each step led to the next steps, and each deception was easier because he had performed the last one and had begun to understand how various bureaucracies worked. Birth certificates led to Social Security numbers and then to driver's licenses, and then to bank accounts and credit cards. Eventually even passports became possible because he could submit the supporting documents by mail.

He stayed angry, but it was about a year before he gave up trying to devise schemes for returning the money that would restore his reputation. He knew he could simply mail the boxes of money to Fort Meade, but that wasn't going to exonerate him. He had hauled the money to Libya and done his best to complete a dangerous mission, and when he had finished, his own superiors had abandoned him and then decided to treat him like a criminal.

He began to invest the money. He would deposit small sums in cash in his bank accounts in various names, then write checks to financial services companies—brokers, mutual funds, and later hedge funds. Once he got started, the whole process became almost automatic. Money deposited or invested became more money, and produced the impression of solidity. Time made new money into old money, and old money into wealth.

It took him seven years to get all of the money out of boxes and invested with financial institutions under various false names. At the end of each year he would have his four accountants prepare tax returns for Dixon and Chase and Caldwell and Spencer, then mail them to a fictitious lawyer who was just a mailing address. He took advantage of legitimate deductions, but always paid the taxes without making questionable claims or forgetting to report income. For over thirty years, he had managed to elude the people who were looking for him. But over the years, one after another of the methods he had used became obsolete. If he'd had to start again now, he had no idea whether he could do it or not.

Caldwell needed to go under the surface as soon as possible. The least troublesome way would be to reach Chicago and stop. It was only about a day away. The Peter Caldwell identity included an Illinois driver's license and a few other bits of identification that he had acquired to pad his wallet—a Chicago library card, a gym membership. On paper he looked like a longtime Chicago resident.

When he reached the city he checked in to a hotel, bought a laptop computer, and began to look for the right apartment. He decided the place should be at least modestly upscale, because police spent less time in affluent places and were less aggressive and suspicious when they were there.

He knew what he was looking for, but he would have to search in the right places in the right way. He started in the northern suburbs—Lake Forest, Kenilworth, Barrington Hills, Winnetka, Glencoe, Wilmette. Houses in the northern suburbs were too expensive to buy invisibly, and there were too few apartments. The southern suburbs were closer to the thing he was looking for, and he looked on Craigslist and found a promising place in Geneva.

It had been many years since he had been in the Chicago area for more than a day or so on the way to somewhere else. He had to do some exploring. He liked the look of Geneva, and the apartment seemed promising. It was 1,800 square feet, with three bedrooms and two baths. When he drove by the building, he was pleased with it. The place was made of gray limestone like a dormitory in an eastern college, with a rounded lintel over a thick wooden front door that looked as though it would be hard to open with a battering ram. There was a back staircase that led to what looked like a kitchen door on the second floor.

He stopped the car and called the number in the ad. He described himself to the woman who answered the phone as a sixty-year-old retiree who wanted the benefits of Chicago but didn't want to live in the center of it. She asked him how soon he could come and see the apartment. The way she said it intrigued him. He said he could be there in a half hour, and went to get a cup of coffee.

When he knocked on the door, the woman materialized in the doorway. She was slim and appeared to be about forty years old, wearing tight jeans and a short black jacket that might have been designed for a male Spanish dancer. She said her name was Zoe McDonald, and she had blue eyes and chestnut hair. He studied her as they talked in the foyer. She had a pleasant, soft voice, no strange mannerisms, and there was nothing about her to make him feel worried.

She seemed satisfied with the way he looked. He was an inch or so taller than average and he had kept himself in the same physical condition since he'd joined the army, because he had the sort of enemies who were physically dangerous. But his training hadn't made him muscle-bound or threatening.

She led him from the small foyer up a set of stairs to the second-floor landing and the apartment entrance. He followed her inside to a large living room with two couches and a couple of armchairs all bathed in light from a set of three large windows.

She explained that she had rented the place for $2,000 a month and wanted two roommates of either sex to defray the costs. His share would be $650 for one bedroom. The bathrooms would be shared or private, depending on the sex of the third roommate. As she talked, Caldwell studied the furnishings, searching for things that would tell him more about her.

In an alcove there was a grand piano, and on it were three framed photographs, turned toward the keyboard. One was a picture of her with a young woman—little more than a girl—who looked a bit like her, and another was of her with a boy and the same girl in a boat with a set of water skis leaned upright behind them at the stern. He asked if she played piano while he looked at the third picture. She and the kids were in it again on a green lawn, but the picture was oddly asymmetrical, because it had been cropped. He knew that the missing person was the husband she must have divorced. He must have been the one who took the other two pictures.

She said she only practiced the piano once a day, and would be considerate to him and the other roommate about when she did it.

He said, "Don't worry. If I were to live here, you could practice whenever you felt like it. I like the piano. My daughter played for about ten years, and it's a good memory." He knew it was a slight risk to mention a daughter, but he took it because he knew this woman would like the idea, and if he lived here he might want to call Emily.

He could tell that he'd made a good impression, so he decided to build on it. "I'd like to make a proposal that might help. I would like to stay for at least six months, possibly a year. And I would like to rent both empty rooms. That way we'd each get a private bathroom, and there wouldn't be a third person to object to your practicing. If you agree, I would pay you the first six months in advance. But I have pets, and you would have to be all right with that."

Her face acquired a look of doubt. "What sort of pets?"

"Two dogs."

"Dogs." Her voice was like a door closing.

"Yes. They're waiting for me in the car. Would you be willing to go outside and meet them?"

"I just don't know, Mr. Caldwell. I don't mind dogs. I like them. But this isn't really the sort of building where dogs are happy. There's not much of a yard. And I have a landlord. Are they small dogs?"

He smiled. "Better than that. They're *good* dogs." He detected a slight tremor of amusement at the corners of her mouth. "Please," he said. "Don't say no yet. Just come out for a minute to say hello."

He was beginning to hope he had judged her correctly. She had rented an apartment she couldn't afford alone, because she had assumed she could easily attract two roommates. But it was now the last day of March. She obviously had not found any, or found acceptable ones. The rent was due. She hesitated. "All right."

They both began to move toward the door, and he used the time to work on her. "I'd like to move in just as soon as I can, because I'm paying for a hotel while I search. And I can pay you in cash."

When they were beside his car he opened the back door and said, "Okay, you two. Come out."

The two black dogs jumped down from the backseat, and Zoe seemed to stiffen, as though she were afraid. But the dogs sat on the grass strip by the sidewalk, studying his face and waiting to hear what was expected of them. He said, "This is Dave, and this one is Carol. Dogs, this is Zoe McDonald." She held out her hand and the two sniffed it, so she petted their heads.

He said, "They're not mean, they're not dirty, and they don't have accidents in the house. They do pretty much whatever I do, or what I ask them to." The dogs brushed against her, letting her pet their backs.

But she said nothing, so he said, "I can post an extra thousand-dollar deposit just for their sake, so you won't have to worry about them doing some kind of damage."

He watched Zoe McDonald's face as she touched the two dogs and tried to figure them out. An hour ago she must have been thinking she was going to have to come up with two thousand dollars. She had no other tenants in sight. Now she had an offer that would pay the whole rent for both of them for three months, and a special security deposit to protect her. The traffic in the living room and the kitchen would be two people instead of three.

He could see that her time with the dogs was helping his case. She seemed to like the feel of their fur, and their affectionate tail wagging was disarming. He said, "There's a big park around here somewhere, isn't there?"

"Yes. It's right down the street that way." She pointed.

"How far?"

"Close. I'll show you."

"Thanks." He took the two leather leashes out of the car and draped them around his neck.

"You're the one who wears the leashes?"

"They look better on me. If the dogs being loose seems to bother anybody, I use the leashes. Does it bother you?"

She shrugged. "No."

He said, "Dave. Carol. Let's walk."

He and Zoe McDonald started down the sidewalk. It was a bright, pleasant early spring day with high, puffy clouds and a breeze that was mild but cool. The dogs widened their wanderings around Caldwell to include Zoe in the circle.

She said, "You told me on the phone you were retired. What did you do?"

"Nothing exciting. I worked for the government for a while, and then went into the investment business for the next thirty years. This seemed like a good time to retire."

"People don't come to Chicago to retire much."

"I like a lot of things about big cities, but I'm happier if I don't live in the thick of it."

"What did you do in government?"

"Pretty much what I did for clients after I quit. I tried to help them use their money wisely. How about you? What do you do?"

"What I still do. I played the piano. Then I taught piano. Got married, had kids, got older, got divorced. Still play the piano."

"I'll bet you're really good at it."

"Better than I was at the other stuff. My kids turned out great, but I suspect they did most of that on their own."

He said, "If they had been screwed up, would you have thought it must be your fault?"

"Probably."

"Then you have to take some credit that they aren't."

"All right," she said. "I will."

They came to the park, which had a small lake and a lot of lawn, with a fringe of trees and some benches. The dogs were delighted with the place, which seemed to be full of new and intriguing smells. They were tentative about straying too far from the pair of humans, but they let their distance grow to about forty feet before they looked at Peter Caldwell to see if he wanted them back.

As they walked, Zoe McDonald's mood seemed to change. She talked about how good it was to walk to a park and to live in a neighborhood with mature trees. Caldwell merely nodded and kept her talking, because it seemed to him that she was beginning to turn her remarks into a sales pitch. She was selling the place to both of them. Only once did he add anything. When she said, "Of course we're right next to a huge city, and walking alone at night isn't a good idea," he shrugged. "Dave and Carol help with that. In daylight nobody thinks it's worth trying to get past them for my wallet. In the dark they grow about fifty pounds each."

She laughed. "I'll bet they do."

She pointed out to him the bus stops, the restaurants she'd tried, the delicatessen and the grocery store.

When a police car appeared up the street, Caldwell said, "Carol, Dave." The dogs trotted up to him and let him snap the leashes on their collars. He patted them and said, "Good work, my friends." He reached into his pocket and produced two bone-shaped biscuits. He looked at Zoe. "Would you like to give them their treat?"

"Yes." She took the biscuits and let the dogs clamp their jaws on them. They crunched them into pieces and ate them from the lawn. She looked at her watch. "We'd better get back. Our rent is due today before six."

7

Caldwell checked out of his hotel the next morning and moved in to the apartment. The process took about a half hour, including the fifteen-minute drive, since everything he owned other than his dogs would fit in one backpack. He bought a suitcase on the way, so he would look less suspicious.

Over the next few weeks Peter Caldwell was as quiet, considerate, and tolerant as he could be. He took Dave and Carol for a walk twice a day, sometimes for hours, and let them sleep in his room as they always had. He formed the habit of being the one who noticed the trash was full and needed to be taken out, and cleaned the common areas of the apartment every second day.

He spent a couple of hours on his laptop computer every day. He checked the news outlets in Vermont and New Hampshire, in New York State, and in Chicago, and then the national news. He checked many of his investment accounts under the names Peter Caldwell, Henry Dixon, and Alan Spencer, looking for some sign that they had been found. For the first five weeks he could find nothing. There was no mention of any of the shootings, and no sign that the authorities had found his extra names or frozen any accounts. For the moment he needed to stay out of sight, and now that he'd found a place to do that, he was very careful to keep it.

Peter Caldwell was a friendly, but not outgoing, tenant. His dogs were better than he had promised, and that was a relief to him and, he was sure, to Zoe. But one day when he and the dogs returned home from their second walk, Zoe was waiting for him on the big couch in the living room that faced the apartment door. "Hi, Peter."

"Hi," he said. "It's nice out. Have you been out this afternoon?"

"No," she said. "I had some things to do around here and got caught up. Are you okay?"

"Me?" he said. "Sure. My health has always been far better than I deserve, and these two make me get out and walk."

"You know, Peter, I've been thinking that you and I should talk. You seem to be doing your best to be completely silent and invisible. That's not necessary."

"I've lived alone for ten years, and I've never had much experience as a roommate, so I'm trying to find the right balance. It's a thin line, so I have to feel around for it."

"You're a mile from being irritating, and an invisible man is kind of creepy. Relax. This is your place as much as mine—more, because you're paying for two bedrooms. You're not just welcome in the living room and kitchen when I'm gone, but when I'm here too. So are Dave and Carol. I like them, and I can tell they like me. At least they don't want to bite my neck and shake me to death. You don't have to be so damned considerate that I feel like I'm living with a ghost." She gave him a look of suspicion. "You're not wanted for anything, are you?"

"Less and less as I get older."

She laughed. "It happens to all of us."

"Well, thank you," he said. "I'll try not to tiptoe around too much."

"Good," she said. "You know, maybe it would help if we got more used to each other. We should go out for a drink sometime. Once you know me, you won't care if I get offended."

"I doubt that," he said. "Let's go now. If you'll just give me a minute to feed these two, I'm free."

"All right," she said. "While you're doing that, I'll get my purse."

He went to the kitchen to feed the dogs. As he watched them eat, he considered. The apartment was perfect for his purpose. Zoe held the lease, and he had never needed to give anyone but her so much as his name. He had already stayed out of sight for five weeks. As long as he remained careful, he was almost impossible to find. He had left no trail. The longer he could stay here the safer he would be. Going out for a drink with Zoe was something he wouldn't ordinarily do. She was too pretty, too arresting to go unnoticed, and having a companion might distract him from watching for trouble. But being with a woman did make him appear more like everyone else, and he needed to keep her happy. He went to his closet, took out a sport coat, and sat on the couch to wait.

When she appeared she was wearing black pants that hugged her body, and a short jacket that was cut like the one she'd worn to meet him. He said, "You look too good for me."

"Once I was in there for my purse, I figured what the heck."

They walked to a restaurant she had recommended to him when she'd shown him around the neighborhood five weeks earlier. It was called John Harmon's Irish Bar and Grill. They went inside and he studied the place. There was a dining room that was all dark wood paneling and booths, with a fireplace. And there was a barroom that was completely filled by men and women in their twenties and early thirties, just off work.

Caldwell took Zoe's arm and conducted her to the dining room, where a young blond woman took them to a booth. They ordered a pair of Jameson 18 black label whiskeys and two glasses of water, and sat across from each other. As soon as the drinks arrived, Caldwell said to their waitress, "Two more please. Just the whiskey."

When the waiter left, Zoe said, "Why?"

"I know we'll want another and I won't want to interrupt our conversation to ask for the next one. And I don't want her to have to interrupt us."

She picked up her glass of whiskey. "Damned sensible."

"Thank you. To pretty ladies." He took a draught of the whiskey and let it expand on his tongue to impart its warmth and flavor before he swallowed it.

"To sensible men." She drank.

"So here's what I know," he said. "You're a fine pianist. I've listened to you. And you have a daughter and a son who turned out okay. I assume you poisoned their father?"

Her eyes widened and her shoulders came up, and she nearly spit out her drink, but managed to swallow and laugh. "You'll never pin that one on me. He's alive and well except for the alimony."

"Why are you divorced?"

"Isn't that a little personal?"

"General terms," he said. "Did he beat you up, or suddenly realize he was gay, or did you just catch him cheating?"

"Cheating. I know it sounds mundane, but it seemed like enough of a surprise at the time. I was a pretty good wife, and I was trying to be a better wife, because it's a little easier to do once the kids are out of the house. When we had it out, I gave him a choice, and he picked the girlfriend." She took another sip of her whiskey.

"Why?"

"I can't imagine. She's twenty years younger than I am, and doesn't know half as many recipes or old song lyrics as I do. All she has is a beautiful face and a great body, and she thinks he's brilliant and sophisticated."

"Got it," said Caldwell. "Sorry to pry, but I wanted to know the general outline, so I'm not an insensitive roommate. You look great, by the way. He's going to be sorry he doesn't have you as time goes on."

"You're sweet," she said. "But now I'm entitled to your story."

"My wife died of an undiscovered aneurism at forty-five. I walked into the kitchen and found her sitting on the kitchen floor with a pot of soup on the stove that had boiled down to nothing and scorched the pot. When I found her, she still looked beautiful, normal, as though she had just fallen asleep. But her skin was cold."

"Oh, I'm so sorry."

"It was about ten years ago, so the wounds aren't fresh. I was lucky to have her as long as I did."

"What was her name?"

"Anna."

"To Anna," she said, and they drank.

"I've noticed that you put a lot of work and time in to the piano," he said. "Are you preparing for a concert or something?"

"Back to me already?" she said. "I'm not really doing it for a practical reason. It was something I did before I met Darryl, and I taught while I was married. I think when the marriage ended it was the logical thing to cling to. Playing gave me something else to think about, and a way to fill the time. I could do something to improve myself—practice. Learn harder pieces that I never had time to learn before."

"Well, those are all good effects."

"So you don't think I'm turning into a crazy old bat who sits in her apartment playing for nobody?"

"You've got a long way to go before you're an old anything. And you can go back to playing for other people. You've already got me. And you could get students. You're good enough to be a concert pianist."

"Thank you. But nobody begins a concert career at forty-five."

"So you gave the career up to marry Darryl."

"I did win some prizes when I was young. I suppose I seem stupid to have given up my shot at success for a guy who was just going to dump me."

"I don't think it's stupid. You still love your kids."

"You're just trying to make me feel better, aren't you?"

He shrugged. "I know some bad, sad things that are true. So do you. But I'm reminding you of some better things that are also true. And since when is it bad to try to make a friend feel better?"

"Are we friends?"

"We will be."

"Why do you think so?" she said.

"Because we've decided to be."

After the second glass of Jameson's, Caldwell said, "It's time to order dinner."

"I didn't ask you to take me out to dinner," she said. "I just said we should have a drink sometime."

"We've had the drink. Now I'm hungry," he said. "Unless you have another commitment."

"No, I don't."

"Then have dinner with me."

She looked at him, her head tilted. "You're kind of a take-charge guy. I didn't think you would be."

"Don't worry. I'm not a bully or a psycho. I am hungry, though."

"I'll have dinner on one condition," she said.

"What's that?"

"I want to sit next to you, on your side of the booth."

"Then come on over."

"Aren't you going to ask me why?"

"I assume it's so you can steal food off my plate."

She moved over to his side and sat beside him. "You know a lot about women."

"I guess I do," he said. "Was that it?"

"No. I'm just afraid that after two drinks, one of us will say something that I don't want overheard. One of us meaning me."

"Well, now you can say whatever you want." He picked up a menu and handed it to her.

She looked at the menu while he beckoned to the waitress.

After they had both ordered Zoe said, "I like this menu. It's friendly food, the kind you don't have to think about or compare to what you had in the south of France. All you have to do is eat it and go back to drinking."

"A wise menu," he said. "So tell me more about you. What were your parents like?"

"They were professors at the University of Chicago. One was a Russian physicist, and one was a Roman historian, but not the one you'd think. My mother was the physicist. She met my father in Rome and fell for him so deeply that she defected so she could have an affair with him. That's what she told me. What about your parents?"

For an instant he considered telling her something that would further his plan to keep her friendly, but decided the story he'd compiled from the lives of several real Peter Caldwells would do that about as well as anything improvised. "We lived in a small town along the shore of Lake Erie in upstate New York. My father worked at the steel mill—Bethlehem Steel in Lackawanna—until it closed in the 1960s."

"What about your mother?"

"My mother had a little store that sold housewares—sort of a hardware store for women. There were pots and pans and cooking utensils, a little cheap china, sewing stuff, knitting stuff."

"Did they send you to college?"

"Yes. I graduated with a major in math and a minor in economics, two truly dull subjects. Then I joined the army. When I got out I went to work for the government. I stayed there a couple of years and quit."

"Why?"

"Why what?"

"Why quit?"

"Because by then I was sure that I knew all about taking orders. I didn't like it. As soon as I started making my own decisions the world got to be a better place for me."

"You made a lot of money."

"What makes you say that?"

"Because you don't care about money. You don't think about it, or respect it, the way people do who don't have any."

"And why did you tell me you'd figured that out?"

"Because I like you and I wanted you to know that I've been paying attention to you and thinking about you. And I guess I also wanted you to know I'm smart."

The admission that she liked him and paid attention made him anxious, but he didn't let it show. "I knew you were smart."

"Oh. I guess I'm too concerned with making sure nobody misses any of my diminishing good points."

They ate and talked and then had desserts that neither of them would ordinarily have ordered. He had often noticed that getting people to talk about their children was an effective way of keeping them from thinking about anything else, so he asked her about her son and daughter.

It was nearly eleven when they began their walk back to their apartment. Zoe put her arm through his and held on tightly, and he suspected she must be feeling the alcohol.

When he unlocked the apartment door and let her in, he could see the dogs' eyes glowing with the reflected light of the streetlamp outside. "Hi, Carol. Hi, Dave."

The dogs circled them in the hallway, wagging their tails and making little noises of welcome.

Zoe patted them and said, "Wow. You guys are so great to come home to."

"I'd better go out with them for a minute," Caldwell said. "They've been inside for a long time." He opened the door again and said, "Come on." The dogs muscled past him and trotted down the stairs to the front door, and he went out to watch over them, then produced a roll of small plastic bags he still had in his pocket from their walk and cleaned up their messes on the strip of lawn. They went around the building to the trash cans and he deposited the bags there, and then the three went up the back stairs.

He and the dogs found the living room was still dark, but Zoe was standing in the middle of the floor. When he came close, she took two steps forward and hugged him.

"Thanks, Peter," she said. "That was the most pleasant dinner I've had in a long time." She stood on tiptoes with her hands on his shoulders and kissed him. It seemed to have been intended as a quick peck, but it landed on his lips. She seemed about to pull back but then she didn't, and instead her arms snaked upward around his neck and they kissed differently. The kiss lasted at least five seconds before they broke apart.

This moment was extremely dangerous. If he tried to be distant, he could make her hurt and angry. He might have to move out of this ideal hiding place, and be on the highway looking for a place to stay. He might even turn her into an enemy who would complain to other people about him and try to pick apart his story. "You're welcome," he said, so late that they had both almost forgotten what had prompted it. He adopted a casual tone. "We'll have to have drinks again sometime. Well—"

She said, "I don't think I've ever shown you my room. I don't suppose you'd like to come for a visit?"

He was silent for a moment. "I would love to, but I'd like you to think about it after daylight. If we take that step, it's pretty hard to undo. If you decide it wasn't such a good idea, then you won't have anything to regret."

She said, "God, Peter. I'm a grown-up. Don't you think you can assume I've been thinking about this all evening? The truth is that I made up my mind before that—perfectly sober, by the way. I decided to make you take me out for drinks because it was the simplest way to get us to this point, here and now."

He shrugged. "I'm sorry. Pretend I never said anything."

"I will," she said. "Now kiss your dogs good night, and come on."

8

He woke at seven, disoriented for a half second, but then he remembered. He blinked a couple of times and looked around. Her room was sunny, with thick white drapes that had not been pulled together to cover the thin white translucent curtains. He looked over at her side of the bed. It was empty, her pillow still in place with an indentation from her head, and the covers pulled back up, as though she had simply vanished.

He sat up and swung his legs off the bed. His mind began to run through a brief inventory of images, sounds, and words. The fact that he was naked brought him directly to the last part of the evening, and prompted visceral memories. He redirected his thoughts and went over the whole evening rapidly, searching his memory for mistakes he might have made. He decided he had not revealed anything he shouldn't have, and he had not offended her. She had given him a last kiss and drifted off to a gentle sleep with an untroubled expression.

Still, the whole episode had brought on terrible danger. Living in the same apartment as a pleasant and pretty female acquaintance wasn't terribly hard. Living in an apartment with a woman who was intimate with him, free to ask all the questions she wanted, and had a right to expect direct answers, was almost impossible to do safely.

His clothes were draped neatly over the back of a chair. He put them on. He opened the bedroom door expecting to see the dogs waiting impatiently for him to reappear, but the hallway was unoccupied. He heard faint sounds from the kitchen, things rattling, and smelled coffee. He walked to the kitchen doorway.

He saw Zoe at the dishwasher, taking out clean dishes and putting them away in cupboards. Dave and Carol were in the kitchen too, eating the last of the crunchy dry food they ate for breakfast. They both stopped and looked up at him, and then stood and trotted toward him. The sound of their metal tags made Zoe turn her head to look, and then straighten to face him. She was wearing a bathrobe that hung nearly to her insteps. It was cinched around her waist and cut in a style that made it look like a gown. "Good morning," she said.

Her smile reassured him—no resentment, no reserve. He said, "Good morning. You look positively regal."

"Now and then my noble pedigree shows. I take it you slept well."

"Great," he said. "How about you?"

She closed the dishwasher with her hip and stepped closer to him. She put her arms around his neck and gave him a small, gentle kiss, affectionate instead of erotic.

He said, "Does that mean you slept well?"

"It didn't make me feel like a new woman. Refurbished, maybe, with the odometer turned back a few miles." She hugged him and stepped back to look in his eyes. "I guess we need to talk again, don't we?"

"Only if you think so." The tests he had feared were about to start. He wasn't ready for an hour with a skilled interrogator. He had to persuade her that all his feelings were positive. That was essential. But somehow he had to slow this down.

"Not a thirty-minute talk. Maybe five. I loved last night. I have no regrets. None. But now, as you tried to warn me last night, things are different. We jumped across that chasm, and now we're on the other side of it, and can't go back. We have to live—or learn to live—over here, where we've been naked together and everything. Your turn."

"We are in a different place," he said. "At the moment I'm pretty comfortable over here. It may just be morning afterglow, but I'm glad it happened. I propose that we try very hard to keep being friends." He smiled. "We made a really good start."

This time they both came together at once, and their kiss was a longer, deeper one. She said, "Friends who just know each other better, or friends with benefits?"

"With benefits, by all means," he said.

"Then the ayes have it," she said. "With benefits it is." They kissed again. "Want to take a shower together, or is that too much me in eight hours?"

"Only one way to find out," he said. "We're kind of testing the waters."

"And saving the planet."

He pulled the belt of her bathrobe so it came loose. She didn't close it, just leaned on him as they walked back toward her bathroom. "One thing, though," she said. "If one of my kids comes for a visit, don't walk in and slap me on the ass, or fiddle with my apparel like that, okay?"

"That goes for you too," he said.

"I'll try to restrain myself."

They spent some time in the shower, dried each other off, and then went out together to walk the dogs in the park. They stopped at a café to buy coffee and croissants, and ate them on a park bench while the dogs chased squirrels into the trees.

As he looked out over the park, he thought about Anna. Several times they had the same conversation about dying. He had told her that she should prepare herself to outlive him by many years.

One time Anna said, "You always assume you'll die first. Did you get a bad fortune cookie or something?"

"I'm five years older. I'm male. And there's a lot of wear and tear on me. Look at an actuarial table. There are also people trying to find me and kill me, which kind of adds to the odds. Remember that I've gotten you several false identities, and hidden money for you."

"I don't want to talk about this," she said, and invented something that she needed to be doing—dusting some books he remembered. "It makes me depressed, and we don't know any more about the future than we did the last time."

He persisted. "I also want you to remember that when I die I want you to find a man again. Get married. Preferably to somebody better than I am."

"Of course," she said. "And I want you to do that too, if I die. I don't expect you to be celibate. That's just stupid."

"You're right," he said. "Maybe I'll start scouting the talent out there just in case you're no longer with us."

"You do," Anna said, "and I guarantee you'll be the first to die."

He could see the expression on her face as she punched his arm. He wondered what she'd say about Zoe. He thought he knew, but he wondered if he was just telling himself to believe what made him happier. Zoe was exactly the sort of woman Anna always admired—pretty, elegant, accomplished but not overly proud about it. He frowned. The one thing that would have disgusted Anna was that he had not slept with Zoe for some straightforward reason—a crush, or even simple sexual attraction. He'd been using her as a blind, for his own protection.

"You're thinking about her right now, aren't you?"

He turned to look at Zoe.

"Your wife. It's okay. I was thinking about my ex-husband after I got up this morning. The sex made it inevitable. I'm pretty sure we weren't thinking the same things, though." She frowned. "What's wrong?"

"That was scary."

"What do you mean?"

"You were exactly right. It's like one of those magic tricks that's just a little bit too good."

"Sorry," she said. "I warned you that I've been thinking about you." She took out her phone and looked at the time on the display. "Do you think Dave and Carol have had enough for now?"

He looked at the dogs. They had stopped paying attention to the squirrels and were lying on the grass a few feet away. "They look that way."

"Then let's start back. I can get in a couple of hours of practice and do some chores while you do whatever you need to do."

"Okay," he said. "Do you want to stop on the way home to pick up some take-out food for lunch?"

She shook her head. "No. I'm starting a diet today. Salad for lunch."

"You don't need to go on a diet," he said. "You look—"

"Shush," she said. "You're going to be my diet inspiration. For the first time in quite a while, I'll know there's somebody who will see if I have a fat ass."

"It's always nice to be of service." They began to walk, and the dogs waited a few seconds and then got up to overtake them.

The first thing Caldwell had done when he moved in to the apartment was to lock his bedroom door and go through his belongings to pick out things he didn't want Zoe to see. He didn't know much about her at the time, but he'd been fairly sure she was not someone who would go up into the crawl space above the ceiling. The access trap was in the ceiling of his closet. He stood on a chair, pushed up the square of wood that closed off the crawl space, and placed a few things up there—the two pistols, the spare ammunition and magazines, money, false identification packets.

He knew that curiosity about him was something that came with intimacy. She would be tempted to look around in his room, maybe when he wasn't present. She might even feel that she had the natural right.

He was sure he had made himself reasonably safe from her curiosity, but when he came home from the walk, he got up on the chair again and checked to be sure Zoe had not opened the crawl space. Then he and the dogs went out into the living room and listened to her practice. His daughter, Emily, had played, but the only practice she had time for now was the medical kind. Emily had played in that way she had of doing things well because she did them hard. Zoe was the sort of person the piano had been invented for.

He sat back in the big chair and read while Zoe played. The dogs seemed to like the sounds except when they were too loud. From time to time Caldwell would look up from his book and let his eyes linger on Zoe as long as he could do it without her noticing. She was intent on her playing. It was a difficult Mendelssohn piece he remembered her telling him was called *Variations sérieuses*. And she was serious. She kept at it for a couple of hours, taking on one passage at a time, repeating it over and over until she owned that passage, and then moving on to the next.

When she stopped, she looked up and caught him. "Do I look weird when I practice?"

"Not at all. Actually, when you're in your head and forget you're not alone you look your best."

"My daughter is coming to visit."

"When?"

"Friday night. As soon as she finishes an exam, she's taking a plane to Midway. I was afraid to tell you."

"I knew when I moved in that she'd come sometime. You even reminded me this morning."

"I was sort of studying you to see your reaction."

"Why be afraid?"

She shrugged. "Another person around, and so on. Two of us with high, girly voices to set your teeth on edge." She paused. "And, it's kind of an inconvenient time, while we're sort of getting used to each other."

"It's absolutely fine. I'd like to meet her."

"There's actually another reason. I was kind of hoping she could stay in your spare room."

"That's fine too. I haven't figured out what to do with it yet anyway. I've been thinking of putting in a handball court, or maybe an Argentinian tapas restaurant. Small plates don't take up much space. But either of those could take months. How long is she staying?"

She said, "Is a week too long?"

"Of course not, unless she's a terrible person. You said she wasn't."

"I'll swear to it," she said.

"All right." He knew he was adding to the danger, agreeing to have another set of eyes scrutinizing him. But he also knew that Zoe would be grateful for his cooperation, and if he got through the visit, her gratitude would make him safer.

Friday came and during the day Zoe was bustling around putting linens on the bed in the spare room and cooking things for her daughter. At about five o'clock he came into the kitchen and slapped her bottom. She spun around in surprise. "What the fuck?" she said.

"You said I shouldn't do that while she's here, so I thought you must be expecting it other times. I thought I'd get it out of the way."

She kissed him and patted his cheek. "Thank you, Peter." She went back to stirring her sauce.

He said, "I'll go out to a restaurant tonight, and let you two be together. It'll also help us look more convincing as just roommates. Let me know when her plane comes in so I can be out of here by then."

"Seven thirty is my best guess for her to reach here."

"I'll feed the dogs and take them out for their walk now."

The walk took them the next couple of hours, to a few places where they hadn't been before, so he used the leashes. He felt comfortable walking them tonight. An older man walking a pair of matched mutts was not especially interesting to people. The new route also gave him a chance to add to his familiarity with the area.

Whenever he was out, he was looking for signs that someone was studying him too closely or following him. He was now operating on the theory that the men who had tried to kill him had not been sent by any part of the government. There would have been no reason for government people not to do what they did best—put on bulletproof vests and jackets that said POLICE or FBI or something, arrive in numbers, kick down his door, and arrest him. He was not exactly guilty of stealing the money, but he was close enough to guilty for a legitimate conviction.

No, these had to be people who had something else in mind. Maybe they wanted to kill him for revenge, or to give themselves lots of time to search his house for account numbers and take the missing money. He had seen three of them briefly, but he hadn't been able to get any of them to speak, so he hadn't detected an accent. He hadn't had time to try foreign languages. They'd had no identification, no phones, no tattoos, not even any jewelry. But they had been very professional, and that made him uneasy.

He brought the dogs home and found that the daughter had not yet arrived. He kissed Zoe, assured her that the sauce she'd made for the chicken breasts was excellent, and left.

His car had not been driven for a couple of days, so he took it into the city to the restaurant. All the way, he kept checking for cars that might be following him. He doubled back three times to be sure, and then had the parking attendants take his car so there would be someone watching it while he had dinner.

The restaurant was called Le Meilleur, and it might not have been the best, but the name wasn't a pathetic boast. It was far better than most. He spent a couple of hours on an excellent meal, a dessert of fruit, and a glass of Armagnac. Then he drove out to the suburbs and stopped at a grocery store for supplies. He wasn't sure whether he was now allowed to buy groceries for both of them, at least while the daughter was visiting, but he was still responsible for feeding himself and his dogs. The only thing he added that he wouldn't usually buy was four bottles of good wine.

When he had put his car in the garage, he climbed the back stairs and went inside. As he came in the door, Zoe called out, "Is that a burglar?"

"Yes," he said. "But I'm not working tonight." He put his grocery bags on the floor and began to load the perishable food into the refrigerator. A moment later, Zoe appeared in the doorway, and a few feet behind her was a girl about twenty-three years old with long, blond hair, but bright blue eyes like Zoe's. Zoe said, "Peter, this is my daughter, Sarah."

Caldwell looked at her, and noted that she was the girl in the photographs, only a little older, and that she was more like her mother in person. Her movements and posture were the same. "Hi," she said.

He smiled as sincerely as he could. "Hello, Sarah," he said. "I'm very pleased to meet you."

"I know. You've heard so much about me," Sarah said.

"Not that much, really," said Peter. "I got the impression that your mother is very proud of you, and has been looking forward to seeing you. Both are good things. And she said you were in school."

"Law school," she said. "At UCLA. Second year. This is my spring break."

"Great," he said. "I hope you'll enjoy it. The weather has been unseasonably good for this time of year, so it's good timing."

"What? No lawyer jokes?"

He shook his head. "Not for a second-year student. You will have heard all of mine during your first year. Have you met the dogs?"

"Yes. My mother introduced us. They're lovely."

"Thanks," he said. "I hope you're not allergic or anything."

"No," she said.

Zoe said, "Okay, Peter. We'll leave you alone now and let you put away your food."

"All right," he said. "I'll just finish this and then take Carol and Dave out for a bit. It's a pleasure to meet you, Sarah."

The two women went back to the living room, and the dogs appeared in the kitchen just as he put the last of the cans into the pantry and closed the door. He took the leashes off the hook, snapped them on the dogs' collars, and took them out the kitchen door and down the back stairs.

They walked the neighborhood for a few blocks, feeling a night chill that reminded him that spring hadn't quite closed the door on winter yet. A late snow was a possibility that didn't seem as remote tonight.

The man simply came into existence forty feet behind him. When Caldwell had last looked no one had been there, but now he heard the footsteps. The dogs took notice too; their ears turned backward to listen. The footsteps quickened and the dogs wheeled around to face the man, so Caldwell turned too.

The man was only a silhouette at first, striding toward Caldwell. The shape was young—slim, supple, and fast. When Caldwell saw him coming, he stepped off the sidewalk and pulled back on the leashes to prepare to let the man pass. But as he did, he saw the man reach into his jacket pocket and grasp something. As the man walked straight toward Peter his hand emerged from his pocket. He passed through a splash of light from a streetlamp and Caldwell saw the gleam on the finish of the revolver.

Peter said, "*Fassen.*" Then he let go of both leashes. The two dogs dashed and then leapt at once, just as the young man began to lift his hand.

Peter charged at him, but the dogs were much faster. They jumped high, baring their teeth at the man's neck. The man stopped and leaned his body back to avoid being bitten, but that put him off balance. The weight of their bodies pushed him backward.

Peter reached him, struck the young man's forearm down, lifted a knee to his groin, and then landed a combination of quick punches to his face and throat. The light was dim, but Peter could see his skin was black.

The man reeled and Peter clutched his wrist and brought his forearm down over his knee to make him drop the pistol, then retained his grip to jerk the man's arm and bring his unprotected face forward to meet a hard punch. He used the back of his calf and swept the man off his feet onto the pavement, where he landed on his back and hit the back of his head. The dogs clamped their jaws on his arms and held him there.

The army had trained Caldwell as a hand-to-hand fighter and he had continued his training through his adult life, but he knew that he never would have prevailed against this opponent if the dogs hadn't done most of the fighting. The man was too fast, too young, and too strong.

Caldwell snatched the gun off the ground and aimed it as the man began to recover his wind and his consciousness. Caldwell used the opportunity to get a close look at the man's face. His attacker was younger than he'd thought. He looked about eighteen. Was this a gang attack or something? Caldwell allowed himself a half second to look up the sidewalk for others, then back at the young man, and then over his shoulder, but there were no signs of other attackers. Caldwell said, "Listen carefully. You get one chance at each question. What's your name?"

The boy looked at his arm and the gun. "James Harriman."

"Give me your wallet."

The young man carefully reached into his back pocket and came back with the wallet. Caldwell took it in his left hand and held it up to catch a little light from a distant streetlamp. The driver's license had the same name. Caldwell noted that it said he was eighteen. He put a finger into the fold and saw there were twelve dollars, a ten and two ones. This wasn't an operative or a hired killer searching for him. He was a delinquent teenager trying to rob an old man. "Is this a gang thing?"

"I needed money."

"This is a stupid way to get it." The shock, the adrenaline, and the exertion were adding heat to his anger, but he fought it down.

Caldwell took a step back. He tossed the wallet on the young man's chest. "I'm going to let you go, but I'll have to keep the gun."

The young man looked relieved.

"But if I ever see you again, I won't be able to let you go. Do you understand?"

"Yes," said the young man.

"Okay, then. Get the hell out of here."

The young man sat up, put his wallet away, and got to his feet. Then he began to hurry in the direction he had come from.

"Stop."

The young man froze. His hands were up at shoulder height and he didn't try to look back at him. Caldwell walked up behind him and stuffed the five twenty-dollar bills he was carrying into the boy's jacket pocket. "Take this money and don't try to rob anybody else."

"All right." The young man started to walk. He called out, "Thank you." Then he walked a little faster, and soon he had gained enough distance to break into a run.

Caldwell waited for about two minutes after the kid was out of sight. Then he turned a corner and moved off too. From time to time he turned down an alley where he would have seen a follower appear if there had been one, and a few times he stopped and crouched beside a porch or stood in a closed store's entrance and watched until he was sure he was alone.

Just before he reached the neighborhood where he lived, he unloaded the revolver, dropped the bullets in a storm sewer, the frame in a second sewer a distance away, and the cylinder in a big dumpster behind a restaurant. He was shaken by the experience. He had come very close to firing a round into a teenager's head because he had thought he was a professional killer. He had spent lots of time many years ago acquiring the skills to protect himself. Now he had to learn to reassess the nature of a threat.

When he reached the apartment it was after midnight. He could hear Zoe and Sarah talking while they watched something on television. He slipped past the living room into the hallway and into his bedroom. Sometime later, he heard Sarah walk past his room, go into the guest room, and close the door. Before he went to bed, he climbed up in the closet again and checked to be sure the guns, money, and identification he'd left were still undiscovered. Everything was intact and undisturbed for now.

9

In the morning he woke to the sight of both dogs' big brown eyes, full of sincerity, staring into his from a few inches away. When he lifted his head, they lifted theirs and rolled to sit up, their tails drumming on the mattress in a syncopated beat.

"Good morning, Carol. Good morning, Dave." He sat up too, went into his bathroom, and then came back to the bedroom, drying himself from his shower. It was early, so he decided to take the dogs to the park. He would buy coffee and a pastry at the place where he and Zoe had gone a couple of days ago.

When he was dressed he went down the front stairs with the dogs to give them a chance to relieve themselves, and then brought them back up the kitchen stairs to have their breakfast.

He found Sarah sitting at the table beside a plate painted with the bright yellow of an egg yolk and a cup of tea with the bag's string hanging out of it. In front of her was a laptop computer.

"Good morning," he said.

"Good morning. I see you're an early riser," she said.

"So are you."

"I'm in school, so I have to study whenever nothing more interesting is going on."

"Don't worry," he said. "I just have to feed these two, and they eat fast. Then we'll be off to the park."

"You sure walk your dogs a lot."

"They like it and it's good for them. It's also good for me."

She looked at him with an appraising stare. "I suppose it would be, at your age. You're retired, right? Do you do anything else?"

He measured the cups of dry food into the two dog bowls, set them down, and then refilled the water bowl. As the dogs began to crunch their food he said, "I don't know. I haven't been in town long. I'm still exploring the Chicago area and getting used to it. I don't really feel in a hurry to do more than that right now."

"Do I seem nosy?"

"It's okay. Curiosity is a sign of a lively mind. That's the only kind worth having."

She said, "I spent some time last night online trying to find out about you. I didn't find much."

He could feel the hairs on the back of his neck begin to rise. "I'm not famous."

"No," she said. "Never dated Marilyn Monroe or anybody like that, either."

"I'm not that old. She died when I was in elementary school. Why did you decide I was worth the investigation?"

"Because you're fucking my mother."

He was silent for a second, and then wondered if he had just stood there during that second with his mouth open. "What makes you think that?"

Sarah shrugged. "I noticed as soon as I got here that she was very chirpy. She's also dieting, and doing a better job with her makeup and hair. And her voice was different when she talked to you." She paused. "And so on."

"She's just happy. Her daughter is home."

Sarah said, "This isn't my home. Or hers either, really. Look, I watched her when she talked about you. Don't get me wrong. I've tentatively decided to approve. She's a magnificent person, and she seems to feel better than she has since she divorced my father."

Caldwell recovered from the shock. "I'm glad that you appreciate her and want her to be happy. That confirms some good things she said about you. But you should direct any questions to your mother. Not me."

"My questions aren't about her. They're about you."

"Well, save them up, and I'll do my best to satisfy your curiosity when we have time. Right now we've both got things to do—study and take the dogs out. See you later." He went to the front door and took the leashes off the hook. "Bye."

"Should I have said, 'Welcome to the family'?"

"Not very funny," he said.

"It wasn't meant to be."

He closed the door behind him and walked the dogs toward the park. He was feeling an uneasiness that grew with each step. First he'd had the scare with the attempted robbery last night. He had come through it all right, but he had barely stopped himself from killing someone who was barely a legal adult, and the experience had left him anxious. Now there was Sarah.

Sarah seemed more dangerous right now than the teenager with the revolver. She had immediately figured out that he and Zoe weren't just sharing an apartment. She had sensed that there was something about him that was off, and researched him online. There wasn't enough online about any one of the real Peter Caldwells to satisfy her.

He had chosen the name partly because there were so many of them, and they lived all over the country and in a few foreign countries. It would be hard for anyone to say he wasn't one of them. But many had social media accounts with photographs. Some had articles about them with pictures: PETER CALDWELL APPOINTED TO GOVERNOR'S COMMISSION. PETER CALDWELL MARRIES NANCY STANHOPE. PETER CALDWELL TAKES HOLY ORDERS. He just hoped there wasn't one that said PETER CALDWELL CHARGED WITH MURDER.

Sarah was bright, she was protective of her mother, and she wasn't shy about asking about other people's personal lives. Even stupid people in her age group were expert at using online sources to find out whatever they wanted. A bright law student like Sarah probably knew ways to search that he'd never heard of. She had already learned how shallow his cover as Peter Caldwell was. How long before she decided to get someone with access to law enforcement databases to dig deeper?

As he walked with the dogs he kept thinking. He didn't know whether she had a good relationship with her father. Maybe she would turn the problem over to him. He could hear her voice. "Mom is seeing someone. Living with him. I don't think she really knows anything about him. He just seems a little . . . I don't know." That would be all it took.

He and the dogs walked around the lake. He felt the leashes swinging from his neck, and it reminded him to look for signs that he needed to leash the dogs. He saw no police cars, and nobody walking who was close enough to feel uneasy about unleashed dogs.

When they were near the café he bought some coffee and went back down to the park to sit on a bench while the dogs sniffed around the area. He thought about the dogs. They had sat patiently while he had been at the café. They loved routines, because routines implied order, and order reassured them. All it took was repetition. Things being the same for a long time reassured people, too. A long history that didn't change much was a person's best credential.

When Caldwell and the dogs returned to the apartment, Sarah was still alone, this time reading a large hardcover law book. When they came in, she looked up. "You know what I'd like to know?"

"Whether I have a criminal record?"

"You don't," she said. "I already checked that. It cost me money, too."

"Sorry."

"I'd like to see a credit report on you."

He felt his heartbeat accelerate, but kept his facial muscles relaxed. "Why would I give you that? Would you give me your credit report?"

"I'm not fucking your mother." She frowned. "Or your father. Or whatever."

He stared at her. "All right."

"All right?" She had not been expecting this.

"May I use your computer?"

Her plate was still on the table. She picked it up and pushed her laptop toward him. He opened it and began to type while she put the plate in the sink. He was glad he had memorized Peter Caldwell's birth date, last address, and Social Security number. After he filled in a grid and clicked a couple of boxes, he turned the computer around and pushed it in front of her so she could see the screen.

As the information appeared on the screen, she began to read it. After a minute or two of silence, she looked up. "Okay."

"Okay what?"

"You don't seem to be a deadbeat or a screwup or something. You've got a whole lot of credit available, but still have a mammoth rating. You pay your bills on time." She scrolled up and down. "Why so many banks?"

"I like banks."

"Not as much as they like you." She shrugged. "Okay, I'm satisfied."

"Thank you." He spun the computer around and terminated the connection. He stood up and started toward the living room.

"Wait," she said.

He stopped. "For what?"

"The apology. Here it comes."

"Keep it. I'm very impressed with you for being so tough and persistent. You're a fine daughter. Now I hope you'll stop invading my privacy."

"I will."

As he walked out of the kitchen toward his room, he hoped she would keep her promise. Since he had come to Chicago he had not yet forced himself to settle certain issues in his own mind, and dealing with Sarah made him think about them. He had been in wars, and he had a long familiarity with the necessity of killing an attacker. He wasn't sure he was as comfortable with killing someone who threatened his life less directly or intentionally, like Sarah and Zoe.

10

The next evening, after his confrontation with Sarah, Caldwell was in his room listening to the radio with earphones attached to his computer while he studied various sources to give him an idea of what his pursuers might be doing, and who they were. Since the night he left Vermont, he wondered how the death of the man who had broken into his house had been kept out of the newspapers. He had called the police and cops had come and interviewed him. Others had examined the crime scene. Men from the medical examiner's office had taken the body away.

He had discovered that the police blotter for Norwich was on the police website, and he searched it every few days, but found no mention of the incident. The only way he knew of for the record to be wiped away so completely was if intelligence officers had gone to the police and persuaded them that the case was a national security issue. But they would have had to do it right away, before word got out, and that meant someone in the government had known about the incident the night it happened.

Suddenly the dogs both lifted their heads at once. He watched them to see if it was simply a reaction to something too distant to be of concern or a developing threat. He took off the earphones. There was a quiet knock, and he stood up and went to open the door.

Standing in the doorway was Zoe, and she was smiling. She was wearing a blue dress with simple lines and no unnecessary ornamentation. It was very pretty on her. "You look very nice," he said. "You don't wear dresses very often. Are you going out?"

"No," she said. "Sarah left a few minutes ago to spend the evening with some friends. They picked her up, and she'll be gone for hours. I thought this dress might be appropriate for this occasion."

"Oh?"

"Yes. Dresses aren't what's uncomfortable. It's all the gear you wear under them." She lifted the hem of her dress so he could see her thigh-high stockings. She lifted it higher, so he saw that she had nothing else under the dress. "I thought this might be better."

"I agree," he said. He scooped her up and began to carry her to his bed.

"Careful," she said. "This is an expensive dress, and I've never worn it before."

He set her on her feet, reached around her, and unzipped the dress. She let it slide down and stepped out of it, and then draped it on the nearest chair. He went to the door, reopened it, and said, "Carol. Dave. Out."

The two dogs jumped to the floor and trotted out. He closed the door and locked it.

Peter and Zoe came together in an embrace, and kissed gently. She unbuttoned his shirt, and he shed the rest of his clothes. In a moment they were on his bed, making love. He was conscious and premeditated, trying to be the most thoughtful and considerate lover possible. He knew this was a chance to make her feel more attached to him, and he tried to work his way into her mind, to manipulate her into feeling pleasure at the thought of him, to make her feel safe and secure, and yet agitated and impatient for each touch. When it was over, they lay together on the cool sheet, the rest of the bedding pushed off the end of the bed. Their hands were clasped, but they didn't speak.

Suddenly, there was a jarring sound, an insistent beep. They both sat up.

"What's that?" he asked.

"Oh, crap," said Zoe. "It's my watch. I set the alarm so I could be sure Sarah wouldn't catch us." She held up her wrist and pressed a button for silence.

"Kids her age don't come home at ten," he said.

She looked at him, her face concerned and apologetic. "She gets up very early to study. Haven't you noticed?"

"Sure. But the dogs will warn us if anyone comes to the door of the apartment."

"I know you're probably right. But there's a hypocrisy factor that you're not taking into account. I'm doing what mothers tell their daughters not to do. I can make a case in my own mind for fooling around with you, but I don't particularly want to talk to her about it." She slipped the dress over her head. "Thanks for tonight."

"I was going to thank you," he said. "Wait a minute and I'll walk you home to your room."

"That's idiotic," she said. "I wish I'd met you years ago."

"Me too."

When the time came for Sarah McDonald to go back to law school, Peter drove her and her mother to the airport so Zoe could see her off without parking and taking the shuttle back to the terminal. Caldwell was prepared for the melancholy that would descend on Zoe once Sarah was through security and no longer visible. He had seen this with Anna every time Emily had gone back to school.

This was going to be another chance for him to manipulate Zoe's feelings and make himself safer. He needed her to trust him, even to come to depend on him. But the first steps had to be small. First he had to be useful and thoughtful.

He wasn't prepared for the fact that he felt a little bereft too. During the vacation he and Sarah had been the ones up early and in the kitchen every morning, while Zoe slept. He and Sarah would exchange a few wry observations about each other before he took the dogs out and she went back to studying. But after a week, the exchanges weren't falsely cynical anymore. The two early risers were like workers on the same shift. They spoke quietly, respected each other's space, and went about their duties.

Zoe chattered while he was driving them to the airport, the same energetic and empty cheerfulness that Anna had managed years ago, and like his own daughter Sarah was mostly quiet. They did that he remembered. Their minds began to leave early, moving ahead of their bodies to the next place, the next phase.

When they pulled to the white curb, Peter got out to lift the suitcase out of the trunk and set it on the sidewalk. He said to Zoe, "I'll wait in the cell phone lot. Call when you're ready."

Sarah said, "Not so fast, bud." She bounced upward and kissed his cheek. "See you."

"See you. Learn a lot so you can sue their asses off."

"Evildoers will fear my wrath."

The two women went into the terminal, the daughter wheeling the big suitcase while her mother carried the shoulder bag with the laptop. Caldwell pulled out and drove into the loop of the airport, but then his phone rang. Zoe said, "I'm ready." Her voice sounded sad.

He completed his circle and pulled up again. Zoe jumped in and fastened her seat belt. He pulled out again.

After a few seconds he noticed Zoe was staring at him. "What's wrong?" he asked. "Did I forget to shave?"

"I'm sorry to see her go, of course. Ignore it." After a few seconds she said, "Why did she kiss you like that?"

"Yeah, why do you all do that?"

"Come on."

"I don't know. When I'm reincarnated as a girl I won't kiss an old bastard like me. You never know where he's been. You could get diseases you don't know the names for."

"If you've got any I'm sure I'll know their names before long."

"Your daughter is a remarkably intelligent person, which means she saw I wasn't so bad. That's all."

"Uh," she said. "Interesting. I didn't think you were her type."

"I'm not. I'm her mother's type."

"Yes, you are," Zoe said. "So now we're empty nesters again."

"A good excuse for us to go out tonight and have some fun. I made reservations at a place I tried alone a couple of weeks ago. It's called Le Meilleur."

"The best?"

"Yes. The name seems to spur them on because they don't want to be embarrassed."

"You're so great." She leaned close and kissed his cheek. "You know just what to do."

He did. He'd known that what she would have done otherwise was to go into her bedroom, lie down, and feel depressed about Sarah for a few hours. Instead, she would be distracted and happy until she got used to her daughter's absence again.

A few days later, he came to the doorway of her room and saw her at her desk muttering and shuffling papers around. She had a pen in one hand.

"Hi," he said. "Can I come in?"

"Sure," she said.

"What are you doing, paying bills?"

"You guessed it," she said. "Boring and painful at the same time."

He said, "You know, there's an easy solution to this problem. We could—"

"I'm not going to marry you, Peter."

He was silent. He had never considered proposing to her. He had just been taking the opportunity to help her with her bills. It would give him another way of making himself essential to her, and at the same time give him a new way of decreasing his vulnerability even further. He could funnel some of his payments through her accounts to transform his financial transactions into hers.

"I know you didn't ask me," she said. "But I've been thinking for a while that we should have this talk. Under normal circumstances —meaning any other time of my life—I would be doing every-thing I could to make you want to ask." She reached out and clasped his hand. "But it's the wrong time for me now."

"Why?"

"For a dozen reasons. For one thing, my ex-husband is paying me alimony. If I get remarried, that stops. It's not a huge amount, and he fought me for every penny of it. It's enough to live on now, and later, my pensions will kick in. In spite of what he says, I earned that money. I raised the kids practically by myself. I cooked and cleaned, did everybody's laundry, drove them, taught them, suffered when they suffered. I was faithful to him for nineteen years. I never flirted or let anyone think cheating might be a possibility. I also worked, giving piano lessons and putting all the money into the family account, so it was spent with everything else. Letting Darryl off the hook would be giving up something I earned over nineteen years. It would also be conceding to him that everything I did or gave up during that time was worthless."

"Okay."

"And then there are the kids. Sarah likes you and Brian will too, but they'd hate it if I remarried. My name wouldn't be the same as theirs. They'd have to go through all that stuff of having to explain it to people, and to print two names on wedding invitations and things. I'm sure you can fill in the rest."

She got up and hugged him. "Being with you has brought me back to life. It's been a very long time since I've felt okay. But I don't see a reason to get married. I can't get pregnant anymore. And I can't give you anything if I'm married to you that I won't give you now. Right now, or anytime you want."

"I have to admit this is a lot to think about."

She laughed. "Come on, Peter. It's a risk-free situation for you. What man doesn't want the sex without the commitment?"

"I've never had much trouble with commitment," he said. "But I want you to have what you want. And I have to assume you know what that is."

She hugged him harder. "Peter, what I want is you. I love you. Just stay here. I don't want you to say anything."

Then she was crying, and holding him so tightly that he could feel her heartbeat against his chest. It was a rotten thing to do to a person.

11

It was clear to Caldwell that he had accomplished what he had been trying to with Zoe McDonald. She trusted him, she was in love with him, and she would do anything he asked. During this period he had verified what his espionage training had taught him. Having a woman with him made people see him differently. People tended to assume that a man who was part of a couple was certified as not dangerous, not crazy, and not criminal. He probably had a paycheck and a place to live. The woman's physical presence was taken as testimony that he was a regular guy. Being with a woman who was attractive and tasteful made him even safer, because she obviously could make other choices.

But it was always possible that Caldwell's time in Chicago might come to an end at any moment. He had to be prepared to leave quickly. It had occurred to him that if Chicago were to turn dangerous, he might want to take Zoe with him. If she could provide him with the appearance of legitimacy now, she could also provide it if he was on the run. And he didn't want to leave her in the apartment for his pursuers to find and interrogate.

She didn't deserve what he was doing to her. She was a good person. As he had gotten to know and like her better, he had begun to dislike himself. He had been behaving like a drowning person who clung to the nearest swimmer and held himself up by pulling her down. If he was going to escape, he had to provide a means of escape for her too.

One morning when Zoe went out to do some errands, Caldwell climbed up in his closet and took down one of the false identity packets he had put together for Anna. He had given her the identity of an imaginary woman named Marcia Dixon, who was the wife of Henry Dixon, one of his aliases. He had built the identity with Anna's help in case they ever had the need and the opportunity to escape. Anna had taken the tests for the California driver's license, and had her picture taken for the front of it. She had gone back a couple of times to the Los Angeles DMV to have her picture retaken to keep her photo up to date and pay the renewal fee.

He had kept the female identities in existence after Anna's death. In addition to the sentimental reasons, he'd had some practical ones. He might be able to buy things on Marcia Dixon's credit. A car registered in a woman's name might not trip any of the alerts for a male fugitive, and if he was pulled over while driving it, show-ing a license with the same surname would certainly get him by.

Now he set aside the items that didn't carry a photograph—birth certificate, Social Security card, marriage license, credit cards. It was only then that he turned his attention to the difficult things—the driver's license and passport. The passport was the first step.

When Zoe came home from her errands that day he took a pho-tograph of her with his cell phone. He posed her against a white wall and said he was going to send a picture to his daughter because she'd said she wondered what Zoe looked like. As he pretended to send the picture to Emily, he evaluated it. The picture was good.

Zoe bore only a superficial resemblance to Anna, but she was about the same age as Anna had been in the picture, and she had brown hair that she wore long, as Anna had. Her nose was thin, as

Anna's was, and her eyes were big, blue, and wide apart. She knew how to smile for a camera and look natural. She didn't look exactly like Anna, but two photographs of the same woman could easily vary that much over time. He took three more shots of Zoe in different poses, and selected the one that looked most like Anna. He sent the photograph to his computer, sized it precisely to simulate a passport photograph, and printed it on his color printer on photographic paper.

Caldwell went online, printed the application for a passport renewal, and filled in the spaces. He submitted Marcia Dixon's old passport and paid the fee, including the extra cost of an expedited return, with a credit card in Marcia Dixon's name. The new photographs he submitted were the ones he had taken of Zoe. He knew he was taking a risk, but requesting renewal of a ten-year-old passport from a new address was such a routine operation that he expected the government employee who processed it would handle it without much thought.

He decided to defer the task of getting Zoe a new California driver's license, because Marcia Dixon's was fairly recent. Anna had never driven a car in California, so Marcia Dixon had a perfect driving record, and her license had been renewed automatically twice since Anna's death. The photo on the license was a woman with long brown hair. If he ever needed Zoe to have a better Marcia Dixon license, he could send her into a DMV office to apply for one.

All of those steps could wait, and he might never need to take them. If the government renewed Marcia Dixon's passport, her identity papers would be solid enough to hold up to any scrutiny they would be likely to get. His own papers as Henry Dixon were perfect, and that would help. For most purposes other than flying, if a man showed his identification, nobody asked his female companion for hers.

Right now, the most important thing he could do to stay safe and to keep Zoe McDonald safe was to live the quietest, least noticeable life he could. So he spent the summer with Zoe and his dogs in the Chicago suburbs. Zoe's daughter, Sarah, came to stay with them for about three weeks that summer. During June and part of July she returned to Los Angeles to take a summer school class, and she had arranged to serve a barely paid internship at a law firm until the end of August, when the fall semester started.

Caldwell and Zoe lived through the long days of summer, sank deeper into their habits, and spent most of their time together. Occasionally Caldwell would board the dogs at a kennel he had found and he and Zoe would take a brief trip. He wanted her to be entertained, and he wanted her to get used to traveling with him. There might be a time when he would have to tell her they were going to take a surprise trip, and have her readily agree to it.

They spent three days at the Grand Hotel on Mackinac Island in Michigan, a weekend at Big Cedar Lodge in Missouri, and a couple of days at the French Lick Resort in Indiana. Any destination they could reach by car was safer for him than flying, and the short trips to resorts seemed enough to energize Zoe.

Caldwell never stopped trying to keep Zoe deluded and happy. He was unfailingly attentive, affectionate, and generous. It wasn't difficult. As soon as he met her he had been sexually attracted to her, and as time went on, he caught himself admitting to other things about her that he admired—her humor, intelligence, emotional strength. He occasionally reminded himself that the important thing was not that he enjoy her company, but that he use her emotions to keep himself secure and ahead of his pursuers.

He could never think about the people who were after him without igniting a resentment that flared into rage. Coming after him after all these years was a mistake, and he hoped that every minute he stayed aboveground was giving them pain. But during that summer, he managed to restore his calm for a time. He was watchful, but not angry.

It was the middle of September before his calm was shaken. Caldwell was out on foot in the daytime without Zoe or the dogs.

He had walked to the post office, and then done some shopping for fall clothes, and now he was on his way home. As he approached a crosswalk, the traffic signal turned green. He turned his head to look over his shoulder and check for cars before he stepped into the crosswalk. There was the same young man. The shock made his body tense to fight or run, and the name James Harriman came back to him as though it had never left his mind.

James Harriman was driving a black SUV, signaling for a right turn. As Caldwell turned and looked through the windshield, they locked eyes for a second, and then the SUV accelerated past him, through the intersection without making the right turn. His sight of the driver was lost in the tinted side window, and in a moment the SUV was gone.

As Caldwell walked, he studied the image in his memory and tried to invalidate his impression. He might have convinced himself he had been mistaken, but Harriman had reacted to the sight of him. Harriman's eyes had widened in startled surprise, and then he had looked away and brought his hand to his face as though to shade his eyes. He had sped up and gone straight instead of turning so he would be out of Caldwell's sight more quickly.

The car had been a Lexus LX 570. Caldwell had been searching new car models recently, so he knew that the list price was north of ninety thousand dollars. This was the car being driven by the kid who'd had twelve dollars in his wallet, the one Caldwell had given a hundred bucks, because he had seemed broke and desperate.

Caldwell went through a list of possibilities that might explain what he'd seen. Was he sure this was the same young man? The young man's reaction seemed inexplicable otherwise. Was there an explanation for his driving that kind of vehicle? He might have found a legitimate job and made his first purchase an expensive car. Maybe, but it wasn't likely a dealer would sell a kid with a hundred bucks in his wallet and no credit cards a car like that on the installment plan. He might have found an illegitimate job, and paid cash for the car. But the kid had tried to mug Caldwell when? During Sarah McDonald's spring break about six months ago.

In Caldwell's limited understanding of the way criminal enterprises usually worked, it was only the older and more secure members who could survive having high-profile vehicles. Ostentation got people arrested or killed. Maybe he was just driving his boss's car on an errand, or acting as chauffeur. The side and back windows were so darkly tinted that another man might easily have been in the backseat. That seemed most likely. The SUV wasn't a young man's car—not sleek and cool with too much engine. It was a rhinoceros with wheels.

Caldwell took all of the possibilities into account, and then returned to the one that had come to him first. Maybe James Harriman hadn't been trying to rob any victim he met on the street that April night. Maybe the reason he'd had a revolver was that he was trying to kill a particular man and make it look to the local police like a street crime. And maybe now he was back, doing reconnaissance for a second try.

Caldwell reminded himself that this sighting might be a coincidence, and Harriman might not have been thinking about him. But then Caldwell remembered a moment about forty years ago, when he had been in a survival course at Fort Rucker, Alabama. The trainer had said, "Most of the people who don't believe in coincidences are still alive. That's not a coincidence, either."

He ducked through the parking lot of a delicatessen, then down the passage between two apartment buildings to the street. He took several shortcuts to reach the apartment, went around the building to the rear stairway facing the garage, and went inside.

It was reassuring that the dogs had been perfectly aware he was coming before he arrived. They were waiting for him at the apartment door with a calm welcome that indicated he had not surprised them. They sniffed his shoes and the bags he was carrying and then escorted him into his bedroom.

As he hung up the new clothes in his closet he thought more about the young man using the name James Harriman. He looked young. But the army often recruited exceptional young men from among the trainees. He could be one of those. The army would give them special training, divert them into some form of special ops for a year or two, and then make the next decision about them—home for more training or out. If the young man was like Caldwell had been at that age, all they had to do was tell him Caldwell was a traitor and a murderer, and step out of the way.

Caldwell locked the bedroom door and climbed up to the access door in the ceiling of his closet. He took down the two compact Beretta pistols, the extra magazines, and the identity packets and closed the hatch. He selected a sport coat that he liked, and put one pistol and two extra magazines in the pockets. He put the rest of his kit into his topcoat because it had deep inner pockets that hung almost to knee level and didn't bulge. Then he hung up the coats on the left side, where he could easily find them in the dark.

He unloaded the second Beretta Nano and put it under the mattress of his bed, lay down, and practiced reaching for it, finding it, and bringing it up to fire. He persisted until he could do it unerringly with his eyes closed. Then he reloaded the pistol and put it back under the mattress.

Caldwell searched the Internet to find out anything he could about James Harriman. He found a site that listed ninety-five of them, but none of them seemed to him to be the one who had tried to rob him. Other sites had more.

From that day on, when he went out he always had one of the pistols on him. It was September, so many days were still too warm for a coat. On those days he wore a loose shirt untucked so he could carry a pistol under it.

On the nights when he and Zoe slept in her room, he would usually leave the pistol hidden from her under the neat pile of his clothes he left on the chaise. He made sure that Carol and Dave stayed close enough to the bedroom so he would notice their agitation if someone came near the apartment. After a couple of weeks, he retrained them to sleep on the floor between her bed and the door when he was with her. They were so happy to be readmitted to the room where he slept that they didn't seem to be disappointed that there was no space for them on the bed.

He began to search the Internet, studying various cities to pick out his next place to live. The cities that looked most promising to him were Los Angeles, Miami, Dallas, and Houston, cities with large, diverse populations. But those were also the cities where his pursuers were most likely to look. He knew he had to consider a wider selection, and so he kept at it.

In the meantime, he decided to improve the security of the apartment. Caldwell bought a set of four small security cameras and a monitor and recorder. He used the extension ladder stored in the garage and installed the four cameras on the edge of the flat roof of the building so that all sides of the building were visible on his monitor. He had no interest in knowing the identity of an intruder, only to know if someone was prowling around the building. When he was alone each day he would speed through the previous night's recordings, looking for a human shape.

He plotted the best ways to drive from the apartment to the nearest interstate highways without getting caught in the Chicago traffic. He tried each of the routes at various times of the day and night.

When he went out now, he was always alert and armed, with an escape route in mind. He was always watching for signs. He returned by various routes, trying to surprise anyone casing the apartment. Weeks passed, but nothing happened. He saw no vehicles parked along his routes that appeared to hold observers or surveillance equipment. There were no hardhat crews who appeared on any of his routes, set out orange traffic cones, and fiddled around without accomplishing much. Nobody betrayed a special interest in him.

In time, he began to feel more optimistic. The young man who had tried to rob him might have been nothing worse than that. Maybe he was a delinquent kid who had fallen into some luck, either an honest job that would save him or a dishonest one that would put him away. Which it was didn't matter. If James Harriman was anything but an army intelligence operator, Caldwell's present hiding place was safe. Panicking and abandoning a perfect hiding place to start a new search for shelter was a very bad idea.

Whatever features a new place might have, it probably wouldn't have a woman like Zoe, whose name was on the lease and all the utility bills, and who provided him with a veneer of respectability and normalcy. Anywhere else, he would be a lone stranger, and he would have to start all over again persuading the locals that he was harmless. He would be presented with a thousand new chances to make a fatal error.

Caldwell didn't stop looking at the recordings from his security cameras, and he didn't stop watching for signs that he was attracting interest. He took one more precaution. He bought a car. It was a black BMW 3 Series sedan, a lower-end model that cost him about forty thousand dollars, but it was new, and it had a powerful engine.

He bought it in the name of Henry Dixon with a check from Dixon's account, because if he ever needed the car, he would no longer be Peter Caldwell. He had the side windows tinted as dark as they would make them, because if he needed the car he would be running. He drove it straight from the lot to the garage he had rented a few blocks away. He visited the car once a week and drove it to keep the battery charged and the engine lubricated. He slowly acquired another twenty thousand dollars in cash and stored it in the well where the spare tire was held.

He did everything he could to get ready, as though being ready for a disaster would keep it from happening. Then he waited and watched.

12

Caldwell was in Zoe's room, lying beside her. The night was cool, maybe an early taste of fall, and there was a steady wind that made the big trees in the neighborhood rock back and forth and their millions of leaves set up a steady hiss and shudder. There was a new moon, so the sky was mostly dark. Caldwell was a little more on edge than usual. When he was in special ops the trainers had taught him to plan operations for nights like this. The additional darkness made it easier to move unseen, the unusual coolness made people shut their windows and muffled sounds, and the wind covered incidental noises.

Zoe's breathing was soft, slow, and regular as she slept, still touching him, her bare arm across his bare chest, her long hair swept back behind her neck.

He closed his eyes and let sleep take him too. When he woke in the darkness, the dogs were both on their feet, staring at the closed door of the room. One of them began a low growl, and the other added to it.

Caldwell slid out from under Zoe's arm, stood, and put a hand on each of the dogs to silence them. He stepped into his pants and shoes, picked up the gun he had hidden under them, then slipped his shirt on over his head. He kept glancing at the dogs. They weren't agitated, just standing alert and ready, staring at the door as though they were awaiting a person's approach. But the dogs wouldn't imagine an intruder. They had heard or smelled something.

Caldwell opened the bedroom door an eighth of an inch and looked out into the hallway and past it to the living room. The room was empty and the apartment's front door was still closed. He opened Zoe's door farther and the dogs slithered out ahead of him. He stayed low as he moved into the open.

He slipped into his bedroom and looked at the monitor of his security system. The screen was divided into quadrants, and when he scanned them, he was relieved at first. What the four cameras were seeing wasn't a street full of Chicago police cars or a federal assault team suiting up in military gear. But he saw movement. It looked like the shape of a man coming toward the front of the house. He tucked in his shirt and put on the sport coat with the extra ammunition, because it was dark gray and would make him harder to see. He looked at the monitor more closely.

Three human figures were on the front steps, one of them kneeling by the door, and the other two standing behind him to shield him from the street. Caldwell watched the man manipulating something with both hands. The dogs lowered their heads. Their approach must have been what the dogs had heard earlier. Now it looked as though the man was moving a pick and tension wrench in the front door lock. The man put something in his pocket, fiddled with the doorknob, and then stood up.

Caldwell slipped out of his room and closed the dogs inside. He hurried to Zoe's room and shook her awake.

"Zoe, there are men breaking into the building. They'll be through the front door and coming up the stairs in a minute. Get dressed, lock yourself in the bathroom, and lie down in the tub. Go!" He snatched up the clothes she had left on the chaise, took her arm and pulled her to the bathroom, pushed them into her hands, and shut the door.

He stepped into the kitchen and turned on the water in the sink, then went down to the end of the hallway and lay on his belly, the pistol in his hand.

There was the clicking of metal on metal, this time at the door of the apartment, twenty-five feet from him, then the clack as the dead bolt retracted into the door. The door opened slowly and a pair of male shapes stood in the doorway, silhouetted in the dim light from a streetlamp shining through the first-floor windows. They each held something in one hand, and he knew the objects had to be guns, but they looked longer than pistols.

From behind Caldwell's bedroom door the dogs began to bark and snarl, and both men turned toward the bedroom and braced themselves for an attack, their guns ready. The dogs scratched at the bedroom door, but couldn't get out. The scratching told the two intruders that the dogs weren't able to get at them, so they stepped deeper into the apartment.

Now the men heard the sound of running water coming from the kitchen, and it seemed to puzzle and distract them. They turned and stepped toward the kitchen, their weapons raised.

Caldwell picked that moment to emerge from the hallway and stop behind them. "Stand still and drop the guns." He squatted and aimed at the man on the right.

The two turned in unison and fired, spraying sparks from the muzzles of their weapons. Both shots went high, and Caldwell squeezed his trigger. He had chosen the man on his right because he knew he could fire and move his aim to the left faster than to the right. The man went down, and before the man's partner could lower his aim Caldwell fired at his chest.

The second man was hit, but he was still on his feet. Before he could slip into the kitchen for cover, Caldwell fired again and the man dropped.

Caldwell checked the two men and found neither had a pulse. He picked up their pistols and set them on the coffee table. The barrels were elongated by the addition of silencers, and it occurred to him that the only shots he had heard were his own. He frisked the bodies and found wallets and passports, but it was too dark to look at them, so he pocketed them and hurried to the bathroom door. "Zoe. It's me, Peter. Come out."

There was a click of the lock and Zoe peered out. "Are you okay? That sounded like gunfire."

"That's why I wanted you in the tub, where you wouldn't get hit with a wild shot. Those two were the shooting team, but there will be other men outside. We've got to get out of here before they realize we're alive."

"Have you called the police? We can wait right here for them."

"We can't wait," he said. "Please. Just do what I ask, without any questions. Our lives depend on it right now."

"What should I do?"

"We've got no more than five minutes. Throw anything with your kids' pictures or addresses into a bag. Don't call anybody, or turn on any lights. If they see you, they'll kill you."

"Why would they kill me?"

"Because it's their job. I've got to go out there for a minute, but I'll be back for you. Don't let the dogs out of the bedroom." He held up the small Beretta he had fired. "The safety is off. If anybody but me comes in the door, aim and fire." He set the gun on the bed and hurried out.

He stopped at the coffee table, picked up one of the pistols he'd taken from the two dead men, and hurried down the stairs to the ground floor landing. He had seen a third man on the security monitor, and knew there might be others. He went to the windows at the sides of the house. There was nobody visible out there. He picked a window, opened the sash slowly, then unlatched the screen, slipped out, and crouched beside the shrubs that grew there.

Caldwell remained motionless for a few seconds and then a few more as he stared into the night in one direction then another, waiting to identify the shape of a man or for a shadow to move. He made his way along the side of the house, crouched again, and looked around the corner. He could see a man in the shadows, leaning against the garage and facing the back stairway of the house. As Caldwell watched, the man took out his phone and checked its screen, apparently expecting a text message from the men inside. In the glow Caldwell could see the man's face. He was the young man who had tried to rob him, James Harriman.

Caldwell thought about trying to go back around the house to get behind him, but the young man had taken a position with his back to the garage, facing the stairs to the kitchen door. Caldwell took a deep breath, let it out slowly, and stepped away from the corner of the house aiming the pistol with its silencer at the man's head. "Hello again," he said.

The young man spun his head to look. "Hey!" he said. It was simply an expression of shock, with no other meaning.

Caldwell could see him lean away from the garage, shifting his weight forward, bending his knees a little as he began to raise his hands. The young man was preparing to make a move. He ducked and lunged toward Caldwell, trying to take him down in a quick tackle.

He was fast and powerful, but Caldwell had been prepared. He sidestepped and batted the young man's arm down with his free hand, so he could keep the pistol aimed at the man's upper body. When the young man's momentum brought him up against the house, Caldwell was still with him, the silenced pistol still between them.

Caldwell said, "Put your gun down and step away from it."

"I don't have a gun."

"Then when I search your body I'll find nothing?"

"Okay, okay," the young man said. He took a pistol out of a shoulder holster and set it down, then stepped back with his hands up. "What happened upstairs?"

"They weren't good enough for this," Caldwell said. "Now I'm going to ask you a few questions. You'll live as long as you answer and don't move. Who were they?"

"They're foreign. I was told to bring them to where you lived and then get them away when they were done."

"You work for the government?"

"Yes."

"Show me an ID."

"I don't carry one."

"Why?"

"You know," the young man said. "I bet you didn't either."

"You're working for military intelligence. What do they want from me after all this time?"

"I think they're trying to do a favor for somebody. Whoever sent those guys."

"How did they know I was Daniel Chase and living in Vermont after all these years?"

"The intelligence guys told me it was time and technology. Even old records got computerized after you disappeared. Now it's easy to find out that the serial numbers of the money you took had turned up over ten or so years, most of them in New England. They found your old service pictures and used a new algorithm to age your face, and then searched public surveillance recordings in New England with face recognition programs for a year or so. A bunch of guys who looked like you got spotted, but agents eliminated all of them but you."

"Why were the two killers upstairs carrying passports?"

"I was supposed to get them to the airport and put them on a plane tonight, right away."

"A plane to where?" Caldwell said.

"They're from Libya."

"If I leave you alive, will you give the intelligence people a message?"

"Right now that sounds like a good deal."

"All I was trying to do from the start was take back the money and return it to the government. My bosses cut my communication, and then set me up to get arrested. The offer is still open. I give them the full amount I delivered to Libya and brought back. They tell whoever sent these guys that they killed me. Nobody ever sees me again. Got it?"

The young man hesitated. "What happened to the two guys upstairs? Are they dead?"

"Of course."

"That means your count is up to five."

Caldwell shrugged. "I didn't go after them. They came after me."

"Look," said the young man. "When you could have shot me or thrown me to your dogs as a chew toy you gave me eating money and let me go. I'll say what you want. But if they don't buy your deal, don't be surprised."

"I won't be. Humor me."

"Suit yourself. But can you at least make me look right?"

Caldwell moved instantly and struck him across the forehead with the pistol. He fell to the ground, unconscious. Caldwell opened the garage, backed in, and came back with a roll of duct tape. He wrapped the man's wrists and ankles, dragged his unconscious body a few feet from the garage, and propped him against a tree. He used a length of baling wire he found in the garage to tie him to the tree. He could see that he'd hit Harriman in the right spot, just at the hairline. It was the hardest part of the skull, but the wound bled freely down his face to his shirt.

Caldwell ran back up to the apartment. He calmed the dogs and let them out of his room, put on the topcoat that held the cash and identification kit, and went to Zoe's room.

She was sitting dazed on the bed. Beside her was a leather overnight bag with a shoulder strap. He said, "Ready?"

"I'm sorry. I'm not going anywhere with you."

"No?"

"Those two men are dead," she said. "You shot two men to death."

"They came here to murder me, and they would have murdered you too."

"Why? Why did they come here? Just because you're rich? There are thousands of rich people in Chicago."

"Please, Zoe. I'm trying to save your life. As soon as we're away from here I'll tell you everything, and answer any question you can think of. But the danger isn't over. It's coming closer and closer."

"Go if you want, but I can't be part of this. And in about two minutes I'm calling the police."

He picked up the pistol she had left untouched on the bed, and pocketed it. He went into his bedroom, put a few things in his coat pockets—wallet, keys, pocketknife—and returned to Zoe's room.

She was standing now, facing the window. She shook, as though she was sobbing, but he couldn't hear her, and in the dark he couldn't be sure. As he approached, she started to spin to face him.

The duct tape was already in his hands. He wrapped the first strip over her mouth and around to the back of her head. As her hands came up to tear it away he spun her around again so she couldn't face him, threw her down on the bed, wrenched her wrists around behind her, and wrapped them with duct tape too. He continued the tape upward to her elbows, so she had no hope of wrenching her hands free. She rolled to try to kick him away.

Caldwell put his arm around both legs and stepped down to her ankles, wrapped them around and around with duct tape, then put the rest of the roll in his topcoat pocket. He took her bag. "Others will be here soon. I had hoped you'd cooperate, but either way I can't leave you here to die."

He lifted her over his shoulder in a fireman's carry and hurried to the door. The dogs ran ahead of him to the back stairway and down to the ground. They went immediately to the young man propped up against the tree, sniffed at him a little, and returned to Caldwell.

He put Zoe in the passenger seat of the car and secured her there with the seat belt. He opened the back door of the car and the dogs jumped up onto the seat. Then he got in, started the car, and drove. When he reached the street, he did not pause to watch for approaching cars. Their headlights would have lit up the block, and stopping for them would have been more dangerous than pulling out in front of them. He accelerated up the street before he turned his headlights on.

Caldwell stared into the rearview mirror watching for a car to appear from around a corner, or to pull out from the curb and follow. But nothing moved. As long as he could, he kept glancing in the mirrors at the long gray strip of pavement, as straight as a surveyor could make it, with pools of light from streetlamps stretching back hundreds of yards. When he came to the turn, he took it, and headed south along streets that were deserted at this time of night.

After a few minutes he pulled into a driveway, then quickly turned up a narrow alley behind a row of buildings. They were all old, redbrick structures that seemed to date back to the building boom after the Great Chicago Fire. When he neared the end of the block he stopped the car.

He reached for the tape at Zoe's mouth. She tried to lean away, but the seat belt held her. He peeled the tape off her mouth, and he could tell from her expression he was hurting her. "You kidnapped me," she said. "Are you going to kill me now?"

"No," he said. "I've only bought us a few minutes, and I'm not going to waste one of them killing you. I'm going to tell you what's happening. About thirty-five years ago I worked for army intelligence. I was assigned to smuggle twenty million dollars to a man in Libya who was supposed to deliver the money to rebel guerrillas trying to overthrow the government. Instead the middleman kept it. He bought fancy cars, started building a big house, and hired bodyguards. The guerrillas in the mountains ran out of supplies and ammunition, starved, and got killed or captured."

"Peter, I just saw the men you shot to death. You tied me up and abducted me. How can any lie you dream up make any difference to me?"

Caldwell kept talking. "I recovered what was left of the money from the middleman. Instead of helping me get back to the US with it, my supervisors cut off my communication and left me to be caught and tortured to death. I brought the money home by myself. When I tried to turn it in, I learned they'd already declared me a thief and a murderer."

"Why would they do that? And what has this got to do with anything?"

"They may have been saving themselves from the blame for a failure. They may have felt that the man who had tried to keep the money was more valuable to national security than I was. It doesn't matter now. Even though I hurt nobody in getting the money back, the official story was that I had murdered Libyans to steal money that was vital to an American operation. Once they were after me, I felt that all I could do was run."

"For all this time? Over thirty years?"

He shrugged. "Once you run there isn't any possibility of not running. I was careful, and lived a quiet life. They found me in Vermont last winter. Instead of arresting me they sent a shooter to kill me. The dogs heard him, or smelled him, just the way they did tonight. So here I am. The people who sent me to Libya were all much older than I was thirty-five years ago. Even if I'd known their names, by now they're all retired or dead. The people who are after me now have no reason to ever stop. The record, if there is one, can never be corrected because the people who wrote it are long gone. It's fossilized."

"You must think I'm really stupid to try to make me believe this stuff."

"You saw those two men in our apartment," he said. "Did you invite them?"

"Of course not."

"Neither did I. You might have noticed that they brought guns with silencers and shot at me. And I swear to you that if you are in that apartment when the follow-up team comes looking for their two shooters, you will die. They can't leave people behind who know about any of this. The two men in the apartment were Libyans. The one outside is American special ops, working for military intelligence."

She said, "How can you do this to me? I was in love with you. I don't know what the truth is, but I know this is a collection of lies. It's crazy."

He patted his pockets. "I took their passports." He took out two bright green folders with gold Arabic writing and a gold heraldic eagle. He held one open in front of her face and opened the car door so the light would come on. Then he held up the other passport for a few seconds, and shut the door. "They were expecting to get on a plane and leave the country right after killing me."

She was silent, not willing to concede anything.

"Our time is up," he said. "I'll let you off, and then you'll never see me again. I'm very sorry that I answered your ad for the apartment. It wasn't fair to you. You're a good person who didn't deserve to run into me. Now I've got to get moving."

"You're leaving me here?" she said. "How would you like to be a woman taped up and dropped off in the middle of the night in an unfamiliar part of Chicago?"

"If you'll promise not to call the cops or tell them anything about where I went, I'll leave you somewhere safer."

"Just get us both out of here now."

He drove to the front of the nearby garage, got out, unlocked the door, and opened it. He went inside, drove the new BMW that was inside into the alley, and then replaced it with the old Toyota. He let the dogs out and ordered them into the backseat of the BMW. Then he lifted Zoe out of the Toyota.

She said, "If I promise to go quietly will you please get rid of the tape?"

"No." He carried her to the BMW, put her in the passenger seat, and strapped her in. He went to the garage, closed it, and locked the door on the Toyota. Then he got into the BMW, restarted it, and drove.

After about fifteen minutes he turned down another nearly deserted commercial street that was lined with warehouses and parking lots. He took out his pocketknife and cut the tape on Zoe's legs and then leaned across to free her from the seat belt so he could cut the tape on her wrists. He put the car in gear again and drove on. "I'm doing this to be kind. Don't make me sorry."

In a moment they were heading southwest on Interstate 55, away from the city. Zoe began the business of pulling the tape off her long hair. "This is really painful. I'm pulling out handfuls of hair."

He said, "You didn't give me any choice. It will be light in about two hours. I'll let you off outside the city with plenty of money so you can take a cab or something. Just don't go right back to the apartment. There will be people watching it, maybe waiting inside. If there's a cleanup crew, you'll be one of the things they'll want to get rid of."

Zoe finished taking the tape out of her hair and began pulling the tape from the ankles of her jeans. Her face was close to the dashboard. "Nice car," she said. "I guess you planned for this night a while ago."

He shrugged. "Once you realize that you can never let them find you, the rest is obvious. I figured this wasn't the kind of car they'd be looking for if I moved on. My last two cars were older Toyotas."

"If you're so smart, how did they find you?"

"I don't really know how they found me in Vermont. Probably I made a mistake. I know they searched the Chicago area for five months before a young operator spotted me."

"The young guy lying by the garage?"

"Yes. I think he figured out that I would try to hide in a neighborhood where there were lots of people who looked like me. He's smart."

"Was smart."

"Huh?"

"You killed him."

"No I didn't. He's the reason I had the duct tape. I wrapped his wrists and ankles. He's tied to a tree by the garage."

"You killed two and left the third behind?"

"The first two shot at me. With him, I had a choice. His people will find him and he'll be okay."

He drove on in silence for a few minutes, and then noticed that Zoe was staring at him with a strange look on her face, as though she were trying to see through his skull. He turned to look at her. "Don't worry. I'll let you off soon. There should be something along this route."

"It's still dark."

"The longer you stay with me, the longer your ride back will be."

"I'm certainly not going back to that apartment. But if I don't come home, they'll start looking for me, won't they?"

"I'm not sure. The two Libyan assassins are dead. I don't know who is making the next decision, or even where in the world he is. You could go straight to a police station as soon as you get to Chicago and report the shooting. They'll examine the crime scene and ask you a lot of questions."

"The police? Why would you want them involved?"

"I don't. But once the police have talked to you, they'll know you didn't shoot anybody, and you should be safer. The people chasing me can't very well make you disappear if the police think you're a witness to a homicide."

"Oh my God," she muttered.

She fell silent. She stared out the car window at the flat countryside for twenty minutes before she spoke again. "Were you really expecting me to come with you?"

"I talked myself into believing this wasn't going to happen. When it did, I was concentrating on making sure you got out alive."

"Is that all?"

"Of course I hoped you would want to be with me if I had to move on, but this wasn't the way I thought it would happen. I can't say coming with me would be a good idea, so I can't blame you for not doing it."

"No, you can't." She went back to staring out the window. "I hate these tinted windows."

"Me too. But I figured they'd make it harder to recognize me." He kept his eyes on the road for a minute or two, and then looked into the rearview mirrors to check for cars that might be following them.

Zoe waited for him to say something, but he didn't. When it became apparent that he wasn't going to tell her anything more, she said, "What will you do with the dogs?"

"I have someone who will take them."

"Where will you go?"

He seemed to come out of a reverie. "Don't worry. I'll let you off this morning."

"I didn't ask that. I asked where."

He said, "You should realize that I'm a very big catch for these people, and I'm getting bigger every hour. Knowing things can hurt you a lot."

"I suppose."

"If they think you know where I am, they'll do what they can to get you to tell them."

"Do you believe they'd torture me or something?"

He glanced at her and turned his eyes back on the road. "I don't know. I've been out of that world for over thirty-five years. But making people like them think you're an accomplice instead of a victim is a bad idea."

Zoe stared out the window for the next hour, looking at the increasingly open country while they cleared the circle of dense population around Chicago. The car left the interstate just at dawn. She could see that they were surrounded by farmland, and Caldwell seemed to be on his way deeper into the country. The road he had chosen was deserted. It intersected now and then with unmarked narrow asphalt roads with gravel shoulders, but in the weak gray light she saw no houses.

Then she felt a deceleration as Caldwell took his foot off the gas pedal. She saw they were coasting onto the gravel shoulder. When he stopped, a cloud of dust caught up with them and blew past.

She looked for signs. "Where are we?"

"We're outside Springfield," he said.

He turned off the engine. "I'm sorry to stop so far from the city. But I've got to give myself a little head start before you talk to the police." He reached into his coat pocket and took out a thick envelope. He held the envelope open while he pulled out a thick stack of hundred-dollar bills.

Her eyes weren't on the money, but on the envelope. "What's that?"

He held out the money.

"Not that," she said. She reached for the envelope. "This." She held the envelope open and took out a California driver's license. "That's my picture. It's the one you took with your phone in the living room." She reached in and took out a passport. She opened it, and looked at the front page, where there was another picture of her. "This looks so real."

"That's because it is," he said.

"How did you get this?"

"A long time ago I got my wife to apply for a passport in that name, so this was just a renewal. When you renew they ask for fresh pictures, so I sent yours. You don't look that much like her, but she had long brown hair and blue eyes like yours. The passport had never been used, and there was no reason for them to think Marcia Dixon was up to something after all these years of good behavior."

She took out a credit card, then another. "Marcia Dixon. Marcia Dixon. When did you do all this?"

"When I took those pictures. You can keep the passport and license. Maybe they'll come in handy. Just don't let anybody catch you with passports in two different names." He set the stack of money on the console beside her. "And put this money away in your overnight bag. Walk back up the road the way we came, and you'll get to the interstate. There are gas stations and fast-food places where you can call a cab. What you want is a ride into Springfield. Tell the driver to let you off at the state capitol building. It's a good place, because there will be hotels and restaurants nearby. If he asks how you got to the interstate, tell him your car broke down and got towed. Your husband is going to wait for the car at the dealer's and meet you in Springfield when it's ready. Mentioning a husband means you don't have to know all the details. Do you understand?"

"You're good at this stuff."

"Thank you."

"I mean you're a good liar."

"Yes, I know. You'd better get started now."

"I'm not going," she said.

"I told you I'd set you free. This is a perfectly good place."

"I'm sure it is. I told you I could see how clever you are. But I've thought this through again since you woke me up in the middle of the night. At that moment I thought you were completely different from the man I knew. But you're the same."

"I don't want you to go with me, Zoe."

"When you did all this to get me a new identity, you must have expected me to run away with you, right? You must have at least hoped I would."

"This isn't a productive conversation. We're wasting time."

"Then let's get going. I'll drive if you're tired."

"Zoe, this isn't something you want to get in on. You picked right the first time. When I got you those papers and cards I didn't know this was going to happen. I thought I'd lost the hunters again, probably for good. The forgeries were just a precaution, and if all went well, we'd never need them." He paused. "It's stupid to even talk about this."

"Probably," she said. "Let's go. Do you not want me to drive your new car, or what?"

"A week from now I'm more likely to be dead than alive. If you're with me, so are you. A hostage is never more likely to die than when the authorities are trying to rescue her. This is your way out."

"I don't want a way out. I want to go with you. I'll be anyone you want, and I'll do anything you say, without question. You can even change the terms, and I won't complain. Just take me along."

"Zoe—"

"Sorry. I don't know her. I'm Marcia Dixon. I'm on a road trip with my husband, What's-His-Name Dixon."

"Henry."

"Henry? Really?"

"Yes."

"It's a respectable name, I guess. So who's driving?"

"Please think about this, Zoe."

"I've thought of nothing else all morning. I'm thinking we have a long drive ahead of us. I know that if you want to get rid of me you can hurt me, throw me out on the pavement, and drive off. If you kill me they couldn't punish you worse than they will already."

"I can't waste any more time right now." He reached across her, pushed open her door, and waited.

"Look, I know that you stayed with me for your own practical reasons. You needed a hiding place, and a woman made it look real and settled and normal—not like a hideout, but like a life. I get it. At first you liked the place, and then you liked the sex, and I wasn't demanding or bitchy or anything, so you stayed, maybe longer than you should have. But I had reasons of my own, and maybe they were mostly selfish too. But over time, something changed for me.

It changed for you too. Otherwise you wouldn't have taken extra risks to make sure I could go with you."

"You're right. I did use you. So get out."

"I know being anywhere near you is a huge risk. But I'd rather take that risk than go back to have the life I would have if I let you drive away without me now. It would be giving up life to give myself a longer time to exist. I would always remember what I gave up. You used me, and I used you too. So keep on using me. I love you, and I can be really useful, and I will be." She reached for the door handle and shut the door.

He sighed in frustration, put the car in gear, and drove. When they reached the junction with Interstate 72, they swung onto it and headed east. After another hour he left the interstate and kept going, taking the back roads, the long, straight highways that had been replaced by interstates but still carried local traffic.

When they reached the first small, pretty town that had a large park, they stopped to feed the dogs and give them a walk. At another town he sent Marcia Dixon into a small store to buy bottled water, bags of nuts, a box of protein bars, a bag of fruit, and more dog food.

Henry Dixon watched her through the front window. He was aware that a woman in her position might have decided to come along solely to get her kidnapper caught. Right now she could easily be telling the store clerk to call the local police. The television news people would call her a plucky little heroine, and she would be invited on morning talk shows. Maybe they would show footage of her in the foreground with the commander of the SWAT team, and on the pavement in the background there would be a body covered with a sheet. This was the test. Either she was telling him the truth or she wasn't. He wasn't sure now why he was so confident that she wouldn't betray him.

He watched her return to the car carrying the bags of supplies. As she approached, he popped open the trunk and took his time putting the bags inside and moving snacks and dog treats and bottled water to the front seat where they could reach them. Then he let the dogs out to urinate again. As he watched them, he kept listening for the whine of distant police sirens.

She said, "I thought we were in more of a hurry than this. Am I wrong?"

He opened the back door and let the dogs onto the backseat. He stood still for another moment, but he still heard nothing. "No, you're right," he said, got into the car, and drove.

After a few minutes of staring into the rearview mirror to reassure himself that there were no cars following, he took out one of his prepaid cell phones and held it out to her. "Call your daughter."

"Really?" She took the phone.

"Yes. Tell her that you're leaving the country for a while. Tell her not to call the police, and not to go to your apartment for any reason. Tell her to let your son know you're okay, and your ex-husband. Tell her you'll call when you're back."

When she was finished, he took the phone apart and tossed the pieces beside the road, one by one.

After another two hours on the road he stopped again and they ate a snack while they let the dogs run. As they were preparing to leave again she said, "I'd like to call you Hank. Is that all right?"

"I guess so. Why?" He let the dogs jump in and closed the back door.

"You look more like a Hank to me. And you were always more of a Pete than a Peter, too. I would have told you eventually." She got behind the wheel of the car and held out her hand for the keys. "Nobody else will call you Hank but me."

He got in beside her. "You know we'll probably be dead very soon."

"It was never going to end any other way. Lovers all die. And no matter when, it was always going to be sooner than we wanted."

13

Three days later at dusk Henry Dixon pulled the BMW into the deserted parking lot for a small vista point off Route 9N on the west side of Lake George in upstate New York. Henry and Marcia Dixon were a few minutes early for the rendezvous, so Henry fed his dogs and let them run free for a while. They sniffed everything in the area with special attention to the trash barrels, and then trotted off to investigate the trees and brush around the lot, but kept returning to Henry and Marcia, who were out of the car and on their feet after a day of driving. Henry knew that they could tell he was sad about something, but they couldn't imagine what made him sad. They smelled no enemies, and their noses told them nothing nearby had died.

The black BMW was pulled back near the hillside leading down from the main road hidden from view. Henry and Marcia were quiet, waiting.

When Emily's Volvo turned down the drive and coasted into the lot, Henry stood still and watched. Emily stopped, turned the car around to face the driveway, and backed up close to the BMW before she parked and got out. She wore jeans and a bulky sweater and a pair of loafers, and her hair was pulled back tight, so the dark hair she inherited from her mother looked shiny and perfectly smooth.

The boys pushed the back door open, ran to their grandfather, and hugged him. Henry swung Adam, the eight-year-old, into the air and held him for a moment, and then put him down. He did the same to Mark, the six-year-old. The two eager dogs galloped up, bumped their shoulders against the boys, ran a few steps off, and then ran back to them. They had always loved the boys' visits to the house in Vermont.

His daughter stepped up and hugged him. "Hi, Dad," said Emily. "I'm so glad I got a chance to see you in person, and not just pick up Dave and Carol somewhere after you've driven off."

"I'm glad to see you too," he said. "But I can't believe you brought the boys with you. You know this is a very dangerous place to be."

Emily shrugged. "Mothers have to make impossible decisions. I decided I had to put them at risk for these few minutes. I want them to remember this." Emily kissed her father's cheek, then let go of him and turned her head. "You're Zoe?"

"Yes," she said. "It's not going to be my name after this. I'm working on getting used to the new one."

"I'm glad to meet you," Emily said.

When her father moved off to play with the boys and the dogs, she said, "He told me on the phone that you were still with him. I never thought you would decide to do this. Nobody would have blamed you for walking away. Least of all, him."

Marcia Dixon shrugged. "He wanted me to leave, but here I am. It doesn't matter why, does it?"

"No," said Emily. "But when it gets to be time, he'll probably sense it. When he says to go, do what he tells you. You won't be able to save him."

They were silent after that, watching the boys and their grandfather playing with the dogs for a few minutes, and then Emily said, "Dad?"

He turned and walked back to her. "I know. It's almost dark. We've all got to go soon." He put his arms around her and held her for a moment. "Thanks for taking Dave and Carol."

"Don't worry," she said. "We'll all take great care of them. When you pick them up you'll see how spoiled they are."

"Do me another favor, and remind the boys once in a while that I love them."

"Of course."

"And give your husband my regards. Oh, what the hell. My love." He went to the trunk of the BMW, popped it open, took out two big bags of dry dog food and a case of canned food, and carried them to the back of Emily's car. When she opened the trunk he loaded them in. "Keep it open," he said, and brought another box from the BMW's trunk and put it in. "Your next three phones."

"I figured."

"They're not preprogrammed this time. Too risky. But I have the numbers."

The dogs and boys noticed that something was happening, so they all drew near.

Emily hugged her father tightly and talked so only he could hear. "Never doubt that you gave me a great life. You did. Now get out of here. And be really nice to Zoe, or whatever you're calling her now. But protect yourself. All she has to do is pick up a phone, and it's over."

"I know," he said. "I gave her every chance, but she didn't."

Henry Dixon opened the back door of Emily's Volvo. He patted the backseat and said, "Carol. Dave." The two dogs jumped up on the seat. He held Carol's face up to his so they were nose to nose, breathing the same air. "Good girl." He held Dave's face up to his the same way. "Good boy." Then he muttered, "That's all there is to say." He took the biscuits he always carried in his pants pocket and gave all of them to the dogs, and then shut the door.

He hugged the boys and watched their mother put them in the car. "Sit up here with me," she said to the older one. "And give your brother a chance to be with the dogs until the first stop. Then you switch."

She took a last look at her father, started the car, and pulled up the incline to the edge of the highway. She let a car go by and then turned left to get back to the entrance to Interstate 87 south toward New York City.

Marcia and Henry Dixon stood beside the BMW, watching them go, and then staring after them at the empty, darkening stretch of road. Marcia turned to him. "I thought she'd be like that."

"Like what?"

"The looks, the voice. The way she is with you and the boys. Whatever gigantic screwups you've done in your life, you seem to have done at least one perfect thing."

"Thanks." They got into the BMW.

She said, "Should we think about hamburgers and a motel, or would you rather put some miles behind us first?"

"I'm ready to stop for the night."

"Is it safe to stop around here?"

"The opposition is looking for an old guy with two dogs about nine hundred miles west of here. Lake George is a tourist area, so we'll be tourists. The season is about over, so we shouldn't have trouble finding a good hotel here."

"What is the opposition thinking about me?"

"There will be some who think that I murdered you. They'll be looking for a body in an Illinois cornfield. Others will think I kept you alive so I can use you as a hostage. If there are any conspiracy theorists in on it, they will have found out your mother was a Russian defector, and they'll be all agitated about that."

"So we're safe here for the moment?"

"As safe as we'd be anywhere."

They drove around the lakeshore until they came to a hotel that looked bigger and fancier than the others. It was called the Georgian. Marcia went inside to the desk and checked them in, while Henry parked the car.

They went to their room, showered, changed into clean clothes they had bought during the long drive to upstate New York, went to the hotel restaurant for dinner, and then ordered after-dinner cognac.

When they were back in their room they made love for the first time since their escape from Chicago. It was a long, unhurried encounter, an unspoken decision to celebrate the first time they were alone and not evading unseen pursuers on a highway. Afterward they lay together on the bed, their bodies still touching.

"That was why," she said.

"Why what?"

"Why I couldn't behave like a sensible adult and get out of your car the other day. I realized that what I really wanted was to live the rest of my life like this."

"I'm flattered," he said. "But it wasn't a smart idea."

"No need to feel flattered. It wasn't actually about you. It was about me. One reason the first part of my life was a disaster was because I was too passive. I waited for things to happen to me. I danced with the one who asked me, and I stayed until he dropped me. No good. But I guess it made me ready for you. I wanted you, and I did the things I thought you would like a woman to do. Until recently I wouldn't have done that. I seduced you. I've been proud of myself since then. And when I had time to see that you really did have to go on the run, I realized I had options. My kids are adults. Nobody depends on me anymore. I can do what I want. Was I going to throw my new life away so I could spend the next thirty years dusting that apartment in Chicago?"

"I want to talk you out of this," he said. "I should, but I'm not in the mood right now."

"You can't. What you can do is try to keep us both alive as long as you can. That seems to be what you're really good at."

14

Julian Carson wasn't allowed into the meeting. This kind of meeting was far above his pay grade. He sat in a booth at the back of the bar at the Intercontinental Hotel on Michigan Avenue drinking coffee and watching the bar traffic. Nobody was likely to pay much attention to a young black man wearing a conservative suit, sitting by himself and communicating only with the cell phone on the table in front of him, so he supposed he was the man for the job.

Of course they hadn't brought him in. He wasn't even an agent. He was a special ops contractor. That meant that he had no title, no rank. He got paid only when he was actually working, a fee for his services, paid once a month through an electronic transfer into his checking account. At first it had been interesting to see the names of the entities that paid him—companies that sounded familiar, universities, city governments, a hospital. But whenever he checked the names online, they always turned out to have no existence outside their bank accounts.

Julian had been spotted for this job while he was in the army in Afghanistan. They had waited until his second tour was over and he had returned to Fort Benning before military intelligence approached him. After roll call the first sergeant had called him aside and told him he was scheduled for an interview. He stood while three officers sat behind a long table and asked him questions about his tour. When the questions were over the senior officer asked him if he was interested in going to a-school for special assignments. He had already been through a few schools, including Ranger NCO school, which was about as rough as the army could make it, so he accepted.

When he was through the training they sent him to several places where his brown skin and his youthful face would help him—Liberia, the Central African Republic, Brazil. He usually worked with a small team, never fewer than three men, never more than five. He had helped close down three smuggling rings—two of them moving armaments and one cocaine—and the money-laundering networks they fed. One of his teams had kidnapped a guerrilla leader; another had stalked a corrupt minister of finance until they had photographed him with so many recognizable gangsters that the president had no choice but to remove him and have him indicted.

It was when Julian was on his way home from that one that they had called him in the airport while he was waiting for his connecting flight home to Arkansas. They had told him to cancel and fly to Chicago for a meeting.

That meeting, they had invited him to. It had been held in a cheap hotel near the airport where he could sit in the bar and watch the women complete their negotiations before inviting traveling businessmen into their rooms. A few hours after he checked in, two agents knocked on the door of his room. When he let them in, one of them held up a tablet and said, "Here is a picture of a man we're looking for. About thirty-five years ago he was supposed to deliver a large sum of money to a pro-America go-between in Libya. The money was to support a group of insurgents who were trying to overthrow the Gaddafi government. Instead of delivering it, he killed a few friendlies and took off with the money. At some point he made it back to the United States. We know he's been here for at least twenty years, but it wasn't until a couple of weeks ago that he turned up again. He had been living in Vermont. An operator was sent to see him—the guy who took the picture."

The blurred picture was of a man walking a pair of big black dogs across a long bridge over a river. It looked as though the picture had been taken from a car passing him on the bridge, and the side window had not been very clean. The face was just a dark spot against a bright backdrop of snow, and the man could have been any age. "What's his name?"

"He was living under the name Daniel Chase."

"What's his real name?"

"That's classified."

"His *name* is classified?"

"Yes."

"Can I talk to the operator who took the picture?"

"He's dead. He was Libyan, and his English wasn't great anyway. Chase killed him and took off. We think he might be living in Chicago for the moment. I'm sending the picture to your phone so you'll have it with you."

There was a knock on the door, and the other agent opened it. The two men who entered were both in their forties, wearing sport coats and baggy slacks. When he heard them talk he realized they must be Libyan, like the agent who had taken the picture.

Julian Carson did not like the Libyans. He had spent too much time in the wars of the Middle East not to recognize their type. They had been part of some kind of intelligence service or secret police, and they were used to seeing themselves as elite. They spoke a bit of English, and they were willing to use it during the meeting with the two American agents, whom they considered their equals in rank, if not in intellect. They looked at Julian but didn't speak to him.

After Julian began to work with them, they always spoke Libyan Arabic to each other. When they spoke English to Julian it was always in the imperative: *Get this. Take us there. Bring it along. Tell them.* They saw him not as a colleague but as a guide and a chauffeur. He was supposed to take care of their needs, and meanwhile to find the target for them, take them to him, and get them away and out of the country afterward. Julian felt like the organizer of a big game hunt, paid to take a pair of privileged beginners to their prey. Whatever the two may once have been in their country, they were now just a pair of overconfident strangers in a place where they couldn't find their way to a bathroom on their own.

When the two Libyans had left for their own room, Julian's contact men told him a little more about the old man's history. He had settled in Norwich, Vermont, which was an upscale town across the Connecticut River from New Hampshire. He had lived comfortably for many years—not like a hedge fund manager, but like a doctor or a lawyer. He had caused no trouble, raised no eyebrows. Then the Libyans had asked their American contacts to begin an operation to find him and make him pay for his crimes. He turned up in Vermont, and a Libyan agent was sent to assassinate him. Instead he killed the Libyan and took off. He was traced out of Vermont, through Massachusetts and Connecticut to New York. Before military intelligence lost him near Buffalo, he had killed two more Libyan agents. A military intelligence analysis had predicted that the place he would go to ground and hide would be to the west, in the Chicago region—Chicagoland, one of them called it. That was why they had all been sent here.

Julian had listened in silence to his briefing, but when they seemed to be about to end the meeting and leave, he said, "Why do we need the Libyans?"

Harper, the senior agent, said, "They need us. This isn't our operation. It's theirs, and we're just here to help, keep it quiet, and make sure they get out. The shooters are standing in for their boss, the go-between who was supposed to receive the money years ago and pass it on to the insurgents. Two or three of his close relatives were killed when the money was stolen. It's a tribal society, and many of the insurgents were members of his tribe, and others were members of other powerful tribes. Because he never delivered the money, the supply line dried up and the rebels were hunted down and killed. He's been living under suspicion and resentment for all of this time. The regime lasted another twenty-five years or so after that—a whole generation—before they got rid of the bastards."

"Why does military intelligence care? Who is this go-between guy who wants Chase killed?"

"That's so secret it's not even classified. It may not even be written down. Nobody has told us the name. I do know that this man has become an important asset to us. Since the regime fell, he's become much more powerful. We need his friendship, and this is the price."

The meeting ended, and Julian got the two Libyans settled in an apartment on the South Side of Chicago and began his search. He had guessed that the two dogs were his best way to find Chase. The dogs limited the number of places where the fugitive could rent an apartment, and even more severely limited the places where he would want to live. He would find a place in the suburbs where there were parks and safe streets where a man could walk a pair of big dogs. It had to be the kind of place where men who looked like him lived, a place where he could get groceries and things without going far. Probably he would go out mostly at night, so Julian decided night was the best time to look for him. Julian was out every night beginning at dusk, searching likely neighborhoods.

It took months, but Julian found him. His first encounter had taught him that this old man was much more formidable than he had anticipated. And the dogs weren't just a risk to the old man, but also a way of ensuring that he couldn't be surprised or physically overpowered. Julian had tried to explain all of this to the Libyans, but they had smirked at him. He had repeated his warnings, but they had ignored everything he said.

He had taken the Libyans to the old man's apartment and set them loose. Now the Libyans were dead and the old man was alive and hiding somewhere out in the world. Julian was the only survivor of the failed mission. Tonight Julian would probably lose his job and his chance to rise in the intelligence world.

He thought about his job. It wasn't even a job. It was a prolonged tryout for a job. He had thought his time out of the country would at least lead to an offer of employment with the CIA. But he'd been at it for six years, and no offer had come. Now it never would. They were holding a strategy meeting upstairs in this hotel, and he was sitting down here in the bar drinking coffee in a booth. This time the agents had told him he was keeping an eye out to be sure the secrecy and safety of the meeting weren't compromised. Who were they even afraid of? Did they think there was actually any security issue in the Intercontinental Hotel on Michigan Avenue in Chicago? No. They were just having him babysit himself.

He wondered if they were even going to fire him. They might just never call him again. Maybe he should quit to avoid waiting for a call that would never come. All he would have to do was give them back the phone they had issued him and say, "Don't call me again. I'm done."

Then doubts came over him like cold waves breaking on a beach. What would he do for a living? He was twenty-six, and had not done anything officially since he was nineteen and been quietly discharged from the army. He had excellent skills, but few that had any applicability in civilian life. He had a solid record of achievements, but nearly all of his work history was classified.

He pushed the anxiety aside and thought about the night at the apartment. The two Libyans had presented themselves as skilled and subtle assassins, but they had turned out to be punks. Chase had told Julian as much—that they weren't ready for Chase's league. Old special ops men were like vampires. Every time a man like Chase killed another adversary, he knew something he hadn't known before. He knew what one more fighter had done when his life depended on using his best tactic, making the right moves perfectly. Each one added another secret to his knowledge, and each one extended his life span and made him harder to kill.

Julian Carson stared at the opposite wall of his booth—the whorls and streaks in the wood—and thought about how he had gotten here. He had enlisted in the army at seventeen because it seemed like a good thing to do while he was looking for a better thing to do.

He had been brought up outside Jonesboro, Arkansas, on his parents' vegetable farm. As he looked back on it now, he realized that farm work had made him the perfect military intelligence man. He had learned to do hard physical labor in a hot climate. He had grown up accustomed to striving to raise crops that took a long time to ripen, working on pure faith because no sign of the crops was visible at first, just dirt that he watered with his sweat. He had learned to take long shots with a rifle at running rabbits, when a missed shot might mean no meat on the dinner table until some other day, when he would see a shot he could make.

He had noticed during his time at war that most highly successful soldiers were, like him, country boys. They knew better than to fight the land or the climate. They endured them. They were also, like him, shorter than average. That part of his education had come by watching friends die. It didn't matter how brave or how well trained, or even how smart you were if your head stuck up where all that superheated metal was flying in your direction.

Julian's phone vibrated and he looked at the text: "Pay your check and come upstairs."

He left a twenty-dollar bill on the table and slid out of his booth, then walked out of the bar. He used the stairs at the side of the lobby because stairs were part of his discipline. One set of stairs was nothing. A thousand staircases were a way to build a lean, powerful body and enough speed to get to an adversary a step before he expected you.

He reached the fourth floor, went to the room, and gave a military knock, a single slap on the door with the palm of his hand.

The door swung open and he stepped in past Waters, one of the two contact men for this operation.

The room wasn't what he had expected. This was a suite, with a long, narrow hallway that opened to a living room with two couches and a pair of matching armchairs. In an alcove to his right was a long conference table. Its surface was littered with coffee cups and saucers, trays that had once held food but now held crumbs and cloth napkins. There were papers and scratch pads and three laptops.

In front of him, seated in the living room, were three men. One of them was Harper, his other contact man. The remaining two men were older, one of them with gray hair, and they were both wearing expensive, well-cut dark suits.

Waters walked past him and sat down. He said, "This is Carson." He didn't introduce the two strangers.

Harper said, "Carson was our man at the fuckup here in Chicago. We found him gift wrapped in duct tape with a bump on his head."

At one time Julian Carson would have felt he had to answer that, but he had learned that it was always better not to say anything unless they asked him a direct question.

"Okay, Carson," said Harper. "Tell us what happened."

"I found the subject a couple of months ago."

"Where?"

"He was out at night walking his dogs. I reported that to you at the time, so you may have the date." He stared at Harper, his face blank. Then he resumed. "I needed to learn where he lived, but because of the dogs I couldn't follow him without his knowing. Also because of the dogs I thought he was likely to live within an hour's walk from the spot, but normal walking speed puts that at up to three miles."

"Skip that. You looked in the area and found his apartment. You drove Mr. Misratha and Mr. Al-Jalloud to the apartment. What then?"

"I repeated the warnings I'd given them. That the subject had a pair of big dogs that would probably hear or smell them coming. And the subject was old, but he was trained, in great shape, and probably armed. I took the Libyans to the building and picked the lock on the front door. Inside was a small foyer, with a staircase leading up to the subject's apartment."

"What did the two say?" This time it was one of the two gray-haired men on the couch.

"They didn't take my warnings seriously. I believe it was Mr. Misratha who said, 'Just be quiet, wait outside, and watch the back door in case he hears us coming and runs.' They screwed the suppressors on their weapons and climbed the stairs."

"And you did what they said? Kept quiet and waited outside?"

"Yes. I was told at the start that this was their operation. I went to the back of the building and stood by the garage so if the subject came down the back stairs and went for his car, I could stop him."

"Did he?"

"No. After a couple of minutes I heard two rapid shots—*bang-bang*. Like one shot, and then one more a half second later. The two dogs barked. I guessed that the subject must have gotten to a gun and double tapped the trigger but missed, and when they shot him with their silenced weapons, a muscle reflex fired off the last round. To me the sounds indicated the subject was dead, since his shots took only about a second and stopped. At least one of the Libyans must be alive and unhurt, and probably both. So I waited for them to come downstairs."

"How long?"

"Five minutes."

"Then what?"

"I took out my phone and text messaged Mr. Al-Jalloud. He didn't answer. It occurred to me that they might be doing something they hadn't told me about, like cutting off a finger to prove they had killed the right man. I sent another text. By then I thought they must be searching the apartment for the money he had diverted. They were very sure of themselves, and it had occurred to me that they might not know how quickly the Chicago police might respond to a call about gunshots and the commotion from the dogs. I wrote: 'Get out now.'"

"Of course Mr. Al-Jalloud didn't answer."

"No, sir. While I was busy with the phone, the subject climbed out a side window of the building, sneaked around to the back, saw me in the glow of the phone's screen, and clubbed me in the head."

"You've been in some tight combat situations," the man said. "You never heard him coming, or noticed a change, a shadow, or anything?"

"I did, right at the last moment. But I was expecting one of the Libyans, not him. Then I was out. I became conscious when I saw him carrying a woman to the garage. He had tied me up with duct tape. He had her tied that way too—arms behind her, ankles together, then wrapped around and around. He put her in the car and strapped her in with the seat belt."

"I hear he talked to you before he left."

"Yes, sir," said Carson. This was the part that Julian had been dreading, but he had given the old man his word. "The subject said to tell you that he had never intended to steal the money. He just took it back to return to the government because the go-between had kept it. When the subject's contact cut off his communication, he felt he was being set up. He got home on his own. He says he's still willing to give back the money. He'll do it if you tell the Libyan who sent the shooters he was killed in the operation. He promises that after that he'll disappear."

"Jesus," said the gray-haired man. "What a load of crap. I can't believe you even bothered to repeat it."

Julian Carson decided to interpret that as a question. "He said he wouldn't kill me if I passed it on. He didn't kill me."

The man stared into Carson's eyes, but Carson stared back, unblinking.

"You got a pretty good deal."

"Yes, I did."

"What did he do then?"

"He checked to be sure the woman was still strapped in the passenger seat with the seat belt. Then he let the dogs into the backseat and drove away."

"That's it?"

"He was in a hurry to be gone."

"I'll bet he was. Where do you think he was going?"

"Wherever he thinks we won't be likely to look for him."

"What do you know about the woman?"

"Her name is Zoe McDonald. Forty-five, divorced, pretty. The apartment was rented in her name only. She was living there for three months before the shooting in Norwich, Vermont, so she couldn't have been renting it with him in mind. She advertised online for two roommates, and then she took the ad down about a week after he left Vermont, so that's probably when he arrived."

"Do you think he's killed her by now?"

"No," said Carson. "I think he carried her out that way—"

"Kidnapped her."

"Kidnapped her that way because he didn't think he should leave her there with the two bodies. He knew somebody would be along to clean up, and they wouldn't leave a witness alive. I think he'll free her in the middle of nowhere so she'll have to walk a few hours to get to a town while he gets away. He might even have done it already and told her if she called the authorities he'd come back and kill her."

"Why do you think that?" the man asked. "If he took her to a remote area, why not kill her? It's much safer for him."

"Killing her on the spot would have been even safer. He had two weapons with silencers he took from the Libyans. He hasn't killed anybody who wasn't trying to kill him."

"You're starting to sound like you believe his story."

"I don't know. But I think he believes his story."

"Why is that?"

Carson said, "Partly just an impression he made on me. But it also occurred to me that if he took back the money, then he must have delivered it to the Libyan first."

"What does that mean?"

"The money didn't get to the insurgents because the Libyan kept it."

Harper and Waters glanced at each other and Waters seemed to cringe for him, but neither spoke.

The older man said, "And you said he only kills people who are trying to kill him. Why are you alive?"

"He wanted me to deliver his message, but he could have left a note. He just didn't pull the trigger."

"Tell us. What do you think we should do now?"

"That's a difficult question, sir."

"Take a crack at it."

"I would do two things at once. I'd go through whatever evidence still exists to find out whether he's telling the truth. And I'd also test him."

"How?"

"He says he's willing to give the money back. Let him."

15

Hank and Marcia Dixon appeared to be relaxed, almost leisurely travelers. The only days when they drove more than five hours were when there was some exceptional delay—roadwork, accidents, weather.

They stopped at resort hotels, or the sort of city hotel that was one or two hundred dollars more expensive than the others in the vicinity. Hank chose the ones where there were plenty of people who were middle-aged or older with money, and few people in their twenties who might get into the sort of trouble that stimulated calls to the police. The hotels had doormen and security people to keep the guests from being bothered.

The Dixons were not the sorts who sought out company or conversation. When they passed anyone in the hallways they smiled. When someone spoke they answered politely. If they liked a hotel and it passed Hank Dixon's standard of safety and anonymity, they sometimes stayed an extra day or two. The first time they did it, he explained to Marcia: "Every day that we're living like this, getting stronger and healthier and more rested, they're out there somewhere standing in the rain or the cold watching for us. Anything that makes their effort a waste of time is good for us."

Every evening, Dixon turned on the television set in their room and watched the news for any mention of the shooting at Dan Chase's house in Vermont, the two men found dead in the parking lot near Buffalo, or the kidnapping of Zoe McDonald in Chicago. He bought a new laptop and looked for anything that might be related to the hunt for Dan Chase or Peter Caldwell.

He had been expecting that the intelligence people would get frustrated and begin to use state and local law enforcement to find him. He had waited to see what the pretext would be. They might say he was anything from a bank robber to a child molester, but they seemed to be putting out nothing. At each stop he looked, found nothing, and then repacked his laptop for the next day's drive.

Hank was premeditated and careful about the way he treated Marcia. He had used romance to manipulate and control her for months, and he had gotten good at it. The deception was not a chore, and her affection for him made her pleasant and pliable. But since the attack in Chicago he had occasionally had an uneasy feeling about her.

She had surprised him when she insisted on coming with him. Running away with a man marked for death was insane. He'd admitted he had been manipulating her, but she acted as though she had given her permission, or even known all along, and found it pleasant. He had tried to persuade her to leave him, and she wouldn't. And if she secretly wanted revenge, circumstances had given her a hundred chances to turn him in, run off with his car, his money, his guns, or do whatever else that would cripple his chance of survival. She had done nothing but try to help him.

He knew that at some point he was going to have to part with her. For now, he still wanted the protective camouflage provided by traveling with a woman who appeared to be his wife. She had offered to be useful, and he would continue to accept her help, but she was more complicated than he had thought, and less predictable. During the months while he had used familiarity and charm to allay her suspicions and penetrate her defenses, she had done the same to his. He had to maintain an emotional distance, and keep himself separate from her.

He took detours that kept them off the interstates and toll roads, where there might be cameras at tollbooths and entrances. Between hotels they paid cash for most of the things they bought. Once, they rented a cottage at a remote lake in Minnesota for two weeks. He gave false names and paid the owner cash in advance. They spent the week hiking and paddling the kayaks that came with the place, and cooking their dinners over a wood fire in the stone fire pit by the shore. At the end of the second week he made sure they had cleaned the cottage, wiped away fingerprints, and returned the keys to the owner before they drove on.

As she watched the telephone poles going by beside the road Marcia seemed quieter and more contemplative than usual.

"Something wrong?" Hank said.

"I was thinking. That's all."

"It doesn't seem to be making you happy. I plan to avoid it."

"We just put fourteen days on the good side. We were happy and got lots of sun and exercise and ate healthy food. Nobody saw the car or our faces. Then I remembered that fourteen days isn't that much. They found you after thirty-five years."

"I doubt that they looked for thirty-five years. They might have searched hard for a couple of years. It would have been a quiet search, because they wouldn't want to explain to a US attorney what I had done, or admit they were conducting operations in this country. After that I might have been on a list. Something happened this year to make me a priority."

"What would it be?"

"At the beginning, my biggest mistake was to come home with the money. That proved that the people inside intelligence who had decided to cut me loose and let me die had given up too easily. Welcoming me home would have made them look bad. So they made up a better story—that I had been in it to steal the money, and had killed some people doing it."

"That's all they wanted to accomplish—just to not look bad?"

"I think that it's also possible one of them was a strategist—that he knew even then that twenty million dollars in the context of the Middle East was going to be nothing. In the end, twenty billion was nothing. What they needed was friends, allies, operatives, and agents there. It's even possible they knew before they sent me that Faris Hamzah would keep the money. They just didn't tell me. Either way, by making it home I put everybody in a bad position."

"Who was everybody?"

"Numbers. Voices on the phone. I never knew names, and what's going on now can't be about them anymore. Something new has happened."

"Do you have any idea what?"

"Somebody has learned the story of what happened thirty-five years ago, and they want it to end differently."

Hank Dixon moved them from place to place, making the time go by pleasantly and without exposing them to much risk. Then they reached a hotel in Spokane, Washington, that seemed to cater almost entirely to businesspeople. Most of the guests were out of the hotel during business hours, and many of them were out again in the evening, probably taking clients and prospects out to dinner. This gave Hank and Marcia a long period of time to use the pool and the gym without having many people notice them.

When they returned to their room, Hank went to work on his laptop computer, as usual. He looked for any reference to the events they had experienced—the shooting at Daniel Chase's house and his disappearance, the two men he had shot near Buffalo, the two dead men in the Chicago apartment of Zoe McDonald, and her disappearance. There was nothing in any of the papers to indicate that any of it had ever happened.

"Any news?" Marcia asked.

"Not that I can see," he said.

"I can't believe this," she said. "I was kidnapped out of my apartment. An unknown man tied me up, threw me over his shoulder, and drove me away, and there's not a word of it anywhere."

"It's not exactly unbelievable," he said. "There must have been agents on the scene right away, before the police. They probably made everything look as though nothing had happened, and cleaned everything up. In these operations, if the police get there and see anything, two federal agents show up at the local police station and say whatever happened is part of an ongoing federal investigation involving national security. If the papers don't already have the story, they don't get it. If they have the story, they're asked not to print it."

After a few more minutes, Marcia went to take a shower. He kept searching the papers. After another hour, he saw the personal ad in the *Chicago Tribune*. It said: "Mr. Caldwell. We've decided to take you up on your offer. Send your instructions to Post Office Box 39281, Washington, DC 20003. J. H."

James Harriman was the young man he had asked to convey his offer, and here was the reply.

He turned off the laptop and said to Marcia, "I'm going out for a walk. No need to get dressed again."

His walk took him through the downtown district. As he walked, he considered. Nobody in any intelligence organization had any particular attachment to the truth. The truth was just one of many versions that was not necessarily superior to any of the other versions.

If he showed up at a prearranged meeting with the money, they'd see it as a chance to end things neatly. He and the money would disappear. But if he devised ways of making it harder for them, they might see this as a time to take what they could get, and move on to the next project. They would keep their word only if they had no power to do anything else.

What he would have to do now was attend to the details. If he was going to do this, he would have to devise a safe way to respond to the ad so they couldn't trace his communication. He would have to find a way to raise the twenty million dollars without revealing where it had come from—which banks and brokerages, in which accounts, under what names. Then he would have to find a way to return it to them without being ambushed.

He began to try out ideas. He could try to get the money in cash, put it in trash bags, and tell them where it was.

He had tried that thirty-five years ago. That much cash had filled ten large cardboard boxes. That would be as many as twenty trash bags. It was easier to obtain cash in those days, too. Now they'd trace the serial numbers to the Federal Reserve District where the bills were released, and then to each of the bank branches. Any cash transaction involving ten thousand dollars or more had to be reported to the government. And bundling a lot of smaller amounts would be even worse. The government would pick that up and jump on it even faster, because it was the way money launderers tried to avoid getting spotted. Maybe using cash had become impossible.

As Dixon returned to the hotel, he kept thinking of ways to give the money to the government without giving them the ability to trace it back to its sources. One way was gold. Melting it wouldn't change it. If he had a pile of gold—say, gold one-ounce coins, he could melt them and make the gold into bars with no markings. If he did that they wouldn't know where the gold came from, at least at first.

But even if he bought the gold from a foreign source that didn't report gold transactions to the US government, he would have a hard time collecting that much gold without getting noticed. Keeping the purchase a secret would only be temporary. Eventually the transaction would be traced to a bank account, even without the cooperation of the dealer. But it might buy him some time.

"Let's see what the price is today," he whispered to himself, turned on his laptop again, and typed in "price of gold today." It was $1,203.00 an ounce.

He used the calculator on his computer. He rounded the price off to $1,200. Twenty million dollars would buy 16,667 ounces. That was about a thousand pounds of gold. He could try to buy a hoard of gold from various sources, put it in a vault somewhere, and send military intelligence the key. But buying that much gold would take time, and there were too many ways to get caught.

He wondered about diamonds. But he knew there was a huge markup on jewelry, and he could hardly deal with well-known, respectable jewelers and expect to be anonymous. He couldn't work with dealers who weren't well known and respectable, either. He wouldn't have a clue what he was buying. He could pay twenty million dollars for a few pieces of glass.

Maybe the answer was to give the government the twenty million in a form that couldn't be moved. He could send them the deed to a twenty-million-dollar piece of land. But buying land took time, and it would require bank information and in-person signings and escrow periods.

The next afternoon the Dixons moved on and checked in to a Seattle hotel, and Hank decided to test an idea. He turned on his computer, and after a few minutes of typing numbers and passwords he began to hum to himself.

Marcia said, "Do you mind if I go down to the pool for a swim?"

"No," he said. He kept typing. "Feel free."

After a few minutes he heard her say bye, go out, and shut the door.

He had been right. It was impossible. Giving the government twenty million dollars in any form couldn't be done without blowing his identity and leading them straight to him. He couldn't move that kind of money in a hurry anymore without the government finding out who was doing it.

Then he tried getting online access to some investment accounts, and a solution occurred to him—to accept what he couldn't change. The government would learn the name of the person who owned the accounts, and the person who performed the transactions. So he would give them information they already knew. The intelligence people already knew that he had once been Daniel Chase and they knew he had once been Peter Caldwell.

The accounts he held in those two names were still open and active. Military intel knew the names, but the government hadn't yet confiscated the money he had invested in those names. Maybe they assumed that for the past thirty-five years he'd been keeping it in cash under the floorboards, or in numbered offshore accounts. More likely, they didn't want to let the federal agencies that blocked financial transactions know about him—the Justice Department, the SEC, the FBI, the IRS. For now, the bank and brokerage accounts of Daniel Chase and Peter Caldwell seemed intact.

He took a deep breath and then typed in an online transaction, a request for an electronic transfer of a hundred thousand dollars from an account belonging to Daniel Chase to the bank account of a corporation called Ellburn Holdings he had founded twenty years ago to store some of his money. He took another deep breath, and then clicked on the box that said SUBMIT.

He watched a circle of dots appear on the screen, rotate counterclockwise for a few seconds, and then vanish. "Your transaction has been completed. Thank you for your business." It had worked.

He opened the next account, and began to type the names and numbers for the next transfer. He submitted the transfer, and moved on to the next account. Before long he was moving much larger sums, but each transaction was accepted. He left some money in each account to avoid any reaction that would be automatically triggered by his closing an account.

Next he opened an account that belonged to Peter Caldwell. The first transfer was another small one, a test. This transaction was successful, so he moved immediately to larger transfers. He kept at it until he accomplished what he'd wanted.

He restarted his computer to be sure that he had closed all of the communications with the firms he'd been dealing with, and then added up all of the transactions he had made. He stared at the screen for a few seconds.

The screen said: $22,000,800.

He heard Marcia's key card slide in the lock and the bolt open. As she stepped in, he cleared the screen. "Hi," he said. "Have a good swim?"

"Great," she said. "You should have come. I'll dry my hair now so we can go to dinner."

"Good idea. I'm hungry."

She went into the bathroom. As soon as he heard the hair dryer he began to look at maps on his computer screen. He studied one, then typed in another request, and then another. Then he found the one he wanted.

He plugged his laptop into the printer on the desk and typed: "To J. H.: It's a deal. Here are the coordinates for the meeting on November 5 at 5:00 p.m." He thought for a moment. Much of the money he had requested would have to be raised by liquidating securities. That often took seven business days. He added three days to be sure the proceeds were transferred and deposited in the Ellburn Holdings account: "November 8 at 5:00 p.m."

Marcia emerged from the bathroom brushing her hair. "About ready?"

"I just have to put on my coat."

16

Julian Carson stood at the cable car stop on Market Street in San Francisco. He had been in San Francisco before, so he'd known this place as soon as he found the coordinates on a satellite map. He was at the Powell and Market turnaround. Tourists loitered here because there was always some chance of getting a seat right after the cars changed direction. Maybe the old man was going to show up on the cable car. The old man would know a cable car was a good place to keep from getting shot, because the cars were full of people, and the stop where Julian waited was crowded.

Julian had not smoked a cigarette except as part of a cover identity since he left the army after Afghanistan, but he was smoking now, using the cigarette as a prop. It made him look older and a little defiant, and clearly not a government employee. He inhaled and let the smoke roll off his tongue and drift away. The strong bite of the tobacco reminded him that he was doing something he would regret.

He took a last shallow puff, exhaled through his nostrils, snuffed out the butt on the lamppost, and then threw it in the trash. As an afterthought he tossed the pack into the barrel after it, and then the matches. Instantly he felt bad. He could have given the pack to one of the three dozen homeless men sitting on the sidewalk on blankets and sleeping bags a few yards off. If the guy didn't smoke he could have traded it for something—goodwill, maybe. They sure as hell needed that.

Carson looked at his watch. It was five fifteen. He had been waiting on Market Street for fifteen minutes already. He had watched the cars, scrutinized the windows of hotels and office buildings. He had scanned the groups of tourists and streams of locals going in and out of stores and other businesses, and seen men who could have been the old man but weren't. Carson knew he had plenty of backup. His worry wasn't that there wouldn't be enough agents to snap up one citizen, or at least to spot and tail him. The worry was that they might have so many out here that the subject would spot them.

This wasn't a normal target, some guy who had been a shop-keeper until he got obsessed with a fanatical movement and went off to another country for a few weeks of half-assed military training. The old man had been trained when a member of the special forces was an expert at moving unnoticed not only through jungles, but also through foreign cities. They all spoke several languages, could do some field surgery, and could operate any piece of hardware they saw. Julian could easily be a breath away, a heartbeat away, from having a bullet plunge into his skin and tear through his muscle and bone before it came out throwing a spray of red mist.

Julian was not afraid exactly, but he was aware that he had a reason to be. He had seen years of combat, and he knew that if the action started he would feel a moment of fear, just the taste of it he allowed himself. Then he would do what he could.

He was in the game now, and there was no way to back out. The men who had been in that hotel suite in Chicago for the meeting were very high-level operational personnel, and they had given him this mission. He had been foolish enough to accept. He could have shut up and said "yes, sir" and "no, sir" until they dismissed him. Or he could have resigned on the spot. But he hadn't.

Thinking about his bosses reminded him that the biggest threat in the next few minutes would not be from the old man. It was unlikely that the intelligence people had told him everything they thought, suspected, or planned to do.

He assumed the pose of a man waiting for a cable car. He leaned forward as though to stare down Market Street, but when he leaned back he felt a hand settle against his spine.

"Don't look surprised and don't turn around." It was the old man's voice.

The old man must not have come in a car or approached from a distance, or Julian would have seen him. He must have been here when Julian arrived. Julian looked down the street in the other direction and used the turn of his head to get a glimpse of him.

The old man had let his facial hair grow into a layer of white bristles on his face. A knit cap covered his head, and he wore a hooded sweatshirt with a down vest over it. He looked as dirty and unkempt as the homeless men who had been sitting on the sidewalk, but he didn't smell like a man who had been sleeping rough in alcoves at the entrances of buildings. The old man said, "Are they really going to take my offer?"

Julian shrugged. "They said to tell you it's a deal."

"They'll leave me alone?"

"That's what they said."

"And they're going to tell the man in Benghazi that I'm dead?"

"I passed on everything you said. I didn't leave anything out."

"I know they agreed. I want to know if you think it's true."

"You have no right to expect me to predict the future. I'd just be making a guess."

"Would you be willing to bet your life on them?"

"I'm already betting my life on you. What's in your hand? A stabbing spike?"

"You're wearing body armor, aren't you?" said the old man. "I'm asking you. Would you make a deal with them?"

"If you give up the money, what will you lose?" asked Julian. "If you walk away, how long before they get the money anyway?"

The old man gave a quiet laugh. "As soon as I saw you here, I used a cell phone to set off the electronic transfer. The money is now in the account of the US Department of the Treasury."

"I don't know how they'll feel about that," Julian said.

"I said I'd deliver it to the US government, not hand it in cash to some faceless agents."

"Hard to blame you. For me, anyway."

"Good. Do us both a favor. Stay where you are for five more minutes and pretend you're still waiting. Otherwise they might think something's gone wrong, start shooting at me, and kill us both."

Julian no longer felt the pressure on his back. He looked down the street with exaggerated impatience.

The old man moved away, holding a dollar in his hand, looking at it as though he were reading the denomination. Then he was among the homeless men again. He stopped to pick up the blanket he must have been sitting on, and kept going. He rolled up the blanket loosely as he limped along Market Street. He was almost to the corner of Fifth when he slipped into the glass enclosure at the BART station entrance. As he moved toward the downward escalator, two men rushed to intercept him.

The nearest one was wearing a short raincoat. He reached out to grasp the old man's hood. "No, you don't," he said.

Henry Dixon threw his blanket over the man's head, swung his arm in a circle to wrench the hand off his sweatshirt, clasped the man in a bear hug, and hurled him down the escalator.

Next was a red-haired man wearing a Giants warm-up jacket. He lifted the back of his jacket with his left hand as he reached for the pistol holstered there with his right. The move put both of the man's hands behind him for a second, which gave Dixon enough time to drive a sharp jab into the man's nose and kick him in the groin. When the man doubled forward, Dixon slammed his face against the railing of the upward escalator. He pushed him halfway down the up escalator, and then bent over to pick up the man's pistol while the moving stairs brought the half-conscious man back up to Dixon's feet. He shoved the pistol into the marsupial pocket of his hooded sweatshirt, knelt by the man, and said, "I thought we had a deal."

The man's eyes rolled and he was spitting blood. "I don't know what you're talking about." Bystanders had begun to gather behind them, some perhaps thinking Dixon was trying to help the man, but most of them seemingly paralyzed, not knowing what to do except wait their turn to go down the escalator.

Dixon pulled the earpiece wire that hung from the man's ear, took the radio, and hurried down the escalator. He skirted the motionless body of the man under the blanket at the bottom and stepped to the turnstiles. He slid the ticket he had brought with him into the turnstile and withdrew it, reached the BART platform, and rushed to the open door of the train that was loading. He ducked in with the crowd and held on to a vertical bar while the train car's doors slid shut. The train moved forward, picking up speed.

He took off the down vest before the train reached the Civic Center station, then took off the sweatshirt before the Sixteenth Street station to reveal a dress shirt, tie, and sport coat beneath. Before the Twenty-fourth Street station he took off the rubbers that had covered a pair of dress shoes. He rolled the extra clothes into a bundle before the car slowed on its approach to the Glen Park station.

The doors opened and he was out on the platform, hurrying with a hundred others to the upward escalators. On the way he dropped the clothes into a trash barrel, then took the next escalator up into the sunlight.

THE OLD MAN

There was a parking lot on Bosworth Street across from the station, but he didn't go near it. Instead he hurried up the other side of Diamond Street to Wilder Street, where there were no signs of cameras. As soon as he was visible on Wilder, the black BMW pulled away from the curb and glided up to him. He got into the passenger seat, slammed the door, and the car moved on.

17

Julian Carson walked along Market Street at a quick pace with the demeanor of a man irritated at the fact that his cable car had never come. As he forced his body to convey the feeling, his experienced eyes were picking out the intelligence people. He saw five men who had been seated inside a restaurant dash across the street toward the Apple store, then into the subway entrance beside it. The tables along the front window of the restaurant were now vacant. A man in a third-story window of the hotel across from the turnaround was looking down at the street and talking into a cell phone.

Here and there pedestrians stopped to talk into cell phones or radios or Bluetooth earpieces—an attractive young couple, the man in a sport coat and the thin blond woman in tight jeans and high boots, a pair of women carrying shopping bags that were heavier than they should be. There was a shout from somewhere near the subway entrance, and each woman put her right hand into the shopping bag that hung from her left, and kept it there until it was clear that the commotion was over. Julian didn't know the women, but he knew that they had not been reaching for new dresses they had bought.

A cab passed with a sign that said OUT OF SERVICE. The driver stopped in front of the BART station and two of the men from the restaurant used a gray blanket as a stretcher to carry a dazed man from the entrance to the backseat of the taxi. Two more men ushered another injured man with a towel wrapped around the lower part of his face and blood on his shirt into the passenger seat. Julian sped up to a trot to see if this one was the old man, but it wasn't. The cab pulled away.

Julian kept walking. He had warned his superior officers. He had told them a couple of times that the old man wasn't just an old man, like somebody's uncle. He was old in the way a seven-foot rattlesnake was old.

Julian had listened to the agents when they told him he was going to be the one to meet the old man and take charge of the money. He had said "yes, sir." He'd certainly had no interest in getting himself killed, and this was the kind of mission that might accomplish that. He had known instantly that the thing to worry most about was friendly fire. He had listened to the plans, but heard nothing to make him expect so many people with guns surrounding him in a crowded public street.

Julian's strides took him to the spot where he had been told to go after the exchange. A fake UPS delivery truck was stopped around the corner with its engine running and lights flashing as though it were making a delivery. He stepped up into the open side door by the driver's seat.

Inside the cargo bay there were three men sitting on a bench wearing UPS uniforms, but two of them held MP5 rifles with thirty-round magazines. The slings that held the short automatic rifles were brown webbing that matched the uniforms. Julian didn't know any of the three.

"Where do we pick up the money?" one of them said.

"He transferred the money electronically," said Julian. "He's already gone."

"Should we go too?"

"Affirmative," Julian said. "It's over."

The man released the magazine on his MP5 and put the gun and ammunition into an open cardboard box that sat in front of his bench, closed it so it looked like something he was delivering, and hurried forward to the driver's seat.

Another man held a radio. He said, "I'm getting the call now."

In a moment the truck pulled away from the curb, went down the street to the next corner, and turned. The big rectangular vehicle made two more turns and headed south of Market. Through the windshield Julian could see warehouses, garages, and small manufacturing operations. Occasionally there were bars that Julian judged were probably even less inviting at night. Then the truck was on the freeway. Fifteen minutes later it pulled through an open gate into a fenced lot adjacent to the vast open space of the San Francisco airport.

The building inside the fence had once been a hangar. The door swung upward and the truck pulled in past a couple of large trucks that looked like appliance delivery trucks and stopped. Julian got out. Beside him were two taxicabs, and beyond them an ambulance, a repair truck for Pacific Gas and Electric, a US Postal Service truck, and four black cars that looked like unmarked police cars, with the distinctive side spotlights.

"Hey, it's Carson." Harper's voice was flat with a hint of sarcasm. "Glad you survived your dramatic mission."

Julian turned to see that Harper and Waters were sitting at a table at the far side of the hangar. They got up and walked toward him.

"Thanks," Julian said. "There didn't seem to be anything dramatic about it that I could see. There seemed to be quite a few people running around tripping over each other, though. Did something happen after the old man left me?"

Harper and Waters glanced at each other, and Waters gave his familiar cringing expression. Harper said, "Maybe that's the problem right there. He wasn't supposed to leave."

Carson said, "Nobody told me that."

"Then maybe you weren't supposed to leave either," said Waters.

Harper's cell phone rang and he clapped it to his ear. "Harper." He listened. His eyes widened and then his jaw muscles began to work. He slowly turned his head to look at Julian Carson, but when he saw that Carson was looking at him he looked down at the floor. "Carson just arrived," he said. "Yes, sir, we'll do that." He listened for a second and then put away his phone.

He muttered something to Waters, and Waters nodded and walked away. Harper picked up the newspapers on the table and began putting them in order and folding them neatly. It looked as though Waters was walking to the back of the hangar.

Harper looked up, put the papers in a pile, and said, "They want to debrief you before we wrap it up here."

"All right," said Julian. "I'm not doing anything else. It's hard to get a date on short notice."

"Well that's fortunate," said Harper. "They want us to wait in the office until they get here."

Julian caught a movement in the periphery of his vision. Waters had opened the passenger door of one of the police cars. He took something off the seat and stood behind the car door holding whatever it was, but Julian couldn't see it. Julian said, "What have you got in your hand?"

"Just cleaning up," Waters said. "Putting away the toys." He held up a short, black MP5 like the ones the UPS men had carried in their truck. "We can't leave the equipment lying around unsecured."

Did they think he would try to escape this meeting? It made him wonder if he should do it. No, he decided. Do your job and the worst you'll get afterward is criticism.

"I'll give you a hand," he said.

"No, thanks," said Waters. "I signed it out and I have to sign it in." Waters didn't move, but he ejected the magazine from the compact automatic rifle.

Carson walked toward the office doorway where Harper waited for him. They entered a room about fifteen feet square with two gray steel military-style desks and a swaybacked leather couch about ten feet long. There was only one door and no windows. The walls were covered with cheap wood-like paneling that had no pictures or decorations of any kind. Harper sat at the farthest steel desk and Julian sat on the couch. "What is this place?"

Harper said, "I don't really know. I think I heard it was shipping and receiving for an import-export company that was off the books. No telling how long ago that was, because I've been here three times now, over a period of about twenty years."

Julian didn't ask about the other times. He didn't want to listen to Harper's story, and he had grown accustomed to the safe policy of not asking questions. Everything was classified. Everything was need to know. He didn't need to know about some shit that happened twenty years ago.

They sat in silence for a few minutes, and Julian watched with satisfaction as Harper began to get restless.

Julian swung his feet up and reclined on the big couch, cradling his head in his hands and looking at the ceiling. He closed his eyes and sighed in comfort just loudly enough for Harper to hear. He thought through everything he had seen this afternoon. For these people a plan was never just a plan, something that everybody on the job knew and followed. There was always a plan within the plan, and probably one or two inside those, like layers of an onion.

He had been assigned to meet with the old man and accept his money. He had known where to go, and known there would be a UPS truck parked around the corner big enough to carry twenty million dollars in whatever form it came. If the meeting went badly, they could carry the old man's wounded or dead body instead—or Julian's.

But that hadn't been the plan, really. That was just the outer layer. He wasn't exactly sure what happened to the other parts of the plan, but there seemed to have been a screwup. Julian thought it over again. Whatever else had happened, he had done his job. Because he had shown up and risked his life, the money had been wired back to the government. He had gone to the UPS truck as scheduled, and been taken off. Those were the facts that mattered—his facts.

Harper's phone rang. He said, "Yes?" Then after a couple of seconds he put the phone into his pocket. "They're here."

Julian Carson sat up slowly, swung his legs off the couch to the floor, and sat up straight. After another thirty seconds the door opened and admitted three men to the room. The two senior agents who had never been introduced to Carson sat behind the unoccupied desk and Waters sat beside Harper on the other.

The gray-haired man who seemed to be the ranking agent said, "Well, Carson. We implemented your suggestion. What did we get?"

"The old man showed up. He told me that he had sent the twenty million dollars to the government."

"We didn't see any money. He screwed you."

"He said he had arranged an electronic transfer to the United States Treasury."

The agent's eyes narrowed and he sat in silence for a moment. Then he took out a cell phone and hit a programmed number with his thumb. He said, "Our operator says the subject wired twenty million dollars to the US Treasury." He listened. "Yeah. Just like a tax payment. Check it out." He looked at Julian Carson. "For the moment, all we've got is what he told you. Suppose it turns out to be true. What then?"

Julian shrugged. "That decision would be above my rank."

"We're all just a bunch of civil servants, trying to feel our way along. What do you think should happen to him?"

"He offered a deal. If he delivered the money, we would tell the Libyans he was dead and leave him alone. We agreed to the deal."

"So, if the money is in the Treasury Department's account where we can't get our hands on it, we should still tell Faris Hamzah: 'Sorry, he's dead and you get nothing.'"

"Faris Hamzah is the important Libyan?" said Julian. "The deal with the old man doesn't prevent the United States from doing something to keep him happy, too."

"That's what we're after? The pursuit of happiness for all of our double agents and informants and contractors?"

Julian noted the inclusion of contractors on the list. He was technically an independent contractor. He said, "If Mr. Hamzah is smart, he'd welcome the news that the old man was dead, so he could stop recruiting amateur hit men. The ones he sent couldn't find their way across Chicago and back. When I drove them to the apartment and let them in, the old man killed them both without raising a sweat."

"Good point. He also killed one in Vermont and two on the way to Chicago," the senior agent said. "In all, he's killed five men in the past year, all of them sent by our friend and ally. That's not counting the guards he killed stealing the money thirty-five years ago, and the guerrillas in the hills who died because their supplies were cut off."

Julian said, "I'm sorry, sir, but I'm still pretty sure things didn't happen the way Faris Hamzah says they did. If the old man could steal the money from Hamzah, he must have delivered it to him first. And if Hamzah had the money, but didn't deliver it to the fighters as soon as he got it, what was he waiting for?"

The senior agent's phone rang. "Yes?" He listened. "Thank you." He looked at Julian again. "He did send twenty million dollars to the United States Treasury."

Julian sensed that the pause was to give him a chance to step into a trap, so he said nothing and waited.

The senior agent said, "Which means it's lost."

Julian's brows knitted, and the agent knew he meant: "Why lost?"

"We can never get our hands on the money. Congress sets our budget. The commanding officer of military intelligence can't walk up to the chairman of the intelligence committee and say, 'Thirty-five years ago one of our own operators stole twenty million dollars from an operation. We hushed it up at the time, and so did everybody since then, but now the money has been returned to the Treasury, so we want it.'"

"I guess we should have told the old man how you wanted the money returned," Julian said.

"Do you know why we didn't?"

"Because we didn't think he would live up to the agreement?"

"No," said the senior agent. "Because it never mattered whether he did or not. This isn't about getting back the money from a thirty-five-year-old operation. Thirty-five years might as well be a million years. We're in the business of furthering our country's interests in the present. Our job isn't to salvage some dismal screwup from a generation ago. It's to move the ball forward a few yards *today*. Our job is about *today*. The objective *today* is to strengthen the bond between the United States and the leader of an important faction in Libya. Nothing else. So what has today's work contributed to that?"

"I don't know," said Julian.

"We've sent the already-bloated Treasury a sum of money that in the three and a half trillion dollars of the annual budget isn't even a rounding error. We also made a scene in a major American city and got two agents beaten half to death in a subway station. We let a rogue agent who has killed five men this year disappear once again like a fart in a hurricane."

Harper's train of thought seemed to have been running a slightly divergent course during this discussion, but it converged with the conversation again. "That guy must have been a beast when he was in his prime."

The senior agent contemplated Harper for a period of two seconds, and then said, quietly, "He's in his prime. Right now."

18

Late that night Marcia Dixon drove south on Route 1 beside the Pacific Ocean. Hank was slouching in the passenger seat looking out at the reflection of the moon on the surface. The black water looked as though it were covered in wrinkles, but he knew that up close they were rank after rank of four-foot swells. Marcia cleared her throat and said, "Do you think there's any chance we can stop to see Sarah?"

"Any chance?" Hank said. His response bought him a few seconds to think. The worst thing he could do now was to say absolutely not, because that would ensure that she would make an amateur attempt on her own. "We'd have to find a way to do it without getting her, you, or me killed. To the chasers you're either a kidnap victim or an accomplice, so your daughter's phone will be tapped and her computer hacked. That's why I had you call her as soon as we were out of Chicago. After that it became too dangerous."

"What if I used a go-between?" said Marcia. "She has a couple of friends she's mentioned a lot since she started law school. One of them used to be her roommate before she started living alone."

He said, "Can you trust her?"

"Yes. They're still good friends."

"What I mean is, can you trust her to say nothing if she's surrounded by four federal agents who tell her being silent will get her sent to prison?"

"I don't think so. That's a lot to ask."

"Sarah knows that you're not in Chicago anymore. She thinks that you're safely out of the country. Visiting her now can only worry her and put you both in danger. And that's if it goes perfectly. You told her to expect to be out of touch for a time."

"When can I be *in* touch?" said Marcia. "Never?"

"No. When it's safe."

"We're heading in the direction of Los Angeles right now. It's night. After what happened in San Francisco, they must think we're as far from California as we can get."

"Maybe you're right," he conceded. "They won't expect me to do anything risky again for a while. Maybe if we keep it simple and quick, we can pull this off."

"You seem different," Marcia said.

"How am I different?" he said.

"This is the first time since we left Chicago that you forgot to mention that we're doomed. What's changed?"

"I'm still doomed," he said. "But at the moment we're free, driving along a moonlit sea. I haven't seen anybody following us away from San Francisco."

"Come on."

"I think it was the money," he said. "Hiding was hard and frightening, and forcing my family to lie and use false names was worse. But now, I realize how much the money bothered me too. I wanted to believe I wasn't the bad guy, but I still had the money. As long as I kept it I was a thief."

"And now you don't have it," she said.

"Nope. The US Treasury Department has the twenty million. It's out of my hands."

"So now you're a happy pauper."

"I'm not a pauper. I invested the money over thirty years ago, and the investments did well. But what's left is invested in names that haven't been compromised yet. If I send the money from those accounts to the government too, then those identities will be burned, including Henry and Marcia Dixon. If we run out of people to be, we'll be caught or killed."

"If we're still in danger, why are you letting me go see Sarah?"

"Because I can't stop you."

They reached Los Angeles late that night and Hank drove to UCLA to look around, but didn't drive past Sarah's apartment. Hank skirted the block and looked down the street from the intersection to try to detect any surveillance operations in nearby buildings or spot surveillance vehicles parked in the street. But Sarah's apartment building was one of several, so there would be dozens of windows that faced hers.

"I don't see anybody who might be watching her place," Hank said.

"Good," said Marcia.

"But I wouldn't necessarily see them from here." Hank decided not to tell her the rest. This wasn't some gang of criminals who had been searching for him. They could be watching Sarah's apartment from one of the geosynchronous satellites that were always over this part of California. Her computer could easily be monitored. They could have planted microphones and cameras in Sarah's car and her apartment, and be using her phone's GPS to track her movements. Equipment hidden in her television cable box could be sending reports every second. They could be watching her a hundred ways at once.

But they might not be. Sarah wasn't connected with him directly. She had visited her mother only twice during the time Peter Caldwell was living in Chicago. Military intelligence had seen him in San Francisco only a day ago, and he had been alone.

If they believed he had killed Zoe McDonald, they would have no reason to watch her daughter.

Hank drove to John Wayne Airport in Orange County and rented a silver Nissan Altima. At a private parking lot for the airport he paid to park his BMW for a few days. Next he drove the Altima to a hotel near Disneyland and slept for the night.

The next morning Hank drove Marcia to the mall in Costa Mesa and helped her pick out clothes for Sarah. She chose clothes that every young woman in the area seemed to be wearing that fall— tight designer jeans, knee-high leather boots, and big-necked loose shirts. She bought a short dark-brown wig and oversized sunglasses. Hank told her not to make Sarah look like anyone, but like everyone.

While they were in the wig store Marcia also bought a shoulder-length wig that was light brown with blond highlights. At a nearby store she bought a black suit and white blouse, a small pair of earrings, and a matching necklace. When she tried on the outfit she looked as though she had just left work at a bank or a law firm. She added sunglasses that obscured the blue of her eyes and made her face seem smaller. At another store she bought makeup that made her skin look a shade darker and her lips thinner. At a giant drugstore she bought dark dye for Hank's hair.

Marcia bought a large bag made of brown buttery leather that could be interpreted as either an overnight bag or a briefcase, wrapped each item of clothing in tissue, and put them all inside. Then she bought a birthday card, wrote a note, and sealed it. "Sarah," it said. "I'll be waiting at 6:00 p.m. Thursday at Jerry's Deli in Westwood. Don't drive and don't bring your phone, computer, or iPad. If you see anyone watching or following you, keep walking, and we'll try again. Love, Mom."

Hank wrapped the bag, sealed it inside a plain brown box, and took it to a messenger service. Hank had it sent to Sarah's address, to be delivered in the evening after 9:00 p.m., but not left if she was out.

On Thursday afternoon they parked in the municipal lot on Broxton and walked to Jerry's at 5:50 p.m. They sat at a table where they could watch the front window, but far enough from it so they could slip out the back door if they needed to.

They sat like what they both had been—parents of a female student who was at a university far from home and had been for so long that she had slipped her moorings. Home was no longer the place where she was from, but the place where her life had taken her. The Dixons drank coffee from thick, heavy white mugs and waited. Hank knew that if he looked around the large room he could find other sets of parents meeting their children here, but he didn't, because looking invited looks.

At 6:04 a young woman appeared in silhouette, her long booted strides bobbing her across the big front window, the sun hitting the street at an angle that illuminated the short dark-brown wig and her very white skin and red lips. She came inside, saw them instantly, and smiled.

She sat at their table and took off the sunglasses to lean close and kiss her mother. "Happy Halloween. What do you think?"

Her mother said, "We didn't want you to stand out. And keep your voice down."

Sarah laughed. She looked at Hank Dixon. "You're still with us? You can't give it up, right?"

"Something like that," he said.

"What does that mean?" said Marcia.

"It's a private joke," said Sarah.

"Sarah, I have to tell you some things quickly," Hank said. "We're not going to be able to see you again for a while." He took out a card. "There's a trust fund set up for you. It's called the McDonald Trust. Here's a business card with the account information. Memorize it today. If you need money, just call them up and they'll wire some to your account. They withhold the taxes, and they'll send you a 1099 to prove it each year at tax time."

She held the card. "You did this? Why would you do this for me?"

"I like surprises. Now I'm going to take a walk and let you two talk." He looked at Marcia. "Don't be too long." He stood up and walked out the front door.

Sarah turned to Marcia. "Did you know about this?"

"No."

"Why would he do this?"

Her mother took a deep breath, and then let it out in a sigh. "He's that kind of man. He likes you. He already set up trust funds for his own daughter and her kids years and years ago. Beyond that, don't try to understand him. There's too much history that's too long to tell, too many complications nobody has time to explain. Just do what he said and let it go."

"But this is all crazy. This getup I have to wear—the boots are nice, but—and you running away from Chicago with him. Why?"

"Running away with him is more fun than most people have in a lifetime."

Sarah stared at her for a second. "So why don't you look happy? Not calm either." She leaned close and whispered, "Did he get caught doing something illegal?"

"I wouldn't say that, exactly," her mother said. "It's complicated."

"But he's a criminal?"

"No, he's not."

"Is he wanted?"

"No."

"What, then?"

Marcia leaned close and whispered in her ear. "Years and years ago he was an undercover policeman. He put some very powerful people away—drug suppliers from South America. Recently the son of one of them, who had been a child at the time, saw him in

Chicago and recognized him. So now he's been told to go away and cool off for a time, while the police handle the criminals."

"Is he—"

"Wrong questions," her mother said. "Wrong conversation. We don't have much time together, so let's really use it. You're a wonderful daughter and always have been. If I die tonight, my life won't have been wasted because I had you. Keep being the same kind of person. Do good in the world. Have babies too, if you can. Part of me would like to simply stay right here in LA and watch you do all of it. But that would accomplish nothing except to intrude on your life, and to waste the part of my life that's left to me—to kind of spit in the eye of the universe. Do you understand what I mean?"

"You love him. You think that this is the last time you're going to be in love. But you're not that old. You could—"

Her mother laughed. "Don't be silly. He didn't tie me up and drag me off. I'm doing what I want to do. I hope you can accept that."

"I'm going to have to, aren't I?" said Sarah. "Can I at least know where you're going from here?"

"I'm going to try to see your brother and then we'll make ourselves scarce for a while."

Sarah looked around. "Are you leaving now?"

"We'll be gone in fifteen minutes. First you and I are going to share a piece of lemon meringue pie. It's a life lesson I learned recently. You never know when you'll get your next lemon meringue, so now is a good time."

Three hours later Brian McDonald walked along the side of his condominium building toward the door. This had been one of the worst afternoons he'd ever had. It had been absolutely insane. When he was a child the McDonalds had always seemed to be a family like everyone else's, except a little better. That had lasted until he was nineteen.

Brian had been away at Stanford, working intently to complete a double major in engineering and computer science. He remembered the day clearly. It had been near the end of fall semester. At 5:00 a.m. he was shaken awake by a small earthquake. It was one of those sharp jolts with a sound like a bang. He had been relieved that it wasn't the kind that sounded like a freight train blasting through walls into his bedroom. He sat up and looked around. It was still not daylight but he could tell nothing had even fallen on the floor. He went back to sleep until seven, when he heard a rumbling in the hallway.

At first he thought this must be the real thing, the start of the quake that had been heralded by the small foreshock two hours earlier. But then he heard the voices and recognized the rumble as the sound of heavy feet running in the hallway. "Get up, you lazy bastards! The semester is over. The rest of exam week is canceled!"

His housemates, Serge and Najib, burst into his room with a laptop and showed him the message from the president and the deans. The earthquake had dislodged a chunk of the 1891 Frederick Law Olmsted façade of the chapel. A county official had declared the campus buildings off-limits until they could all be inspected and cleared. It occurred to Brian that the official must have been better at history than science. He knew that the 1906 San Francisco earthquake had severely damaged the campus, but didn't seem to know that foreshocks before major quakes were rare. But it didn't matter. The decision forced the university to cancel the last two days of final exam week. Brian got up, changed his plane reservation to leave two days earlier, and stepped into the shower.

When he arrived home the next afternoon, he thought he'd be giving his parents a surprise. His mother would be out giving a piano lesson and his father would be at the office. Brian took a cab from the airport, walked in the front door of the house, set his suitcase down, and decided to check the refrigerator. He walked toward the kitchen past the open arch of the den—and stopped.

On the leather couch in the den his father was having sex with his assistant, Steffie.

That instant was like the initiation of a chain reaction. He heard himself say, "Dad?" Steffie screamed and disengaged, and then sprinted toward the only exit from the room, pushing past Brian and across the hall to the nearest bathroom. Brian's father put on his pants with a thoughtful demeanor. Then he and Brian had a man-to-man conversation in the den, staring into each other's eyes over the pile of Steffie's clothes on the coffee table.

Brian's arrival that day dislodged the last pillar that had been propping up the rickety structure of the family. Chunks fell, hit other parts, and those tore away from others as piece by piece the rest succumbed to gravity.

It was about ten minutes before Steffie reappeared. She padded out wearing one of his father's jackets from the hall closet. She snatched up her clothes from the coffee table and went back into the bathroom to dress. Then she reappeared and walked out the front door. She didn't say good-bye and nobody inquired how she planned to get back to the office. When Brian's mother came home about two hours later and saw Brian there, she was very surprised. When her husband pulled her aside a few minutes later to talk to her, she had another surprise.

Brian's mother, Zoe, had a couple of long stony-faced discussions with her husband. By the end of the second one the divorce had been set in motion. A couple of weeks later the last traces of Darryl McDonald had been removed. Within a month, the house where Brian had been carried home from the hospital after his birth and where he'd been brought up—the place he'd imagined he might inherit someday and retire to after a long successful career—had a big FOR SALE BY COLDWELL BANKER sign erected on its front lawn.

His father, Darryl, was living in a small sublet condo with Steffie, who had not only been promoted from secret mistress to fiancée, but also artificially matured by being redubbed Stephanie. Because the incident that had precipitated all of this, when Brian had walked into the den, had not dimmed or lost any of its visual clarity for either Brian or Stephanie, their meetings were rare and uncomfortable after that.

In the years since then, Brian had managed to maintain cordial relations with both of his parents. At first he'd considered himself to be closest to his mother, who represented home, love, and childhood memories. She was the wronged party, and she had always been much more important in Brian's life than his father, who had been largely a figurehead, absent most of the time. Even in the very uncomfortable and treacherous topic of sex that loomed unmentioned but enormous in the background while the family crumbled, she seemed to be in the right. Zoe had always, at least in his presence, been kind and affectionate to her husband. She wasn't exactly an ingénue when this happened, but she had taken good care of herself. She hadn't deserved such outright rejection.

But he could also feel sympathy for the temptation Darryl had felt around Steffie. In the terrible incident, Brian had not been able to take his eyes off her, and he recalled that she was like a ripe fruit, all plump, perfect, rounded curves and sugary succulence. Even as she had charged into him to push through the doorway, he recalled, her face had been beautiful, like a blushing angel. Brian decided it was a sign of his own maturity to concede that his father was only a weak, mortal human being, and that being tempted did not make him worse than most.

There was also the fact that the hand that signed the checks to Stanford, and after that MIT, was his father's. After the initial shock of the divorce wore off, Brian sometimes thought that it was too bad his mother couldn't have done what millions of other women had done and given her husband time to get over Steffie without doing anything overtly unpleasant and destroying the rest of the family's sense of well-being.

The message he'd received from Sarah a couple of hours ago had compelled him to rethink the whole tawdry story. He was beginning to think his mother had lost her mind like a cast-off woman in a Greek tragedy that he couldn't quite place. She had run off with a man who was practically a stranger, and before she went away to God knew where she wanted to bring this man to see him. It was clear that Sarah was taking this thing seriously, because she hadn't called, e-mailed, or sent a text. She had hired a process server from the law firm where she had interned to deliver it.

Brian's relationship with Sarah had been one of the things that the fall of the house of McDonald had brought down. They had been close as children. She was his little sister, and she had looked up to him. But when the breakup had come, they'd argued. She had sided with their mother and expressed contempt for Brian because he had not gone out of his way to be rude to Stephanie. He had told her that she was a naïve, knee-jerk feminist who, paradoxically, hated women, and was incapable of appreciating the complexity of human behavior. After that they had both been busy with graduate school and law school. And there was no longer a home where they would be forced to see each other on holidays.

The letter she had sent him by messenger was their first communication in at least two years. As soon as Brian received it he had closed his office door and read it with dread, and then with alarm, and finally despair. Since Sarah had entered law school she had adopted a measured, seemingly reasonable style of discourse. Reading a letter from her was like watching a philosopher walk calmly up a mountain and step off a cliff. Mom has found love. For the first time since we were children, she's happy. But powerful criminals have a grudge against him, so they have to go away for a while.

Brian rolled his eyes and let out a groan that he'd been unable to stifle. He sat still for a moment hoping nobody had heard, and then began formulating rhetorical questions. I'm a technocrat, Sarah. I work for companies that sell goods and services to the government. They're regulated and watched. How could you send me a letter like this at my office? And what about you, Sarah, you overconfident, presumptuous moron? You've spent the past two years trying to become a lawyer. Conspiring to hide fugitives is a felony. Even if this guy really were in the witness protection program, he would have to be a criminal to know anything about criminals. How's that career going to work out for you now?

He had fumed and fretted for at least an hour and then packed up some work and left the office with everyone else, but he didn't go home. He drove his Audi all over Irvine and Costa Mesa and the Palos Verdes peninsula for about three hours before he realized he was hungry and stopped for a hamburger. Now he was home, having solved nothing and knowing nothing new except that his mother had lost her mind.

As he walked up to his dark apartment building he saw two people, a couple, walking along the sidewalk from the visitors' parking area as though they wanted to intercept him. Here they are, he thought, two FBI agents coming to interview me about my crazy mother. Maybe he could get a job running the IT section of a clothing company or a grocery chain. He stared at the two.

They walked under a streetlamp, and he recognized the walk, the shape of the shorter one.

Then he heard the voice. "Brian!"

His mother. No matter where he might have been—in a blizzard in Antarctica or the bottom of the ocean—that voice would have entered his brain and traveled the thousands of neural pathways it had built early in his life. He walked more quickly to avoid having an illegal conversation in public under a streetlamp, swiveling his head to be sure there were no witnesses nearby.

He beat them to the door and said, "Wait a second while I get this open." He pushed the door inward and stepped aside to get them off the steps, and then shut the door behind them. He hurried to his apartment door and let them in.

He locked the door and said, "Sarah let me know you might be coming."

His mother hugged him. He tolerated it, but he couldn't bring himself to wrap his arms around her as though he approved of her being here.

She released him. "This is Peter. He's my—what? Boyfriend seems to still be the only word we have."

Hank Dixon stepped forward and held out his hand to shake Brian's and Brian gave the hand a perfunctory pump and released it. Hank didn't react to the sudden reversion to the name that had been blown, but it told him there must be something to worry about. He watched Brian scurry to the front windows to tug on the strings to be sure the blinds were closed as tightly as possible. Then he folded his arms in front of him.

Hank said, "Well, I'm sure you two would like to talk, so I'll leave you alone. I'll be in the car." He went out the door and closed it.

Brian said, "Sarah seemed to think you were afraid you might be followed."

"That's true," said his mother. "It's all a problem that goes back a lot of years. The police will take care of it. But for now at least, please don't say anything to anyone about us."

Brian's mind was slapped backward by the enormity of the gap between his mother's understanding of this situation and his own. He actually gave an incredulous chuckle. "Oh, I can assure you your secrets are safe. I'll never say a word about this to anyone."

Brian went to lift one of the blinds and watched the man walking toward his car. Brian felt a bit better. He said to his mother: "What exactly is your relationship with this guy?"

"I know you've had girlfriends, Brian. What was your relationship with them? I hope it was improper."

"I'm not the one who's the problem here," he said.

"Neither am I," she said. "I didn't come to ask you for help or approval. I just dropped by for a brief visit."

"For what purpose?"

"Purpose? You and I haven't seen much of each other in the past two or three years. I wanted to give you a hug and tell you that your mother loves you before we disappear into the night." She saw that he wasn't smiling. "I can see I've made you uncomfortable. I'm sorry. I know you like stability and certainty."

"If you knew that, then it might have been nice if you and Dad had seen fit to stay together, or at least keep up some appearance that we were a family."

"When your father replaced me with a newer model a few years ago, I gave him the chance to change his mind. He didn't, so blame him. I met this guy, as you call him, six months ago. You're not a child. You're twenty-six. And I've been single for years."

"Right," said Brian. "But if you don't think having people like this around puts your adult children at risk, then you're mistaken. I have a security clearance, at least until they find out you're hanging around with a man who doesn't feel the police are adequate to protect him. Sarah, who's just wasted two years learning to become a lawyer, may feel she has less to lose."

His mother studied him for a few seconds, and then said, "I guess we caught each other at a bad time. Still, it's been good to see you, Brian. You have my blessing. Some people find that kind of thing comforting, and even important to them." She patted his arm. "I wish you every happiness." She stepped past him.

He stared at the ugly beige carpet at his feet for a couple of seconds. He was distracted by the realization of how brown everything in his apartment was, all of it selected by the landlord and untouched and unadorned by Brian McDonald. He didn't hear his mother anymore, so he looked up. "Mom?"

There was no answer. He stepped around the corner to the kitchen, but it was empty. He glanced at the bathroom on his way back, but that door was open. He hurried to the apartment door and swung it open. "Mom?"

She was not in the hallway. She was already outside. He started toward the outer door of the building, but when he reached it, his impulse to go out there, to run down the sidewalk after her, seemed to leave him. What did he intend to say—that he wanted her to stay?

19

While Julian sat alone waiting for his plane, he pretended to read the *New York Times*. He was actually thinking about the way his time in San Francisco had ended. The meeting with the old man had been four days ago.

He'd had his debriefing with the senior agents, and then they had stepped out of the office into the hangar to talk. He and Harper and Waters had sat in silence. After about five minutes, Harper got another phone call, and he and Waters left the room. Minutes went by. Julian assumed that the four were conferring about something that he was not authorized to hear. After a few more minutes, he was convinced they were talking about him.

After another half hour, Julian realized he had stopped hearing the background sounds in the hangar—the starter motors of vehicle engines, the constant hums of ventilators, and the buzz of the overhead lights in the open bay.

He stood up and walked out of the little box of an office and stood for a few seconds. The vehicles were all still parked on the tiled floor—police cars, ambulances, mail and UPS and FedEx trucks, even a fire truck. What had changed was that the overhead lights and the ventilators had been turned off. The only illumination came from a row of small, dirty windows high in the wall, and from a single man-sized door that had been left open beside the giant motorized hangar door. The invisible fans that had been running to circulate the air were turned off.

As he walked toward the open door, all he could hear were his shoes hitting the tiles and echoing off the metal walls of the hangar. He stepped outside into the waning sunlight and closed the door. He tugged on the door handle to prove a theory, and verified that it had locked behind him.

From where he stood he could see the San Francisco airport buildings across about a mile of tarmac. He began to walk in that direction along the endless chain link fences, past hangars and warehouses and parking lots. The walking distance was a couple of miles, but he was alone, so he felt calm, and that distance was nothing to a man with his physical fitness and stamina.

At the terminal he stood in the taxi line and took a cab to the hotel in the city where he had stayed the previous night. When he arrived, he found that his key still worked, so they had not checked him out and paid for the room. He opened his small carry-on suitcase and found that somebody had opened it, taken everything out, and then returned his belongings a bit more neatly than he had left them. He called the front desk to ask for a new room and a new toothbrush, toothpaste, and mouthwash.

He made his plane reservation to Little Rock. Then he ate dinner in the hotel's restaurant and went to bed in his new room.

The cell phone that military intelligence had issued him never buzzed or vibrated during that night or the next two days and nights. On the morning of the fourth day he packed up, checked out, and hailed a cab outside the hotel. When the first cab stopped, he stepped off the curb. He said, "I'd like to go to the airport, please." When he was inside the cab he said, "Delta Air Lines, please."

His parents had taught him the value of being polite when he was very young. If he was polite, nobody in the neighborhood outside Jonesboro where he grew up would report his rudeness to his parents and get him punished. The other benefits had come to him one at a time. The most obvious involved women, but there were others. Strangers who had not had a bad impression of a man forgot him as soon as he was gone.

Julian pretended to read his newspaper, and then boarded his plane when his seating section was called. He sat at the window and closed his eyes. By the time the plane rumbled along and lifted into the air, he was nearly asleep. He had acquired the fatalism of people who had flown often to remote places, and the combat soldier's ability to sleep anywhere and at any time. He slept through most of the flight to Dallas/Fort Worth, ate lunch, and stayed awake during the second flight to Little Rock.

He liked seeing his part of the country from the sky. He knew the short flight was taking him over Texarkana and Arkadelphia toward Little Rock. He liked to watch the ground below him changing. The first time he had taken this flight, after he enlisted at seventeen, he had thought of the view as the way land would look to God—green mostly, with ribbons and spots of blue-gray water reflecting the sun heavenward.

The plane bounced on the runway and rattled until the brakes overcame the plane's momentum and the pilot taxied to the terminal. Julian waited for the long line of people ahead of him to stand, open all the overhead compartments at once, and bump into each other. Then they tugged down suitcases and bags that were too heavy and full for the compartments and swung them to the floor, where there was no room for them among people's feet. When the passengers began their lockstep trudge toward the forward hatch, he plucked his small carry-on off the floor and followed at a distance.

Julian rented a car. He was always careful what sort of vehicle he drove when he was home. Nobody had ever told him to do this. That would have been as unnecessary as telling him to think. He selected a white Toyota Corolla, because it didn't look too fancy or too powerful. It didn't have tinted windows or too much unseen space in back. The Corolla was the sort of car that a prudent man might drive to work.

He put the carry-on bag in the trunk because leaving it on the seat beside him might arouse curiosity if a police officer pulled him over. A bag might raise the suspicion in a Southern cop's mind that Julian had a hidden weapon or other contraband. The danger was probably intensified by the fact that Julian looked much younger than he was—not the sort of man who might be a state legislator or judge. Instead he looked like the sort who might mysteriously injure himself while in custody.

Julian had fought battles, including a few with people who believed that dying would lift them to heaven in an instant. He no longer felt the urge to prove his bravery to himself, and he had lost interest in persuading anybody else of anything. He believed in arriving quietly, avoiding confrontation, and moving on without notice. His family was the only reason he ever came back.

He felt better once he was outside Little Rock and beyond its suburbs. He drove along Interstate 40, took the exit for US 49 North, and kept going toward home. His part of Arkansas was the northeast in the Mississippi Embayment, where the land was rich alluvial soil from the Mississippi's tributaries. The rocky range of hills along Crowley's Ridge, where Jonesboro had grown up, was a border for him. There were oak and hickory forests where he had hunted, and then the flat plain where his family had built their vegetable farm.

He drove to the farm, parked the car, and got out. The air smelled the way air was supposed to smell, as though a summer rain had just fallen and the droplets had exploded into mist. The late afternoon sun was warm and comforting on his shoulders. In many of the places he had been sent over the past six years, the sun had been another enemy. Today it felt the way it had at the end of a day when he was a kid coming home from working with his brothers and sisters.

As he went to open his trunk, the front door of the farmhouse opened and his mother stepped out on the wide wooden porch. He remembered sleeping on that porch sometimes as a kid. It was enclosed in screen to keep out mosquitoes and deerflies, and had a pair of ceiling fans to keep the air moving on hot evenings.

"It's about time," his mother said. She was the one from whom he had inherited his short stature, young complexion, and slim body. Her serene expression made her look about half her age.

"Sorry, Mother," Julian said. "I got called back in at the last minute for a project."

"You already told us your excuse," she said. "And I still say it's about time you got here."

His father appeared on the porch too. He was tall and lean, with square shoulders. It seemed to Julian that he was aging much faster than his mother. The upper part of his spine seemed to be contracting to bend him forward a little. He grinned. "I had to eat your pie, or it would have gotten stale. Nice to see you, though."

Julian climbed up to the porch, set down his bag, hugged his mother, and shook his father's hand.

"Welcome home," said his father. "How long can you stay?"

"I'm not sure. I'll stay until I have to go."

There were more empty bedrooms now than there had been when Julian was young. He went to put his bag in the first one, but saw it had become a sewing room, so he went to the next and set down his bag. Then the three sat on the porch.

When the sun was low enough below the porch roof to be in a person's eyes when he looked to the west, Julian's two youngest brothers, Joseph and Noah, and his youngest sister, Leila, walked in along the farm road that ran between the vegetable fields. At first they were just three small, dark silhouettes in front of the harsh light, and then they grew as they came closer and the sunlight began to weaken to orange.

He could see they had been weeding, because each of them had a hoe over one shoulder and a strap over the other for the big canvas bag. He thought of those as harvest bags because when he was a boy he remembered gathering vegetables in one to dump into the baskets. He knew that right now each would hold a lunch box and a big plastic bottle for water, both of them light and empty at this time of day.

When Leila noticed the unfamiliar rental car he saw her point, and they all seemed to walk a little faster, their feet lighter. When they arrived, Julian hugged Leila, then Joseph, and then Noah, smelling and feeling the sweat on their shirt backs. "I'm so glad to see you," he said.

"I see you got here just in time to see the workday end," said Noah.

"Just the three of you are doing all of it?"

"Of course not," Leila said. "We were just out there with the weeding crew. We've got twenty people working every day right now."

"Plenty of room out there if you're still up to it, though," Joseph said.

"I'll be out there with you tomorrow morning," said Julian.

They all went inside, and while the others took turns showering, Julian set the dinner table and talked with his parents in the kitchen. The old dining table had only about half of its places filled now that the older brothers and sisters were gone, and he asked about each of the absent ones—how they were doing, whether they visited often, when the last time was.

Julian was up with the others before dawn, ready to go out to join the crew weeding the next patch of the farm. This one was asparagus, and if they worked hard, they could get the green beans done too. Everything on a farm came in cycles. By the time the crew got through weeding the whole farm, it would be time to start the first patch over again. Over all was the cycle of seed, weed, and harvest. Irrigation wasn't necessary except a few times in midsummer, because the rest of the time there was enough rain, but there was a big tank at the highest point on the farm that served as a reservoir for the water pumped from the well.

At breakfast they continued the conversations interrupted the night before. The three youngest siblings were all dating local people, and they teased each other about the beloved's appearance, prospects, and intelligence. This went on for a while, and then Leila's big cat's eyes turned to the side and settled on Julian. "I heard Ruthie Straughan got a divorce."

There was silence for a couple of seconds. The others, all at least five years younger than Julian, waited. Leila added, "But I suppose you knew that already, or you wouldn't just happen to think of coming home."

Julian said, "Where did you hear that about Ruthie Straughan?"

"I'm not sure," she said. "I guess it must have been at church. Did you hear it there too?" All three of her brothers laughed.

"I have to get all my gossip from you," he said. "I don't recall having been to church in a while."

Leila said, "The Lord finds many ways to make things known. I do my part."

When they finished breakfast they put the dishes in the sink to soak, picked up their lunches and water bottles, and went outside to get into one of the trucks and drive out to the fields. This was the coolest part of the day, and it was the best time to get the hard work done.

Joseph, who served as foreman, lined up the hired workers at the end of the asparagus field, and then the Carsons picked up hoes and bags themselves, and the crew began to move along the spaces between rows, digging all the weeds on one row and then heading up the next row. They worked steadily and methodically, as people did who had been raised to work.

They all worked until the sun was directly overhead and their shadows pooled at their feet. Joseph checked his watch and they all went to sit in the shade beneath the fruit trees and opened their lunch pails. Most of the hired hands went to get their lunches from coolers in the trunks of their cars.

As the Carsons ate, the siblings started on Julian. "You know, Julian," said Joseph, "I always figured you had a great big job in the Pentagon or somewhere. But I can see you're better at weeding than you ever were. Is that what they have you doing?"

"I can't tell you much because it's classified," said Julian. "I'm sort of like the director of the CIA, except younger and better looking."

After a few minutes the others turned their attention to Noah, who had been refusing to tell his siblings who he was taking to a cousin's wedding.

They went back to work, and the stream of banter and gossip filled the afternoon, and then the sun began to go down. Leila stopped at the end of a row and said, "I'm going home. I don't know about you, but I've got things to do tonight." She shouldered her hoe, and emptied her canvas sack on the compost heap one last time. The others did the same and got into the truck, and they all drove back up the farm road to the house.

When they made it to the house it took time for all of them to shower, change clothes, and eat the dinner their mother had made. The dinner was much as it had been when Julian was growing up. The exact combination of spices his mother always used made him remember nights twenty years ago.

After dark, Julian spent an hour or so chatting with his parents about local people, politics, and the condition of the world. Then Leila came out to the porch and said, "Julian, can you give me a ride into town?"

When they were in his rental car, moving along the highway toward Jonesboro, Leila said, "I don't know if you want to know this, but she wants you to stop by and see her."

It was as though their conversation from before dawn had never ended, just gone underground and surfaced again. He had no confusion about whom she meant. He looked at Leila. "I don't know if I wanted to hear that, but I do appreciate your passing it on."

"Are you going to go?"

"I don't know yet. When and where do you want me to pick you up?"

"I'm meeting Meg and Latrice at choir practice. Then James is going to pick me up in his car."

"You sure?"

"Of course I'm sure."

He opened his wallet and found a receipt. "You got a pen?"

She handed him a pen from her purse.

He held the receipt against the steering wheel and wrote down his cell phone number. "If you need a ride, call me." After a moment he added, "If you want me for any other reason too." He handed it to her with the pen and she put them in her purse together.

In a few minutes, he stopped in front of the church. Leila got out of the car, and then leaned back in. "That house where the Deckers used to live, next to the corner market?"

"I remember."

"That's where Ruthie is staying now."

"You think I ought to go see her?"

Leila frowned. "I don't know what your life is like now, Julian. As you said, it's classified. If you want to, go ahead. If not . . ." She ended her sentence with a shrug. "Got to go. I love it when you're home." She hurried to join her friends, and Julian drove off.

As Julian drove the streets of Jonesboro he passed the high school. Sometime in the 1970s it had been demolished by a tornado and rebuilt low with a peaked roof and gables on the front and a steeple that made it look like a big Howard Johnson's.

Soon Julian noticed that in his aimless drive, his rental car had made several right turns, and that the last one took him near the old corner market. He considered calling the farm to see if his mother wanted anything from the store, but then thought better of it. If he bought something frozen or likely to go off, he'd have to rush right home with it.

Julian pulled up on the street far enough from the store not to be recognized in a car he didn't own, and sat for a minute. His eyes settled on the market as he thought. There was Ruthie coming out of the market with a brown paper bag in her left arm.

She was wearing a white cotton dress and flat sandals. She paused in the parking lot. She seemed not to see him, but to know he must be there and look where she expected him to be. She walked across the parking lot and up the sidewalk to the passenger side of his car. She pointed at the lock button on that side and he hit the switch to make it pop up. She opened the door and sat beside him.

He looked at her, not pretending he wasn't staring. He was taking in the sight.

She smiled. "Can we go for a ride?"

He started the car and drove.

"I wasn't sure you'd come," she said.

"Leila told me."

"I got divorced this year," she said.

"Are you sad about it?" he said.

"No. A little embarrassed. People look at me, and I can see behind their eyes. They're trying to guess why it happened. They wonder if he cheated on me, if I cheated on him, who we would have cheated with. They wonder if I'm cold, or bitchy, or selfish. They wonder if he hit me. Whatever anybody ever got divorced for, they try on me to see if it fits."

"What does fit?"

"Nothing. People get along or they don't. If they don't, then one day one of them sees the future all laid out ahead. And they realize that it's almost exactly like the present. And they don't want it to be."

"I understand," he said.

She gave him a look that had a bit of skepticism, and he knew what she was thinking: *Either you've been divorced or you haven't.* So he thought about how foolish he probably had sounded. It wasn't that he'd had the experience or really understood. What he'd meant was: *I don't want to think about that anymore.*

They drove on for a couple of miles before she said, "How long are you going to be here?"

"I don't know." He took out his phone and held it up. "When this rings again, I'll have to go. If it never rings I'll be here until I die."

"If it rings, can you say no?"

He thought for a few seconds. "Not if I want to keep working for the government."

"Has that been so great?"

"Not really, to tell you the truth."

"Okay," she said, and then stopped because he could draw his own conclusions.

"Why did you want me to come and see you?" Julian asked.

"Before I divorced Taylor I did a lot of thinking, and after the decree I kept thinking."

"What about?"

"About a lot of things. Mostly about what I know, and what my life has been like so far, and the choices and decisions, and how they worked out. And I've thought about what went wrong and what I should do next. Taylor has always been a drinker, and so I went to a couple of Al-Anon meetings. He wouldn't go with me."

"It wasn't a bad idea, though. Did you learn anything?"

"Some things. They have these steps you follow to straighten yourself out. One of them is to go around and find all the people you've harmed, and try to make things right."

"I've heard of that," Julian said.

She turned to look at him. "You're one of the people I harmed."

"I don't remember that," he said.

"It was when we were young—like seventeen. I knew you had a big crush on me, but I pretended I didn't."

"That's not taking anything from me."

"I knew that you were serious when you tried to ask me to go to the prom with you, and you really wanted me to go. I knew that you would have been so happy if I would just say yes. But I pretended I thought you were just joking around, so I could laugh and say no in a way that would make you stop, but not be able to say I was being mean."

"That's not being mean. You just didn't want to go with me. That's no harm."

"It hurt me," she said. "Not right away, but later. I kind of knew it would then. Most girls were looking forward to going to the prom with somebody, but I was mainly interested in staying unclaimed and seeing who asked, and how many there were, and picking the best one. You were the first one to ask, and at that age I was two inches taller than you, and we had known each other since we were three. After I said no I had second thoughts because you were the only one who really cared about me. But I told myself that no matter what I did, you'd still be around. So I went with Lawrence Coles. Then right after graduation you were gone. A couple of years later, you were back from the army for a few days, and everybody could see who you really were. I was sorry then—but not for you. For me."

"Just forget it," he said. "If you go around to all the guys who wanted you and say you're sorry, you'll be apologizing to everybody in Craighead County."

"It doesn't say that."

"What?"

"The twelve-step thing. It doesn't say you apologize. It says to make amends."

20

Hank Dixon swung the ax, brought it down on the end of the upright log, and split it. He set the next one upright on the stump and took another swing. After about ten minutes he had filled the bin with split pieces he could use to start fires. He carried the wooden bin to the porch under the roof, and then went back for two loads of larger pieces from the cord of wood in the yard. Then he tugged the tarp back over the woodpile and tied it down to keep the wood dry.

He saw Marcia coming back up the path from the lake. She said, "Does this mean we're in for a cold night tonight?"

"I think so. The forecast says that places over six thousand feet will drop into the thirties tonight."

"It sounds cozy," she said. She stepped close and kissed him, and he could feel the cold of her nose on his cheek. "But try not to hit yourself in the shin with the ax."

"Wood chopping happens to be something I'm good at," he said. "All those years in New England made me an expert at fire starting, walking on ice, and snow shoveling. I never thought I'd need that knowledge in Southern California, but here I am." He paused. "Run into anyone down the hill?"

"No," she said. "Things looked pretty deserted." She looked down the mountain at the small town below. "Tell me the truth. How do you think we're doing at this? I mean living here and everything."

"All you ever know is that they haven't got you yet."

Marcia shrugged. "No sense in running up the score beyond that anyway, right? It's poor sportsmanship."

They walked to the porch of the cabin and went inside. The cabin was bigger and fancier than most houses. A Los Angeles stockbroker and his wife had built it as a mountain retreat. The stockbroker told Hank that he had imagined they would be retreating to the mountains during the summer to escape the heat, and coming during the winter to ski. Maybe they would visit during the fall to see the leaves on the deciduous trees on the lower altitudes and smell the sap of the tall pines up near the house. In the spring they might come to do some trout fishing in the mountain streams that fed the lake. This fall the cabin was for rent.

When Hank had looked online and seen the photographs of the interior of the house and its furnishings, he had e-mailed and then called the owner to strike a deal. He wondered why the rent was so reasonable.

Shortly after the cabin was completed, the stockbroker's wife had observed that coming all the way up here from Los Angeles took nearly all day, and the homeward drive took most of another day, much of it through places that weren't scenic. That meant weekends were too short to make the trip worth taking. After that she had announced that the longer trips he proposed had turned out to be boring. There was nothing to do, with just the two of them in such an isolated place.

The cabin had not decreased the man's stress. He had spent so much money and effort to build the cabin that he had no choice but to try to recoup the expense by renting it. It was easy to rent out a cabin on a mountain lake in August when it hadn't rained in Los Angeles for eight months and the temperature on Wilshire Boulevard was 105. It was even easier to rent during the winter holidays, when people wanted to ski. But it was not so easy after the kids were back in school and the weather in Los Angeles had reverted to being paradisiacal.

When Hank drove Marcia up to Big Bear to the cabin for the first time, he said little about the place except that it was "just right." He appeared to be preoccupied during the shopping trip in San Bernardino. Hank had stayed in mountain cabins before, so he knew enough to bring all the supplies he could fit in a car.

When he drove up to the right address, they could see the view of the lake was beautiful. Hank said nothing as he took Marcia up to the front door. He simply unlocked the lock and swung the door open so she could see the gleaming black Steinway grand piano sitting across the large living room.

Marcia stepped past him in silence like a woman stalking something that might get up and take flight. She walked across the room, ran her hand along the mirror-smooth black wood, sat on the bench, opened the keyboard cover, and sounded a note. Then she played about seven bars of Chopin's Nocturne in E-flat Major. Finally, she stood up and ran to Hank. She hugged him hard, and when she pulled away from him, he could see she was crying. After a few seconds she whispered, "I love you."

The log house was well designed, well made, and pristine. The place had probably been occupied no more than sixty days since it was built. The furniture, fixtures, and appliances had barely been used. The stockbroker had bought the piano in Los Angeles in the hope that his daughter would come up with her parents frequently and play, but she had come a few times and used the trip as an excuse to give her fingers a rest. Hank and Marcia moved in to the master bedroom upstairs, where there was a window that had been designed to frame the view of the lake.

They hiked the trails in the mornings. In the afternoons Marcia played the piano and Hank read, and occasionally took the canoe out to explore the lake. In the evenings they cooked, watched the cabin's television set, and used the computers. They took baths in the oversized whirlpool tub and slept on the new California king bed.

Hank made Marcia spend a few hours each day practicing ways he had devised to deal with emergencies. He coached her in telling the life stories of Henry and Marcia Dixon so she would never be caught with a version that contradicted his. When she was flawless at it they tried it again, this time to be sure they didn't tell stories using the same words.

Hank took care to remain vigilant. He kept the three unused prepaid telephones in their original wrapping so he could be sure Marcia didn't get tempted to use them to call her children. When she was in the shower or practicing the piano, he would examine the laptop computer's history to be sure she hadn't used it to get in touch with her daughter or with anyone else. He even made sure that none of the computer's history had been erased since he'd last used it. He also kept checking for any sign of news. He checked the *Chicago Tribune*'s personal ads once a week for any communication from James Harriman.

A month passed in the mountains. The trees at the altitude above the lake were nearly all pines, so they didn't change colors or lose leaves. But the mornings were all cooler now. The Dixons wore jackets for their early walks, and brought knitted caps and leather gloves that they sometimes put on. Later in the day the sunshine bored through the clouds and burned off the mists, but there was no question that fall had taken possession of the mountains.

One day Hank drove them out of the mountains and into San Bernardino, where they shopped for things that would help them extend their stay at the cabin into the winter. They bought tire chains, antifreeze, ice scrapers with snow brushes on them, pairs of boots, and jackets rated for subzero weather.

On the way home Hank stopped at a gun store and bought two sets of ear protectors and plugs, a pair of shooting glasses for Marcia, and a supply of 9mm and .45 ACP ammunition. On the drive home Marcia said, "Why all the ammunition? Have you seen something I should worry about?"

Hank said, "I thought you and I might go out and get some target practice to keep us sharp."

"Who said I was ever sharp? I've never held a firearm in my life. And where could we even do that?"

"I found a few ranges," he said. "But I thought maybe we'd be better off just going out into the wild country. Otherwise you have to provide identification and all that."

"Won't just going out and shooting get us arrested?"

"San Bernardino County has a lot of space where you can fire a weapon legally. It's the biggest county in the whole country. It's got more area than Connecticut, Delaware, and New Jersey combined. Once you're ten miles outside of any town, you're pretty much by yourself."

"You still haven't told me why we're doing this."

"It's something I want you to learn," he said. "You said you would be useful. Having a second armed person to cover me in an emergency would be useful."

The next day Hank drove out Route 38 to the east of Big Bear, and eventually found a flat dirt road that must have been a firebreak where they could pull off the highway about a mile before the country got too rocky and uneven. He parked among some scrubby trees and walked.

When Hank judged they had gone far enough he studied the area until he found a low hillside he could use as a backstop. He set up a dead tree limb and anchored it in the sandy dirt at the foot of the hill. "This will have to do as a target."

"Okay. What do I do?"

"First you learn a little bit about semiauto pistols," he said. "They're not wildly different from each other." He unzipped his backpack, took out a small pistol, and held it up. "This is a Beretta Nano. It's about as small as a good 9mm pistol gets, and it will probably fit your hand pretty well. This catch releases the magazine. On this model there's another release on the other side of the grips, but that's unusual. The magazine holds six rounds, and you can also put a round in the chamber if you want to carry it that way. I don't. If I really expected to have to shoot seven times, I'd go somewhere else instead."

"All right," she said.

"You pull the trigger and the trigger bar pushes the striker back against its spring. Right near the end of your pull, the cocking lever frees the striker and it pops forward, hits the primer, and the round in the chamber is fired. The slide recoils, ejecting the brass casing, and comes forward again, letting the next round be pushed up into the chamber. You get to pull the trigger six times, and then there are no more rounds in the magazine. On the last round, when the slide goes back it stays there, with the chamber open like this."

"Got it."

"Watch how I load it." He released the empty magazine and loaded six rounds into it, then pushed it upward under the grips. "You have to charge the weapon like this." He pulled back the slide and released it. "That lets the first round into the chamber."

He had her put in the earplugs and fit the ear protectors over them, and then put on his own.

He turned toward the upright branch he had set up. He held the pistol in a two-handed stance and fired a round into the center. Then he handed her the pistol, grips first. "Your turn."

He watched her imitate his stance, then adjusted her hands. "The left hand will help your right to hold it steady. You want the front sight dot to sit between the two rear sights. Put it on the target and you're ready to fire. Don't drag the sight off the target with your finger. Just use the last joint of your finger to pull it straight back. When you're ready, fire."

She fired and the round knocked a chip off the tree limb.

"Very good. Now fire the rest." He watched her fire, and noticed that she looked more comfortable each time.

When she fired the last round and the slide stayed back, he took the pistol, reloaded it, put it in his coat pocket, and lifted another pistol out of the backpack. "This is a Colt Commander. It's bigger and heavier, obviously. It's chambered for .45 ACP, and it's not designed for concealed carry. It has a little more stopping power than the 9mm. Its magazine holds seven rounds and you can carry one in the chamber. As I said before, I don't usually do that."

He went through the whole process again for Marcia, showing her the parts and the mechanism, and then how to load and fire the weapon. He handed her the Commander and let her fire it. After each shot he made a comment, either a correction or encouragement.

After she had emptied the magazine he taught her how to clear the pistol and reload. Then he had her return to the Beretta Nano, release the magazine, check the load, reinsert the magazine and charge the weapon, and then fire those rounds. When she'd fired the last round she reloaded the magazine, then fired through that magazine.

He made her alternate weapons, firing a magazine at a time. He changed targets, finding smaller branches and placing them farther away, always watching her form and accuracy until she had fired a hundred rounds.

"Are you confident that if something terrible were happening, you could pick up either one of these, load, and fire accurately?"

"I know I could," she said.

"All right, then," he said. "Reload them both one more time and then help me collect all the brass."

"I can help you pick it up first," she offered.

"No," he said. "Reload first. We're not people who can afford to have all our weapons unloaded at once."

He knelt to pick up the brass casings that had been ejected from the pistols. Then he took both pistols, checked to be sure they were fully loaded, and put them in the backpack. When they had picked up the brass they headed to their car. When they were back at the cabin he cleaned the weapons and put them away.

The next day Hank checked and modified his bugout kits. Each contained a few thousand dollars in cash, a Beretta Nano pistol with two spare magazines, and the licenses, credit cards, and passports of a Canadian couple named Alan and Marie Spencer. He set aside the two pistols with silencers he had taken from the two killers in Chicago. He loaded them and put them both in the nightstand on his side of the bed.

Just as he was finishing these tasks, Marcia came in. She could see that the kit he was filling now had a driver's license with her picture on it, and the pistol. "What's going on, Hank?"

"Nothing," he said. "We're in a good, comfortable place right now, where we have privacy and time. If we don't use a little of it to get ready for trouble, maybe we're not earning the chance to keep going. If we don't earn it, maybe we won't get it."

Over the next weeks Hank prepared for events that might occur—another attack by Libyan assassins, a raid by police with tear gas or flash-bang grenades, a house fire, a car accident, a neighbor who thought they seemed suspicious or recognized a picture that they didn't know had been publicized, a robbery—anything that might put them in danger. He began to train Marcia to perfect her responses, so each of them would know what the other was going to do.

He bought an emergency rope ladder and kept it rolled up by their bedroom window and bolted to a six-foot pipe. He bought a pair of standard binoculars and a pair of night-vision binoculars. He studied the roads and the houses around the lake from the cabin's upper windows. He explored the forested areas to pick out trails and dirt roads. In the evening he used the night-vision binoculars to pick out cars, pedestrians, boats on the lake, and animals moving along the trails.

Hank identified the routes a person could use to outrun or evade attackers. He favored the troughs of dry streambeds for invisibility. He looked for outcroppings and piles of boulders for vantage points. But always, he preferred the pine forests, which offered protection from above and floors of pine needles that wouldn't hold a footprint.

Next he began to test the escape routes. For weeks he used their early morning walks to determine the viability of each route and to get Marcia to memorize it too.

When he was satisfied, he identified a series of rendezvous points where he and Marcia could meet if they got separated. The points were established all the way to San Bernardino and then to Los Angeles on the south and west, and to Las Vegas and Salt Lake City on the east and north.

When the escape routes had been settled and memorized, he kept looking for other ways to elude the chasers. He knew that the most likely hazard was that he would slip away and Marcia would be captured. A skilled interrogator could get her to reveal a great deal about him without realizing it. He was sure she would try very hard not to say anything, but eventually she would weaken.

She had been very useful so far. Having a respectable-looking woman with him made anybody who saw him assume that he had not come to rob them or pick a fight. Nobody brought a woman along when he had something like that in mind. He was also aware that he owed her some hope of escape if things got rough. And he couldn't help knowing that having a second armed, healthy, and well-rehearsed person trying to escape when he did made his survival much more likely.

He hoped that if they were separated Marcia would do exactly what he'd trained her to do. She would run hard over familiar ground, expecting to rejoin him. He knew that when he didn't arrive, she would be shocked. But after the shock wore off she would notice that she wasn't wondering what to do next. She already knew, because he had drilled it into her brain.

He had forced her to memorize and practice the first parts of her route dozens of times. After that, her job was just a question of reaching a series of particular buildings in increasingly distant cities. As soon as she found herself really alone, her need to survive would take over. Once that emotion overcame her attachment to him, she would be okay. An armed, intelligent woman with two unassailable false identities, thousands of dollars in cash, and millions in banks could go pretty far without a man.

21

Julian's eyes opened. He heard the phone buzzing, but it was too early for the alarm he'd set to be going off. He rolled to the side of the bed away from Ruthie and snatched it to turn it off. But as he did, he saw the number on the display. The area code was 202—Washington, DC. The phone buzzed again and he slid the arrow with his thumb and heard a voice like a tinny, distant radio voice. He pushed it under his pillow.

"Julian? Who's that?" Ruthie said.

The tinny voice from the phone said something else, but he managed to click the OFF switch. "Go back to sleep, baby. It's just my alarm." Then he was up and moving. He rolled the clothes he'd left out into a bundle and hurried out of Ruthie's bedroom and down the stairs.

He stopped in the living room and got dressed. The room was dark, and the world outside the windows was dark. The five-year-old white pickup truck he had bought after he returned his rental car sat in Ruthie's driveway with a ghostly glow, waiting for him. As he dressed he noticed that against the glow the dents and marks showed up even more clearly. The street was empty and still, as though all the people had left town.

He sat down on the hassock in front of the easy chair to put on his socks and shoes. No matter what else was going on, he had told

Joseph he would be at the farm by dawn to help bring in the broccoli. It was a big fall crop for the Carsons, and it was time to cut.

Julian made it out the front door before the phone vibrated again. He got into the truck and backed out into the street before he swept his thumb across the screen to answer.

"Who's the girl?" It was Harper's voice.

Julian said, "That's got nothing to do with you."

"Where are you, Julian? I get the feeling you're in Jonesboro, Arkansas. You're supposed to let us know where you are at all times."

"Nobody said anything like that to me. In fact, nobody said anything to me. Everybody just left me in that building near the airport. And it's been over two months since this phone has rung."

Harper's voice hardened. "It's time to come in."

"Come in where?"

"Fort Meade, Maryland. Drive in the Reece Road gate and tell them your name and that you're expected at military intelligence. Anytime today will be okay."

"I won't be there. I have a previous commitment."

"You want me to tell them that?"

"Yes," Julian said. "I'm not a soldier and I'm not an agent. I'm an independent contractor."

"All right. But I have a feeling I'll be seeing you very soon," Harper said.

"It won't be today."

"I'll make your apologies for you, Julian," Harper said. "But don't lose your phone." He hung up.

Julian drove out to the farm. When he turned onto the long gravel road to the farmhouse, he could tell that nobody else was up yet. Getting out of Ruthie's house without letting the phone wake her had forced him to get out the door without breakfast or even brushing his teeth.

He parked his truck out of the way beyond the barn and walked to the house. He used the key that was up on the lintel to open the front door and then replaced the key. He turned on the kitchen light and began to make coffee and a large pot of oatmeal.

Coming home was not only to arrive in the house's space. It was also to arrive in the house's time, an unchanging moment around his eighth birthday. The thick china plates and cups all looked as they had when he was a small child, and the pans were heavy black iron and ageless.

When he had some oatmeal in a bowl and a pot of coffee made, his mother came in. "Good morning, Julian," she said. She stepped up and kissed his cheek. "It's so nice to have you around messing up my kitchen again."

"It's nice to be here."

"You know, if you want to be with Ruthie, you could marry her and stay here with her. You wouldn't have to drive all the way into town."

"But she would. She has a job."

His mother shrugged. "I'll bet she'd think about saving on the rent if you offered her a ring."

He laughed, and then began to eat his oatmeal while she packed lunches for the day in the fields. After another minute Leila came downstairs, kissed her mother, took a bowl and filled it with oatmeal, and sat with her brother. After a few seconds Leila's big eyes moved to the side to hold him in her sight without moving her head. "Julian, you're looking a little peaked. I hope you haven't been staying awake too late and missing your sleep." She asked her mother: "Doesn't he look skinny and tired?"

Her mother said, "Mind your own business, Leila. You don't hear him complaining."

"Oh, he might be. We just can't hear it because he's too weak."

"Thank you for your concern," said Julian.

"Concern about what?" Noah and Joseph were coming in the doorway. They picked up bowls and went to the stove.

"About nothing," their mother said. "Leila is just being Leila."

"She does that a lot," said Joseph, and sat down to eat.

"All day long, practically," Noah said.

Julian finished the oatmeal and coffee and stood up to rinse his bowl. When he'd set the cup and bowl in the sink, he took his lunch box and said, "I'll drive out there and get the crew started on the broccoli. Did I see the baskets already in the stake truck?"

Joseph said, "Both stake trucks. We stacked them up so they'd be ready to go. We'll take the other truck and meet you out there."

"Good." Julian went out and took the keys off the hook on the wall by the door.

Julian drove out of the yard and down the farm road to the broccoli field. He could see in the predawn haze that the broccoli was ready. The buds were firm and tight, but none of them was already in flower. It was a good crop. There would be side shoots to harvest for weeks.

Julian's arrival caught the attention of the work crew, and they got out of their cars, took baskets and big knives out of the back of the truck, and went to the broccoli field. Julian joined them to help set the pace.

From long practice he took a single hard slice through each stalk at an angle and put the head in his basket as he moved to the next stem. It was smooth, flawless work. When the basket was full he loaded it on the truck and took another.

His brothers and sister arrived in the second truck within minutes and went to work around him. About once every two hours his cell phone would vibrate in his pocket a few times. He would take it out and look at the screen and then put it away unanswered.

They worked until the truck was full, and then drove it back to the barn and unloaded the baskets, placing them in neat rows. Then they got more baskets and drove back out.

At lunch Leila kept coming up with more and more outrageous theories about who Noah's secret girlfriend was, ending up unable to decide between Mayor Constance Wittles and Judge Joan

Harker. Noah asked Joseph whether the new aftershave he'd been wearing had been inherited from the world's oldest lady, who had died in New Orleans at the age of 114 a week ago, or was a concoction of his own. Joseph told Leila that the pastor was collecting votes to move the church across town so Leila couldn't sing in the choir, because her voice made the children cry during services. The only one everyone left alone was Julian.

He barely noticed. He worked with an intense concentration and speed that the Carsons usually adopted only when a frost threatened a crop. He worked tirelessly and spoke little. Every time his phone buzzed, the others watched his expression as he looked at the number and put it away.

When the sun sank and lost its power they didn't stop. The broccoli would be in better shape if it was harvested at a cool temperature, and they wanted to finish the patch. They worked until nightfall and then got into the two loaded trucks and drove back up the farm road. This time they locked the trucks up for the night with the produce still loaded. They would drive the trucks into town to the predawn market for sale.

Julian made a special effort to say good night to his brothers and sister, his mother and his father. Leila looked at him with a puzzled look on her face, then hugged him. "I'll see you when I see you," she said.

Julian climbed into his white pickup and drove into Jonesboro. When he pulled up in front of Ruthie's house, it didn't look right. Usually when he arrived the lights in the house were few and dim, but the curtains were open. Tonight the lights all seemed to be on, but the curtains were closed. He looked up the street. Parked just beyond the corner he could see the front end of a big black SUV.

He sat behind the wheel of his white pickup and looked at the house. The short period of unreality was over. The past two months had been as though time had gone backward to when he was seventeen. He had not liked that period of his life, but ten years later, circumstances had put him back in the same place with the same people, and life felt right this time. He had been living in the illusion that he had another chance, and that this time things were different. Ruthie didn't say no and go off with someone else.

How could he have let himself believe that this could be permanent? People didn't get to redo their lives so everything was right. That was a delusion. He got out of the pickup, walked to the front door, opened it, and stepped inside. There were four men in Ruthie's living room waiting for him.

He considered punching someone, but there was Ruthie, sitting on her couch five feet from Harper. He considered running, but there was Ruthie, looking up from the couch, searching his face for an explanation. He couldn't leave her here alone with them. Two of them were men he had never seen before. They both had buzz-cut hair and that look that soldiers had in suits, like dogs stuffed into clothes.

Julian closed the door behind him and stood still.

Waters said, "Hello, Julian. It's good to see you. We stopped by to give you a lift to the briefing." He looked at Ruthie appreciatively. "Mrs. Straughan graciously allowed us to wait here for you."

"Miss Davis," she said.

"Oh, I'm sorry," said Harper. "Your divorce was so recent that I guess the records haven't been updated."

Julian looked at Ruthie. She was clearly waiting for him to let her know what was happening, and what he was going to do. He said, "I hadn't planned on going anywhere tonight. Miss Davis and I haven't had a chance to talk about it."

Harper said, "Well, the time is running a bit shorter than we had anticipated. That's really all I can say at this time. Miss Davis, I apologize again for the inconvenience and the lack of notice, but the country is at war."

Julian said, "Let me get my bag." He took Ruthie by the hand and led her to the bedroom.

Once they were inside with the door shut she said, "I thought you were out of the army, Julian. So how can they come and get you, like you were AWOL or something?"

"It's hard to explain," he said.

"It's hard to explain?" she said. "That's what you have to say to me after your friends bully their way into my house and sit right down like they own the place?"

"I told you the situation the first night I came here. I'm a civilian but I work for military intelligence. As soon as this is over, I'll be back."

She studied him. "I guess I've been stupid. You did explain the situation. You were here to have a short visit with your family and have a break from the secret, highly serious work you do."

"It did start that way, but—"

"Good," she said. "I hope I helped make your visit more fun. I've read how spies—I mean intelligence experts—like to have a new woman to sleep with whenever things get slow. But things seem to be getting busy again, so I'll help you pack."

She went to the closet and tossed his carry-on bag on the bed. Then she went to her dresser, opened the first wide drawer, and took out a neat stack of his underwear, and then a double handful of rolled socks, and set them on the bed. "Good thing I washed your clothes today."

"Stop, Ruthie," said Julian. "I don't want to fight."

"Why not?" she said. "You seem to be great in a fight. Men come from God knows where just to tell me there's a war on so you have to go."

"Because I love you," he said. "We're finally together like we should have been all along."

She seemed to be paralyzed for a second, and then she stepped closer so he could put his arms around her. Then her arms came up and she hugged him harder and harder while she cried. "Come home. Then we'll fight."

In another minute they were out of the bedroom. He followed Harper and Waters to the front door. When they stepped out he stopped. He put the keys to his pickup truck on the table by the front door, and said, "Bye, Ruthie."

She whispered, "Bye."

He stepped out onto the porch and then down the steps after Harper and Waters.

A big black SUV pulled up at the curb. Harper opened the back hatch and Julian set his bag on top of the others already in the cargo space. The two men he didn't know waited until he was seated inside the SUV and then closed the doors and stepped back. Julian saw them turn and walk toward another black vehicle that had appeared a hundred feet away.

The SUV made a turn at the end of the block and headed out toward the Jonesboro Municipal Airport. Twenty minutes later, when the SUV pulled up in front of the terminal, Harper said something to the driver while Waters took his carry-on bag and went inside to get the tickets.

Julian and Harper got their bags out and went into the terminal. Waters came toward them holding three boarding passes, but he put them in his coat pocket instead of giving each man his own. Before the passes disappeared, Julian saw that the top one said Baltimore-Washington International.

The three men went through security and then walked to the far end of the concourse where only a few airport workers ever passed. They sat for a minute or two before Waters began. "Well, thanks for modifying your busy social schedule to join us, Julian. I figured you would man up and come along without a lot of coaxing."

Julian didn't say anything. He was staring down the concourse. In his imagination he was running along the shiny, highly polished floor. Far down the length of it he could see the escalator that descended to the main entrance. Now and then a person would come upstairs from the security barrier. In his imagination, Julian was swinging an elbow into Waters's face, feeling the snap of the small bones at the bridge of the nose. Then he was launching himself from the bolted-down row of seats like a runner at the starting blocks. He could be back at Ruthie's in fifteen minutes.

"Mr. Harper was not as sanguine about the chances, which is why we had those two extra personnel. There were also two more in the car behind. Mr. Harper does not like to have to persuade people of their duty." Waters paused. "Julian? You awake?"

Harper spoke. "He's just feeling sorry for himself. The summer's over, but the summer romance isn't, I guess."

"You think?" said Waters.

"You made the right decision, Julian," said Harper. "It's not even a decision at all."

"No?" said Julian.

"Not yours, anyway. This mission will get done. We will succeed, because no mission ends until it's a success."

"Why do they want me?"

"Probably nothing we can't do without you."

"Then why are you here?"

"Mr. Bailey, Mr. Prentiss, and Mr. Ross told us to."

Julian sat in silence.

Harper leaned closer. "When the mission is complete, you'll come back here to Jonesboro and she'll be waiting for you just the way you left her—freshly fucked."

Waters chuckled, but Harper had already taken out his phone and begun reading texts and e-mails to signify that he was no longer interested in the conversation.

An hour later their flight was announced, and they boarded. The airport was sparsely populated after ten on a weeknight. Most of the people Julian could see were making their way to the same flight they were taking to BWI.

Waters had given Julian a ticket for the window seat. He assumed that was because it put both Waters and Harper between him and any opportunity to cause trouble, but Julian didn't care. The moment had passed when he might have slipped away, and the impulse had passed with it. He was too angry to sleep this time, but he shut his eyes to keep from having to talk to Harper and Waters.

He opened them two hours later when the pressure in the cabin changed as the plane descended.

At Baltimore-Washington another pair of soldiers in civilian clothes waited at the bottom of the escalator. The two men identified themselves to Harper, escorted them to an SUV, and drove them to Fort Meade. Fort Meade was not only the home of three military intelligence units, but it was also the headquarters of the National Security Agency, so Julian was glad they were all driven in as a group. It made getting through the security at the gate quick. It was much easier to be one of five intelligence personnel arriving in a group than to be "a young black guy here at the gate, and he hasn't got a government ID."

The men parked the SUV in a lot beside a large barracks complex, and then escorted the others inside. Waters and Harper had apparently already been occupying rooms, and they disappeared into them. Then the men led Julian to his. He found that permanent party barracks had improved since his active duty years. They had been made less austere by the application of paint and the addition of better furnishings. One of the two soldiers gave him the key to his room and they both left.

At dawn there was a knock on the door. A soldier said, "Mr. Carson, your briefing is in one hour."

"Where?"

"I'll be back for you in fifty minutes."

Julian showered, shaved, and then waited. The soldier reappeared on time, and walked with him across a road and a parking lot, past a number of other buildings like his until they reached a redbrick office building. The soldier led him to an unmarked door on the fourth floor and knocked once, then opened the door. Julian thanked him and went inside.

"Good morning, Mr. Carson."

Julian saw the gray-haired older man he had met at the hotel in Chicago and the hangar in San Francisco. "I'm sure you remember us. I'm Mr. Ross, this is Mr. Bailey, and this is Mr. Prentiss."

"Yes," Julian said. He repeated the names to himself. He had memorized them when Harper had said them, but wondered which was which. Now, hearing the man say them, he could tell the names were false. It was always like that. Each bit of information was a reward for great effort, one ring closer to the center of the circle. But there never seemed to be a ring where the information was true. It was only truer than the information in the last ring.

For now, the man Julian thought of as the highest in rank was Mr. Ross. He looked at Julian, his cheekbones resting on both fists. "I think it's time we had a frank discussion, Mr. Carson."

"Yes, sir."

Julian noticed that in front of him on the table was a manila folder. He sensed that Mr. Ross had just closed it.

"You are a very impressive operator. You've worked in teams and alone. You've worked in South America, the Middle East, Africa, and at home. But now we're in the middle of an operation that you seem reluctant to complete. Why is that?"

"After San Francisco nobody said anything to me about the operation. I waited for more than two months to hear from intelligence. Nobody called. I assumed that if the operation wasn't over, I was no longer part of it."

"You went home to Arkansas, and I understand you made good use of your time off. You spent part of the time being with your family and helping out on the farm, and part of the time reconnecting with old friends. That about right?"

"Yes, sir."

"During your time away, we were following other avenues."

Julian said, "You were watching to see if the old man would get in touch with me again."

Mr. Ross's mouth turned up and he showed a perfect row of small porcelain-white teeth as he turned to Mr. Bailey and Mr. Prentiss with a look of triumph. "You see that, Mr. Carson? That's what I meant about you. We can train people for years and years, give them loads of time in the field. What we can't do is make them smart."

Julian felt the pride expand in his chest as he savored those words. He knew the words were calculated but he didn't find the strength to resist. He knew that acknowledging his abilities was a confidence trick, but he longed for it not to be.

"Do you know why you figured out what we were doing? Because it was just what you would have done in our place."

Julian was silent. He wasn't sure whether he wanted to admit that.

Mr. Ross said, "You look at guys like Harper and Waters. They each have at least ten years on you. Harper probably has fifteen. They're competent, loyal, and responsible, but they're pretty much all they're going to be. You're not. Whether you stay in military intelligence or go on to the CIA, you'll run into both of them again over the years somewhere. They'll still be perfectly okay, still doing the jobs they're in now. But you'll be something else—somebody else. You see?"

"I think so."

"I know you do. I've got my eye on you." He paused to impart significance to the next words. "And so do other people."

Julian longed to know which other people. Who? But as always nothing clear and specific was to be said aloud. To ask would be to disappoint, and would prove that you weren't ready after all.

Mr. Ross opened the manila file. Julian could see that his photograph was attached to the first page. Mr. Ross moved the page to the back of the file, and all Julian could see on the page below it was paragraph after paragraph of small unreadable print.

"You're wondering why we're here," Mr. Ross said. "As you know, Fort Meade is not only military intelligence. The biggest part of it is the National Security Agency."

He took the next sheet of paper out of the file and pointed at an address printed in a paragraph near the bottom. He held the paper out to Julian. "This is your contact at NSA. Our fugitive is still out there somewhere. This time you're going to have a whole lot of help finding him."

22

It was winter and Julian had been living in a barracks at Fort Meade since early fall. He had been home to Jonesboro only twice. The last time he was called back early to check out a theory that the old man was living in a safe house in Montreal that had been set up forty years ago but seldom used.

He couldn't blame the National Security Agency people for coming up with bizarre theories. They had all the data in the world. Sifting through it to find and connect the threads of a single story was the problem. There had to be something that explained how the old man could make himself so scarce, something like a safe house that old intelligence people had set up and forgotten. The only clear photographs of him had been taken when he was Julian's age. And every operator except Julian who had gotten a close look at the old man since Libya was dead.

Julian was sitting in the office he'd been assigned at military intelligence when his phone rang. He heard the voice of Goddard, his NSA contact. Goddard said, "I think you're going to want to come over here. We found him."

The call was so unexpected that Julian said, "Who?"

"Who else?"

Julian closed his office and hurried over to NSA. When Julian arrived at Goddard's office, he waited until Goddard had shut the door before he said, "Where is he?"

Goddard was a heavyset man with a dark beard and thinning hair. He leaned back in his desk chair with his hands behind his head, the chubby fingers laced. "He's living in a cabin up in the San Bernardino Mountains at Big Bear."

"How did you figure that out?" Julian was buying time, because he felt sick to his stomach.

"If you look at enough facts in enough different ways, you'll find things that stand out. And we have everything."

"I know," Julian said. "But this guy makes no phone calls, makes very few purchases that aren't cash, and barely shows his face."

"But that's now."

"Yes," said Julian. "That's now. We're looking for him now."

"It wasn't always now. He wasn't always running under such pressure. He used to make phone calls. He used to use credit cards, own a house, move money around in bank accounts, and so on."

"So what?"

"Nothing goes away. Every phone call he made five years ago, every purchase he made on a credit card or a debit card, it's all recorded and stored. Nobody looks at it until we have a reason to. We had the name Peter Caldwell, the name he used last year. And we had the name Daniel Chase, the man he was for at least twenty years before then."

"What led you to him?"

"It doesn't really matter which line of inquiry pays off first, because that's only a matter of chance. Eventually everything will work, because each thing you try eliminates people. If he only drinks single malt scotch and only uses horseradish mustard, we can eliminate hundreds of millions of people who don't like both of those things. If we notice somebody has an idiomatic pronunciation of a particular word, we can search our archive of phone calls for instances of that pronunciation of that word."

"But what was *his* mistake?"

"No mistake," said Goddard. "The method doesn't require a mistake. It just requires that one person be different from another. And we all are."

"I understand what you're saying," said Julian. "All I'm asking is which it was this time."

"When the old man gave the Treasury Department twenty million dollars, he was being smart by transferring the money from the accounts of the two aliases military intelligence already knew. He realized he had nothing to lose because the names were already blown. And he was too smart to have transferred or paid any of the money to his next alias. We also noticed that the accounts in the two names Daniel Chase and Peter Caldwell had never been mingled before. All very smart."

"But?"

"But the root accounts were started at about the same time, and built up in the same way, beginning with small cash deposits. Because he hadn't used either name since he made the Treasury payment, we concluded that he must have one more identity, probably begun about the same time as the others."

"And you found another account like the first two."

"Yes," said Goddard. "Here." He handed Julian a piece of paper with a name and address typed on it.

"Henry Dixon," said Julian.

"And Marcia Dixon," said Goddard. "Judging from their purchases, he and the woman from Chicago are still together."

"Thanks very much for your work."

"Don't mention it," said Goddard. "Now comes the caution. The reason we helped you is that we were told the old man is a traitor and a murderer—one of our own intelligence guys who's turned into a monster. In order to help, we ignored the rules. A lot of the methods we used are illegal."

"I won't compromise your methods," Julian said.

"I know you won't," said Goddard. "I didn't tell you enough for that."

Julian arrived at the condominium in Big Bear as a snowstorm was beginning. The flakes were big, and stuck to the windshield of his rental car, so he needed to use his wipers and headlights to find his way.

The condo had already been booked online, and the keys were waiting for him at the rental office. When the rental agent looked up from his desk and saw him, Julian saw the man's face lose its look of expectancy and go flat and expressionless. Julian ignored the man's involuntary reaction, signed the agreement, and took the keys. As Julian had driven into town he noticed that nearly all the faces were white.

Julian went to the condominium, unpacked, and prepared. He was aware that this moment was the peak of his career. This was his chance to become a success and an insider. But his mission was a mistake.

The old man was not what they said he was. He had seen covert aid money being diverted—and taken it back. He was not a traitor.

About twenty minutes after Julian arrived, the soldiers drove into town from Yuma Proving Ground in Arizona in a pair of black SUVs and an oversized pickup truck. They wore civilian clothes, but all of the clothes looked new, and the men were too well matched to be anything but some kind of team. The first man to the door was Staff Sergeant Axel Wright. He looked like a retired quarterback, tall and blond, with long arms and a thin, permanently sunburned face. When Julian came to the door, Wright introduced himself and said, "Mr. Carson, sir. Do we have your permission to bring in our equipment?"

"Of course. Come in."

Julian sat in the condominium's kitchen and watched the members of the squad spread around the living room, the stairway, and the dining room. They took their weapons out of their padded transport cases, assembled them, and loaded rounds into the detached magazines. Julian hadn't seen anything quite like this since Afghanistan.

They were a ten-man squad that included a medic, and Staff Sergeant Wright as team leader. One of the eight riflemen was a radio operator-maintainer. For this mission he was equipped with other devices besides a radiotelephone. He spent a few minutes plugging in a couple of olive drab army-issue laptops, hacking into the Wi-Fi network, changing the password, and adding his phone and some other equipment to the network. Then he went to work.

The radio operator began studying the screen of his laptop and relaying weather information to Staff Sergeant Wright while Wright looked out the window at the falling snow. The snow was steady, with big white flakes floating down past the window and already building a layer of white on the ground. The flood lamp mounted on the eaves of the building threw enough light to make the flakes fifty or sixty feet away glow against the dark sky, obscuring the view.

To Julian, Wright's confidence was a bad sign. The sergeant wasn't paying attention to what his men did, and that meant they had worked together for a while and Wright knew he didn't even have to look anymore. The old man up the mountain in the cabin might be clever, but in a confrontation he would have no hope against men like these.

After about five minutes Wright turned away from the window, and his men looked in his direction in silence. He said, "The snow is going to get heavier and the air colder, and it won't stop coming down until morning, guys. Pelham and Slavin, go get the pickup configured to plow. Kelly and Oldham, take one of the SUVs and find something heavy to weigh down the truck bed for traction—bags of gravel or sand, or whatever you find."

The four men put on their winter gear and went outside. Sergeant Wright went into the kitchen to the sink and drew a glass of water, and then sat at the table across from Julian. "Mr. Carson. You're sure you'll recognize him when you see him, right?"

"I've seen him three times," said Julian. "The first time he seemed to be a creaky old guy walking his dogs. The next time he suddenly turned up in the dark to show me he had his gun in my face, and the third time he was disguised to look like a crazy old homeless guy living on the street. He's well trained, and he hasn't forgotten any tricks."

"I understand that you want to take him alive. Is that right?"

Julian nodded. "Yes. And there are two of them. He has the woman, Zoe McDonald, with him. We'd like to take her alive too."

"Of course, if we can," said Wright. "Alive or dead, though, he's the priority. And he's a killer. You know what an armed assault on a building can be like."

"Yeah," said Julian. "I do. I'm wondering if this operation has changed since I was briefed. I wasn't expecting to conduct a heavily armed frontal assault."

"When I was briefed they said he had killed some foreign agents who had tried to take him quietly a couple of times in different cities. So military intel cranked up the heat."

"If we get the two of them alive, what do your orders say happens next?" said Julian.

"Then we get to go back to Yuma, where it's warm, and you go on to your next assignment," said Wright.

"We have to turn them over to somebody first," said Julian. "Whom did they tell you we give them to?"

"After we get them, we'll report and get our orders at that time."

Julian nodded as he studied Wright. Military intelligence must have uncharacteristically realized that Libyan agents weren't going to do anything up here in the dead of winter but get themselves killed. So they had sent a force equipped for war. He understood.

Maximum force meant less likelihood of casualties. And Julian knew that if he went through the soldiers' equipment, he would find body bags. He doubted that he would find handcuffs or restraints for moving prisoners.

Big Bear was crowded in the winter. When it snowed, Snow Summit and Bear Mountain filled up with people from Los Angeles. Right after the Thursday night weather report they began to call for reservations. Skiers and snowboarders came up in long convoys, pulled into parking spaces at the lodges, resorts, and condos, and began to fill every room. Houses that Hank and Marcia Dixon had never seen occupied suddenly had five or six cars parked in front of them and lights in every window. High trails the Dixons had hiked in the fall were passable only on snowshoes now, but nearly every morning they would see people struggling in deep drifts.

As soon as the first snowfall, Hank talked Marcia into going cross-country skiing with him. Hank had taken Emily and Anna every winter in Vermont until Emily was through college and had begun medical school, and he had continued after they were both gone. The attraction now was that Hank and Marcia could ski miles from the village, where the visiting flatlanders seldom ventured and there were no trails.

Nearly everything Hank did was intended to contribute to their security. Buying Marcia a diamond engagement ring and a wedding band seemed likely to make the Dixons look more like who they pretended to be, and therefore safer. Buying a long-range rifle in .338 Lapua and a good scope would allow Hank to take a position in an upper window of the cabin and shoot an attacker from a thousand yards. But if he and Marcia were a thousand yards from the nearest enemy, it would be far wiser to run. He bought the rings but didn't buy the rifle.

To Hank, the hours of darkness were the most dangerous. Each time an assassin had been sent for him, the killer had arrived late at night, so in Big Bear Hank Dixon slept lightly. Nights made him miss his dogs more than ever. Whenever he heard a sound outside he would get out of bed and quietly slip out of the bedroom. Then he would walk to the window and look out on the snow-drifted hillside that led down into the sleeping town.

He would look for a vehicle parked along the narrow winding road, or maybe moving toward the cabin from below. Then he would go across the hall to the guest room with the best view of the hill and look up toward the crest. He knew that a sniper would prefer to fire into the window from above, where he would have a good view of the rooms and a superior firing position. When Hank felt particularly uneasy, he would use the night-vision binoculars to search the forest trails. Then he would pad back into the bedroom and slide under the covers into the space where Marcia's body kept the bed warm. He would remind himself that there had been no car, there had been no men, and in time he would sleep.

The morning after the big snowstorm, the air was cold but the sun was bright, obscured only for seconds at a time by passing clouds blown by winds at high altitudes. Whenever the sun broke through the clouds, the glare of the snow brightened enough to hurt the eye.

Hank stood in the living room and saw an oversized black pickup truck with a snowplow blade mounted on the front. The truck had big tires with chains, and what looked like sandbags piled in the bed.

He watched the truck move up the right side of the road, its plow shouldering the snow to the edge of the pavement in a long, serpentine ridge. When the truck came to a cabin's driveway it swept the snow across the front, blocking it. The truck wasn't a municipal vehicle.

It had been snowing at Big Bear since the end of October, and he'd never seen this black truck come up the road before. He supposed that the owners of the other cabins in this section might have hired a local entrepreneur to plow their road and driveways to open them after the storm.

Hank went away from the window to get a cup of coffee. As he poured it in a mug, he considered it likely that one of the owners had hired the plow. But he decided to keep an eye on the truck. He had learned over the years that things that didn't seem right often weren't. He could hear Marcia playing a few bars from the Chopin sonata she had been learning. She stopped, then played the same passage again.

He returned to the front window and saw the truck moving on the far side of the road, heading downward again, leaving the same winding ridge of snow all the way along. The driver never stopped to clear any of the driveways. Odd. Hank sipped his coffee and looked out at the roads below in the village while he listened to Marcia play. There were few cars out after the big snowfall. He stood for a few minutes, set his coffee on the table, and went out to the mudroom. He put on his quilted jacket, found his gloves in the pockets and his knitted cap in a sleeve. He picked up his sunglasses and opened the door to grasp the shovel and bring it inside.

He stood in the entrance to the living room and held up the shovel so Marcia would look up from the piano to see.

She stopped playing.

"I'm just going to dig us out," he said. "I'll be back soon."

"My hero," she said, and went back to playing.

He went out and began to shovel. He had picked out the shovel himself, and he respected it. It was a black steel scoop shovel on a thick ash shaft, which he thought of as a coal shovel. It was heavier than a flat snow shovel and nearly as broad, but it didn't bend and would slice under ice instead of bouncing over it.

As he worked, his breaths were thick white puffs in the crisp air. He cleared the barrier of snow at the bottom of the driveway and looked down on the village and the lake. He was concentrating on the shoveling, but part of his mind was still thinking about the truck. The only two cabins beyond theirs on this road were unoccupied. He hadn't seen anybody, or even a parked car, in a month or more. He decided to watch for cars coming up the road toward the other cabins. Maybe one of the neighbors had seen the weather reports and had the plow come because he was on his way up here to ski the fresh snow.

Julian Carson walked quickly through the pinewoods above the three cabins that sat along the newly plowed road near the top of the mountain. He saw the target Henry Dixon standing on the driveway in front of the big cabin with a shovel. Julian recognized him immediately. Some part of Julian's mind had kept alive the hope that Goddard had made a mistake, but it was the same man. Dixon looked as though he was clearing the way to drive the car out. Julian couldn't let him do that. Julian sped up, walking only under the pine trees above the deep snowdrifts. He couldn't afford to make noise or leave clear tracks, so he stayed in the woods. The pine branches formed such a thick thatch of needles under the trunks the forest ground was only dusted with thin powdery snow that would be difficult to read for tracks.

He came to a fallen pine tree and walked atop the trunk, moving quickly but keeping his balance, until he could step off into the path already pressed into the snow. The path led him to the back porch, a concrete block with three steps leading up to it. He went low and peered in the window. He could see the kitchen was empty. He knelt on the porch, took off his gloves, and reached into his pocket for his pick and tension wrench, then went to work on the bolt. The hardware on the door was practically new and very sturdy, and had a wide steel overlap to prevent anyone fitting a knife or screwdriver into the crack to jimmy the lock. Everything about the mechanism was big and thick, but the size of the keyway made the lock easier to pick. He lined up the pins quickly and opened the door. He heard classical music. A piano.

He moved swiftly through the kitchen into the living room, using the music to cover the sounds his feet made on the floor. There was the woman he had seen the old man carrying out of the apartment in Chicago. He came up behind her. He put his forearm around her neck and stifled her first jerk of surprise, holding her tightly as he said softly, "Stay still, Zoe. Stay quiet."

Hank finished clearing the mound of snow off the edge of the driveway and started toward the house. As he stopped at the side door and set the shovel against the wall, he took another look. The truck was gone. The town still looked deserted. He opened the door and noticed the piano had stopped.

Marcia was standing in the entrance to the living room. Her face was pale and her expression frightened. A hand pushed her aside, and Hank could see that the figure that stepped away from the wall behind her was James Harriman, the young special ops man.

Marcia said, "I'm so sorry. I never saw. I never heard—"

"It's all right," Hank said. His arms began to float away from his sides. "Where are the others, Mr. Harriman? Or are you going to do it?"

Julian said, "I sneaked up here to warn you, and there's not much time."

"Then warn me."

"NSA found you. They store more information than they did in your time. They ran some instant searches, looking for anything that makes you different. Two days ago they figured out you were Henry Dixon, and you were here. Now there's a rifle squad in the village suiting up."

"Why are you warning me?"

"Because you lived up to the deal. You told the truth."

"That's it? I'm not a murderer or a thief?" said Hank.

Julian looked at him in surprise. "Well, yeah."

"Neither is the average person. Would you risk your life for him?"

"I have. And so have you." Harriman glanced toward the front window, an involuntary reflex. "We've all got to get out of here. They plowed the road so—"

"I know. So they could drive up here in cars to take us fast and get out. How soon?"

"A few minutes. No more than a half hour. Don't try to take your car. They'll be blocking the road."

Hank said, "Thanks, Mr. Harriman."

"You're welcome. I hope you make it." Julian went to the back door of the cabin and stopped. "I didn't tell you this so you could kill a couple of our own guys."

"Of course you didn't," said Hank. "I don't want that either. I just want to stay alive."

James Harriman turned away, stepped down into the path of footprints, and then along the fallen pine log into the woods.

Hank closed and locked the door and turned to Marcia.

She said, "I'm so sorry, Hank. I was playing, so I didn't hear him."

"You wouldn't have anyway. This is what he's trained to do. Now it's time to get out."

While she put on her warm jacket, hat, boots, and gloves, Hank ran to the coat closet and took the two backpacks that contained their bugout kits. He collected their cross-country skis and poles and bundled them tightly with bungee cords in the middle and both ends. He put their ski boots in the backpacks. Then they went to the back door and sat on the steps to put on their snowshoes.

Hank said, "Here. Put them on like this. Use the strap to go across the instep here."

"That's backward."

"That's right." He stood up and walked a little. He left tracks that looked as though he were going in the opposite direction. He stepped on the tracks that James Harriman had made, making them unreadable. After a few seconds, Marcia was up with her snowshoes on backward too.

Hank led the way. He started up the hillside carrying their cross-country skis and poles. He set a strong pace, heading up the mountain at an angle into the pine forest above the cabin. Their tracks were not possible to hide, but these tracks looked as though they marked someone's approach to the cabin.

When he was just below the summit of the hill he could hear Marcia's breaths coming in windy gasps. He stopped and they sat in the snow to let her catch her breath.

Finally he said, "If this turns out to be the end, you'll have to split off and go your own way. You're still a kidnapping victim, and you can get out of this."

She looked terrified, but said, "I want to stay with you."

"That's not smart," he said.

"I made my own stupid decision for my own reasons, and it's not going to change. Let's get up and get moving." She stood and began stepping up the hill at an angle to keep the snowshoes from tilting to the side and slipping.

Hank overtook her and kept climbing until they reached the ridge. They looked down at Big Bear Lake and the road leading up to their rented cabin. Hank pointed. Two black SUVs were stopped at the foot of the hill, preparing to make their way up the road.

Hank sat down and said, "It's time to get our ski boots on."

They set their ski boots on the snow in front of them, took off their snow boots, brushed off the snow, and stowed them in their packs. They put on the ski boots, and then Hank used two of the bungee cords to hang the snowshoes from their backpacks. They used their poles to steady themselves and stepped over the summit. He pointed with one of his poles.

"Look over that way. I want to head eastward along the high ridge as far as we can go. Follow me."

* * *

A few minutes later, the snowplow truck with its plow raised to shield the truck from gunfire sped up the road to the mountain cabin with the two SUVs directly behind it. The vehicles stopped in front of the cabin and Julian and the rifle squad poured out and entered the cabin from both doors at once. They found the cabin empty. There were two half-filled coffee cups that still felt warm, a refrigerator full of fresh food, and a bed upstairs that had been slept in and remade. But the two occupants were gone.

Sergeant Wright sent out four men as scouts to find tracks and follow them while the other men established a working headquarters in the cabin and began to search for any indication of which direction the pair had taken. In an hour, the two men who had gone up the mountain to search for tracks reported by radio that the snowshoe impressions leading down to the cabin were backward. The subjects had gone up wearing their snowshoes reversed.

Sergeant Wright ordered the two scouts to keep following the backward tracks through the snow, and sent four others down to the village to rent snowmobiles. He told his radio operator to man a communication post in the cabin with two searchers, maintain radio contact with all parties, and keep track of their GPS positions.

While all the other men were occupied, Julian loitered by the side of the pickup truck with the plow on the front. He leaned against the truck and let his bare hand hang above the truck bed, where eight sand bags had been piled. He could see that one of the bags had leaked a thin stream of sand onto the shiny black surface. He casually brushed off some of the sand, but kept some of it in his hand. As he walked away, he put his hand into his pocket and deposited the sand there.

The SUV returned from a sport rental store in town, but only the driver was in it. The other three men came up the hill a hundred yards behind it on three snowmobiles. Wright told two of the men on snowmobiles he wanted them to head up the mountain, following the snowshoe trail, and rendezvous with the two scouts on foot. Wright and Julian would follow on the third snowmobile. As the first two headed upward Julian noticed that they towed short plastic sleds, the sort that were used for towing game home from a hunting trip. Julian didn't have to strain his imagination to know what those were for.

Within a few minutes the three snowmobiles had reached the spot where the scouts were waiting. At this point the backward snowshoe tracks ended, and ski tracks appeared. The tracks were long and thin, with the marks of ski poles at intervals, the tracks of cross-country skis.

The two scouts climbed on the backs of the two snowmobiles towing sleds. Now their party consisted of Wright and Julian on one snowmobile, and two men on each of the others—six fully armed men on three machines.

The three snowmobiles moved forward, following the ski tracks into the mountains. They were able to go fast over the open stretches, eating up ski tracks in a few minutes that must have taken a half hour to make.

Hank skied through a wooded area. The snow was untouched and drifted. He could see the distance between the tall trees was wide enough so they could maintain good speed. In the fall he had chosen skis that were a size short for both of them. The slightly shorter skis were easier to control and to keep on the path, but they were a bit slower than longer ones would have been on the straight, open inclines.

Hank knew that the backward snowshoe trail would not fool an army rifle team for long, and they would soon pick up the ski trail. He headed into a denser part of the forest, where branches brushed his shoulders as he passed. Top speed for a cross-country skier at his level was probably fifteen miles an hour on flat ground. Through the woods he judged they were traveling about ten.

He had seen that there were tree wells, areas around the bases of big trees where the snow cover was too sparse to ski on, so he stayed away from them. He knew that he and Marcia could go much faster on a downslope, but that the trees at lower altitudes would be closer together. He tried to navigate and keep them at the right level.

They had gone a few miles in silence except for their heavy breathing and the scrape of their skis over the snow, when Hank's ears began to pick up another sound. At first it was a buzz, like the noise of distant chain saws. Hank tried to tell whether it was somebody cutting wood or something else. As they went on, the noise didn't fade. Instead it grew louder and deeper. He stopped and let Marcia catch up.

"What is that?" she said.

"It sounds like snowmobiles," he said. "We can't outrun snow-mobiles, but we can try to go places where they have to slow down." He pushed off and led them downward into thicker woods, where the lowest branches of some of the trees nearly swept the ground and others intertwined at shoulder level. Hank had driven snow-mobiles in Vermont and New Hampshire, and now he looked for places that would slow the vehicles down.

Always he looked for spots where he could set up an obstacle. At one stretch where the spaces between trees had been wide for a time, he found a slope that led down into a narrow space between trees. He stopped, took out his pocketknife, and cut a small slice in the lining of his jacket. He unraveled a length of loose nylon stitching, stretched it from one tree, across the path, around the opposite tree, and then bent a flexible pine branch as far back as he could, and held it there against the tree trunk with a forked stick. He tied the nylon line to the forked stick, so if the line was hit by a snowmobile, the forked stick would be tugged away and the pine branch would whip forward toward the head of a snowmobile driver.

From time to time when he saw the opportunity he would pick up a long, straight pine branch, strip it of twigs, and stab it into the snow between two trees where they had just passed, so it looked like a spear set there to impale a snowmobile. What he hoped it would do was slip under the snowmobile and strip it off its track like a tank trap, or at least jam the track for a few minutes.

Twice he found a rock in the space between two trees, and widened his stance slightly so one ski would pass on each side of it. Then he would shake a bit of snow off the branches above to cover the rock.

He led Marcia on, deeper in the woods and lower in altitude. After another half hour they came to a rocky canyon where they put on their hiking boots and carried their skis.

In the middle of the canyon, where the brush was thickest, Hank stopped and opened his backpack. He pulled out a shiny metal rectangle with smooth sides and a couple of vents on the removable top. He opened the top, took out a lighter, and lit the wick at the top, waited for a moment, and then restored the top.

"What are you doing?" Marcia asked.

"This is the best hiding place we've passed. This is a hand warmer. It burns lighter fluid, and lasts for hours." He set the device down, propped between two rocks in a sheltered spot.

"What's it for?"

"This is an army rifle squad. If they have infrared scopes, they'll pick up the heat."

When they had made it across and climbed up the other side they put on their skis and resumed their skiing to the east. The sound of the snowmobiles had faded and became inaudible. Hank said, "I don't hear them anymore. Maybe one of the traps worked."

This time their course was on an open plateau with a gradual eastward slope. Their most difficult task was to keep from accelerating to a dangerous, uncontrollable speed. Crashing into a tree could be fatal, and injuring a leg at this distance from a town would mean freezing to death. He hoped Zoe could stay upright in the center of the open slope. Then he thought he heard the sound of a snowmobile again.

23

As the three snowmobiles followed the ski tracks through the woods, Julian could see that the old man had left tracks in the narrowest openings between trees. Julian suspected that the old man had faked some of the tracks to lure a snowmobile into a space where it would get stuck. He said nothing about it, but waited.

In one of these passages the lead snowmobile driver got too eager. He drove too fast, scraped a pine tree on his right, caromed to the left, and hit a tree. The front cowling of the snowmobile was dented but, worse, the left ski at its front now pointed inward. The snowmobile became difficult to steer, and the driver had to keep wrenching it to the side to go straight. He stopped.

The other snowmobiles pulled to a stop around him at the side of the forest trail. Julian got off his snowmobile and went to take a look. While the driver and his passenger examined the ski, Julian looked at the dented hood. He opened it and examined the engine while he pushed out the dent. He pretended to finish the dent removal while he used his left hand to spin the wing nut to lift the air filter. He pushed on the butterfly valve of the carburetor and dropped in some of the sand he'd brought. Then he replaced the air filter, closed the hood, and stepped away. His sabotage had taken no more than five seconds.

Sergeant Wright called the radio operator at the cabin. He told him to look online for instructions for fixing this model snowmobile. They waited for about ten minutes before the radio operator called back with the instructions.

Julian heard the radio operator's voice say, "Loosen all steering tie-rod jam nuts."

One of the soldiers said into the radio, "Confirm locations of steering tie-rod jam nuts."

Wright and the driver of the other remaining snowmobile restarted their machines and resumed their speed, following the trail of the cross-country skis.

Going through the pine forests was slow and dangerous because the paths were narrow. A person on cross-country skis could glide through a two-foot gap, but a snowmobile could not. Even a three-foot space made a narrow passage, and if the ground under the snow wasn't level, the vehicle could slide sideways into a tree, just as the first one had.

A couple of times the forested areas became so thick that Wright began to suspect, as Julian had, that the tracks leading into them might have been faked to get the snowmobiles trapped. At the next forested area Wright ordered the other working snowmobile to race ahead around the woods on open ground. But the men on the other snowmobile were unable to find the place where the ski tracks emerged into the open, and had to return to the spot where they had left the woods and inch onward with Wright and Julian.

Then the other snowmobile driver saw ski tracks reappear a hundred feet ahead, turned aside, and sped up to take a shortcut. He reached a place where he had to go through a narrow space between two trees. There was a shout, the bottom of the snowmobile scraped some hard object, and then bounced over it and stopped.

Wright and Julian pulled up beside the snowmobile as the two men got off to investigate. Wright dismounted and looked at the spot. "It's a rock, Slavin. You hit a rock. Is that thing still okay?"

"I don't know." The driver restarted it, and it seemed fine. He moved the snowmobile forward a bit.

Both snowmobiles went forward very slowly, and Julian called to the driver of the other snowmobile: "Does that engine sound funny to you?" The driver stopped again and dismounted. Julian stepped closer and opened the hood. He looked closely at the exhaust assembly that ran from the engine toward the exhaust pipe. "The exhaust is too hot to touch," he said. "But it seems to have a good connection." Then he took off his gloves and ducked down to examine the engine.

Beside the exhaust duct was the chain case. He felt under it and found a plug like the ones under a car's oil pan. He opened it until he felt chain lubricant leaking, and then closed it just enough for the threads to catch. Then he closed the hood and knelt to look under the aft part of the snowmobile. "I don't see anything wrong," he said. "Maybe there's just a little rattle from the bump." He closed the hood and got on the other snowmobile behind Wright.

They restarted their engines and resumed their search. Then the radio operator called Wright, and they stopped again. He said that the snowmobile with the damaged ski was repaired and realigned, but now the engine was malfunctioning. The engine would start, but then it would cough and sputter and stall. They had better assume it wouldn't be fixed in time to be of use. Wright ordered the driver and his companion to try to drag the malfunctioning snowmobile to a place where they could load it onto the pickup truck.

Julian's hope grew as the two remaining snowmobiles inched along the trail through the forest, sometimes hooking around the narrowest spaces and then finding no way to rejoin the trail. Sometimes they would begin to speed up, but then bounce over roots or rocks that made it too dangerous to continue in a straight line, so they moved in arcs in and out of the forest, taking up more time.

Wright drove to a stop and turned off his snowmobile. He said to Julian: "That rock was a trap. The ski tracks went right by on either side of it. That old man didn't learn to move through snow in Libya. Has he ever served in country like this—maybe with the Tenth Mountain Division?"

"He lived in Vermont for a long time," said Julian. "Maybe that's where he got good at this stuff. I haven't seen his military records."

"You chased him for a year without ever seeing his records?"

"I don't even know his name," said Julian. "This mission is about as secret as it can be."

Wright stepped a few feet away, unzipped his snow pants, and urinated near the trees. He said, "Just a day ago we were in Yuma receiving a briefing. We were to hunt down a military traitor in California who had committed several murders. We were ordered to do it using plain unmarked gear with zero help from any civilian authority, and no contact with local police. We were told we'd be meeting a man from army intelligence who would be our source of information."

"I guess they meant me."

"But you don't have much information, do you?"

"Not much. I don't think they want either of us to know much more than we do. I can recognize him if I see him."

"That'll have to be good enough." Wright zipped up and walked back to the snowmobile. There was a radio call from the other snowmobile. Wright said, "We'll be right there." They climbed back on their snowmobile and made their way to the spot ahead where the other two men had stopped.

The snowmobile driver had come through too fast, with his eyes on the ski tracks. A limb bent back and rigged as a trap to swing into the opening between two trees had hit him across the forehead. The two men were examining the limb that had hit him. Wright looked at Julian. "What do you think, Mr. Carson?"

Julian saw the chance to introduce doubt and uneasiness. "That's the kind of thing he'd do. I don't know the details of his record, but in his day just about all the combat was in jungles. They used snares and bungee stakes and tiger pits."

"He could have killed me," said the injured man.

"He could have, but he decided not to," said Julian. "The way they did it was to add a sharpened ten-inch stick at a right angle to the branch so when it hit you it would kill you. It's a warning. We may not see the next one either, and that one could be placed so it'll break a neck or spear one of us. He knows how to do it."

Wright leaned closer and spoke so only Julian could hear. "I do not relish having any of my squad killed out here in the woods by some crazy traitor."

"I don't want that to happen either," said Julian. He was secretly rejoicing. The old man had given Julian another opportunity to slow the team down and make them cautious.

Wright had a solution. "All right. The tracks are still headed due east. We'll get out of the woods, go east in the open, and try to pick up their tracks again. Keep up, and don't slow down. We don't want to give him an easy shot."

The two men mounted the other snowmobile, and the driver started it. The engine whirred, caught, and roared to life, but then there was a horrible noise. There was smoke coming out of the air intakes on the hood and out of the exhaust, and the engine stopped. Julian knew that the plug at the bottom of the chain case had finally vibrated enough to fall off and the chain oil had leaked out. The chain had heated up and failed.

The driver opened the hood, stared uncomprehendingly at the smoke, fanned it out of his face, and then reached for the chain case and recoiled from the heat.

Julian stayed where he was, but put his hand on the pistol in his pocket. "Wow. I thought that engine sounded funny."

Wright looked at the engine and nodded. "Yeah, you did." He turned to his two men and said, "Damn. Where the fuck did you guys rent these snowmobiles? They're absolute crap."

Wright got back onto his snowmobile. "Okay. Take the cargo sled off that piece of junk and hitch it to the back of this one. Do a good job, because there's nowhere else for you to ride."

The two soldiers attached the flat sled and then sat on it. The front man held on to the towrope and the other held on to him. Wright moved slowly at first, out onto the open snow. He tentatively added speed, but when he reached about fifteen miles an hour, one of the men called out: "Sergeant Wright!"

Wright looked back and saw they were getting bounced around too much to hold on any longer. He slowed down drastically.

Then they moved east along the edge of the forest. Julian clung to the snowmobile seat behind Wright. They went along for some time, trying to avoid rough spots and irregularities in the terrain. They came to a spot where the wind had blown away a layer of snow to reveal a double layer of cut pine branches laid crosswise in a grid. Wright got off the snowmobile and kicked aside the pine branches. Below them was a three-foot-deep, rock-lined natural depression that looked like part of a frozen streambed. Wright said, "That man is starting to get on my nerves."

Now the sun was low behind them. At the next spot where they were shielded a bit from view, Wright stopped again. He said, "We've run out of ski tracks. I think that means we're ahead of them. Night comes early in the mountains. The old man and his girlfriend won't be able to ski through these woods in the dark. They'll be out in the open on the slopes. And they'll be tired as hell. I want to stay ahead and find a place to wait for them."

For the last of the sunlight and into the early darkness the one remaining snowmobile limped along, carrying Wright and Julian, and towing the two men in the sled. And then they reached a sight Julian had not expected. They came over a rise and saw lights. Below them was a highway, and on it were a seemingly endless stream of white headlights snaking up into the mountains and down to the flatland below.

Wright gathered his men. "All right, guys. We'll park the snow-mobile in the woods over there." He pointed to the left. "We'll watch for our two fugitives." The men got off the sled and moved on foot into the thick woods while Wright drove the snowmobile in after them.

When everything was quiet again, Wright took out his radio and called his radio operator at the cabin. "Group leader to base. We've reached a major road here. It's got to be Route 38. Get a call into HQ. Request a chopper with an infrared scope be sent to our location to sweep the area behind us and beyond the road to the east. Advise when you have an answer."

Wright turned to Julian. "If they have body heat the chopper will see them. If they don't have body heat they're dead. That would be good enough for me."

The sun had set, and the Dixons needed to get as far as they could before the light was totally gone. Hank kept them moving along at a speed that felt as though it must be their maximum.

As the light disappeared behind them and the shadows on the snow ahead blended into the general haze of blowing snow, they heard another engine sound. Still very far away, it was louder and deeper than a snowmobile. Hank knew exactly what it was. He made a gradual turn toward the woods to his right. He kept going until he was at least two hundred feet in, and under thick branches.

Marcia, following in his tracks, caught up and stood there beside him. "What can we do?"

"Wait and see what the chopper does. Stay in the thick part and don't move. If they have infrared scopes, all we can do is dig into deep snowdrifts, cover ourselves completely, and hope they move on."

Julian saw Sergeant Wright's call for air support for what it was, a fighter making his last big swing a powerful one, knowing that if it didn't connect he was finished. The men were cold, tired, and frustrated. They were sheltering among the trees, saying very little.

The helicopter appeared from the east a short time later, moving fast at a high altitude, and then descended and began to make its sweep of the area beyond Route 38. It looked to Julian as though the land on that side was rougher, and the hills steeper.

Julian spoke even less than the other men. He volunteered no opinions, which seemed to him like offering medical advice in a morgue. He followed Sergeant Wright's strategy and stayed in the cover of the trees to stare over the snow-covered expanse to the west to discern the approach of the two skiers. He was not subject to Wright's command, but it was the least he could do at this moment, and he hoped it would help direct suspicion away from him. The cover of the woods kept the cold west winds from punishing him the way they had in the open, and the rest was welcome.

When the helicopter was gone, the world was silent again except for the constant radio chatter between Sergeant Wright and his radio operator back in the Dixons' cabin. The men listened to the conversation, which was a series of reports that the helicopter had found nothing up to some set of coordinates, and then, minutes later, nothing up to the next set.

Suddenly, the helicopter reported a heat signature in a valley some distance to the west. Wright grinned. "There you go, guys. They've got something."

There was a pause in the transmissions for several minutes. The helicopter was landing to send two men to get a better look. After a few tense minutes the pilot radioed back, "The heat signature was from a pocket warmer."

"Say again," said Wright.

"The heat source was not a human being. It was a pocket device that burns lighter fluid. It's for staying warm in cold weather."

"Roger," said Wright.

He stomped around in the snow for a few seconds. "That's perfect. The son of a bitch figured we'd use infrared scopes to find him."

Ten minutes later, the helicopter pilot reported that his aircraft had been recalled to its base. As it came over their position, the helicopter hovered for a moment, circled once, and then kept going to the east.

Wright said, "All right. That's it, gentlemen. Get on the sled. We're going to head back. We're going to take the open spaces this time and skirt the woods. If you see anything, sing out. There aren't going to be any innocent bystanders out in these mountains tonight."

24

A few hundred yards away, Hank Dixon crouched in the woods and watched the helicopter reappear from the west, complete a circle over a stand of trees, and hover over a spot near where it had first appeared. Why would a search helicopter fly over the same spot twice? He guessed that the pilot must be flying over the rifle squad, a kind of informal good-bye as it flew back to the east.

He said, "Okay. Time to get out of here. We'll go this way."

"Ready," said Marcia. She pushed off with her ski poles and followed Hank. "Where are we going?"

"Away from the people who are chasing us. I think they must be waiting for us back there, where the chopper was just now." He skied to the south for a mile or more, and then resumed his progress toward the east.

They came to a hill, glided partway up, and then walked on, pointing their skis to the side, leaving a herringbone pattern in the snow. When they reached the top they looked at the drop on the other side. There was a long line of automobile headlights creeping along a road like a glowing river. Hank stopped and Marcia pulled up beside him. "Cars!" she said.

Hank said, "We've made it to Route 38."

Hank led the way, skiing cautiously down at an angle, slowing their progress as they moved toward the road.

Marcia was laughing. "I can't believe it. I thought we were lost in the wilderness. I thought they'd catch us. Then I thought we'd freeze to death tonight."

"We still might," he said. "Let's get our ski gear packed away and get down to the road."

They stowed the ski boots in their backpacks and put on their snow boots. Hank rebundled the skis and poles and carried them on his back. They reached the shoulder of the road after a few minutes of walking.

Hank stood at the side of the road, stretched out his arm, raised his thumb, and leaned just far enough into the road to be in the glare of the oncoming headlights. Several cars went by, but the drivers ignored him. The next three seemed to speed up at the sight of him.

He stepped out of the glare and put his hands on Marcia's shoulders. "You give it a try."

One more car passed, but the driver of the next SUV switched on his turn signal and coasted to a stop. They could see through the rear window that there were two heads in the front. Two men in their twenties jumped down from the big SUV.

The driver called, "Are you okay?"

Hank said, "We weren't quite sure. We got turned around on a cross-country trail. We were lucky to find the road."

"Where's your car?" the other man said.

"We got a ride up to Big Bear with some friends. Now I'm afraid we both have a touch of hypothermia. Where are you headed?"

"Down to San Bernardino," the driver said. His eyes were on Marcia every time he spoke. "If you want to come too, we'll take you."

"Thanks so much," Marcia said. "We're really cold and tired."

The two young men took the skis and poles from Hank and slid them under the tie-down straps over the ski rack on the roof, then pulled the straps tight. Then they climbed into the front seats.

Hank swung the back door open so Marcia could slide in on the backseat. She leaned forward to shrug off her backpack. Hank saw the driver's eyes in the rearview mirror. He saw them focus on him, and then saw the driver's right shoulder dip downward. He seemed to be reaching for the shifter.

As the car lurched forward, Hank pushed off with his legs to launch himself toward the seat. He grasped the back of the front passenger seat with his right hand, and strained to drag himself aboard the accelerating vehicle. Marcia shrieked, "Hold it! He's not in!" She clutched one of Hank's backpack straps, and set her feet against the doorframe.

Hank hoisted himself in as the car accelerated and the door slammed.

He saw the driver's eyes meet his in the mirror. "Oh, I'm sorry," the driver said. "I thought you were already in."

"That's okay," said Hank. "I'm in now." He settled into his seat and swung the backpack into his lap. His hand slipped inside the backpack pocket and grasped the Colt Commander pistol.

The car moved along Route 38, hugging the curves as it went, the grade adding to its speed.

"You know," the driver said to Hank, "I didn't really notice you at first. What I saw was a pretty woman along the road."

"That's all?" said Hank.

"Yep," the driver said. "I was moving fast, it was dark, and there was a lot of glare from headlights. So I stopped."

The driver was a big guy. Those were the words Hank knew the driver would have used. He was a big guy. He was about six feet three, and he weighed about 250 or 260. He had a round head with a cap of very curly brown hair. The baby face—with fat cheeks and a rosy complexion—must have caused him some embarrassment, and certainly so did the fact that his muscles were obscured by a layer of fat. He went on. "What I saw was your lady friend back there. She's hot."

"Derrick," said his friend. "Let's talk about something else."

"What for?" said Derrick. "We're all friends here. Bros. We're giving them a free ride in a remote area of the mountains. She is hot. Isn't she?"

Nobody answered.

Derrick waited. "Isn't she?"

"Yes," said his friend. "She's hot. Can you please just keep an eye on the road?"

"I wasn't asking you," Derrick said. "I was asking *him*."

"Me?" said Hank.

"Yeah, you."

"Then yes," he said. "She's my wife."

"Your wife?" Derrick said. "You and her? You must be really rich."

"Jesus, Derrick," said his friend.

"Jesus, Kyle," said Derrick.

Kyle's voice was tense now, high and whiny. "Just cut it out."

"We're just talking to pass the time. It's a long, long way down that dark, freezing road before we get to San Bernardino, and talking helps keep me awake. My bro back there probably goes to sleep early every night, given his age, so I'm helping him out too."

"Stop it," Kyle said. "This isn't funny."

Derrick persisted. "So bro. I know this doesn't bother you because you're a good sport. Is your wife a good sport too?"

"Not particularly," Marcia answered.

"That's okay," Derrick said. "I don't blame you for feeling that way. You're married to an older man. He can't possibly keep you happy. Not by himself, anyway."

Hank said, "Your friend Kyle is right. This stuff isn't funny, and it's offensive. So stop."

Derrick shrugged and laughed. He drove on in silence for the next half hour. From time to time he would look to his right at Kyle. Then Derrick's eyes would flick up to the rearview mirror, verify that Hank was still watching him, and then settle on the road ahead.

They continued down the dark highway. There was steady traffic going down out of the mountains at this hour, but fewer cars coming up. It was mildly reassuring to Hank, because if Derrick abruptly became unable to control the car, they would be less likely to have a head-on crash. Each minute was taking them another mile away from the squad that was hunting for them and closer to a warm, safe place somewhere. He dreaded what might happen soon, hoping to put it off as long as he could.

"I should apologize," said Derrick. "I didn't mean to offend anybody."

"Fine," said Hank.

"I was just trying to be friendly. I've heard that a lot of guys your age have trouble, you know, performing. That's the term. And the little woman cries herself to sleep every night. A lot of them would love to be with a younger guy. Or even two of them."

"Please stop this," said Marcia.

"Are you sure, though?" said Derrick. "There are three of us and only one of you. Maybe your husband would like to watch you get really satisfied."

"No."

"Well, keep it in mind while we drive. There's plenty of time to think. It's a long way to San Berdoo."

"That's enough," said Hank.

"If you don't like it, you're welcome to leave. You can get out and walk."

"You're right. Pull over and let us out."

The two men in the front seats leaned closer and exchanged a few words, and then Derrick began to slow down. When he reached a wide shoulder, he stopped. Kyle got out to remove the skis from the roof. "Okay," Derrick said. "Last stop. Don't forget to tip the driver."

Hank opened his door. When Marcia tried to do the same, Derrick hit the lock button and her door locked. Kyle gave Hank a push, intending to push him to the ground so they could drive off with Marcia. But Hank had been prepared, and he shrugged off the push. He brought his Colt Commander out of the backpack and swung it across Kyle's head. It hit his forehead and blood instantly began to flow down his face into his eyes.

Marcia dived across the backseat and scrambled out Hank's door.

Derrick was paralyzed for a moment, not sure what to do. He wanted to drive off, but Kyle was outside the vehicle, apparently hurt.

Hank aimed the gun through the open door at Derrick's face. He said, "If you try to move that car you're dead. Get out."

Derrick got out, but kept the big vehicle between him and Hank. "Hey, dude," Derrick said. "What's that for? We didn't mean anything. We weren't really going to take her. It was just to scare you a little."

"Come around to join your friend Kyle."

"Now, just think about what you're doing," Derrick said.

"Or I'll kill you where you stand," Hank added.

When Derrick and Kyle were together by the side of the road, Hank said, "Now toss me your cell phones."

Kyle tossed his, which landed at Hank's feet. Derrick said, "I don't have mine."

"Then I'll shoot Kyle first, then you."

Kyle scrambled to his feet, reached into Derrick's pocket, and threw a phone that landed at Hank's feet beside his. Marcia picked them both up and put them in her jacket pocket.

Derrick sounded more angry than frightened. "Look, we didn't do anything. We were just joking."

Hank said, "You found two strangers you thought were helpless, and decided to do us harm. You're going to die for it. Take a second to say your prayers or whatever you do." He aimed the Colt Commander at Derrick's head and moved his finger onto the trigger.

Derrick's eyes widened. He went to his knees in the cold, salt slush, and ice. "Please!" he said. "Please don't do this to me. I'll do anything, give you anything if you'll just let me live."

Beside him, Kyle began to vomit. Some of the liquid splashed in front of Derrick. He put his head in his hands and began to sob.

Hank nodded to Marcia and she climbed into the front passenger seat and closed the door. Hank said, "Get up. Start walking this way, into the woods."

"Please," said Derrick. "Don't."

"Go!" Hank shouted. The two men stood up and began to walk into the woods. As they went on, they seemed to go slightly faster, moving a bit more quickly than when they began. Once they had put a few trees between them and Hank, they seemed to hope they could get far enough so Hank couldn't see them and fire the shot. In a moment Hank heard what sounded like running.

Hank got into the driver's seat beside Marcia, eased the vehicle into the traffic, and drove down Route 38. "Take the batteries out of the phones. Wait five miles before you throw the pieces of the phones away."

25

Hank hid their skis, poles, and boots beneath a layer of trash in a dumpster behind a supermarket in San Bernardino. In the flat country, even after 3:00 a.m. the temperature was forty-four degrees and the wind was calm. The radio in the stolen SUV said it had been seventy degrees during daylight. They kept their ski jackets, caps, and gloves because they both still felt chilled from the long hours in the snow.

Hank found the train station on Third Street and then stopped at a nearby apartment complex. He and Marcia cleaned their prints from the SUV and left it in an empty parking space behind one of the big buildings, put on their backpacks, and walked back to the station. He bought them two tickets for the 4:06 a.m. Metrolink train to Union Station in Los Angeles.

This early in the morning there were only a few dozen people waiting, but that was enough to keep them from standing out. A few of the passengers were wearing suits and ties or other business attire, but the rest were dressed in synthetic quilted jackets like theirs and casual pants. At least half wore backpacks, probably containing their work clothes.

They arrived at Union Station just after 5:30 a.m. It was still barely light, but the station was already busy. It was full of people coming into the center of the city, leaving it on the red, purple, and gold subway lines, or preparing to take long-distance Amtrak trains or Metrolink trains to other cities.

Hank went to a ticket counter and took a printed Amtrak schedule, and then went to sit with Marcia.

"You seem to have a plan," she said.

"I have the beginnings of one."

He looked around them to be sure nobody was near enough to overhear them. "We've reached a point where we have to be somebody new."

"All right," she said. "How does it work this time?"

"There's a northbound train leaving at ten ten."

"That makes sense, I guess," said Marcia. "We are in a train station, after all."

"I'm going to see if I can get us a sleeping compartment. There might not be any at the last minute, but we'll see." He went to the counter and came back with tickets. "Got it. We've got a sleeper all the way to Seattle."

"Great. Sleep would be nice."

"And the train will give us time to talk and prepare for what comes next."

At 10:11 a.m. they were on the Coast Starlight in a private sleeper compartment pulling out of Union Station. They were still exhausted, so by the time the new passengers had boarded after the first stop in Burbank and the train moved out again, they had both fallen asleep.

It wasn't until afternoon that Marcia woke up. She whispered, "Are you awake?"

"Now I am," Hank said.

She said, "Now that we're alone, I want to thank you aloud, and not just inside my skull. The past thirty-six hours have shown me what a big difference there is between saying I wanted to go with you and actually trying to do what you do. Thank you for keeping me alive."

"You're welcome."

"And you said this morning that we have to be somebody else from now on. I've been wondering about that."

"Okay," he said. "I'm sure you know the Dixons are through. The intelligence people have the car that's registered to Henry Dixon, and the credit cards and checks we used are all in the names of Henry or Marcia Dixon. But I put another complete set of identification documents in the bugout kits."

"The Canadians."

"Yes. Alan and Marie Spencer," he said.

"Is that why we're going north?" she said.

"One reason. On the way, there are a lot of little stops, and three big ones. We stop in San Francisco tonight, and then get another train to Portland, and a third to Seattle. For the next couple of days, we've got to stay as close to invisible as we can. Being on the train will help."

"I understand," she said.

"There's something else to think about during the trip from here to Seattle. They know we're traveling together, but you can still get out of this. You haven't broken any laws yet—at least that they can prove. I might still be forcing you to go with me. When we get to Seattle you can step off the train and go back to being Zoe McDonald, while I go on to Canada. Once we're separated, there won't be any point in chasing you anymore."

"Please don't push me away," she said. "I can still be useful. The Spencers live in Toronto, don't they? When we get there, having a wife will help make your identity more convincing. And we'll have to find a place to live. I can do that without your ever showing your face."

"I've got a place," he said. "I rented an apartment about twelve years ago in the name of one of Alan Spencer's businesses. I rented it because I knew if I needed it I'd be running. The moment when people are hunting for you is never a good time to start searching for a new place to live."

"That's pretty smart."

"It's only smart if it worked," he said. "I can't be absolutely positive that the place hasn't been discovered or that the Alan Spencer accounts haven't been found by the NSA with the others. I won't know that until I get there."

"Until *we* get there? Please?"

"Until we get there." He had done his best to give her a chance. He couldn't tell her the truth. If she wanted to stay with him he had to keep her feeling safe and optimistic. She would feel better if he let it appear that what they were doing would make them safer and prolong their time together.

26

Julian Carson, Sergeant Wright, and the two army riflemen returned to the cabin late the next morning. They had been awake for thirty-six hours, and had been outdoors in bitter cold for at least twenty-four. The man who had driven a snowmobile into the old man's trap and gotten hit in the forehead said he was fine, and he showed no symptoms of a concussion, only a bruise and a cut, but he and the others were exhausted.

When the four came down the hill above the cabin, Julian could see that the two damaged snowmobiles had been loaded on the pickup truck. When he and Wright pulled up in front of the cabin, Wright ordered two of the men who had been stationed in the cabin to return the three snowmobiles to the rental company.

The radio operator was at the door of the cabin when Wright, Julian, and the others went inside. He had been on the radio and the phones for so long that his voice was hoarse. The four men left at the cabin with him had spent much of the night patrolling the area beyond the top of the mountain on foot in the hope that the fugitives might double back.

Staff Sergeant Wright listened to the radio operator's report, and then began giving the rest of the men their orders. "All right, guys, listen up. We were never here. Wipe down the whole place for fingerprints. Walk it completely to be sure nothing that belongs to us is in the cabin. Lock it up and meet the rest of us down the hill at the condo."

Wright drove one of the SUVs. Julian sat in the passenger seat, and the two other snowmobilers sat behind them. There were two more men in the third seat. At the condominium Julian had rented, the men climbed the stairs, cleared their weapons and stowed them, removed their winter gear, and found places to lie down—beds, couches, piles of down jackets—and slept.

A few hours later Sergeant Wright was up again and stalking around the condominium waking up his men. When he reached Julian, he said, "I feel as though I ought to apologize to you, Mr. Carson. We didn't do much to solve your problem."

"No apology is necessary," said Julian. "This just wasn't the old man's day to get caught."

They shook hands. "See you next time around."

Julian nodded, but said nothing more. Within a short time the soldiers had packed up and loaded their gear in their three vehicles. They left in three stages a few minutes apart, trying not to look like what they were.

Instead of checking in with his employers, Julian used his phone to reserve a flight out of the San Bernardino airport for the next morning. He was certain his phone would be monitored, so they would know what he was doing anyway. That evening he walked to the center of the village for dinner. He drove up to the old man's rented cabin after it was late on the slim chance that he and the woman had sneaked back, and then he returned to the condominium and slept.

The next morning when Julian went to the rental office to return the key, the manager insisted on going back to the condominium with him to inspect it for damage. Julian was not surprised. He occupied his mind with the thought that this man had foolishly assumed a young-looking black man only five feet eight inches tall couldn't hurt him. He also didn't know that the men who had cleaned the place were accustomed to making their gear and their dwellings gleam.

When the man declared himself to be satisfied, Julian grabbed his hand before he could anticipate the move or evade him. Julian shook his hand hard and grinned. "I'll be sure and tell all my friends about this place," he promised.

Julian flew to Baltimore-Washington International with a stop in Houston. While he was waiting in the George Bush Intercontinental Airport he looked at his phone and saw a confirmation that he had received an electronic transfer for his pay. This time it was from Zinnia's Baby Services, but the amount was the same as usual.

He rented a car and drove to Fort Meade. He arrived after 9:00 p.m., went to his barracks, cooked himself a frozen dinner in the microwave, and went to bed. The wake-up call came at 7:00 a.m. He showered, shaved, dressed, and packed his bag, and then waited for the knock from the soldier on orderly room duty. He was the same one as last time. They walked together to the same room on the fourth floor of the office building three rows away, and then the orderly knocked, opened the door for him, and went away.

Julian entered and saw three men sitting on the other side of the conference table, as before. Mr. Bailey and Mr. Prentiss sat on either side of Mr. Ross, who was engaged in reading an open file in front of him while the others sat with yellow legal pads and pens, but not making use of either.

Julian watched Ross perform the familiar bit of theater. He closed the file and looked up at Julian. "Hello, Mr. Carson," he said. "Have a seat."

Julian had never been invited to sit before, and he knew it was intended to be another reward, a gesture of politeness that had to be earned before it was given. He sat.

Mr. Ross said, "I understand from Staff Sergeant Wright's report that you were an asset to the team."

This could only be ironic. Julian was supposed to understand this, so he pretended it didn't matter. "He's a good squad leader. His men trust him and they're well trained and disciplined. He must be good in military situations."

Mr. Ross had to know that Julian was asking him why he'd been sent such an inappropriate form of help. Mr. Ross pretended it didn't matter. "But nobody got the old man and his girlfriend."

"No," said Julian. "I think the old man must have noticed there was an army rifle squad in the middle of that little resort town."

Ross studied him. "They were that obvious?"

"Buzz haircuts. Brand-new winter clothes. Their physiques—necks about as thick as their heads, straight, stiff posture, not one beer belly. They're all about the same age, too old to be in college. No women."

Mr. Ross looked at Mr. Bailey and then Mr. Prentiss. Both of them looked down and made notations on their yellow pads. "So he spotted them and took off?"

"It might have been later. On the night the squad arrived Sergeant Wright saw the snow was already deep and falling steadily. So Wright had two men take a pickup truck in the morning and plow the road up to the cabin."

"What did he have in mind?"

"He wanted to drive up and take the targets by surprise instead of hiking up through snowdrifts."

Mr. Ross said, "This whole thing was a screwup from your point of view, wasn't it?"

"Yes, sir."

"You think we should have waited for optimum conditions?"

"It wouldn't have hurt," said Julian. "The old man's cabin looked like he'd been there for a while and planned to stay."

Mr. Ross said, "The assessment was made that it was better to complete the mission right after the storm than to risk the old man slipping off the next night."

Julian shrugged. "I see."

"So now we've got another botched operation to our credit," said Mr. Ross. "We've involved two other government agencies and embarrassed ourselves. This reflects on you."

Julian was silent.

"What do you think we should do now?" asked Mr. Ross.

"My opinion doesn't matter anymore, sir."

"It doesn't? Why do you think that? If I'm asking, I want to know the answer."

"I'm removing myself from the issue."

"What the hell does that mean?"

Julian stood. "I've decided to end my government service. I'm an independent civilian contractor, and as of now I quit. I don't want any further employment. Thank you for the consideration." He held out his hand toward Mr. Ross, who ignored it, and then offered it to Mr. Prentiss, and then to Mr. Bailey. None of them took his hand. He pulled his government cell phone out of his pocket and set the device on the table in front of his chair. Then he turned and walked out the door.

Julian Carson walked down the sidewalk past the rows of buildings, across the two large parking lots filled with the private cars of military intelligence and National Security Agency personnel. He felt buoyant, a feeling that grew stronger as he got farther away from that office. He controlled the feeling and walked on, looking around him at Fort George Meade. This would certainly be the last time he would ever see this place.

27

The Canadian passport looked a lot like her American passports—dark blue with gold writing and a seal on the outside. This one said CANADA, of course. The gold symbol was a fancy crown design, and along with PASSPORT below it there was PASSEPORT. The photograph and identity data were on the same page as they were in the American passports.

She read the name again. Marie Angelica Spencer. She said it aloud. It was okay. Probably his . . . Anna had thought of the name. She had caught herself thinking: *First wife*. He would have let Anna choose something she could imagine living with, and the name sounded compatible with the way Anna—and she—both looked, northern European, probably of Irish, English, or French descent or all three.

Changing—even being a person who was amenable to change—was confusing. She supposed that it wasn't as big a deal to her now as it would have been before she took her husband's name, McDonald. She had taken that wholeheartedly and without reservation, and then nineteen years later had learned it wasn't her name after all, not really.

She had very quickly gotten comfortable being Marcia Dixon. It was a common and familiar name, like putting her feet in a worn-in pair of slippers. And being Marie Spencer was not going to be any less comfortable for her. Marie Spencer was another good name for a person who didn't want to be noticed or wondered about.

But being Canadian was going to take some thought and some research. She remembered they had a parliamentary government with ministers, they had provinces instead of states, and they had the Queen of England. They had two official languages. She had studied French in school and wasn't bad. She could still read pretty well, and the fluency would come back.

As she thought about the change she didn't mind so much. If you had to change your nationality, Canadian wasn't a bad choice. Years ago, she remembered, some friends of hers—really her husband's—had gone to Europe and always told people they were Canadian to avoid political hatred. Everybody liked Canadians.

The Pacific Ocean appeared on the left side of the train. Now that she was on her way out of her own country she regretted not learning much about California. She didn't know the names of any of the other mountain ranges besides the San Bernardino Mountains where she and Hank had been hiding. Yes she did—the Sierras. But this life, her new one, was full of quick escapes and things found and relinquished before she could really examine them.

Although she had not realized it then, the day Peter Caldwell had arrived at her door in Chicago her new life had begun, and time had sped up. Now she burned through sights, places, and names.

She knew she had lost some things as the old life ended. Her son, her firstborn, seemed to be one of them. She remembered how much she had loved him when he was born, and then more and more as she devoted all of her attention to him. He had been intelligent. She had been pleased with his intelligence at first, and secretly relieved that he would have an easier time than people who didn't have that. And she had, even more secretly, been proud. But as he got older he reminded her sometimes of the terribly precocious children in horror movies, with their soft, sweet faces and penetrating, pitiless eyes.

In recent years she had realized that his father, Darryl, must have been like that too—very alert, very intense about things like winning and being the one who was right, and also free of any inclination toward humility. As Brian grew older he became more unaffectedly calculating, like his father. Darryl was a person to whom the odds, the risks, and advantages were instantly apparent, and who could conceive of no reason to resist them.

She turned a little and looked beside her at Hank. No, at her husband, Alan Spencer. She loved him so much that as she inhaled she felt her chest expand and the air rush in. She had never felt as strongly about any man in her life before. She could see he was asleep and she wanted to touch him, not in spite of the risk of waking him, but because he might wake. She wanted to hear his voice again because his calm voice made her feel warm and safe.

Feeling that way was important to her, because although Alan didn't know it, Marie had no way of returning to her old life as Zoe McDonald, even if she had wanted it. That was over forever. Big Bear had been terrifying, and then the ride with those two awful boys had been something out of an old nightmare, but being with him had saved her.

The monotonous *clackety-clack* of the train going along the level tracks beside the shore made her tiredness return. She wriggled closer to her pretend husband, Alan, feeling his body touching hers, his chest moving in slow, restful breaths behind her. *Like this*, she thought. *When we have to die, let it be like this.*

28

As the Coast Starlight train moved northward near Monterey, Alan Spencer looked out the window at the familiar country. When he was young they had sent him to the Defense Language Institute in Monterey. The train must be somewhere near Lewis Road now. That was the route. The school was on the bluff above Monterey Bay at the Presidio. He glanced at Marie. He felt the urge to tap her shoulder and say, "Look out the window. I spent a couple of years here once." But that would have come too close to a topic he needed to avoid.

The highly accelerated Arabic course at the language school was sixty-four weeks. He had stayed beyond the basic course to master several regional dialects. After that he had spent another six months working on intelligence analyses with a team of expatriate Libyans at Fort Bragg, North Carolina. Since most of their discussions were in Arabic, his fluency had increased dramatically.

He had not known, while they were developing plans to mount a mission to support a rebel faction in the Nafusa Mountains of Libya, that the mission was going to be his.

Alan watched Marie turn her head to stare out the window. "It's pretty around here," she said. "Ever been here before?"

"No," he said. "I haven't even seen all of Canada yet, let alone the US."

"Very correct of you," she said. "We'll have to get busy traveling once we're back in Canada."

The brochure Alan had gotten with the tickets said that the train trip took about thirty-six hours. Marie had decided to use the time wisely. When the train stopped at the small station in Santa Barbara she had taken a cab up State Street to a bookstore, bought four travel guides to Canada, and rushed back. She had been reading much of the time since then.

At breakfast in the dining car the next morning they met an older woman who said she had booked her trip all the way to British Columbia. The final leg would be on a bus, but it would take her to Surrey and then Vancouver. After breakfast, Alan found the conductor and booked extensions of their tickets to Seattle so they would be on the bus with her. Customs officials would talk to this sweet elderly woman with hair curled like white floss, and it might make her traveling companions, the Spencers, seem innocuous too.

The Spencers practiced being Canadian, but for the moment Alan would allow Marie to rehearse the role only with him in their compartment, where nobody could overhear her mistakes. He had spent time years ago learning to pass as a Canadian before he had first arrived in Toronto as Alan Spencer. He told Marie that they weren't ready to be Canadian in public, but they would work on it together.

Marie soon saw that the differences were not extreme. Most Canadians didn't say "aboot" for "about" or end every sentence with "eh?" But there were subtler signs and differences for which she would have to prepare. For the moment they were only people from somewhere in English-speaking North America, and they should avoid saying anything about their origins.

Alan was relieved that the bus across the border existed. He had not had time to research this trip in advance. It had simply been an option he'd noticed at Union Station in Los Angeles. He had been assuming they would have to cross the border on foot in some remote spot between official border crossings. But during the years since 2001 there had been a proliferation of agencies and federal employees who watched the borders and the adjacent areas to prevent illegal crossings. Once it would have been an easy trip. Now, the Spencers might not have made it.

As the train approached the station for their stop in San Jose, Alan saw a big Sears store, so as soon as they could get off they went to the store and bought some fresh clothes, toiletries, and other essentials.

Their last night in the United States, Alan went through their backpacks and jettisoned things that they couldn't bring across an international border. He dismantled the Colt Commander and the two Beretta Nano pistols, and emptied their magazines. He made a pile of barrels, springs, unattached trigger and sear mechanisms, slides, grips, and frames. Any part he could remove, he did. Every few miles during the night he would throw a piece or two out the window as far from the tracks as possible. When the train went over a bridge spanning deep water he dropped more.

He split the money into packets and counted it, so that neither of them would have more than ten thousand Canadian dollars or the US equivalent. That way neither would have to declare the cash.

Alan Spencer cut up their Dixon identification and credit cards and fed the pieces into the wind. By the time they reached the King Street Station in Seattle they were as clear of contraband as they could be. He took Marie to the bus they would be taking to Canada and sat with his arm around her, because he knew she would be nervous as they prepared to cross the border.

The bus driver handed out Canadian Customs Declaration Cards to the passengers who had booked themselves through to Canada. The Spencers had nothing left to declare that would prompt questions.

Shortly after they filled out the cards and the bus was in motion, Alan went into the bus's restroom. He took from under his shirt a small canvas tool bag he had bought in the Sears store in San Jose. He took out a screwdriver, unscrewed and removed a wall panel that allowed access to the toilet's water supply pipe, tied the bag to the pipe, and replaced the panel.

The bus crossed the border at Blaine, Washington, and then stopped at Surrey, British Columbia. He had prepared Marie for Canadian customs by telling her to steel herself to look calm, a little bored, but alert. There was a primary inspection station where a man from the Canada Border Services Agency examined their documents, and then a baggage claim where they took possession of their backpacks, and a secondary inspection station where other Border Services people inspected the backpacks and asked questions.

Alan said they had flown to Los Angeles three weeks ago, done a great deal of sightseeing and hiking in parks around Southern California at Joshua Tree and Death Valley and the Angeles National Forest, and were planning to return home to Toronto by train.

As Alan had expected, the inspector showed little interest in their story. The clothes he had chosen for them in San Jose were right—cheap and utilitarian, bought because they'd run out of clean clothes on a trip. The worn hiking boots and gloves they'd had in Big Bear, the lightweight ski jackets for cool mornings and evenings, helped bolster his story that they were hikers. Alan had included brimmed hats to wear in public places where there were surveillance cameras, and shorts. The trip through customs took only about ten minutes, but the tension made the experience seem much longer.

After the luggage had been reloaded into the bus, they climbed in, returned to their seats, and got moving again. Alan returned to the bus's restroom, removed the wall panel, took his canvas tool bag, and put it into his backpack. From the shape and the weight, he could tell the pistol, silencer, and magazines were intact. Then he replaced the panel. Soon the bus pulled into the station in Vancouver.

They took the ferry from Vancouver to Victoria and checked in at the Empress Hotel. The hotel was old and formal and luxurious, so Alan took Marie to a department store where they bought more formal clothes and a pair of suitcases.

Marie said, "What are we doing next?"

"Listening to Canadians talk. Looking at what they wear and buying some of it so all of our clothes will have the right labels. Making ourselves into the least likely people to be troublesome."

"So we're killing time again?"

"Not killing it. Just slowing down a bit while we get used to things."

He decided to stay at the Empress Hotel for five more days. They went to museums, shopped, and explored, always listening to the people around them. Most of Alan's attention was devoted to assuring himself that nothing had changed. Nobody was following them, the Canadian police were not waiting for them when they returned to the Empress each afternoon, and their pictures had not begun to appear in newspapers or on television.

On the fifth day, they took the ferry back to Vancouver and boarded the Via Rail Canadian Snow Train.

For the ten days of travel to Toronto, Marie listened and practiced. She studied other people on the train and in hotels, observing customs, mannerisms, inflections, and pronunciations. When they were alone he drilled her. Canadians used the metric system for temperatures and distances, but they expressed their height in feet and inches, their weight in pounds. When they bumped into you they said "soary" for "sorry." Marie had a good ear, and soon she was repeating entire anecdotes that she'd heard Canadian women tell, pronouncing each word exactly as she'd heard it.

When they arrived in Toronto, Spencer didn't immediately take possession of his apartment. Instead he checked in to a hotel across the street. The apartment was at Yonge Street just south of Queen, and he spent a lot of time sitting near the Yonge Street window overlooking the apartment building and watching.

Alan Spencer knew that if US military intelligence had discovered that he was the same man who had been Daniel Chase, Peter Caldwell, and Henry Dixon, they would have found the apartment on Yonge Street. The rent had always been paid by Weyburn Dynamics, an entity he had invented in the second year after he set up his American identities and begun to invest the twenty million dollars. His main hope of anonymity now was that the insularity he had given the identity of Alan Spencer would hide him.

He had resisted the temptation to let any of his American identities blur into this one. He had never given Chase, Caldwell, or Dixon a financial interest in the Weyburn Company or had them serve on its fictitious board of directors.

Alan Spencer and the Weyburn Company held no money in American banks, invested in no American corporations, and did no business in the United States. The money was invested broadly in Canada and in companies in various commonwealth nations and a few European ones. He owned stock in Canadian "hydro" producers, Canadian real estate, shopping malls, mining, lumber, oil. His investments had at first been intended as a series of ways of storing money that didn't belong to him. Weyburn was essentially a lawyer's office and a bank account that paid a few Canadian businesses to provide services—including filing Canadian taxes and financial reports, paying for the apartment, and providing the company with a mailing address in Toronto. His investments had done well, but not well enough to attract the attention of American business interests.

Next Spencer began to watch the apartment through the windows of Toronto buses. He studied Yonge and Queen Streets as his bus passed the apartment building. The area was always bustling and full of traffic, and its sidewalks were crowded with pedestrians.

The apartment was a few blocks north of Lake Ontario, and only a couple of blocks from the entertainment district, close to thousands of businesses in the glass skyscrapers that had grown up in the southern part of the city in the past twenty years.

The apartment was on the ninth floor. He had chosen it in person about a dozen years ago, had the rent and services charged to Weyburn Dynamics, and made sure that only the company was listed as the tenant in the building's records, and that the suite number was not on any directory. His lease included an in-house cleaning service that came in once a week to dust, vacuum, and clean the windows, but otherwise nobody entered.

The glass of the large windows was opaque and reflective from outside. The building had a lobby where security people made visitors show identification before they could reach the elevators or the stairs.

He went past on the bus at 6:00 a.m., noon, and 5:30 p.m. the first day. He took the bus the next day at 7:00 a.m., 1:00 p.m., and 8:00 p.m. He took pictures through the bus windows with his cell phone. Each day he altered his schedule. He studied everything—possible observation posts in vehicles that were parked in this busy area too often, the presence of people who stayed on the street for too long. He walked the area at various times of the night. He found nothing that made him suspicious.

On the fifth day at 6:00 a.m., Alan Spencer made his first entry into the apartment building. He signed in, showed one of the security men in the lobby his passport, rode the elevator to the second floor, and then went back down the staircase and watched the two security men through the small window in the stairwell door. Neither had picked up a telephone or left his post at the reception desk. He watched for five more minutes and then walked up to the second floor and took the elevator to the ninth.

The apartment had not been altered since he'd last visited five years before. The three bedrooms, three baths, kitchen, dining room, living room, conference room, and office all appeared the same. He made a quick tour and verified that the tables had been polished, the bed linens were fresh, and the windows cleaned. Then he began his work.

Spencer removed each of the electrical socket covers, light switch covers, and light fixtures searching for bugs or cameras. He took the slipcovers partially off each piece of furniture. He examined each cupboard, took all the drawers out, and studied the insides and undersides of counters, tables, and desks. He opened the bottoms of telephone receivers and appliances. He examined the objects on shelves to see if they contained electronic devices. As afternoon arrived he took the grate off each vent, hood, or heating fixture. He took apart the smoke detectors, thermostats, and sound system speakers. He spent time opening the television set and cable box, looking for parts that didn't belong. He found nothing in the apartment that was not as it should be.

He walked through the apartment taking cell phone pictures of all the disarray, and then prepared to leave. He pulled and teased a bit of synthetic wool from the carpet to make some lint. He placed a bit of it on the tops of the doors to the bedrooms, the bathrooms, and the closets. He left a small battery-operated camera running under the front of the couch that faced the doorway.

On the way out of the building he stood at the apartment doors beside his, below his, and above his to listen for sounds of occupancy. He heard television sets in three, classical music in one, and an angry couple quarreling in one. There was only one apartment door where he heard nothing. As he turned to leave he heard the *ping* of the elevator arriving down the hall, and walked toward the doors. The woman who emerged from the elevator was short and elderly. She smiled as he passed her in the hall.

He pushed the elevator button to reopen the doors, stepped in, and then held the "door open" button. He listened until he heard an apartment door open. He waited a second, and then looked back.

He saw the door of the apartment beside his swing shut. He let the elevator close and rode down to the lobby.

He made his way back to his hotel across the street by taking a circuitous route that took him behind the hotel, around a block, and through the front door of a bar. He ordered a Macallan scotch over ice, drank it, and then left through the back door near the kitchen. There was nobody following him.

When he entered their hotel room, Marie kissed him, and then pulled back to look at him. "I missed you. How did it go?"

"Good so far," he said.

"I figured. You taste like single malt scotch."

"Sorry," he said, pronouncing it as a Canadian.

"No, it's a good taste," she said. "What time do you want to go down to dinner?"

"Give me a half hour. I just need to shower and change."

She moved the tip of her tongue to her lips. "Maybe I'll order one of those at dinner."

After three visits to the apartment he still found the bits of carpet lint had not been disturbed and the only image recorded on the hidden camera was his own. He reassembled everything he had dismantled. The next day he waited for the woman who did the cleaning in the apartment once a week. After she had been in the apartment for a few minutes he entered and found her at work cleaning the windows. That satisfied him that she was who she claimed to be. He decided that he and Marie could move in to the apartment.

Two days after that, while Marie was out having her hair done, he began to refresh his Arabic.

29

By February Julian Carson was already a familiar sight in Craighead County, and particularly in Ruthie's neighborhood in Jonesboro. He had taken a job at Arkansas State University in the Department of Chemistry and Physics ordering, issuing, and assembling various pieces of equipment for the laboratories. Ruthie had finally finished her nursing degree in January and was working in labor and delivery at St. Bernards Medical Center on East Jackson Avenue.

Julian used most of his days off to help on the family farm. He was good at maintaining and fixing tools and machinery, and winter was the time when most of that work had to be done. Ruthie had grown up on a farm outside town too, so she was used to the work, and put in some off days with him.

The wedding was scheduled for March, because all of April, May, June, and July had been spoken for by other couples, and they didn't see much point in waiting. The church was free on March thirtieth, and so was the minister, so they took the date.

When March thirtieth came, the Reverend Donald Monday presided. He had known Ruthie since she was baptized, but the Carsons didn't make it to church, because they made the rounds of the farmers' markets on Sunday mornings. Julian's father had often said, "If everybody else went to church on Sunday mornings

I would too, because there wouldn't be anybody out to buy my vegetables."

Mr. Monday was not a strict minister, and he understood that people had to sell whatever they sold when other people were available to buy it. He was a scholarly and benevolent man.

He tended to select the biblical texts for weddings that fell on the optimistic side. He favored leading off with Genesis 2:18–24: "It's not good for man to be alone; I will make a suitable helper for him." In keeping with science, religion, and personal experience, that led naturally to: "Be fruitful and multiply" from Genesis 1:28.

Because he was a sincere admirer of good, strong women, the sort of woman Ruthie manifestly was, his thoughts turned to Proverbs 3:15, the virtuous wife. "She is more precious than rubies. And all the things thou canst desire are not to be compared unto her." He wound it up with John 2:1–11, the story of Jesus at the wedding in Cana, where he turned water into wine and a good time was had by all.

Mrs. Finlay, the church organist, accompanied the children's choir, which Ruthie's cousin Ayana directed. Nearly all of the relatives and a good number of the congregation turned out for Ruthie's wedding, because that was the sort of place the town was.

The wedding proceeded with the precision that Ruthie had hoped for. Her father was dead, so her uncle David the lawyer walked her down the aisle. Reverend Monday's weddings tended to be smooth and practiced, without a false note or a hesitation. There were people sitting in the pews who would have caught a change in the wording the way a teenager would hear a change in a popular song's lyrics. It had been said of Mr. Monday that he had you married and celebrating your third anniversary before you could stop to think.

All seemed to go flawlessly through the last "I do" and Mr. Monday's "I now pronounce you." Then the bride and groom turned to each other in a brief but tender kiss, and then completed the turn to face the congregation. Among the many happy faces in the pews there were two faces that were not smiling. They belonged to Harper and Waters, who sat near the back of the church.

Julian knew that they must have slipped in during the processional, while the voices of Ayana's choir sang and Ruthie, resplendent in her wedding gown, had every eye on her, particularly Julian's.

Ruthie stiffened and tightened her grip on Julian's arm. He whispered, "It's okay. They don't matter."

At the reception, Julian and Ruthie both watched for them, but Harper and Waters never reappeared. The Carsons left for their honeymoon in Sarasota that night, but the two men didn't show up there either.

Mr. and Mrs. Julian Carson stayed for a week in Sarasota, walked on the fine white sand beach and swam in the hotel pool because the Gulf wasn't warm that week and seemed untamed to Ruthie. They ate at good restaurants and spent a great deal of time in their room. Julian woke each morning with the thought that life was very good.

When they returned to Jonesboro, Julian entered the house alone, and found no sign that agents had been inside while they were away. "That's the end of that," said Julian. "If they had wanted to, they could have come in. But they didn't."

"How do you know?"

He brought her inside, got a flashlight from a kitchen drawer, and led her to the bedroom. There was a jewelry box on Ruthie's dresser with a smooth lacquer top. There was a very thin layer of flour that he had blown onto it from his palm, and when he moved her finger across it the finger left a mark. He showed her places on the hardwood floor near each of the doors where he had blown puffs of flour to make footprints show, and they were undisturbed. Nothing had been touched.

Ruthie turned to him, smiled, and said, "I'll never cheat on you, Julian."

He said, "Didn't we just promise that in church?"

"Yes, but this is practical. With all your tricks and traps you'd catch me."

"Keep believing that," he said.

She hugged him. "So they're done, right? They'll leave you alone now."

"I quit. I guess they're convinced."

What Julian knew was that until the old man was found, his case would remain active. What it meant was that Julian was on a long leash, but it was still a leash.

It was possible that the high-level people, the ones like Mr. Ross, Mr. Bailey, Mr. Prentiss, and whomever they reported to, suspected him of helping the old man escape. If so, they would be listening to Julian's phone calls and reading his mail in case the old man tried to reach him. What they were doing beyond that was hard to know.

Mr. Ross knew that Julian had talked with the old man in Chicago and in San Francisco. Did he suspect that Julian had warned the old man at Big Bear? Mr. Ross knew Julian wasn't an enthusiastic member of the team. Julian had told Mr. Ross that he believed the old man had never intended to steal the money. And Julian had not hidden from Mr. Ross that he was quitting because of the hunt for the old man.

Julian had confidence that the old man would be too smart to try to communicate with James Harriman, and he would have no way of knowing that James Harriman was Julian Carson, or where Julian Carson was.

But Julian remained alert. Watching for military intelligence agents had become part of his daily routine, just one of the things he did. His long experience living in chaotic and dangerous countries made watchfulness a reflex.

When he was driving he checked his rearview mirrors and noted each car behind him and how long it stayed there. When he woke at night he would listen until he was sure that what had awakened him had not been a footstep or a tool moving in the keyway of a lock. He scanned every crowd for faces that were familiar and for faces that were not but seemed interested in him.

About once a week he inspected the house to look for anything new plugged into an out-of-the-way socket, any change in the configuration of the phone junction box or the circuit box. Each time, he would prepare a trap, a particular arrangement of objects on the workbench in the garage or on the seat of his truck that would show him if someone had touched it. He draped a length of black thread across the space between the side of his house and the fence about two feet from the ground, and checked regularly to see if it had been dislodged.

He knew that there could be someone watching him at the university too. The old man would be just as likely to try to speak to him at work as at home, because at the university there were always people coming and going, and he might think he would not be noticed in a crowd.

Julian studied people within the department—professors, secretaries, lab assistants, graduate students—trying to pick up a hint that one of them had agreed to help the government keep track of him. During his own intelligence work he had recruited civilians and used them that way. Often all it took was a little flattery. People liked to feel important.

After a few months without another visit from the military intelligence people, he began to wonder if the old man was already dead. Maybe they had caught up with him and killed him on the spot or rendered him to Libya and Faris Hamzah. Maybe the whole operation was over and Julian's penalty for quitting would be that he would never find out.

30

Alan Spencer looked at his watch. It was nearly six o'clock. He put down his glass of red tea and said in Libyan Arabic, "It's been a pleasure to see you again. But now my wife will have returned home and be expecting me. Please excuse me." He bowed to Abdul Othmani, and then to Mahmoud Tanzir, stood, and left the restaurant.

He had never mentioned to his Libyan friends that Marie was a pianist, and that she spent most afternoons in a practice room at the music academy near their apartment. He was always aware that the people hunting for him would be using everything they knew about Zoe McDonald to find him. They would know she could never give up the piano for long.

She had cut and dyed her hair, changed the way she dressed, her name, and her nationality, but people in intelligence knew that as soon as a fugitive stopped feeling that every second of life was a desperate pursuit, her own tastes and preferences would begin to reassert themselves.

He had told her that having a piano in the apartment was out of the question. Any intelligence man would periodically check the records of the high-end piano manufacturers and pay visits to a few recent purchasers. But in a big city there were alternatives. She had visited a number of places around Toronto where it was possible to rent a space with a good piano. She had settled on a music studio where few children took lessons, but adults practiced for Royal Conservatory–level examinations or prepared for regional competitions. The academy kept her surrounded by people who were talented, and that prevented her from standing out. The studio was comfortable and had a couple of break rooms where she and the others could chat or rest. The building was a reasonable walk from their apartment, and in the rain or cold it was a one-stop subway ride.

He would probably not have agreed to this arrangement, but the place had the advantage of keeping her out and busy every afternoon. Alan used his time each day on activities that he didn't let Marie know much about.

Alan spent a portion of every day reviving his fluency in Arabic. He began the reawakening of his linguistic memory by completing online commercial language courses. They included some modernisms and slang he had not heard before. The people who had designed the courses seemed to be heavily interested in Middle Eastern business language, customs, and modes of address. Alan found a few Libyan films. During the Gaddafi era it became dangerous to make movies, which all had to be approved by Gaddafi himself, so few films were made. He found one made in 1972 called *The Destiny Is Very Hard,* and another called *The Road,* both made by Libyan directors using Libyan actors, so he watched them over and over again, trying to recover his accent.

After a few months of intensive study, he was ready to search Toronto for Libyan exiles. Toronto had always been one of the places where people who fled dictatorships, wars, and chaos stopped running. And in his experience, as soon as exiles came to rest they began to seek each other out.

He knew that most Libyan exiles would attend a Sunni mosque of the Maliki school. He put together a list of Sunni mosques and began to visit them, listening for Libyan-accented Arabic. There was a concentration of mosques and Islamic schools around North York, so he walked the neighborhoods in the district. Muslims tried to live within walking distance of a mosque, so he spent many hours simply walking, looking, and listening to people speak.

He found a small halal restaurant that served good *kefta* and Moroccan *merguez* and *fattoush*. The restaurant attracted people accustomed to sitting at tables in the afternoon talking and drinking tea. He spent his first few visits drinking tea alone and eavesdropping on conversations while he held a book in his hands. After a few visits sitting at a table near a group of men about his own age, he noticed that one of the men brought a friend, and there were not enough chairs for all of them. Another man who seemed to be the host asked Alan in English if he minded if they took a chair from his table.

Alan replied easily in Arabic, "I would be happy to give up as many chairs as you like. I'm alone."

The man switched back to Libyan Arabic. "If you would like to join us, we'll move the two tables together and we can all stretch out a little." This man introduced himself as Abdul Othmani. He took charge and asked Alan his name, which he said was Roger Thorne, then introduced him to each of the others, one at a time.

They behaved as though Alan were an honored guest. The conversation was about the persistent cold this winter. When the conversation turned to local politics, a few of the men became reticent. Abdul Othmani's friend Mahmoud Tanzir whispered to Othmani, who laughed. Othmani said to Spencer: "Roger, you aren't a government informant, are you?"

"Me?" said Roger Thorne. "I'm too old to be a government informer. I'm here because I'm particular about my food."

They seemed to be willing to take a chance on him after that, as though they realized how ridiculous it would be to plant an agent to spy on a group of elderly men drinking tea. He learned that they were all exiles from the Gaddafi government crackdowns of the 1970s, and most of them had completed their working lives as skilled tailors in Toronto men's stores and retired. Mahmoud Tanzir and Abdul Othmani had emigrated at the same time from the same street in Tripoli, and were old friends.

Roger Thorne's fluency in Arabic had to be explained. He said his parents had been Canadian archaeologists who had been based in the eastern part of Libya near Benghazi. When he was a young child they had left him in the homes of Libyan friends while they were away in the field. They had spent months at a time studying the twelve-thousand-year-old rock paintings in the Acacus Mountains.

Roger Thorne began showing up at the Salaam Restaurant nearly every day to join the conversations at the table. Othmani and Tanzir were always there, joined by a constantly changing group of friends and acquaintances.

During the same period Alan Spencer began to devote time to relief organizations. He visited a number of Toronto groups, talked to administrators and volunteers, and read everything he could find on the subject of Canadian relief efforts in the Middle East. Finally he selected the Canadian People's Relief Corps and became a member. He began by giving the group a five-thousand-dollar donation. It was large enough to bring him a personal thank-you note from the director, but not enough to cause much curiosity.

The Canadian People's Relief Corps' mission was to organize, fund, and equip teams of relief workers and send them where humanitarian aid was most urgently needed. They provided water purification systems, generators, food, clothing, and materials for temporary shelters. If the country was infested with mosquitos they brought mosquito netting. If the region was hungry but stable they brought well-digging equipment, seeds, tools, and even imported livestock. And no matter where they went, they brought medical supplies, doctors, nurses, technicians, and trained volunteers.

The organization had been operating for over twenty years, and Spencer saw references in the literature to teams that had been to

Bosnia, India, Timor, Bangladesh, Mozambique, Mali, Rwanda, Nigeria, Liberia, Ukraine, Syria, Eritrea, Sudan, Algeria, Tunisia, and Libya.

During his second month Spencer donated another five thousand dollars. After the third month he made the monthly donation permanent and began attending meetings. He never spoke during the business portions of the proceedings, which were usually reports on current missions in various countries or deliberations about future missions, but he sometimes stayed after with a few others to discuss the issues without speaking publicly.

On one occasion he happened to be talking to some of the board members about missions to the Middle East when the president brought out a letter from an official in Iraq. Spencer said, "I can probably tell you what it says."

When the president handed the letter to him he read it aloud in English and handed it back. The director asked him why he spoke Arabic. He repeated the story he had concocted for Abdul Othmani and his friends about his parents bringing him to Libya as a child.

A month later, after a regular meeting of the Toronto group, the director introduced Spencer to a pair of doctors who were planning to take a large group on a mission to North Africa in a few months. One of them was a woman named Labiba Zidane. While they were speaking about the difficulty of operating in Libya, Dr. Zidane unexpectedly switched to Arabic.

"The director says you're fluent in Arabic," she said in Libyan Arabic. "Are you?"

He replied in Arabic. "I am only a poor student of the language, but I can get by in most situations. And you are a physician. May I ask what your specialty is?"

She smiled. "My practice is in pediatrics but I have some experience in infectious diseases."

The other doctor, Andre Leclerc, was French Canadian. He looked at them in amused puzzlement. But the pair kept talking in rapid Arabic.

Dr. Zidane said, "How old are you?"

"I'm sixty," Alan said.

"Healthy? No trouble with your heart or lungs?"

"No trouble."

"Would you consider coming with us to Libya in the fall? We desperately need volunteers."

"I'm not sure. What sort of work would I do?"

"Triage, most of the time. Often people in the remote areas or the poor in the cities don't see a doctor from one year to the next, so they come in large numbers. You would greet the patients and ask them if they have any specific problems, ask them their names, then make them understand where to sit to wait, and take their temperature and blood pressure. Obviously, if someone is terribly ill you would take them to the front of the line."

"Let me think about it."

"You'll need a few weeks of training, and you can think while we train you. It's several months away."

Dr. Leclerc said, "You two sound as though you've known each other for some time."

"No, but we have a common acquaintance—with Arabic. This is someone we want," she said. She turned back to Alan. "Do you have a passport?"

"I do," Alan said. "But I'll have to see if it's even current."

"Our staff will take care of that for you," said the director. "Bring it with you this week, and we'll include you in the request for all of the entry visas."

"But I haven't decided," said Spencer.

"Having a visa is a precaution," said Dr. Zidane. "And we'd better see which shots you need. I promise they won't hurt a bit."

THE OLD MAN

As Alan Spencer walked to the subway station he thought about what had happened tonight. He had gotten the invitation that any clandestine operator would have wanted at this stage. Later, if Dr. Zidane doubted him, she would not fail to remind herself that Spencer had not come to her and Dr. Leclerc. They had approached him and tried to talk him into going. He would make sure they asked him again in English in front of more witnesses before he assented.

31

It was summer. To Marie Spencer the Toronto winter had seemed harder than the ones in Chicago. The snow had lasted into April, and then there was a period of cold rain and dark skies that seemed to last a long time before the sunny days arrived.

She had always loved summer—not just the gentle weather, but the celebration of renewal. Now she lived with a man who never had to concern himself with whether he could afford something—a play, a concert, a train trip across a continent. He let her spend summer days working at things she loved to do, and the long, mild summer evenings with him enjoying the city.

During the summer she had made good progress at the academy learning the piano pieces she had wanted to master, and Alan always seemed to be reading and studying, or going out to work with Canadian charities. He never said much about the charities, but she knew enough about him now to understand what he must be doing. He was very premeditated, and he was probably burnishing his legend. She'd read somewhere that was what they called a false identity in his old line of work—a legend. If he were ever under suspicion by the Canadian authorities, he couldn't just be a reclusive businessman. He had to be a person with acquaintances and contacts, and a record of virtue. During that summer he seemed to be thriving, as he had not been since Chicago. Physically and mentally, he was at a peak.

She appreciated the care that he took to remain healthy and strong. She also appreciated the fact that he didn't bore her with the details. She knew he lifted weights and worked out in a gym somewhere on King Street. There was also a martial arts dojo where he trained, but she didn't know precisely where that was either, other than the fact that it was near a restaurant that he liked. He had been going to the dojo, taking lessons or classes or whatever martial arts people did, for at least four months before she knew it. She had noticed a few bruises on him, and some scrapes, and asked him how they'd happened.

They talked about everything—or, she did, really. He spent most of their conversations listening. He would comment or ask questions, say he understood, and let her move to another topic. He almost never offered the details of his own day. His talk tended to be about things he had observed or learned while out in the city, or interesting articles he had read. She liked these anecdotes because they widened her view of the city without forcing her to do much work. At that time she was learning the Rach 3, the Rachmaninoff Piano Concerto no. 3 in D Minor, and that was enough to think about.

On September 30, Marie came home at six and discovered that Alan was not sitting on the couch waiting for her, as she had expected. She closed the door and walked through the apartment calling him. Then she looked at her cell phone, but found no messages or missed calls from him. So she put away her music and went to the kitchen to see about preparing to cook dinner.

Then she noticed that Alan's laptop was open on the dining room table and plugged into a wall socket. She was curious, so she walked to the table and looked. There was a disc in the laptop, its jewel case sitting beside it, but the computer was asleep. She refreshed it, and played the disc.

Alan had recorded a videodisc of himself sitting there at the table. When she first saw his face, there was a half second of pleasure, but then she saw that his expression was not happy.

"Hi, Marie. I'm aware that leaving a recording is a terrible way to tell you this. I can only promise you that there was no way that wasn't terrible. I am on a plane right now, about ten hours into a fourteen-hour flight. I'm part of a mission to deliver aid and medical care to some people who need it and deserve to receive it. The work is real. There are forty-six of us, and I'm certain that none of the others have ulterior motives.

"As for my motives, I'm sure you know what they are. The morning when we had to get out of the cabin and try to escape through the snow, I realized we were about to move to our last option. We both knew by then that my giving the money to the government had not changed anybody's mind. And we knew that they would never stop looking for us. But that morning, I realized that I couldn't let things go on much longer. Beginning that day, I changed what I was doing.

"I apologize for the secrecy. I had to hide my plans from you. I knew that you would never agree. And I knew that if I told you in person even ten minutes before I was on the plane and in the air, you would try to stop me.

"I've now reached the point where if you called anyone or made any attempt to get the plane stopped, I would certainly be caught and killed. I don't know how long this will take. This trip is supposed to last for six months, but where we're going, plans have to be made day to day.

"I've left you the things you'll need if you have to leave the apartment while I'm gone, even if it means leaving Canada too. You'll find a pocketbook in a drawer in the bedroom with Canadian and American cash in it. There's also a Vermont driver's license and a bank card in the name Julia Larsen with your picture on it. There's a balance in that bank account of a little over two million dollars.

There's also a safe-deposit box key in the purse for the box at that bank. The American passport is the last one I got with your picture in it, so don't lose it.

"I hate to sound corny, but destroy this DVD. It could get us both killed. The only good way to do it is to burn it. Thank you for everything, and good luck. Good-bye."

While the image dissolved into static emptiness, Marie cried. It wasn't the sort of crying that made a small drop or two well up in a woman's eyes that she blotted with a piece of Kleenex. She wept with deep, shuddering spasms, rocking back and forth.

She knew exactly where he was going, without having to look up the possible destinations of a fourteen-hour flight or the excursions of Toronto relief organizations. He was going back to that horrible place because he liked the odds. If he killed Faris Hamzah, then Faris Hamzah would stop demanding his death and sending killers, and she and his family would be safe. If Faris Hamzah killed him, then Hamzah would stop sending killers, and she and his family would be safe.

She loved him, but she hated him. He didn't have to do this. They had been in a new country, safe and happy, for six months. He had manipulated her, fooled her again. He had never stopped manipulating her. And now he had left her totally alone in a foreign country, and she was scared and angry.

She ejected the DVD from the computer, broke it in her hands, and broke it again. She carried it to the kitchen, put the pieces in a small iron frying pan, slid the pan into the oven, and turned on the broiler to melt them. She turned on the stove-top fan to get rid of the smell. Then she began to search the apartment for guns.

She found herself annoyed at Alan for not having guns in the apartment. If he had any left, he must have taken them with him. He undoubtedly thought she would decide to kill herself, and so he would try to make it less likely that she could carry it off.

Her frustration and irritation grew as she searched. She looked in every drawer, every cabinet, and everyplace she had ever seen him hide a gun. She was at it for hours, and then realized it was nearly midnight. She was tired, and she was hungry. She went into the kitchen and ran water in the frying pan. She tried to scrape the charred mess out of the pan. She pried most of what was left of the plastic into the garbage, then conceded that the pan was now unusable, and threw that in the trash too.

She sat and thought about the relationship, from the moment he had called to ask about the room she'd advertised in Chicago until now. The big moment, the time when everything had changed, was when he had kidnapped her from the apartment and driven away. That was when her secret had begun to matter again.

He had asked her a hundred times what had possessed her to insist on coming with him when he ran from Chicago. Why would a woman whose only crime was having an affair with a man she barely knew decide to become a fugitive, to run away with him from the government? Why would she be so stupid?

She wondered if she should have told him. She could have. He would never tell anybody else. He had been eager to know, and he almost certainly would not have blamed her. But telling him would not have changed anything for the better. It was better to let him think that she was in love and easily controlled than to know what she really was.

Her father had been in the air force, so the family moved every few years. She was born when her father was stationed at Edwards Air Force Base in the California desert. The family lived in a house seven miles west in Rosamond. She didn't remember anything much about the place because they moved on to Arnold Air Force Base in Tullahoma, Tennessee, when she was six. Then there was a long period when her father was stationed in other countries. She made friends in Tullahoma, learned to play the piano, had her first dates, and even got to be secretary of her class in school. She had been happy on and off, as teenaged girls were. Then her father came home, and they had to move to Ellsworth Air Force Base near Rapid City, South Dakota.

It had been hard moving away from a world she liked, and to some extent tamed, to a new, alien place during the summer before her senior year. Families of enlisted men didn't usually live on base. Instead the air force paid her father some money for "separate rations," so he could live off base with her mother and the kids. Air force bases had ten-thousand-foot runways, so they tended to be in flat, empty places. But in South Dakota, for once they weren't in the middle of nowhere. They rented a house outside Rapid City, which she'd thought of as a big, interesting city.

It happened in July, when the family had just moved in. The house sat on a large yard, but the building wasn't really big enough for them. There was some vague promise from her parents that they would keep scouting for a better one. They assembled the beds, hung up what they could, but most of the family's belongings were still piled in the attached garage or the living room. Her father was working nights to start. As she'd thought about that night since then, she guessed the night shift was probably something they did to newcomers.

At around 4:00 a.m. she woke and heard a noise. She wasn't sure how she knew it was a hostile noise, but she did. She got up, crept to the doorway of the room she shared with her younger sister Katy, and looked up the hall. There were two men in the house, and one of them had tripped over the pile of belongings in the living room. He got up, whispering swear words.

She slipped into the next room, where her parents' delicate or important things had been put until permanent places could be found for them during the next few days. She saw her father's uniforms on hangers, her mother's good dresses, the television set, the sewing machine. She moved to the closet and felt for the shotgun. The cold, smooth barrel came to her hand. She found the box of deer slugs on the floor, knelt, and pushed the shells into the bottom of the gun one by one, sliding them into the tubular magazine. She remembered loading four, because there were two men and she would probably miss.

She got up and went to the hall. The two men were just stepping into the hallway toward her. They seemed huge in the dim light. She said, "Stop and put up your hands."

The men stopped, and then one turned, planning to dash into the room where Katy was sleeping.

She fired hastily, hoping to hit the middle of the man's body, but the slug hit the side of his head. The second man turned away and ran toward the living room, but she pumped the shotgun and fired again. He pitched forward and lay there facedown.

Her mother reached her about a second later, and then everyone else was up, running to her and asking what had happened in frightened, whining voices. Her mother took the shotgun from her and sent the younger kids into the parents' room, where they wouldn't see any more horror than they already had.

The two men were an awful sight. The man who had fallen into the bedroom where Katy slept had the contents of his skull spattered against the wall and the doorjamb and the floor. The other had a huge hole in his back and a pool of blood growing on the floor around him. The door in the kitchen that led into the garage was still open, with her father's crowbar lying on the floor beside it, and she knew that was how they got in.

At 6:00 a.m. her father returned, and saw what had happened. He and her mother had a conversation alone in their room, and then came out. Her mother and the other children were all fully dressed now. Her father rolled one of the men into a tarp he'd bought to paint the new house, and dragged him into the garage. Then he rolled the other into another tarp, and dragged him out into the garage too. A few minutes later he drove away.

Her mother scrubbed the floors and walls, working with cleaners that smelled like bleach and then going over and over the same areas.

She had asked her mother if her father was hiding the bodies, and her mother said, "You shot one in the back, and the other in the side of the head when he wasn't looking. What else can we do?"

Her father returned a few hours later and began the interior painting he had planned to get to over the next few weeks. He got the hallway and the girls' bedroom done the first day, and when he came home from the base the next morning he put on another coat of paint, and then completed the hallway so everything matched.

About two weeks later, her parents waited until the small children were asleep, and then had a talk with her alone. Her mother told her that her father had taken the men out and buried them. He had wiped the fingerprints off the shotgun and thrown it into the grave with them. He had thought that was the end of the horrible incident. But about a week ago, a couple had been running their dogs in the field where he had dug the grave, and the dogs had smelled the bodies. The state police had dug up the bodies and the shotgun. They had declared the cause of death a double murder.

The shotgun had belonged to his grandfather originally, and so there was not much chance of connecting it with the family after all these years. But the police had checked the serial number, found the gun had been sold in the 1930s at a Sears store in Wichita, where his grandfather had lived, and the store had looked up the name of the purchaser after all these years. The surname matched the new man on the base.

Today her father had been summoned to his commanding officer's office, where two state police investigators were waiting. They wanted to know about his shotgun. They said that while the gun had been cleaned of fingerprints, there had been very clear prints on the shotgun shells still in the magazine. They had already compared the prints with his and his wife's, but there was no match.

Her father had told them that he'd had the shotgun in the U-Haul truck he'd driven from Tennessee, but he'd just arrived a few days ago and hadn't unpacked everything. He hadn't noticed it was gone.

He said to her, "I'm so sorry. I didn't think to check if it still had any shells in it."

Her mother said, "I know this is really bad news. But there's a good thing too—a way out. They told your father they'd checked the records of all the people whose fingerprints they have and not found any matches. It occurred to us that this is our chance to save you. Nobody anywhere has your fingerprints. They can run them for matches until the end of time and not have any luck."

"Okay," she said. But she wondered why they looked so sad.

"But you're going to have to leave us," her father said. "This isn't the end of it. They'll come here in a day or two, and they'll take the fingerprints of anybody old enough to lift a shotgun."

"We can't let them see you," her mother said. "You would go to prison for the rest of your life. We've put together all the money we can spare so you'll get a start. And your father has signed over the car to you. We'll get by with just the pickup until we can buy another one. We'll have to tell them that the kids they can see are the only ones. If they learn that you exist, we'll tell them you ran away a couple of years ago in Tennessee."

Her father said, "We just got here, and you're not registered for school yet. Nobody knows you, so they won't be asking where you are."

She studied her parents, and said, "This can't be real." But the tears running down their cheeks were real.

She left that night. She drove the family car to Denver, got a job as a waitress, and found a cheap apartment to share with another waitress.

Just over a year later, when she met Darryl, there was no question she had been too eager. She had married him, hoping that her infatuation with him would grow and grow. It hadn't, but being his wife had kept her safe for nineteen years. She had never dared to have her fingerprints taken. She had never tried to teach music in a school, or apply for a license to do anything else, because that meant fingerprints and background investigations. She would have been charged with two murders.

Last fall, when the two Libyan assassins had broken into the apartment and Peter Caldwell needed to run away, she had not wanted to go with him. He was a killer. But once he had kidnapped her from the house and she had time to think, she realized that she had to leave that night too, and she could never go back. If there was a police investigation of the two Libyans' deaths, how could the police not find her fingerprints? They were on every surface, every object in the apartment. The long-unsolved shotgun murders of two men outside Rapid City, South Dakota, would be solved. So she had gone with Peter, hoping that when he said the intelligence people would clean the apartment completely, he was right.

She'd had sympathy for Peter, and gained even more as she ran with him and he became Hank, and then Alan. It had never occurred to him that he wasn't the only one who was being hunted for murder. She had often been tempted to tell him, but that wouldn't have helped him. It might even have made him think being with her threatened his life. It was just as well that she had not taken on the task of explaining it all to him. She had loved being with him, but now he was gone and he was going to die.

32

It was 2:00 a.m. when the charter flight touched down on the runway in Tripoli. The pilot had come in slow, giving it just enough speed to keep from being swept sideways by any sudden wind, and then he hit the brakes hard. Tripoli's runway had been part of a major battlefield at least twice in the past couple of years, and Alan Spencer didn't blame the pilot for his caution. Mortar and tank rounds had undoubtedly hit the pavement, and there was no way to predict how well the holes had been patched.

Spencer knew that when their plane had taken off from Toronto, this airport had been in the hands of the opposition government army and the Misrata pro-Libya Dawn Militia, but in twenty-four hours anything could have happened. There had been air attacks from the Tobruk-based government in the spring, and the Zintan militia had held the airport for a couple of years before that.

As the plane shuddered and rattled to a halt at the end of the runway and began to taxi, Spencer looked over at the dark silhouette of the main terminal. As they taxied closer, headlights came on and he could see that the building that had once served three million passengers a year was now pockmarked with bullet holes and shrapnel scars. Some of the windows were still broken.

The plane didn't pull up to the terminal, just stopped a hundred feet or so away, the nose turned toward the end of the runway for the return trip. The male flight attendant opened the hatch and lowered the stairs to the ground. Stepping out of the hatch to the steps was like walking into a furnace. Spencer had judged that it would be too late in the season for the Ghibli, the hot wind from the southern desert that raised the temperature a couple of times a summer. But here it was.

The aid workers had been sitting for so long that they felt desperate to get out the door. Then it seemed to occur to them, one at a time, that it might be a long time before they were in air-conditioning again. Glen McKnight, one of the volunteer doctors, said, "What do you think the temperature is?"

Spencer translated his thought into centigrade. "I wouldn't be surprised if it were forty," he said. "It happens here sometimes." He smiled. "It doesn't last, usually."

As they walked away from the plane toward the terminal, several men wearing combinations of military battle dress and civilian clothes loitered nearby. All were carrying AK-47 rifles and a variety of other gear. Most wore the *kaffiyeh*, but a few were bareheaded and others wore baseball caps or camouflage-print fatigue hats.

Alan was relieved to see that they paid little attention to the passengers, which meant they weren't hostile, and they were mostly occupied in watching the middle distance around the airport.

The navigator and the flight attendant opened the bay beneath the plane and the aid workers began to unload the cartons of food, medicine, and supplies. There were no airport workers to handle baggage, and the sentries showed no inclination to help, so the Canadians worked at it themselves. They piled their cargo about fifty yards away from the plane near the terminal building. When they had removed all of the small boxes and cartons, they were able to reach the larger heavy wooden crates that had been loaded first.

Many hands lowered each large crate to the ground. Some were heavy, and others were full of medical equipment that was delicate and expensive, donated by companies or bought by contributors. The unloading took about twenty minutes of hard labor, and while that was proceeding, the fuel truck that had been parked in the shelter provided by two large buildings pulled up on the other side of the plane and a man began refueling it.

The men with guns had their eyes turned away until the plane was unloaded, and the fuel truck pulled away and went back to its sheltered space. Then the driver got out and parked a car in front of the fuel truck so the truck would be harder to hit with small arms from a distance.

The plane's pilot and copilot performed a hasty walk-around inspection of the plane, and then boarded it. The flight attendant raised the steps and closed the hatch, and the pilot started the engine. The control tower had been hit by something big and explosive in one of the battles, and whatever had taken its place was not evident to Alan. The pilot was visible in the cockpit in radio communication with someone, somewhere, and then he moved the plane forward, heading for the end of the runway.

Some of the volunteers watched the plane turn at the end of the runway, and then roar along the tarmac at a slight angle to avoid the worst of the shell craters and burn marks on the pavement, and then rise into the air. Alan listened for sounds of small-arms fire, but heard none, and saw no streaks of light moving toward the plane. In a minute it was high enough so it became just a set of blinking lights fading into the distance.

The air became quiet at that moment. The arrival or takeoff of a plane was a rare occurrence. The militiamen seemed to relax now that the plane was gone, but it didn't seem to Alan that they were entirely secure or at ease. He noticed that there were also at least a half dozen of them on the roof of the ruined terminal with binoculars and night-vision scopes. He could see they were protected by debris camouflaging a wall of sandbags, and he thought he saw the barrels of heavy machine guns.

A dozen members of the militia on the ground performed a customs check as the volunteers watched. They inspected a few of the cardboard cartons that held bags of rice, beans, and wheat flour, canned vegetables, and halal meat. They moved to the wooden crates of machinery and pried a few open. As he had expected, they paid most attention to the crates that held heavy equipment. Well-drilling rigs, irrigation pumps, water purification machines, and hand tools piqued their interest most because they were made of steel and dismantled for shipment, so the crates looked, felt, and sounded as though they contained weapons.

The medical equipment was light and tended to be electronics sheathed in plastic consoles. There was lab equipment to analyze blood, urine, and dissolved blood gases. There were an X-ray machine, an ultrasound machine, and a PET scanner. There were sterilizers, EKG machines, infusion pumps, anesthetic machines, and monitors to track patients' vital signs. The militiamen opened a few of the boxes, but shut them almost immediately and moved on to the next ones.

Alan noticed that there seemed to be some kind of commotion beginning near the far side of the main pile of boxes. He recognized Dr. Zidane immediately, and Dr. Leclerc, and they seemed to be unhappy with the man Alan had decided must be the head of the militia contingent. He moved closer and listened.

In a few seconds Dr. Zidane noticed him. She said in English, "He wants to take food and supplies. Can you believe it?"

Alan said, "How much?"

She said, "Who knows? We can't spare any of it."

Alan stepped closer and bowed to the leader. "I am Alan Spencer," he said in Arabic. "Are you the commander of the militia?"

"Abdul Hamid, colonel of the Misrata Militia. I've been speaking with this woman, and she doesn't seem to understand anything she wasn't taught in an American school."

Alan said, "American? Dr. Zidane is Canadian, like the rest of us."

"That difference means nothing here."

Alan could see that one thing hadn't changed much in the past thirty years. This was not a part of the world where men—at least men like this militia—were accustomed to arguing with women. Alan said, "Maybe I can help clear up the misunderstanding."

"You were able to land a plane here because we fought for this airport in two great battles. We're here to protect you because the plane brought food and other supplies that the people need. We're not going to sell it or throw it away. The people around here are our relatives. We know how to get it to them."

Alan smiled, he hoped, convincingly. "Oh," he said. "Thank you for explaining. Please give me a moment." He stepped to the two doctors. "I think he feels insulted."

"He's insulted because I'm a woman," said Dr. Zidane. "For that and because I won't let him steal food and supplies. We didn't bring this here to support a war."

Alan said, "He wants to distribute some to the people around here, who are his relatives or members of his faction. How much of the food can we spare?"

"None."

"Would his tribe and its allies get some of the supplies if he didn't ask?"

"Of course. We don't choose sides or tribes. We give aid to whomever we can reach who needs it."

"Maybe we could trust him to deliver the supplies that are going to his people anyway."

She scowled. "I don't trust him. Why do you?"

"Several reasons. He can't steal the supplies from his men's relatives, and he knows it. He's not a king. Nobody who is surrounded by men carrying machine guns is a king. He'll just be doing some of our work for us."

Leclerc looked at her. "This sounds logical to me."

She threw up her hands in a gesture of frustration. "All right. Do it."

Alan turned to Leclerc and said, "The other reason is that we can't stop him. If we say no, he can take everything."

Alan returned to the colonel. "I'm sorry for the delay. If you would be willing to distribute the goods intended for your friends and relatives, it would save us time and effort, and we would be grateful. Take one quarter of the food and supplies, but please leave the medical goods here for the clinic."

The colonel looked hard at him for a couple of seconds. "That woman. What about her? Does she agree? What if I take it all?"

Alan shrugged. "If you have skilled doctors, you might do some good. But Dr. Zidane is an expert on North African diseases, the only one we have with us. Dr. Leclerc is a famous surgeon. Dr. McKnight is a great anesthesiologist."

The colonel smiled. "I see why they brought you with them."

"Thank you. I'll ask some people to help your men pick out the cartons you need."

Alan joined the nurses and volunteers waiting nearby. "Give them a quarter of the food. Nothing else. Keep all the medical supplies and the agricultural machinery and so on."

The work went quickly because the militiamen wanted to travel while it was still dark and their convoy wouldn't attract attention, so they did much of the lifting and loading. Meanwhile, Alan began an informal inventory of the items that the soldiers were not supposed to take.

He was careful to locate a crate he had packed personally in Toronto. It held the diagnostic X-ray machine and some stands and associated equipment. Inside he had placed a Czech-made .45 caliber pistol with the barrel threaded for its silencer, and four spare loaded magazines. He had taken the pistol off the body of one of Faris Hamzah's assassins who had come for him in Chicago. He had chosen this pistol as the one to retain, because it was high quality and had no purchasing history that could possibly lead to him.

He had hidden the pistol and the rest wrapped in two of the lead-lined aprons that went with the X-ray machine, and then restored the original packaging so that even if the machine were subjected to a physical search, his additions wouldn't be noticed. He slipped the pistol and magazines into his travel jacket. When he found his duffel bag he took off the jacket and hid it inside the duffel.

Alan worked with a few other volunteers to place the pile of supplies and equipment inside the terminal's damaged waiting area and then set up enough folding cots so they could all sleep as a group and watch each other, their bags, and boxes. When Alan got the chance to pick a cot, he chose one on the perimeter. He reached into his duffel bag, took out a towel, rolled it to use as a pillow, and then reached back into the bag and felt for the weapon he had hidden there. He screwed the silencer on the barrel, engaged the safety, and buried the gun among the clothes.

He studied his own reaction to the long flight, the layover, and the physical labor in the heat. He wasn't twenty-five years old anymore, but he seemed to be all right—aware of no signs of dehydration or muscle aches.

He lay there thinking about Marie. She would have found the laptop and the videodisc a few hours ago, so she knew what he had done. He felt a painful mixture of affection and regret grip his stomach, and then waited for it to pass. When it didn't, he spent a few minutes reviewing the provisions he had made for her. They should be sufficient to keep her safe and comfortable for the rest of her life. He reviewed everything again, and soon he dozed off.

Around 5:00 a.m. growling engines signaled the arrival of the three trucks that were to take the aid workers to their first clinic. The volunteers stowed their cots and their belongings, and then began loading the trucks. The wind had shifted while they were sleeping and the temperature had dropped about ten degrees.

The Canadians relaxed and regained their optimism. These were men and women in their twenties through forties—a generation or two younger than Alan—and they had recovered from the long flight overnight. They set up a line like a bucket brigade to pass the cardboard cartons of supplies from the terminal to the trucks. Alan took a place in the line and began to pass boxes.

After a few minutes he sensed someone behind him and turned. It was Dr. Zidane, and she pulled him out of the line and led him a few yards away.

"Alan, I want to express my thanks for the way you handled things last night. I guess what I mean is, how you handled me. I wasn't thinking clearly."

"I wasn't handling anybody," he said. "I was just trying to bow to the inevitable, and people let me do it. I find the gray hairs help."

"I made a foolish mistake," she said. "I was tired and irritated, and I think I've gotten too used to living in places where people wouldn't think of breaking the rules. Here you have to be flexible and patient. My parents moved to Canada in the seventies, so I never lived here as an adult."

"Well, I was glad to help. And thanks. It's nice to get a pat on the back from the boss."

"Well, I'd better get over to the trucks before somebody puts a generator on top of an ultrasound machine." She hurried off, and he returned to work on the loading line.

As he worked, he thought. He had made himself visible, and that was a risk, especially being visible to men like the colonel. He might suspect him of being a plant from a Canadian intelligence agency. Alan was fairly confident that the Libya Dawn fighters wouldn't care if he were. They were allied with the remainder of the old Parliament, and they were opposed to the extreme Islamists to the east, and to the internationally recognized government beyond them in Tobruk. Canada wasn't much of a threat. But in civil wars it was difficult to know who all the players really were, and which side they might be on tomorrow.

He had also felt a chill from talking to Dr. Zidane. She and Dr. Leclerc were in charge of this mission to Libya, and she was the one who had most of the knowledge of the place—the language, religion, and customs. She should have been able to deal with the commander. But something had gone wrong last night, and he thought he knew what it might be.

Dr. Zidane was clearly a member of a rich, high-status family, the sort who might have once expected to order an army officer around. But things had changed. The country was divided into five or six major factions, and people of every shade of opinion were walking around with military weapons. She might have been right that the colonel was simply unable to tolerate a structure that put a woman in charge. But there might be more to his animosity too. The fighters had no reason to love the aristocracy.

What Alan was most afraid of was that he might have sparked resentment in her. He had unexpectedly come between her and the nearest Libyan authority, and maybe even between her and Dr. Leclerc. He resolved to fade into an unnoticeable blur in the mission as soon as possible.

At nine the trucks reached their first stop and the Canadians set up the first clinic in a village fifty miles from the outskirts of Tripoli. The lines of patients formed while the volunteers were still hauling boxes around and setting up tents and canopies. The registered nurses and trained technicians supervised and set up the diagnostic equipment and prepared the supplies for vaccinations, pap smears, deworming, and other routine procedures. At least half of the relief workers had been deployed in remote countries before, so there were plenty of people who were capable of deciding what went where.

The clinic was in operation within an hour, and patients were being seen in an orderly, timely way. Alan was one of the four

Arabic speakers who wrote down the names of the patients and their complaints, took their blood pressure and temperature, and then directed them to the triage nurses.

The clinic hours started at first light each day and went on until the four doctors had worn themselves out around dusk. For the nurses and volunteers, the work continued until late evening. They cleaned and bandaged minor injuries, gave shots, and handed out food and clean water.

There were several volunteers who were engineers and specialized in electricity, hydraulics, or sanitation, and they ranged away from the clinic, invited into the villages by local people to solve problems or repair old systems. Alan Spencer quickly learned who they were and what each did, in case the information should become useful.

The clinic remained in its first location for three days, and then the trucks, which had been hidden in two garages and a warehouse, arrived again and they loaded up and left. They drove eastward, but immediately had to swing south into rough country controlled by the Tuareg, because the strip of land along the Mediterranean in the north-central part was controlled by ISIS, and they would have been eager to behead a couple of dozen Canadian humanitarians in front of a web camera to help their recruiting efforts. The Canadians made five six-day stays among the Tuareg at known oases.

As they moved eastward again they entered the area controlled by the national government. The regime was based in Tobruk, and consisted of the country's Council of Deputies, combined for the moment with the remnants of the former national army. The government army was carrying on a campaign called Operation Dignity. Its primary opponents were the other national government in Tripoli and Islamic militias of the Libya Dawn faction. At that moment both sides were fighting over Benghazi, but a cease-fire was holding south of there, where the Canadian relief mission was headed.

They had avoided the area to the north and west where ISIS was holding out against air strikes from Egyptian fighter planes. The Canadians had also avoided the Tunisian border, where a group of Al Qaeda fighters were operating a base that they used as a training camp and a stronghold for staging raids.

Every region had its own militias, each with its own weapons, its own tribal hatreds, and regional rivalries. Spencer knew that Libya had about 140 tribes. The national army still seemed to be in charge in the east, but they could not pacify it, so lines shifted. Some of the eastern Libyan Islamist militias—Ansar al-Sharia, Libya Shield 1, February 17th Martyrs Brigade, Rafallah al-Sahati Brigade—had banded together into the Shura Council of Benghazi Revolutionaries to oppose the Tobruk forces.

Changes came abruptly in a modern civil war, and the chance of heading for a safe destination and arriving to find it taken or retaken by a hostile force was high. But the relief mission's leaders kept themselves and the staff informed about what was ahead as well as possible by satellite phone and radio. They stayed out of the large cities, where bad things were most likely to happen. Cities were the big prizes for attackers and the lifelines of the defenders.

As the mission headed eastward, Alan Spencer began to carry on quiet conversations with his Arabic-speaking patients. He would ask about their tribes, how their relatives and friends were surviving, the state of their businesses and home villages. He noted the names he heard, their factions and groups. And sometimes, he would work his way around to asking: "Have you ever heard of a man named Faris Hamzah?"

33

Fall was busy at the university, but Julian Carson enjoyed the work. The university was the most reliable and stable employer in Jonesboro, and he liked the science faculty and students. They tended to be polite but preoccupied, and not especially pretentious, and they were too busy to be curious about him.

But what he liked more was Ruthie. He had not gotten over his secret shock that somehow the course of his life had twisted around so that she had come to love him.

His life was almost perfect. He had been able to quiet his own conscience about most of the things he had done for the army. He had been part of a forward covert team sent to protect the personnel and the interests of the United States in several countries. He could have made a good argument that each operation made sense and probably saved the lives of civilians in the countries where he'd worked. If his career had ended when he'd been recalled from Brazil, he could have closed that part of his life without regret. If it hadn't been for his final assignment, he could have been at peace. What made that impossible was the old man.

Everything the senior agents had said the old man had done was logically impossible, and had to be lies. The old man couldn't have stolen the twenty million dollars from Faris Hamzah unless he had delivered it to him first. And if Hamzah had given the money to the rebels in the hills instead of stealing it, the old man couldn't have taken it back from him. The old man's superiors in military intelligence had never charged him with anything, and neither had anybody since.

Julian couldn't help wondering where the old man and his girl-friend had gone after Big Bear. He had no idea how they were liv-ing, now that the old man had returned the twenty million dollars to the Treasury, or what names they were using. He had no way to help them, but what he could do was distract and mislead the pursuers. He needed to make sure that the military intelligence people would be watching him.

Last time, he had reached the old man by putting an ad in the *Chicago Tribune*. He knew that the old man's interest in Chicago would have lapsed during the months since then. But he also knew that the intelligence people would not have lost interest. They would still be monitoring the want ads, and still searching for anything that carried the name James Harriman.

He composed a classified ad for the *Chicago Tribune* just like the one he had used to set up the meeting with the old man in San Francisco. "I will be available to talk in the same way at the usual time. J. H." He asked that it run for a week, and enclosed payment in cash.

Julian made everything he did look suspicious. He went to an Ikea store and bought furniture that came unassembled in large, flat cardboard boxes. There were a queen bed, a couple of nightstands, and a dresser. On the same trip he bought a set of blackout drapes to hang behind the regular curtains in the guest room. As he left the store with the boxes on a flat cart, he noticed that there was a man he had never seen before standing inside the building a few feet back from the sliding glass doors, watching him. As he was loading the boxes into his car in the lot, he saw the man getting into a dark blue Mustang. Twice on the way home he saw the car again. They were still watching him. He made several quick turns, came back the same way, and passed the man, then lost him.

Julian had bought the furniture because Ruthie's niece from Louisville wanted to come for a visit, but he did his best to make his watchers suspect that he might be planning to hide the old man and his girlfriend for a time. When he had finished assembling the furniture and hung the blackout drapes, he saw a black SUV parked across the street with two men inside. After a few hours a second pair relieved the first. The shifts went on for over a week, and ended when Ruthie's niece arrived and moved into the room.

The next week he bought a pair of prepaid cell phones that could be used and discarded and had them delivered to his office at the university.

At frequent intervals Julian did things that would indicate his plan was to help the old man. The next week he began a series of computer searches of travel agencies, airlines, and hotels. He studied Antwerp, where the diamond wholesalers operated; Luxembourg, where the old man had assembled the money to take to Faris Hamzah thirty-five years ago; Geneva, where banks might harbor numbered accounts old enough to have existed when the old man had first taken the money out of Libya.

Anything Julian could do to keep the eyes of military intelligence focused on him, he did. He knew he could rely on their overconfidence to help them fool themselves. They knew that he had found the old man twice when they had failed. Now he tried to make them believe that he was secretly in touch with the old man and making arrangements for him to sink deeper out of sight.

Julian e-mailed cryptic messages to men whose names he found online—men in their sixties who owned businesses, ran organizations, were mentioned in articles, or wrote them. He often used the names of donors or graduates he found in online Ivy League university alumni publications. Sometimes Julian's messages looked like word code. Some were numerical, and others were symbols arranged in patterns. None of them meant anything.

Julian made sure agents would have to get on an airplane, fly to some city, and investigate. He picked addresses all over the country and mailed puzzling things to them—keys that no longer opened any lock, tickets to plays or sporting events in distant cities that might serve as meeting opportunities.

Julian was fairly confident that he could keep one small corner of the intelligence world occupied—Mr. Ross, Mr. Prentiss, Mr. Bailey, Waters, Harper, and a few unseen colleagues. Their operation—trying to deliver a rogue American agent to a Libyan asset—seemed to Julian so incriminating that the number of people who knew anything about it must be very small.

There were some encouraging signs. If they had already found the old man or killed him, they would have no interest in Julian anymore. As long as they were watching Julian, the old man must still be alive and free.

During a break at work he completed searches about banking practices in the Cayman Islands, and the extradition laws of various European countries. He started with France, and then moved to Ireland, and then east to countries that had once been part of the Soviet Union. That would give the people monitoring his computer plenty to think about.

One evening when it was nearly ten he picked up a backpack, slipped out the back door of the house, and went through a couple of yards to where he had parked his truck after work. He took the truck to the hospital to pick up Ruthie from her shift and drove her along the dark highway to Lake City, where he made a series of quick turns and then backed into a space behind a building and watched for the car he had noticed following on the dark highway to catch up.

He and Ruthie went to an ice-cream shop in Lake City where they and their friends used to go in high school and were delighted to find it was still there. They split a sundae and drove home, followed all the way home by the same car.

When they got home, Julian did his usual his walk around to see if anyone had been inside the house, or outside trying to get in, but there was no sign of intruders. Then he and Ruthie showered and went to bed.

Now and then he would let a period go by when he did nothing suspicious, and he let one of those times occur next. Then, early in the morning a week later, he went to the university library and borrowed some language practice tapes in Portuguese and books about Brazil. He was sure that whoever was watching him must know that he had posed as a Brazilian for over two years before he'd been recalled to the United States to look for the old man.

Julian went to the Chemistry and Physics Building and began work. He had to set up an apparatus for a chemistry demonstration to be performed at a morning lecture, fill a series of written equipment requests for physics research, and fill out the forms for the purchasing department.

He set the Portuguese tapes and the books about Brazil in his desk at odd angles and photographed them with his phone, so when he returned from lunch he could see whether they had been touched. When he returned he found they had.

That night before he went to sleep he wondered where the old man really was. He hoped it wasn't Brazil.

34

Alan Spencer had begun to dress like a Libyan after two months in the country. On most days he wore a pair of loose white pants, a white shirt that hung nearly to his knees, and a pair of sandals. Sometimes he wrapped a scarf around his neck and pulled it up like a hood over the skullcap he wore. On hotter days he wore the *kaffiyeh*, keeping his neck, shoulders, and head protected. His face and hands had tanned, because he spent most of his days interviewing patients outside the medical tents.

He began to notice that the patients, particularly the ones in the remote rural areas, were more likely to approach him first, because his clothing put them at ease.

Spencer assumed that a few of the Canadians probably thought he was going native, or masquerading, but others seemed to respect him for adapting to the climate. In time a few other volunteers followed his lead. But his motives were not what they imagined. The long, loose shirt and pants made it easy to conceal his pistol and the flat pocketknife he now carried. He knew that if terrorists were to open fire at the clinic, the first shots would be aimed at the highest-value targets. They would aim for the doctors, then the nurses, all in hospital scrubs, and then anyone else who didn't look Libyan.

Spencer's new appearance might give him time to pull out his silenced pistol and kill one or two attackers before they realized where his shots were coming from.

As the months went by, the Canadian relief mission moved farther east, and slightly northward toward Ajdabiya, Benghazi, and Tobruk. The team encountered increasing numbers of refugees from wars and migrants hoping to reach places where they could earn a living. There were groups of Eritreans and Somalians fleeing Al-Shabaab, traveling on foot toward the Libyan port of Ajdabiya. The travelers he interviewed said that they hoped to get on boats to Greece or Italy, but if that failed they would keep going to Benghazi and try again there.

Many needed medical help, and had been in need long before they reached the clinic. All of them needed food and water. Groups would stop to rest for a day or two before they moved on, trying to marshal their strength for the big push to the Mediterranean.

As the clinic moved closer to Ajdabiya, they began to meet Syrians, Senegalese, and even a few Libyans from regions where the fighting had been heating up. All it took to explain why they were converging in the northeast was a glance at the map. Libya was the obvious place to cross the Mediterranean to southern Europe. The smuggling routes were centuries old, and the human trafficking business had been thriving for decades. The logic of getting out of the Middle East and North Africa was unassailable, obvious to everyone. The wars of the past ten years had left poverty and chaos, and the extreme danger of the escape routes deterred no one.

Nearly all the refugees spoke Arabic or had someone with them who did, so Spencer's language skills were more in demand than ever. Traffic increased as they neared Tobruk, the stronghold of the government forces.

Because of the press of patients the Canadian relief mission exhausted its supplies two months earlier than they had expected, so they asked that the scheduled airlift to resupply them be moved eight weeks ahead. They drove into Tobruk to wait for the airlift at the airport, which Alan remembered had still been the old El Adem air base when he was in Libya. When they reached the airport, Dr. Zidane received a phone call that said there would be a three-day delay. The supplies had to be purchased, packaged, and loaded.

Spencer waited until the group had unloaded the trucks and set up camp inside the airport fence. Then he went to find Dr. Zidane alone. He said, "I know this is an unusual favor to ask, but I'd like to take a little time off."

"Time off?" she said. "That's a novel idea. What would you do?"

"I think I told you that when I was a child I came to Libya with my parents, who were archaeologists. When they worked in particularly remote sites, they sometimes had me staying with Libyan friends between here and Benghazi. I'd like to go and visit some of the places I remember."

She shrugged and said, "I don't feel I can say no to you, Alan. You're absolutely irreplaceable, but we're stuck here for a few days, and we don't have enough supplies left to run at full strength anyway. But please, be very careful. You're in the middle of a civil war."

"I'll be careful," he said. "And I'll be back in seventy-two hours, when the plane arrives."

"Do you want to take one of the satellite phones?"

"No, thanks," he said. "Carrying around expensive, sophisticated technology won't make me any safer."

He found a driver outside the airport waiting for his next passenger. The man's pickup truck reminded Alan of the small Japanese truck he had used thirty years ago to drive himself to Morocco. The memory made him trust this truck not to break down. He asked the driver if he could take him to a village just outside Benghazi, about 250 miles away. The driver countered that Benghazi was at least 300. Spencer said the village was closer than Benghazi. They arrived at a price, and Alan climbed in beside him.

The driver's name was Abdullah, and he was a cheerful companion. He drove with great confidence and talked about his family, his village by the sea, and his hope that the fighting would end so he could go to Benghazi and open an electronics store. Spencer could see he was watching the road for anything ahead that might harm his tires, break his springs, or blow up.

Spencer told him he was a Canadian relief worker who happened to speak excellent Arabic. He told the practiced lie about coming to Libya as a child with his parents. He said he had volunteered for the relief mission to give a little bit back to the country.

He directed Abdullah to the village near Benghazi where he had met Faris Hamzah. The road that led to the place from the south was the same one he had used to bring the money to Faris Hamzah and to take it away again. The boundaries of the village had crept outward, and now it seemed to have become a town.

Spencer looked from a distance at Faris Hamzah's complex. Now, over thirty years later, the wall around it had been built up and buttressed and was about ten feet tall. The house had been enlarged and raised to two stories with a flat, rectangular roof. He could see there were two other two-story buildings on the property—possibly housing for Faris Hamzah's guards or servants—and a garage.

The couple of dusty, scraggly olive trees of thirty-five years ago were now a couple of dozen trees. They appeared to be grouped around the space where he had once seen a half-finished fountain, so he guessed the space must be a shaded garden now.

The big house was not a surprise. Hamzah must be a powerful man if he was sending teams of killers to the United States. In Libya, power meant military power, religious power, or factional power. Hamzah had not been a soldier, and had never been even remotely pious. But he did have a family and a tribe, and a connection with the local people. His great-grandfather, grandfather, and father had built a food stall in the village market into a store, and then added a few more stores in other villages. The intelligence report on Hamzah that he had read mentioned that the family's fortunes had not been diminished by excessive honesty, but they did not seem to have suffered for it.

Spencer guessed that Hamzah had to have kept an unambiguous connection with the cluster of villages his tribe controlled, and especially this one. In the old days, he'd held no office, and probably didn't now. After a first attempt by Libyans in the post-Gaddafi years to hold elections, the Islamic fundamentalists had announced that they had no intention of accepting their loss. After that there were no elections for Hamzah or anyone else to run in, and no offices to win. All a man like Hamzah could be doing was promising to deliver his faction to one side or another in the civil war. Right now, he must be on the side the United States supported, the Tobruk government. Otherwise US military intelligence wouldn't be doing favors for him.

The car passed the block and Alan Spencer made a quick decision. "Abdullah," he said. "Please drive on this way for another quarter mile and let me off. I'll find my way back to Tobruk later."

Abdullah stopped, and Spencer gave him the fee they had agreed upon and another third as much.

Abdullah thanked him for his generosity, and Spencer said, "Thank you for your kindness and your patience. May Allah protect you."

"And may he protect you," said Abdullah. He turned the car around and drove off.

"*Aameen*," Spencer muttered. "May it be so." He stepped away from the road and onto the dusty, weedy ground. He selected a route a distance from the first buildings and walked it, staying far enough away from the village to escape notice. He avoided a junkyard and then made his way upwind of a municipal garbage heap. He found a hill he remembered that overlooked the dry river and the village on the other side. He climbed up and sat down to wait for the world to get dark.

35

When Julian Carson returned to his office in the Chemistry and Physics Building after lunch he found an e-mail waiting for him on his computer. It was from the chancellor's office, and it had all of the formal boilerplate that was automatically added to anything originating there. There was Office of the Chancellor of the Arkansas State University and the address, phone number, and e-mail address of the chancellor's office.

At first Julian wasn't very interested because the chancellor's office included pretty much everything that went on in the administration building, including the budget, the contracts and grants office, and the recruiting office.

He began to scan the message lazily, but then he sat up and read it carefully. It was addressed to Mr. Julian Carson, and it was from the vice chancellor for Campus Support, the administrator in charge of facilities.

"Dear Mr. Carson," it said. "Please come to the Campus Support Office, Admin Room 310, at 2:00 p.m. today, December 12, for a meeting. You will be engaged for approximately one hour, so please clear your schedule from 2:00 p.m. to 3:00 p.m."

He looked at his watch. It was after one. He checked his schedule for the afternoon to be sure he was free, and then printed the e-mail and went to the Chemistry and Physics Department office.

He knocked on the door of Helen, the chairman's administrative assistant. She called, "Come in." And he entered. She was, as usual, running figures on her computer and scribbling notes on a scratch pad, trying to devise ways to make the department's budget accommodate everything—faculty, supplies, scientific equipment. "Hi, Julian. What's up?"

"I got an e-mail that says I've got to go to a meeting at the vice chancellor's office, from two to three."

She glanced up at him and held out her hand for the paper. She read it quickly and handed it back. "Safety," she said. "That's my guess. You're the designated person to handle and store dangerous chemicals and fool with high voltage and all that."

"Would all the people who do that fit in his office?"

"The English Department doesn't usually have anything that blows up. Maybe they're organizing an emergency planning team for disasters or something. You're not in trouble, or they would have told me too. Do I need to assign somebody to take your place while you're gone?"

"I don't think so. I thought I'd put a note on my door that I'll be back at three."

"Good idea. Enjoy the extra hour of sleep."

"Thanks."

He left Helen's office, went back to his own, and posted his note, then walked across the campus.

When Julian got to the office of the vice chancellor at 1:55 p.m., he entered and found himself in a waiting room with a receptionist's desk without a receptionist. He sat down in one of the chairs along the wall.

At 2:00 p.m. the inner office door opened and the vice chancellor came out. Julian stood, but the vice chancellor walked past him as though he were invisible and went out the door. Julian heard a sound, turned to look in the direction of the inner office, and saw three men come out—Mr. Ross, Mr. Bailey, and Mr. Prentiss. Apparently he was in trouble after all. But he had been misleading them and wasting their time, so the only real surprise was where they had turned up.

"Hello, Mr. Carson," said Mr. Ross. "How have you been?"

"Okay," said Julian. He glanced at the door where the vice chancellor had gone. He was making sure nobody got between him and the exit.

"Vice Chancellor Halgren was Captain Halgren once. He was happy to lend us his office and his employee for one hour."

"What for?" asked Julian.

"Just a little chat," Mr. Ross said. "Come on in."

They went into the inner office. Julian looked at the dark wood furniture and paneling, and the full bookcases. All of the books came in identical sets, and no book looked as though it had ever been touched. He sat at the table and waited.

Mr. Prentiss lifted a hard-sided briefcase to the surface of the table, and then worked a combination. He opened the briefcase, took out a thick blue file, and set it on the table in front of Mr. Ross. Then he set the briefcase on the floor.

Mr. Ross tapped his fingers on the thick file. "This," he said, "is something we had to work very hard to get our hands on. We wanted to give you a chance to take a look."

"What is it?"

"The old man's army personnel file. It's got his service record, from his signed oath to preserve and defend us from all enemies, foreign and domestic, all the way to a copy of his DD-214. It's also got records of his contract work for military intelligence, including his final mission, the one to Libya."

Julian kept his face blank. "Why would I want to see that? I'm not working for military intelligence anymore. I don't care about the old man."

Mr. Ross stopped drumming his fingers on the file and held it with both hands. "I don't really claim to understand you, Mr. Carson. You did a good job of finding our man twice. You took a pair of Libyan agents to his house in Chicago. You got him to a meeting in San Francisco. You nearly froze to death taking a special ops rifle squad to his cabin in the mountains. Then you got frustrated and quit. You came back to your hometown and married a pretty girl. That's not you."

"What doesn't fit me?"

"You haven't forgotten about the old man. You're still looking for him."

"No I'm not," Julian said.

"You're on your computer every day checking out places where you think he might be hiding. You pick out men on the Internet who are about his age and description. You send fake coded messages to the ones you can't eliminate by looking at their pictures."

"Why would I do that? If it's a fake code, it doesn't mean anything."

"You and the old man both know how the game is played. You didn't think he would tell you where he was. You wanted him to know where you are. You want him to realize it's you, so he knows how to get in touch and arrange another meeting."

"I didn't pretend to quit the government," Julian said. "I quit. It's not my job to care where the old man is now."

Mr. Ross frowned. "Quitting only means you're not on the payroll. You don't quit a war and go home to spend your life counting beakers and test tubes. I knew when you handed in your scrambled phone that you were still in. You just didn't feel like taking orders anymore."

"So you brought me his file."

Mr. Ross nodded. "We brought you his file. This is the most highly classified set of documents you've ever touched. The file wasn't in the National Personnel Records Center in St. Louis. Since the giant screwup thirty-five years ago it's been archived in a facility in the middle of the Air Force Intelligence installation at Patrick Air Force Base in Florida. The building isn't on any list of buildings or on maps of the base. The base perimeter is patrolled, and the building is guarded by people who don't know what they're guarding."

"And you're going to just hand it over to me."

"You know better than that."

"What, then?"

"The vice chancellor has given us exclusive access to a room on this campus that conforms to the security requirements for storing highly classified technical information. The room has one steel door and no windows," Mr. Ross said. "The file will be locked in a safe except while you're alone in there reading it for one hour a day. Then the file gets locked up again until you come back."

"Why would I want to read it?"

Mr. Ross shrugged. "Because you want to know the truth."

"And why do you want me to read it?"

"Because I think once you know everything about him, you'll figure out how to find him. If you do, you're the one he might talk to."

Julian looked straight into Ross's eyes. "I think he was framed."

"That's what you think now. Maybe when you know more about him you'll think something different. But it doesn't matter what you think. What matters is that you can't let this alone."

Julian looked at the other two men. "How much is redacted?"

Mr. Ross said, "This isn't some copy released under the Freedom of Information Act. This is the real thing. Nothing is redacted."

36

Julian sat in the single folding chair at the folding table in the small utility room beneath the stands of the football stadium. A row of four-inch pipes that ran floor to ceiling was the only adornment to the windowless concrete walls. Each had a five-inch valve that looked like a little brass wheel. There was an overhead fluorescent light mounted on the concrete ceiling. The only other piece of furniture in the room was a safe. He opened the thick blue folder. It was the standard military personnel format with a thick sheaf of papers speared and held on the left and right by metal pieces folded down and secured. Julian began to read.

The old man's last name was Kohler, first name Michael, middle name Isaac. He was born in Bay Village, Ohio, on July 10, sixty-one years ago. Julian looked up from the blue folder and thought. Bay Village sounded like a suburb of Cleveland on the shore of Lake Erie. He pictured it as one of those old places that had a park with a white wooden bandstand at its center and a ring of redbrick buildings that held stores and restaurants.

Michael Isaac Kohler graduated with a BA in economics and political science from Cornell University in Ithaca, New York. That meant he had won a scholarship or that his parents had been rich, or nearly rich. Julian had never been able to place the old man's accent because it conveyed only the north-central part of the country, and he used standard grammar. What had Kohler wanted to be, in those days when he came home after college? Whatever it was, he didn't get to do it. He was drafted that summer, and sent through the machine—basic training, infantry school, advanced infantry with courses in hand-to-hand, sniper training, and survival school, and then off to Vietnam. Two tours, and then home. Why two? Why didn't he take his discharge after surviving the first tour?

Julian leafed through the pages secured to the right side of the folder. They contained the dates and locations of Kohler's training and the certifications he'd earned, and copies of the orders to report to various places.

Julian lifted another page and found copies of citations. Two Purple Hearts, a year and a half apart. Bad luck there. He made a good target. But after that: a Bronze Star and, later, a Silver Star. They gave you the last two only for gallantry under fire. The old man was a war hero, somebody who had not only done something but saved people while he was at it.

Julian remembered watching the old man in Chicago, and again in San Francisco. He had seen him burn whatever fear he must have been feeling and convert it into alertness, energy, and motion. There was never a second when he hadn't known what to do.

Julian leafed through the rest of the thick file to get a quick overview. There was the transfer to military intelligence. He'd spent the next year at the Monterey language school. No, a year and a half. And there were the honorable discharge papers, just like Julian's. That was where the military part of the record ended.

Julian turned back through the pages of the military record to the recommendation for the Silver Star. There was the usual businesslike description of what Kohler had done, written by Kohler's company commander, Captain J. W. Marks. Kohler had been one of the men who arrived in Vietnam early in 1972, just before the

Easter Offensive. That was the moment when the enemy chose to stop relying on the patient Viet Cong guerrilla campaign that had pecked away at the Americans for years, and began the North Vietnamese Army invasion, complete with tanks and heavy artillery.

At the time of the invasion, Kohler had been out in the jungles north of Quang Tri with ARVN rangers searching for small Viet Cong units. One night, after the rangers had found signs of enemy activity, Kohler and the rangers had blacked their faces and hands and gone out to sneak up on the enemy guerrillas, capture one, and bring him back to be searched and interrogated. They captured four.

What they discovered was that something big was coming. These troops were from far away in the north. They weren't locals wearing black pajamas and sandals made from tire treads. They were soldiers with full military uniforms and gear.

Julian looked for the next part of the story. It wasn't in the citation, but he could easily supply what wasn't said. Kohler must have conveyed his concern to Captain Marks, who had reported it up the chain of command, but the reports had gone unnoticed among the thousands of pieces of intel that a war produced every day.

Kohler went out alone to search for more evidence that a major attack from the north was coming. Two days later, as he came in from one of his solo night recons, he found himself behind several platoons of North Vietnamese troops moving in on three sides of the ARVN camp, preparing to massacre the rangers. Kohler began a one-man attack, firing at the enemy, exhausting his ammunition, throwing his grenades, and taking a North Vietnamese machine gun, which he turned on the attackers. Kohler drew the enemy's fire, which led his ARVN rangers to the enemy soldiers' positions and gave them somebody to shoot at. The rangers rallied. They suffered light casualties and retreated successfully, taking their wounded with them.

The North Vietnam Army troops recovered very quickly from their minor, momentary setback in this single action. Tank divisions rolled into the central highlands from several directions, including Cambodia. The North Vietnamese Army advanced, slowed only by fierce and costly resistance from the Americans and the ARVN. They got as far as Kon Tum City on June 9, and were stopped there by hard fighting and devastating American air strikes. The date on Captain Marks's recommendation for the Silver Star was July 1.

Julian had read about the Easter campaign when he was in Ranger NCO school. It was a long, hard holding action, but stopping the invasion at Kon Tum probably delayed the inevitable loss of South Vietnam by three years. Julian wondered. If Michael Kohler had known the future that day, would he have wanted to prolong the Vietnam War by three years?

Knowing the future wouldn't have mattered, Julian decided. Given the chance, Kohler could only have done the same thing. He wasn't trying to preserve a strategy, or hold some worthless land a little while longer. He was trying to save men he knew from dying.

Julian stood up from the small table in the concrete room. He closed the blue folder and left it on the table. He went to the door, knocked, and watched the door open. Waters and Harper came in, took the file, and frisked him again. When they found no paper hidden on him, Waters took the file and locked it in the safe in the corner, and they all left the little room. As Waters locked the steel door, Harper handed back Julian's phone. "See you tomorrow, Julian."

"Right." Julian walked down the concrete hallway past the electronic circuit room, and then through the visiting team locker room, and out another steel door that locked behind him when he closed it. Now he was behind the stadium, walking toward the parking lot.

The old man had a military career a lot like his, he thought. They both got sent to fight wars that were lost before they got there.

37

It was after midnight. Alan Spencer leaned against the slope of the hill above the dry wash north of the town and looked up at the stars. The sky was black, but there were enough stars to make an explosion of light, maybe twice the number he could see on the clearest nights in Toronto. He saw a meteor streak across his vision and disappear, and decided to take it as a sign.

He sat up and shifted the burden of the .45 pistol, its suppressor, and the extra magazines in his belt. He stood and stared at the road and let his eyes follow it to the town. He could see the buildings, looking like a pile of boxes. Most of them were low rectangles, but there were a few now that had three or four stories, and even two he could spot far off on the south side that looked like office buildings.

It was late enough now so he could take a look at Faris Hamzah's compound. He walked toward the paved road into town. As he went, he found a stick about four feet long and used it as a walking stick, guessing that it would help make him look from a distance like a harmless old man.

When two sets of headlights approached behind him on the road from the north, he sat and waited for them to pass. They were probably trucks on their way in from Benghazi, but they both had closed-in cargo bays, so he couldn't tell what they carried. Neither driver seemed to see him, and the trucks rumbled past without a change in speed.

Spencer walked into the village without seeing anybody else. He made his way to the street where Faris Hamzah's compound was. He stood still for a time and searched for people, but nobody was out on foot tonight, so he began to walk. He stayed far from the compound as he walked up nearby streets, studying it from all sides. While he made his circuit, he searched for guards, and for any monitoring equipment that might have been installed to protect the place. In the thirty-five years since his last visit, the age of cheap alarm systems, surveillance cameras, and other devices had come, and Faris Hamzah would be the ideal customer.

Spencer found cameras. They were all installed at the corners of the buildings, aimed outward at the wall that circled the compound. He looked for glowing lights along the walls that would be the two ends of an electric eye beam six or eight inches above the tops of the walls, and he found those too.

Since he had last seen the place, the gate into the compound had been widened to about twelve feet to accommodate cars and trucks. It was now a set of iron bars with what looked like steel plates welded in behind them to give the gate armor. He stepped close and looked in through the half-inch space between the two sides of the gate. There was an electric motor to open and close the two sides. He supposed that in an emergency the gate could be barred.

The house was grander than he had anticipated. Whatever Faris Hamzah had done since the fall of Gaddafi, he must also have been doing something lucrative earlier, during the regime. The building reminded Spencer of the palaces in Iraq where Saddam Hussein had hidden from assassins and air strikes. The entry had fifteen-foot marble columns, and the walls were stone for the first eight feet from the ground and stucco above. The building missed being luxurious only by the omission of windows on the ground floor. The ones above were small and high, like the gun ports on a fort.

Spencer walked to the dark space between two buildings about 150 feet away across the road, and sat down in the shadows to watch. After a moment he realized the façade of the one beside him was a bricked-in rectangle that had once been open, and then recognized it as the old mechanic's shop where he had watched the compound thirty-five years ago.

He sat there staring at the gate of Hamzah's compound, and then he realized that he knew the way in. The walls were too high and smooth to climb and there were electric eyes along the top. But the gate wasn't smooth, and there were no beams of light running along the top. He had been close enough to study the house through the space between the two sides, and the space between the door and the wall. There had been no wiring, no beams of light.

Spencer ran his eyes over the buildings in the compound. There were no lights on in the second floor of the house, or the other two buildings. There was only a dim light that seeped under the front door of the main house. The occupants, other than the night watch, if there was one, seemed to be asleep.

Spencer thought about his situation. If he didn't do this tonight before the town woke up, he would be giving Hamzah's friends and relatives a chance to notice him and report that a suspicious character had appeared. But if he tried to accomplish his purpose tonight, he was probably going to fail. He would get one chance.

He looked at his watch in the moonlight. It was nearly 3:00 a.m. If he was going to make his attempt, this would be the best time to begin. He stood and walked across the street outside of the wall and reached the iron gate. He grasped two of the vertical bars and used the horizontal bars of the frame as footholds, crouched near the top, pulled himself over the gate, and dropped to the ground. He stayed on his belly and crawled into the garden beneath the olive trees. In seconds he was in the center, where the tiled fountain, the big potted plants, and the low, thick canopy of the trees hid him from the cameras.

He had been tense, waiting for the blare of an alarm. Now he waited for the rapid footsteps of a squad of armed bodyguards pouring out of the buildings to kill him. He lay still for a long time and then turned his watch toward the moon so he could read it. Ten minutes had passed. He began to crawl again.

He crawled beside the fine path of pulverized gravel, among the potted palms and agaves. He never lifted his head, simply made for the side of the big house, where the security cameras were turned outward and wouldn't pick him up. When he reached the side of the house, he sat there resting and rubbing his knees and elbows after his long crawl. He stood and listened, and then moved on.

He stayed beside the house, touching it most of the time to remain in the cameras' blind spot. It took him another few minutes to reach the back of the house, which had not been fully visible from the streets he had walked earlier.

There was a balcony above him. It was on the second floor, overlooking a small ornamental pond. The pond was a surprise. He ducked closer and saw in the moonlight that there were lily pads on the surface, and he thought he caught the silvery flash of a scaly fish as a slight ripple disturbed the surface.

Spencer looked around him, and noticed that there was a tiny toolshed about the size of an outhouse along the wall, and near it a long, narrow wooden bench, where a person could sit and watch the fish. He opened the door of the shed and tried to see, but it was too dark to make out much. By touch he found a workbench, and on it was a toolbox that consisted of a metal tray with a handle, and some tools. He found a long, narrow screwdriver and stuck it in his belt. He went out again and looked up at the balcony.

He tried lifting the long, narrow bench, and found he could. It was just a thick board with a support at each end. He used the screwdriver to remove the support at one end. He lifted the end that still had its support, rested it on the roof of the toolshed, and climbed it like a ramp. When he was on the toolshed he dragged the bench up there with him.

Spencer stood on the roof and lifted the bench so its remaining support hooked over the railing of the balcony. This time, his ramp was a bit steeper, but he was able to climb hand over hand on the long board as his feet walked him up to the spot where he could grasp the railing.

He climbed over the railing to the balcony, and then looked through the sliding glass window into the room. It was a bedroom, large and luxuriously furnished. He could see into it fairly well because the bathroom had some kind of night-light, and the faint illumination was much brighter than the rest of the compound tonight. This had to be Hamzah's room. He stepped to the side and looked at the corner near the window. There was nobody in the bed.

Spencer was overwhelmed with disappointment. He felt a weight in his belly, and a sick sense of futility. He had come so far, tried so hard, risked so much to throw away his life because he'd come on the wrong night. Spencer thought about going back the way he'd come. After a moment, he decided that was wrong. He would almost certainly be caught and killed. And maybe he'd simply come to the wrong room.

He tested the sliding door, but it was locked. He used his stolen screwdriver to bend the metal trim around the sliding door outward so he could slip the blade of his knife beside the door and pry the latch up. He slipped it off its bar and slid the door open. He entered and closed the sliding door.

Spencer took out his pistol, screwed the silencer on it, and went to the door that led to the interior of the house. He opened it a crack, looked, and listened. The house was designed in a European style, with a hallway upstairs lined by doors that probably led to bedrooms. But at the center of the upper level the rooms ended and there was a curved staircase leading down to a foyer. He could see that the dim light he had detected from outside came from a chandelier hanging above the foyer. He moved to the railing to look down and see who was awake.

In the light, just inside the large double doors of the front entrance, two men sat on identical armchairs. They wore military battle dress, but their only weapons were holstered pistols. Spencer was sure that somewhere very close to them, possibly in the closet by the door, there would be assault rifles. There was a buzz, and one of the men took a cell phone from his breast pocket and spoke quietly.

Spencer could tell from the rhythms of his speech that he was speaking Arabic, but he couldn't hear the words from where he was. The man ended his call and said to his companion, "Ten or fifteen minutes."

Spencer retreated from the railing and moved up the hallway, quietly opening the doors of the rooms. If Hamzah was sleeping in one of the other rooms, he had to find him now. He looked in each room he passed. Only three of the eight rooms were furnished as bedrooms. The others were an office, a conference room, a couple of storerooms, and a lounge of a sort, with a big-screen television, a couple of couches, and a refrigerator.

Spencer slipped inside the nearest of the storerooms, to see if it contained any munitions he could use to rig a bomb. If Hamzah wasn't here now, sometime he would be.

Spencer heard an unexpected noise, the sound of engines. He stepped to the narrow window of the room and looked out to the courtyard. He saw the automatic gate swing open slowly. As the gate opened inward, vehicles began to nose their way in.

There were three cars, three identical black SUVs. Spencer knew security men liked that method of transport, because it was a shell game that made the enemy guess which cup held the pea. Somebody important was in one of the cars. Was a dignitary about to visit Faris Hamzah, or did he rate this kind of treatment?

Spencer watched the first two SUVs clear the gate and follow the paved drive to approach the front of the house. The first two

SUVs pulled forward to the second building and stopped, but the third stopped in front of the main house's entrance. The headlights went out, returning the courtyard to night.

Spencer was mesmerized. He had been imagining a moment like this for the past two years. He had pictured this compound and thought of ways of getting in, and what he would do if he had the chance. But the place had changed, and there were so many men in these vehicles, and now there were cameras. He had come to the compound tortured by the idea that he might simply study the place all night and not find a way in. Then he was sure he had chosen the wrong night. But maybe this was the time.

He heard the car doors open and watched the occupants jump to the ground, and then step away from the vehicles. He watched men emerge from the first two vehicles before they shut the doors and the dome lights went off. They carried assault rifles as they walked to the farther two-story building and went inside. The first men into the building turned on lights, and he could see through the open door that the place was furnished like a barracks, with rows of bunk beds.

Spencer counted six men in each vehicle. The routine, the way this convoy had been organized, reminded him of the day when he had seen Hamzah going ahead of time to the place where he had agreed to meet. He had a growing hope that the important man in the vehicle parked below by the entrance to the house was Faris Hamzah.

The pair of watchmen he had seen on the first floor opened the main entrance's double doors, letting a patch of light from the house spill out to the courtyard. Then they stood on the portico stiffly with their eyes straight ahead like an honor guard.

The two front doors of the SUV opened and the driver and a man in the front passenger seat got out carrying rifles. They took positions facing each other a few feet apart in the eight-foot space between the front steps and the side door of the SUV, their eyes scanning the middle distance, rising to look at nearby roofs, then to the side.

The side door of the SUV opened. Spencer could see a pair of legs wearing low black shoes and pressed khaki pants like a summer dress uniform ease out so they dangled from the seat. A thin metal shaft came out beside the right leg. A rifle? It extended farther. A cane?

Spencer stared. It was a cane. Faris Hamzah had been at least forty-five when he had met him more than thirty years ago. Of course he would be old. The two feet and the cane reached the ground. The man was visible from above, standing in the light from the open doors of the house, but Spencer couldn't see his face.

He wanted to be sure. If this man wasn't Faris Hamzah, Spencer was about to die for nothing. He gripped his pistol with his left hand and waited.

The man took a step, and then another. He pivoted to his right, toward the barracks, and looked at it for a moment. Then he turned to the left toward the rear of the SUV, and Spencer could see his face.

The face was old, and the hair, beard, and eyebrows were white, but he was Faris Hamzah.

Spencer slipped out of the storeroom and moved quickly down the hall to the space at the railing near the staircase, then looked down at the front entrance. Faris Hamzah stepped into his foyer and watched the two night watchmen close and lock the big double doors, and then slide the dead bolts into the floor. He spoke to them in low tones, and the two of them nodded, turned, and walked to one of the hallways leading away from the foyer.

Spencer hurried back to Hamzah's bedroom, went into the walk-in closet, and shut the door. He knelt behind the large island that held drawers for clothes and shelves for shoes. In the darkness, he set the pistol with its silencer on the floor beside him and took out his knife. He had been hopeful for a minute that Hamzah would be alone in the house. The building was all stone and stucco, and he was sure he could fire his silenced pistol without being heard outside. But he couldn't be sure that the two men downstairs would not hear a suppressed shot.

He waited. He heard footsteps, and then the door opening. A light came on in the room. He heard feet passing on the way to the bathroom, and then heard the door close. The toilet flushed and he heard the feet walk out and approach the closet.

The closet door swung open, and he heard the footsteps enter. He heard a drawer open, and then he stood and moved toward Faris Hamzah. There was a folded pair of pajamas in Hamzah's hand when he half turned and saw Spencer. His eyes widened, he dropped the pajamas, and started to turn to run. Without his cane, he was too slow, and Spencer was on him in a second. Spencer pulled Hamzah's head back and said in his ear in Arabic, "You should have left me alone." Then he drew the blade of the knife across Hamzah's throat and dropped him to the floor.

Hamzah lay on the floor bleeding, gripping the wound in both hands. At first the arterial blood spurted between his fingers, squirting the white dresser, blond hardwood floor, and white walls a few times, but he lost consciousness quickly and the blood flowed into a growing pool beside him.

Spencer wiped his hands and his knife on a suit that was hanging from the clothes rack, closed the blade, and put it in his pocket. He looked in the mirror to be sure his clothes hadn't been painted, but they had. His left arm was red, and there was a streak of blood across his chest. He noticed a row of civilian outfits that looked like his own hanging nearby, and decided on the solution. He went through the bedroom into the bathroom, took off his bloody shirt and washed his hands, arms, and face. He checked his pants and shoes, and then he went back into the closet, took a long Libyan-style shirt, put it on, and then picked up his pistol and turned off the light as he left the closet.

There was a knock on the door, and then the two men from downstairs swung it open and stepped inside. One carried a tray that held a plate and some food, and the other held an open bottle of red wine and a glass. When they saw Spencer, the man with the tray squatted to put it on the floor to free his hands, and the other dropped the glass and wine and tried to draw his gun.

Spencer fired once at that man and saw a hole appear in his forehead, and then shot the other man twice and saw him fall backward.

Spencer dragged the two the rest of the way into the room and closed the door. Then he went through their pockets. One of them had a key fob with a silver stripe along the edge that said RANGE ROVER. Spencer pocketed it, and then stepped back into the closet and fired one round into Faris Hamzah's head.

He hurried to the storeroom where he had watched the cars arrive, and looked out the window. He could see no lights in any of the windows of the other two buildings in the compound. He could see the three SUVs—two parked by the barracks building, and one still parked at the front entrance to the house. Maybe it was parked there intentionally because Faris Hamzah walked with a cane, or maybe the watchman was supposed to park it somewhere else. It didn't matter. He made his way down the stairway to the front of the building. He unlocked one of the twin front doors, stepped out, and closed it.

He went to the driver's door and found it unlocked. He climbed in, started the engine, and drove toward the gate. As the car moved forward he searched the dashboard, the wells on the door panels, and finally found the remote control for the gate clipped to the sun visor. He pressed the button and the gate swung open toward him.

The mechanism seemed incredibly slow, and as the gate inched its way inward, he steered to the center so he would not waste a moment. As soon as there was enough space he steered between the two sides and pressed the button again so the gate stopped and began to close.

He glanced in the rearview mirror to see if anything had changed inside the compound. There were no new lights, no sounds of gunfire, no figures running yet. He drove on, adding speed as he could.

He was afraid someone had heard him driving out, and would run to the house and notice the men lying in Hamzah's bedroom. He hoped that the bodyguards would assume the man who had murdered their employer was a member of a rival faction, and Spencer knew those factions would be fifty miles to the northwest of the village, engaged in the competition to control Benghazi. He must head east for Tobruk, the place that was held by Faris Hamzah's friends and allies.

Spencer kept his speed conservative for a few blocks until he reached the turnoff toward Tobruk, the same route that he and Abdullah had traveled early this morning. Then he began to add speed, driving with both hands on the wheel and his eyes ahead.

The distance to Tobruk from Benghazi was nearly three hundred miles. But Abdullah had not taken him all the way to Benghazi, so he didn't know how much closer than that he was now. He pushed the speed as hard as he dared, paying more attention to controlling the car than to the speedometer.

Minutes went by, and each time he saw another one pass on the dashboard clock he celebrated. He wished the SUV could fly, or that he could take it off the road and head east across country instead of bouncing along and twisting and turning. He strayed from the center of the highway only to hug the curves. As he came out of one he would aim for the next one he could see ahead, making as much of his head start as he could.

His minutes became an hour, and he was sure now that Hamzah's men must have sped off toward Benghazi to pursue his killer. He couldn't be so lucky that they had all fallen asleep and not heard anything.

Spencer was at the end of his second hour of driving and judged he must be nearly halfway to Tobruk when he came around a curve and saw lights about a quarter mile ahead on a long, straight stretch. After a few seconds he could see the lights were a military checkpoint. There were two Humvees parked a few feet apart with a wooden bar between them, and two uniformed men visible in front of them.

Spencer slowed down and opened the glove compartment to see if there were papers for the SUV he was driving. He felt under the seat, glanced for more storage wells in the doors, but found nothing. He quickly shoved the silenced pistol and its spare magazines under his seat.

He knew his best chance was to bluff. Maybe his age and his good Arabic would make him seem innocuous. He slowed to a stop at the roadblock and kept his hands visible on the steering wheel.

A sleepy-looking man in camouflage fatigues stood and walked to Spencer's window. Spencer opened it and smiled at him expectantly.

The man said, "Where are you going, uncle?"

"I'm driving toward Tobruk, sir," he said in Arabic.

"I can see that. What is the purpose of your trip?"

"I want to see the doctors at the Tobruk airport from a Canadian relief organization. I heard they'll be there for another forty-eight hours."

"Let me see your identification."

Spencer thought about how carefully he had planned his trip. He had made sure to carry no identification so the Canadians would not be arrested as accomplices if he were killed. Now he regretted the precaution. "I don't have any with me," he said. "But my name is Mahmoud Haruq."

The soldier looked weary. "Get out of the car."

Spencer got out and stood beside the car. The soldier patted him down, and found nothing except a thick sheaf of Libyan dinars in his pocket.

"You have a lot of money and a new car. Why don't you have papers?"

"It's an emergency. I'm supposed to drive to Tobruk and bring back one of the doctors."

"For whom?"

"For Faris Hamzah."

"Is that who owns this vehicle?"

"Yes, sir."

The soldier smiled as he turned to face his companions. "He works for Faris Hamzah."

The others grinned and shook their heads in disdain. The man sitting on the rock by the road stood up, slung his rifle over his shoulder, and approached. "You work for Faris Hamzah?" he said. "Faris the Great?"

It was clear that these men were not fans of Faris Hamzah. He couldn't decide how far the enmity went. Would they harm him just because they had contempt for Hamzah?

The second man walked to the side of the SUV and looked in at the empty seats, and then walked to the rear door. He pounded on it with his fist.

Spencer leaned into the open door, grasped the fob of the keys, and pressed the button that opened the door locks. The man lifted the back hatch and said, "Ah. Take a look."

The first man walked back and joined his comrade at the rear of the vehicle. The men began taking things out. There were three M4 rifles. Spencer glanced at the roadblock ahead, where there was only one man left in front of him. The men in the back leaned the rifles against the bumper and lifted a couple of olive drab ammo cans. He could see they were heavy, which meant they were full.

Spencer scrambled into his vehicle, started it, and threw it into reverse. The two men behind the SUV dived to the side to avoid being hit, and then scrambled to rise as Spencer threw the SUV into drive and roared away from them. He hit the wooden barrier so it swung into the front of the right Humvee and bounced on the ground.

Spencer never let the vehicle slow. As he sped off, there was some yelling and then a burst of automatic weapon fire. He heard the staccato reports, the bang of bullets hitting the steel of the

SUV's interior, its bumpers, its roof. The unsecured hatch flapped up and down as he drove. It absorbed one burst, some of the bullets punching holes in the sheet metal and others pinging up into the sky. Then another short burst came just as the hatch flew open again. Bullets hit the windshield, leaving big blooms of pulverized glass in front of Spencer's face and to his right.

As Spencer reached the first curve in the highway the hits were fewer, and then there were none. He drove as fast as he dared along the dark highway, trying to put some miles between him and the roadblock.

In his rearview mirror, far behind him, a pair of headlights appeared, and then another. He switched off his headlights and turned the SUV off the road. He drove between low, dark hills that looked like piles of rocks strewn across the hard, dry surface of the Jabal Akhdar plateau. He bumped over slopes, always taking them head-on to keep from tipping the SUV over on its side. He got into ruts so deep that he had to stay in them until he could wrench the wheel to the side and bump out of them.

After a short time, he swung between two low hills and his SUV tilted to the side. The wheels spun and began to dig him in deeper. He rocked the vehicle forward and back, but couldn't get it out of the holes the wheels were digging. He looked around, and realized the SUV was hemmed in and surrounded by rocky hills that hid it from the road. He reached down to find his pistol, silencer, and magazines still jammed under his seat. He took them and ran around to the rear of the vehicle to see what was left of the weapons and ammunition the soldiers had found. There was nothing.

He stepped on the rocks near the foot of a pile, then hurried along the side into some thick brush. He began to run. Spencer ran hard, asking his body to forget its fatigue for just this hundred yards, and then for the next hundred. When he was a mile from the spot where he had left the SUV, he could see headlights on the road he had left.

As he watched, he saw them drift along, and then stop. Slowly, the first Humvee, and then the second, turned off the road and began to bounce across the open land. They were following his SUV's tracks.

He ran on below the endless glittering specks of stars. He found the Big Dipper, and then followed the line from its cup to the North Star. For a long time he trotted and then he walked, using the last hours of darkness to make his way northeast toward Tobruk.

When the sun came up he slept in the shade of a rocky shelf. When he woke it was afternoon. He stood and walked to the east, stepping toward his own shadow, the western sun falling on his shoulders and his head scarf.

Spencer knew he had not traveled far since he had declared himself to be halfway to Tobruk. He was at least two hundred kilometers from Faris Hamzah's compound, but he was still that far from the airport at Tobruk, where the Canadian People's Relief Corps would be waiting for their resupply flight. He had used up half of his seventy-two hours.

His night had left him dehydrated, and he could not go on much longer without water. He was on a stretch of land where he could see no buildings, no sign that human beings had ever been there. There was nothing in sight that suggested he was near water—no trees, no green brush of the sort that grew near wells and streams. His only possessions were a pistol with a suppressor and two full magazines, a good pair of shoes, and his white Libyan clothes. The soldier at the roadblock may not have intended to rob him, but he had never given back the two thousand dinars that Spencer had been carrying. He had only eleven dinars in his pocket, left over from tipping Abdullah.

He would have to keep going a few hours to get far enough from the roadblock he had escaped, then try to find a village where he could get water. If he failed, he would die. The rule of thumb was that it took three days to die of dehydration, but he had spent much of his first night running.

Spencer set a marching pace by counting cadence. He kept his head up and picked a hill that lined up with his shadow and walked toward it so his course would be straight. The road to Tobruk was an arc that swung to the north and then back down, all of it roughly parallel to the sea. If he aimed his steps correctly, then at some point he would intersect with the road.

It was late night when he saw something new ahead of him and to the left. A set of headlights was moving along, the beams shooting into the darkness. From this distance he couldn't actually see the vehicle. He had no idea if it was a car, a truck, or a bus, but it didn't matter. It was what the vehicle was driving on that mattered. He had met the road.

He kept walking, unable to resist swinging farther to the left to meet the road sooner, and then he was there, stepping onto the pavement. He felt the luxury as he walked along on the pavement toward the east. Now there was nothing to trip him, no irregularities or loose stones to turn his ankles. He walked steadily and made better time, always listening for the sound of an engine.

At five thirty in the morning another set of headlights illuminated the road ahead. A car was about to overtake him.

He was starving and parched, and he knew that if he didn't get help he would be dead by midafternoon. He stepped into the middle of the highway and waited. He watched the headlights grow nearer and brighter, and when the car was close enough to see him he waved his arms.

The car slowed to twenty miles an hour as the driver looked him over. When the car reached him, it stopped.

Spencer leaned over to look into the car. The man behind the windshield was dark, with a short beard and close-cropped hair, about thirty-five years old. He was a little bit chubby, certainly not a laborer.

The passenger window whirred down. The man said in Arabic: "What are you doing out here?"

"My car got wrecked," Spencer said. "I lost control and it ran off the road and crashed. Praise Allah I'm alive. I thank you so much for stopping." He bowed deeply.

"If I take you to the next village, what will you give me?"

"I'll buy gasoline, and if you'd like me to, I'll drive your car so you can rest," said Spencer. "If you're going all the way to Tobruk, I would give you two hundred and fifty dinar to take me with you."

"Did you say two fifty?"

"Yes. Two fifty."

"All right. Get in."

"On this side or the driver's?"

"That side. If you crashed your car, I don't want you driving mine."

Spencer got in beside the man and felt his legs release their tension in the soft cushion of the seat while the man accelerated, moving along the road toward Tobruk.

They drove for a few miles, and then the man said to Spencer: "You must be rich, huh?"

"No, not really," Spencer said.

"You must be. You smashed your car and you walked away from it, as though it meant nothing to you."

Spencer looked at him. "I'm sad that my car was wrecked, but I'm very happy that I could walk away from it without dying or having a serious injury. Now I'm even happier that a kind and good man was the one to come along the road at night and pick me up."

The man nodded and drove on.

Spencer distrusted and disliked this man. The driver knew that Spencer had been walking through wilderness all night, but he had not offered him a drink of water or even asked about his health. But Spencer needed him to stay alive, so he was determined to keep him friendly.

Spencer decided that the best thing he could do was to lean back and appear to fall asleep, so he wouldn't risk irritating or alienating him. He leaned against the door, his eyes closed, and he began to breathe slowly and deeply. The way he kept it up was to count. He would count to sixty slowly and call it a minute, and then count the next sixty and call that two minutes. He got to nine minutes and started the tenth, when he awoke in full sunlight, startled.

The car was stopped off the road. The driver was touching him, feeling his pockets for his wallet.

Spencer stiffened and started to sit up, but the man held a knife in his free hand, and it hovered above Spencer's chest, where he could see it. The knife was about four inches long with a symmetrical blade like a boot knife.

"Where's the money?" the man asked.

"What's the knife for?" said Spencer. "I'm planning to pay you."

"I'm taking the money you promised me. It's my money now."

Spencer wondered where they were, and how long he had been sleeping, but he had no idea. He said, "I'm going to pay you the two fifty as soon as we get to Tobruk. That's where it is. Most of the money I had with me got burned in my car."

"You didn't say the car burned. You've been lying to me. I'm taking you nowhere." The man raised the hand that held the knife.

Spencer's left hand batted the man's forearm to the side while his right moved to the pistol in his belt. He grasped the pistol through his loose shirt, twisted his torso, and fired through the cloth.

The heat burned Spencer's belly as the round tore through Spencer's shirt and into the man's chest. Spencer opened the car door, rolled out onto the gravel shoulder, crouched, and pulled the gun out from under his shirt.

The man was not moving. He had been kneeling on the driver's seat above Spencer while he frisked him, but now he had collapsed facedown onto the passenger seat that Spencer had vacated.

Spencer held the gun on him, stepped closer, and poked him hard. He didn't move.

Spencer pried the knife out of the driver's grip, used his left hand to grasp the driver's wrist, and pulled. The man offered no resistance, and there was no sign of consciousness, so Spencer dragged him across the passenger seat and out onto the shoulder of the road. He touched the man's carotid artery and he felt no pulse.

Spencer closed the passenger door and looked around. He stuck the pistol back in his belt and dragged the body off the road into the field of weeds beyond. The land was bleak, another series of low hills and fields, but no sign of people or buildings. The driver had chosen a deserted place to rob and murder him.

He knelt beside the body and searched it. The wallet had only six dinars in it. There was also a driver's license, but the picture didn't look much like the body at Spencer's feet. He took the six dinars, but put the wallet back in the man's pocket.

He went back to the car, removed the keys from the ignition, and opened the trunk. There was no suitcase, no extra clothes. There were only a few rags, a spare tire, and an unopened one-gallon plastic bottle of water.

He took the mat that covered the spare tire in the well, put it over the passenger seat to cover the blood, and used some of the water and the rags to clean off the blood that had spattered his face when he'd shot the man. Then he got into the car and drove. As he drove he drank. He was not sure where he was, but the clock on the dashboard told him it was nearly ten o'clock in the morning.

The man's wallet had not contained enough money to buy much gas. The first thing he had said was to ask Spencer what he would give him for a ride. And the photograph on the license did not belong to him.

Spencer was almost certainly driving a stolen car, and judging from the way the driver had already had the knife in his hand when he'd started searching him for money, the true owner of the car was probably dead. Spencer glanced at the gas gauge. There was a quarter of a tank of gas. What was that, fifty miles?

Spencer had eleven dinars. The wallet had held another six. If there was gas available for sale to civilians, he might still reach Tobruk. He kept driving. Every mile down the road was a mile he would not have to walk.

An hour later he could see he was approaching a city. And then, to his left, the sea appeared. Derna. It had to be Derna. Soon there were a few buildings. He began to see the word Derna in Arabic script. A Derna hotel, a Derna construction company, a Derna restaurant. The one thing he didn't see was a Derna gasoline station.

He was wary about stopping. He was running very low on gas now, but the car could tie him to at least the killing he'd done, and probably the one he hadn't. He passed an apartment building that had been bombed out, one wall gone and the rooms and staircases on that side opened like a child's dollhouse. He knew that Derna had been taken by the Islamic State forces for a time and then won back.

The city seemed to have recovered from the fighting, and there were no sounds of gunfire, but this was not a place where he wanted to be stranded. It would be very difficult to get out if he were stopped.

He remembered that Derna was about seventy miles from Tobruk, so he decided to keep going. He drove along at a reasonable speed that he thought might stretch his gasoline supply and not attract attention from soldiers. He passed a checkpoint on the opposite side of the road with soldiers stopping and inspecting cars and trucks coming into town from the other direction.

A mile farther on he saw three armed soldiers walking along the highway. He pulled over to the side of the road near them and called out in Arabic: "Do you need a ride?"

The three men trotted to join him. Two got in the back and the other sat in the passenger seat. The man beside him said, "Thank you for your kind invitation."

"It's the least I could do. How far are you going?"

The soldier said, "Four kilometers straight ahead. It's a long walk, and it feels good to ride."

Spencer nodded sagely. He was familiar with the feeling. Then, only about a mile on, they reached another checkpoint on his side of the highway. Spencer pulled over at the checkpoint and a soldier started toward his car, but when he saw the three soldiers he opened the barrier and waved the car through.

In another few minutes the man beside Spencer said, "Leave us by the road up there. We don't need to have the lieutenant know we didn't walk all the way. He might think of more work for us to do."

Spencer pulled over and said, "Allah protect you."

The three soldiers went on their way. Spencer managed to drive forty miles farther before the engine coughed and then ran out of gas. He kept his foot off the brake and coasted a hundred feet before the momentum was used up. He got the rags out of the trunk, wiped the surfaces he had touched, and left the car unlocked with the keys in it.

He looked at his watch. He was reaching the end of his second day, and he still had about thirty miles to go. Before this time tomorrow the Canadians would receive their supply flight and be off without him. He began to walk.

Spencer walked about five miles before he reached a farming village a distance from the south side of the highway. He could see melons and some green vegetables growing on acre-size plots all the way into the village. It looked like a place where he could buy a melon and some water.

As he came into the village, he saw a young man about twenty-one or twenty-two years old. He was riding a new bicycle up and down in front of his house, apparently testing the adjustment of the chain and the gears and giving the bicycle its first lubrication. The bicycle had thick, knobby tires like a mountain bike, and it had a couple of big baskets mounted on the sides of the rear wheels so he could carry a load without affecting his steering. Spencer guessed he probably used it to deliver melons to a market stall.

Spencer stopped and stood nearby with his arms folded, watching the young man riding. He said in Arabic: "That is an excellent new bicycle."

"Thank you," the young man said.

"May I ask what happened to your old bicycle?"

The young man looked puzzled. "How did you know there is one?"

"Because you're a skilled rider. This is not your first one."

"The first one is old. It belonged to my uncle for years and years before it went to me. I still have it, but I think I'll save it for the parts."

"I only wonder . . ." Spencer trailed off.

"What?" said the young man.

"Well, the new bicycle is very good quality. If it ever needs a part, it won't happen soon. And no bicycle ever needs every part replaced. Meanwhile, the old one is just taking up space in your house and rusting. The rubber parts are getting hard and brittle. It's worth something, and that value is going to waste."

"What do you suggest?"

"If you could show it to me, I might consider making an offer."

At four forty-five on the afternoon of the third day of Alan Spencer's absence, the people at the Tobruk Airport saw a figure on a bicycle pedaling along the road toward the cargo terminal.

The man wore Libyan clothes and he was dirty and ragged, but when he saw the row of Canadians standing by their trucks watching him, he waved at them and began to pedal harder, standing up on the pedals and pumping to build up speed like a racer at the end of a long course. He bumped up over the edge of the concrete pavement at the entrance and coasted to a stop in front of them.

"I'm sorry if I'm late," he said. "The distances here can be deceiving."

38

Julian Carson walked behind the visiting team locker room and along the hallway to the small concrete room. As he stepped to the steel door it opened and Waters and Harper came out, wheeling the room's safe, which was strapped to a two-wheeled dolly. Harper held the door while Waters pulled back on the handle of the dolly and steered it out into the hallway.

Mr. Ross, Mr. Bailey, and Mr. Prentiss came out after them. Julian noticed that once again, Mr. Prentiss held his hard-sided briefcase.

Mr. Ross acknowledged him first. "Hello, Mr. Carson. You're right on time."

The hairs on Julian's arms rose. He had been trying to delay the manhunt by taking as long as possible with the old man's file. Had he kept up the tactic too long? This would have to be the moment. "I think I know where to find the old man."

Mr. Ross stopped. "Really?"

"Yes. He was in Vietnam in 1972 working with a platoon of ARVN rangers in the central highlands when the Easter Campaign began. He got his Silver Star because he was out alone on a scouting mission when the North Vietnamese regulars were moving in to massacre his men. He engaged the enemy by himself to sound the alarm and saved his men. They all got away alive because of him."

"Good for him," said Mr. Ross. "So?"

"Some of those ARVN soldiers are sure to still be alive. Any of those men or their families would be glad to hide Michael Isaac Kohler. And there will be a record in this country of who they all were. Military intelligence probably has it. All we have to do is pay each one a visit."

"Interesting," said Mr. Ross. "But this show is over. Time to fold up our tents and go."

"What? Why?"

"Our guy is dead."

"The old man?" said Julian. His mouth felt dry. He had known it was almost certainly going to end that way, but he had hoped that this time, this once, it would not.

"Not him. Faris Hamzah. His enemies assassinated him right in his house when his bodyguards weren't looking. There's nothing to be gained by going after the old man anymore. If he's in Vietnam, then *xin chuc mung* to him. He's not our problem. Or yours."

"I suppose not," said Julian.

On his way back to his office, he decided he would write an obituary for the *Chicago Tribune*. It would announce the death of Faris Hamzah, and it would be the last thing he placed in the paper with the initials J. H.

39

"Mom!" There was silence. Then: "Mom!"

Dr. Emily Coleman closed her eyes. It had been a long day and she was at the kitchen island cutting up vegetables that she knew the boys would only pick at and pretend to eat.

"There's a car in the driveway."

"Who is it?" she called back.

"I can't tell. It's a big black car with weird plates."

"What do you mean, weird?"

"White."

She stopped moving and listened, begging God or the universe that he wouldn't say "US government."

"White with a big mountain on it," he said. "Washington."

She set down the knife, wiped her hands on a dish towel, and went into the living room. It occurred to her that Carol and Dave weren't barking, but she didn't dare draw the obvious conclusion from that. She could barely breathe.

She stepped to the door and opened it. There he was. He looked fine—tanned and in shape.

"Hi, Doc," he said. "I thought I'd come by and pick up my dogs."

He got the word "dogs" out, but barely, before the two black beasts shot through the doorway, whirled, and leapt around him like dancers, and then the two grandsons arrived and hugged him at about belt height, making it difficult for him to take a step inside and hug his daughter.

40

Bill Armitage walked along the beach, staring out at Puget Sound. He loved taking this walk in the morning, and he'd been doing it nearly every day at six for over a month. He always scanned the Sound for the sight of black dorsal fins, hoping to spot a pod of killer whales. It hadn't happened yet, but he was pretty sure it would. He was a patient man, he was very watchful, and he knew the ways of predators. They appeared after you got tired of looking.

He liked to start at the parking lot of Fort Casey State Park. As soon as he got there, he would get out of the car and go to the back door, open it, and let Carol and Dave jump out and run around a little, then scout ahead of him as he made his way to the beach. After a few minutes they would get used to the salt air laced with the strong smells of seaweed and washed-up sea creatures and fall in with him, orbiting him as he walked.

Armitage liked to go at least as far as the old Admiralty Head Lighthouse before they turned and made their way back. At low tide he could easily pick out his own straight, steady footprints and the meandering, circling, zigzagging prints of the two big black dogs. A few hours from now, the prints would all be washed away by the rising tide as though nobody had ever been here.

He wore two leather leashes around his neck, and he felt them swinging as he walked. He almost never needed to use them, because he and the dogs were usually alone on the beach in the early morning. He knew that in time he and the dogs would use up this walk and move on to others, taking each for a month or two before they were satisfied that they knew it. Whidbey Island had a great many possible walks, and if those were ever used up the world held others.

THE END